Clawing

By Robin Kirby-Gatto

Table of Contents

Foreword

When I was asked to write the foreword for this book, I was very excited as I had the privilege of reading this book before it was published, being extended to me. I've had the pleasure of reading Robin's nonfiction books, which are deep reading, indeed. Two of her books, *At His Feet* and *Destiny*, feature fiction and nonfiction together, giving a taste of what a full fiction by Robin could be.

Years ago, I was introduced to *Piercing the Darkness* and *This Present Darkness* by Frank Peretti. Prior to this time in my life I had read mostly nonfiction, biographies in particular. Shortly after the two Peretti books, I was introduced to *The Bourne Identity* by Robert Ludlum. Initially, I had not wanted to read it, protesting that it was simply *not my kind of book*. However, it developed within me, a thirst for action and suspense. My interests soon spilled over to thriller and sci-fi fantasy, especially with books by Ted Dekker. Once I read Dekker's books, I became hooked.

If you like Ted Dekker or Frank Peretti, or authors who have similar works, you will love this book. Robin's book, *Clawing and Gnawing*, has successfully fused several genres together. She takes a story that combines the supernatural with sci-fi and fantasy, then adds conspiracy theory for good measure. If that isn't enough, physics is added in the mix to stretch your brain a little.

This book doesn't baby you, handing everything on a silver platter; it makes you think. However, it is not so highbrow that you can't understand it unless you have degree science. I have heard Robin speak many times, and one of the things that she elicits from her audience is an excitement for subjects that a person might not have, otherwise. For example, I found myself fascinated by anatomy when that subject was used to illustrate another point being presented by her. Prior to that, I found anatomy to be uninteresting and difficult to understand.

Robin has successfully created an introduction to her story that captivates right from the opening. The beginning paragraph is reminiscent of *Twilight* Zone. You are then introduced to the main character, Milly Teschlon, who is not your typical heroine. She lives at home with her parents and actually has a good relationship with them. On the surface, just a nice Midwestern girl living the status quo. You soon discover that she not only seems like the typical *girl next door*, but also has insecurities that should keep her from stepping out.

On the other hand, she accepts the circumstances she finds herself in, taking each in stride and rising to the challenge encountered. She teams up with her best friend, Parker, who is a fellow college student like herself, but is also linked by a common cause with several of the college faculty.

The story wouldn't be complete without a connection to the past. For Milly, that connection is to her great grandmother whose name she shares. She discovers that her great grandmother, Mildred Lee, has recorded events, along with codes in a diary, which has direct effect on Milly's present determining her future and the future of mankind.

If you like supernatural or sci-fi fantasy, or you find yourself following the latest conspiracy theories, or just want to be entertained with a good story line about good versus evil, and enjoy a little challenge along with that entertainment, you are sure to find all of that and more in *Clawing and Gnawing*. Who knows, it may give you a perspective you've never considered. Without a doubt, however, you will enjoy this story finding it hard to put the book down.

With each chapter comes the thought, how much more can possibly happen; and yet, it does. Throughout the book, momentum builds until the crescendo of the great finale. My excitement increased with every chapter, leaving me captivated until the end. Hang in there through the more brainy stuff that brings logic to Robin's story, you will not be disappointed. Enjoy!

Richard Gatto

Preface

Go into this book open minded, not using a past fiction read that you have enjoyed, but rather, let this work stand on its own. I have written many teaching books, eleven of which are transferred onto Amazon, and I still have another 70 workbooks to convert into books. I have some distribution of fiction throughout two of my works, and recently found myself drawn to write this trilogy, *The Ancient Language Seekers*, for those who are given over to unique types of fiction, which cross-pollinate with many genres.

You will either love this book or hate it; there will be no fence sitters with *Clawing and Gnawing*. My gift, in bringing in the sciences with the works I do, is in this book as well, giving a unique spin on the plot. *Clawing and Gnawing* is the first book of the trilogy and will be followed by two prequels, *The Prophet* and *Awake*.

Please know that I mean no disrespect to anyone who might be in this book and have passed. I have wrestled with what all to put in this particular epic, and believe I have used wisdom to stay true to my belief and revelation. Also, any diet or medical information within, please see your doctor about.

It is my hope that you will come to know and like the characters, as well as appreciate the complexities of blending the different genres, bringing to life a small town that is riddled with mystery, fantasy, and the supernatural.

In each of us is a desire to be greater than we presently are, and I believe in this work you will be compelled all the more to be bent towards that end, as you are stretched with Milly, the main character, who finds herself in a unique position of choice, of whether or not to be a hero or a hermit. Each of us daily have this choice, and with this writing, I believe it will encourage you all the more to take risks that you wouldn't normally consider, while reaching for the stars.

Enjoy!

Robin Kirby-Gatto

Chapter 1

Since many do not have familiarity with the supernatural, it is with utmost certainty that it be related to you the specific occurrences those in a particular community have recently encountered. The thin veil of what we know as *reality* has merged into another dimension, which is absolutely phenomenal. Most people perceive the world through the narrow scope of what their senses are able to pick up, not realizing that there is so much more. Their *normal* does not involve the supernatural; their brains have not been expanded into the other realm, where they can perceive that which is *abnormal*. When there is a confrontation in a person's soul, between the normal and the abnormal, everything changes.

Here, we will see the *abnormal* enmesh with the subconscious, flooding into the conscious mind more and more, bringing enlightenment of the *abnormal*, which in time becomes a person's *normal*.

This is what happened to Milly Teschlon, a sophomore Philosophy/History double major, who finds herself awake to both a thinking and antiquity which precedes time as we know it, confronting the dimensions of this present age. Similar to Einstein's theory of light, breaking the mold on what science knew of light, it brought a new compass.

"Compass" comes from two Latin words, ***com*** meaning "together" and ***passus*** meaning "a step or pace." Therefore, a compass denotes the ability for people to step together into *the place of knowing that which they did not before*. Milly Teschlon became a compass to her small town, influencing others to walk with her into the supernatural, which is where our journey begins.

Let me preface this with the fact that it is easy to be overwhelmed, with *this knowledge* of what is revealed by the compass.

With Milly, the many series of events and encounters have been extreme and intense. Therefore, it will be necessary to be patient while the information is relayed through the many happenings that she and others have experienced, so that you gain better understanding of the *supernatural.* The words to describe these events might come off as pretentious, and the language may seem a little out of the ordinary, in didactic patterns throughout, but all of this is necessary so that you consider the inner workings of what has occurred in this small town, before you fully comprehend that which many have come to know as *truth.*

"Mildred Lee Teschlon," named after her Great Grandmother, Mildred Virginia Lee, is the young lady whom may at first glance, seem ordinary, however is anything but. Milly's Great Grand, helped many get through the Great Depression, being a servant not only to those whom she was kin, but also to the community at large, in Springfield, North Dakota.

A placard is set up in the city center, where a street is named after Milly's Great Grand. Many say if it had not been for Mrs. Mildred Virginia Lee, Springfield would have never survived one of the darkest times of our nation. Now seeing the history of Milly's Great Grandmother, it is not surprising to see where strong character and emotional stamina run rich in the family. These qualities provide strength to others in times of difficulty. Uniquely, it is these traits that seamlessly cause the entire town of Springfield to cross over into a new era, a greater time.

Mildred Lee Teschlon, who goes by the nickname, "Milly," has attended Strytan University of Springfield, North Dakota, since her freshman year, and now in 2012, is a sophomore. Milly, stands at 5'4" with a medium build, having brownish hair tinted with natural herbs, giving her hair a slight glisten when the light hits her shoulder length cut. Her normal attire is colored tennis shoes, different sports tops and blue jeans, layered by a blazer over her t-shirt.

She has lived in Springfield, since her family moved there, when she was two-years-old, from Newark, Missouri. Her mother, originally from Springfield, wanted to return, and the door opened when Milly's father was transferred there with his accounting firm. Springfield is all Milly has known, outside of her few travels, and is the basis of all that she would consider as *her* reality.

Milly, gifted with high-intelligence, continually made honor-roll throughout elementary, middle school and high school. Her father, Daniel, wanted her to get a degree in mathematics and go to MIT. He liked to believe that Milly was her father's daughter, designed with his smart intellect. However, Milly found her passion given to the things of antiquities and philosophy. With her mother's steering, she was led to double major in Philosophy & History, specializing in antiquities.

Milly loves her parents dearly, feeling fortunate to have such a cool mom and dad. Her father, Daniel, stands at 5'10" and is proud of his premature grey hair, which is more pronounced in his trimmed beard and mustache. His devout workouts at the gym each week, keep stress off of him. He makes it a point to implement his philosophy on having a healthy home, so that Milly does not get caught up in all the fad foods that are bad for you.

Milly's mother, Lavern Teschlon, is what one would picture of as the *perfect* stay at home mother, caring for Milly and her father, as a general, caring for his troops. She has administrative gifts and runs a tight ship at the Teschlon home. Lavern's hair is a light auburn, in a short French haircut, as striking as a model on the cover of Vogue. She is a trendsetter in the area, and is always jumping on the latest fashion in clothing, as well as design in interior decorating. Her short frame of 5'2" on her petite body makes her more youthful than her now, 49 years of age.

The Teschlon family has been quite happy in Springfield. Although they had hoped for another child, ten years earlier, the three of them have been content, enjoying a life of what many in this world would hope for. Debt free, home nearly paid off, cars paid in full, Milly's college fund paying for all her college expenses, and her father's great job, making life very easy, allowing them to travel and acquire things that others would have to save to buy. They have quality time together and enjoy life as much as possible.

Milly still lives with her mom and dad while attending Strytan, and enjoys staying at home. It has taken her a good 10 years to get her room perfect to her liking. She has decorated her *Cave,* which is what everyone refers to when it comes to Milly's room, with memorabilia from different museums, galleries and showings that she has attended. Her cave feels much like a treasure trove of different artifacts she prizes from times past in their travels, mixed in with her own personal trophies from her soccer days in high school. Getting old T-shirts to rag her room, she and her mother, painted the walls and ceiling with a wall treatment of deep apple-red and a hint lighter tone of red, on top. The red wall treatment all over her room, gives it the ambiance of a secret coffer, an antiquities vibe.

Milly's Cave, unknowing to her, is actually a depiction of her soul, where the great things of who she is, is hidden from the real world. She has a long-standing issue with her self-worth from different times in her life, where others have bullied her about being *different* or *odd.* These incidents in her past were more than mere teasing, but rather they have been continued verbal harassments, as well as social media reputational homicide. The instigator of these horrific experiences is the one whom Milly considers her nemesis, Dana Dryer. They have been in school since kindergarten, and from that time, Dana has tormented Milly.

As a result of the long standing bullying, Milly has *voices* inside of her head that speak to her in order to put her down. These voices are not in a schizophrenic way, but instead seem to conjecture ideas in her mind, pulling up negative memories from her subconscious. Milly, unsure if the voices are the opinions of others from her past, knew that the bullying created a deranged thought pattern, about how she thinks about herself.

Hard for her to put explanation to this torment, Milly wrestles continually with it, and has not shared about this inner struggle with others; she puts on a mask so everyone remains an arm's distance to this fight of survival. Milly's parents, clueless to this inner turmoil, have been kept from her dark secrets. It is safer for her to wrestle this alone, in her own mind, keeping her concern of what others might think, at bay. It is her fear that people might consider her a mental case, or worse still, her parents may send her to a psychiatrist, where she will find out that she actually is mental. What makes matters more difficult is that she has the long-standing reputation of her Great Grand to live up to, in the Springfield community.

The University

Strytan University, one of the oldest universities in the States, has a grand reputation in the Liberal Arts cross-pollinating with its Sciences. It is renowned for its graduates that have lived abroad and traveled throughout the world, influencing communities of different nations. Priding itself on being a pioneer in different areas of study, Strytan has majors that branch off and cross-pollinate, creating diverse and unique fields of studies.

The new semester kicking off, students were hustling and bustling all over The Quad, getting to their first class, as they looked at their fall schedule. Anticipation was in the air, as freshmen finished orientation the week before, fraternities selected their new pledges, and classes were in session. New notebooks, pens, pencils, folders, calculators, notecards, and textbooks were the paraphernalia in most of the students' backpacks. This was the week that they would get their class syllabi, identifying the planning of each individual class.

The campus was buzzing, with freshmen throughout, chiming in about the prior week's events, as pledges wore their new shirts. Returning students felt a little more seniority, as they deemed themselves more mature, especially Milly, who was now a sophomore, and no longer a *newbie*. She was glad to be finished with her freshman year, and now excited to be taking higher-level classes in both philosophy and history, along with the regular required classes of math, science and writing. Her fall schedule was full and she liked it that way; there was nothing more that she loved, than studying her favorite subjects.

While walking throughout campus, she could hear the conversations of those whom she passed, realizing how much she had missed the invigorating chaotic mornings during school; she was now glad to be back. Milly caught a waft of the perfumes and colognes on most everyone. It seemed to be a ritual for new students to chose a signature scent as a calling card, which this day, left lingering smells in the hallway where the different fragrances ascended into the atmosphere, giving an aroma of *life*.

Milly was thrilled about the new philosophy class, and could not wait to attend, as well as see her best friend Parker, to tell him the dream she had last night. Parker and Milly had been friends since their freshman year of college, having met each other during orientation.

Milly entered the Truman Building, which is where most of her classes were, housing the History, English and Philosophy departments. She sensed the excitement of the freshmen, as they stood in the front of the building like a hive of bees gathering honey into a honeycomb. They lingered around recounting what happened during orientation, laughing with each other, and giving the "sign" of acceptance, by patting each other on the back or shoulder in approval.

Milly knew some of the professors well, having participated in open houses with the Philosophy and History departments, as well as monthly events throughout her freshman year. Most of the offices for the professors on each floor were at the end of the hall, either the west or east end, depending on where their office was stationed. Stairways on each end, made it easier for students to filter through the building, up the appropriate wing. The Truman building was three stories, with the English department on the first floor, the Philosophy department on the second floor, and the History department on the third floor. For the moment, Milly was headed to the second floor to begin Philosophy 201.

Bearing down the west wing of the building, Milly trotted up the steps, excited to see her favorite professor, Norman Kaufman, who had become an all time favorite with the students at Strytan. His character was by far, more distinctive from the other professors, with his sly wit in what seemed like dry deliveries of words, and his contemplative looks as he examined students while they spoke. In addition, his different postures of standing, leaning on walls, sitting on top of his desk, and hovering over students like the sun over a flower that was ready to blossom, made him stand out. Professor Kaufman considered himself, as one, who would bring out the *great thoughts* in others, which he dubbed *life's philosophy*.

Being only 42 years old, he seemed an old soul, standing at 5'10" with a lean build. His brownish curly hair fell over his ears nearly covering his eyes, making it more of a game to see what color his eyes actually were. Looking at him, you would think that he most likely surfed in California in his younger years; he was a carefree spirit.

Milly entered the room, seeing Professor Kaufman writing on the board, as he meticulously wrote in the most stylish way, putting quotes up from the philosophers that they would be studying. All first classes were usually boring, where the students would get their syllabi and basically talk about the overview and what was expected for the course. Not this one though; Professor Kaufman's first classes for the semester were always memorable, as they inspired, provoked, and challenged the student's thinking. He turned to see Milly come into the room, nodded, and then returned to writing the quotes.

Milly looked around and saw some of the other students from the prior semesters, and gave her good morning and hellos, as they too sat with anticipation of what was to come.

"Milly," she heard a voice calling her from the door. It was Parker Knight, her best friend, who was a Philosophy/Science major. Parker believed that Philosophy always turned to science and enjoyed the study of biology, anatomy, botany and the like, along with the study of philosophy. It amazed Milly each time that Parker spoke to her about his scientific studies; melding them into the different philosophies they studied their freshman year, intrigued her. Being around him was like a breath of fresh air. Who needed television, when Parker Knight was your friend?

Milly grinned, as Parker glided towards her desk, plopping his books on the one beside hers. He had a huge smile across his dark colored face, with eyes as brown as his skin, making his teeth whiter, as he smiled that winning smile at his best friend. "So, are you excited today about what Professor Kaufman will bring us this first day of the semester?"

Milly replied, "You know I am; I have been waiting all summer for this moment, and am starrrrrrving for more philosophy; it's like I am addicted to it. I believe I have Philosophism and there is no hope." She giggled at her own wit.

"Milly, it is weird; when I woke up this morning, I just felt something different was going to happen this year." Parker, with his eyes wide looked at Milly, while in thought, to which she could have sworn he was doing "a Kaufman." That is what they called their silent stares after taking his course their freshmen year, almost considering *it* a "philosophy thing."

"What is it Parker; what is going on in that brilliant mind?"

He responded with anticipation, "I had excitement before coming here to school my freshmen year, but *this* that I am feeling is like that multiplied by 10, Milly. As much as I liked orientation, and then beginning classes here, I am even more expectant about something new happening that neither one of us have ever experienced in our lives."

"Whoa there partner," Milly said with a slight chuckle. She was unsure how to take her friend. "Something that we have never experienced?" she asked.

"Yeah, you know like how you felt when you first came here to school? You never knew what college was, because you had not experienced it before then. But later, you found it to be greater than you ever thought, especially when you got connected to the philosophy department, and of course, ME," he said grinning with his white teeth gleaming through the conversation.

"Yes Parker, I remember, but man, I cannot imagine something ten times greater than that, which we have never experienced." She was completely clueless as to what he was referring to.

Professor Kaufman took control of the class, as he motioned for one of the students to shut the door. All eyes were on him, as the students sat there, some leaning forward in their chairs, while others were sitting straight up, and a couple leaning back in their seats. Hot piping coffee steamed out of the cups of those who brought their latte or Americano to class, getting freshly brewed coffees from *The Grind*, the campus coffee shop.

Sneakers could be heard squeaking on the floor, as people were stationing themselves in place at their desk. Most students on campus, would go on about Kaufman's first day classes, and believed it was the best discourse of their life. Therefore, the students now, were expectant of the greatness that was soon to flow from Kaufman's lips.

His eyes straight ahead, were locking in on the new crowd. Kaufman had a sensory gift of seeing behind him, as he pointed toward the quotes on the board at his back, beginning Philosophy 201, while making eye contact with the students. It was the intellectual *first kick* of the football season, as Kaufman threw out a pass to his students, like a quarterback to a wide receiver. He was looking for someone who would be brave enough to go long.

"Let me quote the following," Kaufman stated, as he straightened his shoulders. With great skill of oration, he began to speak.

"That which is crooked cannot be made straight: and that which is wanting cannot be numbered.

I communed with mine own heart, saying, Lo, I am come to great estate, and have gotten more wisdom than all they that have been before me in Jerusalem: yea, my heart had great experience of wisdom and knowledge.

And I gave my heart to know wisdom, and to know madness and folly: I perceived that this also is vexation of spirit.

For in much wisdom is much grief: and he that increaseth knowledge increaseth sorrow."[i]

Students were stunned as Kaufman spoke with great ease, as though he was delivering a line in a movie, moving his head and hands with inflections, while slowly speaking these words, like that of a virtuoso. Milly felt as though she should know it, especially when Kaufman said *Jerusalem*. It was as though her gut responded to the resonance of the word, Jerusalem, and it felt like she was being painted as the wall of her room, with a special color of antiquity that seemed to cover her, almost enveloping her in what she perceived was *ancient*. She was captivated, as were the others, as Kaufman looked at his speechless crowd, his hands touching one another, his contemplation look, with his glasses magnifying his blue eyes, as the room was silent. He asked, "Does anyone know who the philosopher was who spoke this?"

"Socrates," said one student, as others giggled in the background. The student slumped as if their entire being was deflated like a balloon that was popped, hoping that people knew it was an intentional joke, as they laughed and then straightened their shoulders a bit, so as to not give themselves away.

Kaufman walked towards Milly's desk, as she spoke in her heart, "Please do not come to me Kaufman, please, please, please."

She felt a slight wind blowing over her, as she realized that it was no wind at all but Kaufman hovering over her desk, like a gardener waiting for a flower to bloom. "Milly Teschlon, does this infamous quote bear with your soul? What do you consider, when you hear the words of this great poet and philosopher?" Breathing and waiting, Kaufman, stepped back two feet so as not to crowd her, in order that she could be heard.

"Well, Professor Kaufman," Milly cleared her throat, hoping that something would flow out of her mouth brilliantly, "I believe that this philosopher finds himself in a quandary with wisdom and knowledge; he desires to have it, but although he has it, at the same time, it is like a burden and pain to his soul." Milly was awed at the response that came out of her mouth, feeling as though what she really had in her heart, was "I have no clue what this means." She felt like a dubbed over Chinese movie in English, except it was Milly being dubbed by the Philosophism, which was her own word for being addicted to philosophy, it was a good disease to have, she thought.

"You are exactly right Milly Teschlon," Kaufman replied with a minute grin.

Stepping back, he looked at the class, and began repeating the quote, in demonstrative gestures and flow, pulling the students into a different place, at which time *it* happened; Milly felt *painted* with that which was ancient, a voice calling her from outside of time.

That is the way she put it, when her soul felt carried to a different place, leaving what she had known as *normal*, moving into the *abnormal*, experiencing what words meant. It was crazy! Some called this mindset "three-dimensional thinking," which is what Einstein experienced, being considered outrageous to those around him, who were quite normal. Therefore, to Milly, *it* was good.

"That which is crooked cannot be made straight: and that which is wanting cannot be numbered,"[ii] Kaufman repeated. Pacing in front of the room slowly, he then provoked the students even further, "This line from the philosopher declares that there is both a good wisdom and a bad wisdom. We see here, the bad wisdom is reflected by the 'crooked and wanting.'"

Students were shifting in their seats, trying to comprehend fully what Kaufman was saying.

"In the next line," Kaufman said with a slight pause, "The philosopher states: *I communed with mine own heart, saying, Lo, I am come to great estate, and have gotten MORE WISDOM than all they that have been before me in Jerusalem: yea, MY HEART HAD GREAT EXPERIENCE OF WISDOM AND KNOWLEDGE."*[iii]

Kaufman turned to stare at the rising philosophers, grabbing their ears with his words, "This brilliant soul, had COMMUNION or can we say, 'common union,' with wisdom and knowledge; more than anyone before him."

Kaufman walked back to the front of his desk, and continued, "Obtaining knowledge became *an experience* in his soul. The philosopher was taken into a place, where he was *painted*, with something more ancient than time."

He remained hushed as students gasped, with a few who could be heard saying, "wow."

Milly's ears were perked, since she heard him say what no one else knew she was thinking, about, which was *being painted*! "How could he know that word," she thought, unless he had the same disease she had too, philosophism. She smiled, hoping it was notable to others that she was one of those who were *painted*. "Surely Parker saw it."

Kaufman walked up to Milly, looking into her eyes, "Yes, it is good to be painted in wisdom, don't you think?"

She almost melted in her seat when he spoke the words, "painted in wisdom." It did something to her stomach. She knew that the gut was the second brain, with all the neurons operating within. Her "gut instinct" was her second brain letting her know that there was an ancient call connected to her soul for this wisdom.

Kaufman spanned his eyes around to the other students, "How awe-inspiring of an experience to have more wisdom than others, to the point that you cross over into another dimension that very few have ever entered, where your normal world becomes this experience, which is totally abnormal." Students marveled and knew that they had gotten their money's worth already for the semester.

"The next line, the philosopher states, is," he said in a softer tone, "*And I gave my heart to know wisdom, and to know madness and folly: I perceived that this also is vexation of spirit.*"[iv]

Kaufman poised himself against his desk slightly on the edge. Leaning forward to whisper life's greatest secret, as he said, "Here, we see the reality of the philosopher's failing, as he now depicts the two wisdoms he came to know, one which is of another dimension, eternal, and then a wisdom of this world, which he calls folly and madness."

"To know the two of them was much vexation to his soul, leaving him in anguish. The culprit of his pain, is revealed in the final sentence, '*For in much wisdom is much grief: and he that increaseth knowledge increaseth sorrow.*'"[v]

You could tell that Kaufman inhaled the solution to the philosopher's quandary, and through extended vocabulary, assimilated this point for his students to comprehend. "To know both dimensions of a wisdom, one which appears wise but is folly and madness, and then to know a wisdom that is so ancient that it precedes time itself, causes one anguish if they have disregard for the higher realm of philosophy."

Hushed, the students were bent in their seats, as if to hear a whisper from the ancient time, waiting on Kaufman to give them more. Then he spelled it out to them, "When you know this wisdom and what is right with it, which we know is truth. Then to know it and do that, which is contrary, is absolute madness. This is where this great philosopher's soul was, bent between two dimensions, two wisdoms. We know this philosopher as King Solomon."

The students were surprised, some having heard of King Solomon by their upbringing, and others never having heard the name, unsure what he was king of.

"He was King of Israel," Kaufman said. "King Solomon ruled in Jerusalem, what many have deemed as the gateway to eternity."

Milly pondered, remembering from her childhood, how King Solomon wrote most of the book of Proverbs, which she had studied. Ruminating on the quote, she thought about her dream from last night, wondering if there was a connection to King Solomon's quote about wisdom, and her dream.

The sound of all the other voices in the class drowned out, as she felt covered with paint again, existing in what felt like a bubble in time. There was no other way to describe what she was feeling, other than *painted*. Her curiosity was peaked and she thought, "What is it with this *painted* term, that continually turns over in my head? Why *painted*?"

Snapping his fingers in front of her face, Parker spoke like a robotic voice, "Earth to Milly, earth to Milly."

She turned to see what was going on and realized that class had ended. It was time to move on, to the next juncture of her Sophomore year, knowing that she had a 50 minute window before her next period class of history, after which, would then be poetry for her English requirement.

Now realizing that she had been lost in her own thoughts, she could not help but wonder how much time she had missed. "Wow, that was fast," she said, "is class already over?"

"Uh, yeah, why do you think I am snapping my fingers in front of your face?" Parker asked as he tilted his head to do a "Kaufman," examining her like a botanist scrutinizing a new insect. "Seriously Milly, where were you for those last 5 minutes of class; you were not with us."

"We'll talk about it at *The Grind*, do you have a few before your next class?"

"Yes I do. Also, it seemed as though you were going to tell me something when I first came in, is everything alright?"

She remembered that she had not told him about the dream. "Yes, I do have something, and yes everything is alright. In fact, everything is better than alright; I believe this lesson with Kaufman's class correlates with what I wanted to share with you."

"Cool, let's go."

Kaufman looked at Milly and Parker, and nodded as they went out. The two of them came down the stairs and exited the Truman building, to head towards the campus coffee shop, *The Grind*.

The Grind

Coffee smells, toffee, caramel, vanilla and hazelnut danced in the atmosphere, like a rhumba to the nose, where even the particles of aroma passed through nose hair, pulling its guests toward the coffee bar. This was everyone's favorite place on campus. Milly and Parker usually met once a day at *The Grind*, to discuss their new classes, as well as to study for upcoming exams.

"What's your addiction?" said the young man behind the coffee bar.

Milly and Parker laughed and said simultaneously, "we've never heard that before."

"Jinx" said the young man, and all three began to laugh. Then he pointed to his T-shirt that had a coffee cup with steam coming off the top, saying, *MY CHOICE OF ADDICTION IS COFFEE*. Milly replied with excitement, "I absolutely love it, I have to have one of those shirts; it would look great with my navy blazer!"

Parker joined in, "Well, once I graduate and become a well known neurobiologist, I will buy you every color that they have." The two of them chuckled as the young man behind the coffee bar waited for their order.

"Right," Milly replied, "my addiction is a small vanilla latte with sugar free caramel drizzled on top, hold all sugar please."

Milly then looked at Parker, who gave his order, "Well, my addiction is a large cheesecake latte with chocolate drizzle." The young man looked at them, nodded as he pointed for them to sit at the coffee bar while he finished their drink order, asking them if it was for "here" or "to go?"

"Absolutely for here," replied Parker, looking at Milly, extending his arm towards her, "right Mill?"

She nodded and did two thumbs up in a *cheesy* way, "That is to go with your cheesecake latte, Einstein." She could not resist using her odd sense of humor to tease him about his choice of drink.

The importance of them staying at *The Grind* to splurge on an overpriced hot drink, was because it brought them the indulgence of feeling as though they were at a posh place. The Grind had the coolest coffee cups ever, made of a thick tall clear glass that looked like an oversized lab experiment vial, allowing people to see where the foam met the dark coffee. Observing people drinking from the cups was hilarious, like watching people drink a lab experiment.

The young gentlemen handed them their drinks, and they took them outside to the patio. *The Grind* was the trendiest place in Springfield, made out of a container. An extended roof, overhanging the conspicuous silver corrugated container that was trimmed in chrome, added more space for people to sit. The roof, made of black industrial material, had columns supporting it, which were made of industrial steel. The ten garage doors were placed between the columns all around *The Grind*, with two doors on each end, and three doors on each side. On beautiful days the garage doors were lifted, bringing the outside in.

Although the coffee shop itself was made of only one 8 x 40 foot container, with the bar all around it, the roof overhang and the garage doors made the space feel much larger. A huge hangout for students on campus, and even a local gathering place for professors, *The Grind* was the center of all social life on campus.

Milly and Parker's favorite place was right outside of the garage doors, on the patio area, where they could sit and enjoy the sun. The two of them walked out to the patio, sipping on their drinks, making sounds of delight. They could not help but be grateful for the addition that the coffee shop brought to the campus just two years ago. Thank goodness it was brought on campus before they started their freshman year.

As they sat down at the table, Parker looked at Milly and nodded his head. She could have sworn that she was seeing more of Professor Kaufman's mannerisms in him. "Wow, do you realize that you are turning more and more into Kaufman with your nods and stares?" she asked.

Parker looked at her, and shrugged, "How do you know that he's not turning more and more into me?"

"Ok cowboy, hold it there and let's get to the real particulars of why we are having this conference today." All their meetings at *The Grind* were a "conference."

"What is it Mill?" That is the term Parker used for Milly when they were in their intellectual mode in drumming out coursework with one another or when they were in conference.

"I had a crazy dream last night that was clear, like a high definition movie with sensory overload, that seemed so real."

"Ok, that's a good start to this semester!" Parker said excited. "Especially since we just left Kaufman's class with a blowout, so what was your dream?"

"I was walking down these old stone steps, into what seemed like a cave in the earth. As I continued down the steps, I saw more stone steps that were then lit up. Not from a light like in a room, but from this warm light coming all around, that seemed like the sun setting in the evening or rising in the morning."

She continued on, "After I descended down the steps, I then came to a room filled with warm light, and in it was a bed, desk and chair. On top of the desk was this old paper, rolled up like a scroll, and I heard a voice say, '*I will give you understanding of what is on the scroll.*'"

Milly had Parker's attention, as he sat there mesmerized. To which she motioned for him to continue to drink his latte. He took a sip and listened on in awe.

"Immediately, I was then taken up to what seemed like the universe, as an astronaut in outer space, except I needed no suit. I could see the Milky Way, nebulas and even a singularity. Afterwards, a voice spoke to me and said, *'Mildred, I have much to show you that is to come.'* Then, I saw a huge door in the heavens, slowly opening with this brilliant light, like that of the sun, coming from behind it." She stopped, took a deep breath, another sip of her latte and looked across the table at Parker's face, seeing his jaw dropped, and his eyes wide open.

"Well Park," which was Milly's term for Parker in their conferences, "What do you think?"

"Gosh Mill, that is absolutely the wildest dream I have ever heard. I have no clue, what do *you* think it means?"

"I wasn't sure at first. But, when Kaufman began speaking this morning in class, for some reason I kept telling myself during his delivery, that I felt 'painted.'"

She paused before proceeding further, making sure that she could accurately convey her experience to Parker. "Right after I said that in my head, Kaufman gave us King Solomon's quote, then stared right at me as he talked about being *painted* in wisdom." Milly was confidant that Kaufman's actions were confirmation to her dream.

"I don't know what to say Mill; you know I am a deep person, but man, I have to think about this one." Parker was being stretched with his friends dream and had no direction to give her, other than to agree.

She continued, "There is more; I think that it was not by accident that I had the dream last night and we started Philosophy 201 today; I believe that the dream relates to King Solomon's quote, about a higher wisdom, and that this dream was showing me that the way to this higher wisdom is not the way that I think, but rather down an ancient pathway that's rarely traveled."

Parker sat in disbelief, no longer doing his Kaufman stare, but instead shaking his head from side to side, "Gosh Mill, I believe you could be right. It is freaky though to think that this could be the case."

The two sat and finished their coffee and were joined by the young man behind the bar. "So was your choice of addiction today right on?" he asked.

They assured him that he was on target with the flavors, and then got up to go to their next class, Parker had Biology 202 and Milly had History 310.

History

Next to philosophy, history was Milly's second favorite subject in school. She enjoyed history and especially the study of antiquities, which was the class that she was taking this semester under Dr. Anjali Mercer.

Milly did not know Dr. Mercer well, but her reputation preceded her, from the rave reviews the upperclassmen gave. A wonderful teacher in antiquities, the only thing Milly need do, was to get past Dr. Mercer's strong dialect. Originally from, New Delhi, India, Mercer came to the States when she was 14 years old with her family, to pursue the American dream. Having five sisters, her parents believed there were greater opportunities for educational advancement in the States.

Dr. Mercer married a medical student, Dr. Alan Mercer, while pursuing her undergraduate. She obtained her masters during her husband's medical residency training, and then pursued her Doctor of Philosophy (PhD) when her husband finished his residency. The two of them are fondly referred to as "the Doctors Mercer." Both are well respected, and give a good bit of their time to charity work, with unwavering dedication to help others. Therefore, Milly felt as though she was about to be in the presence of greatness.

She arrived back at the Truman building, scaling up to the third floor for History 310. Unsure of what Dr. Mercer's class would bring with it, she entered, and felt she was among the upperclassman. Those in attendance were juniors and seniors. They greeted her to make sure she felt welcomed to the "antiquities club."

"Take your desks," Mercer said as she strolled into the room. She was neatly dressed, in a long charcoal pencil skirt suit, with her long black hair up in a bun, and her face accented by her red-framed glasses. Mercer looked the part for sure, Milly thought, for an antiquities professor.

She could not help but imagine Dr. Mercer as a superhero, ready to come out of the suit to save the world. Relaxed after her short conference with Parker, Milly was readying herself to have her ears trained to Mercer's dialect. Although others had warned her of the difficulty they had at first listening to her, Milly discovered Mercer's dialect was not as bad as others had made it out to be.

"It is time for your favorite subject, which is why you have showed up in History 310 for this semester," Professor Mercer said. "We will be studying antiquities, which are things of ancient origin from human remains and artifacts. Although many see this area as the study of archeology, the wonderful thing about Strytan is that they have cross-pollinated with History, making this a more rounded study of things of ancient origin. Antiquities is a 'far away history.'" She pulled the projector screen down, picked up the remote to begin her slide show, and told the students to turn to the first chapter of their text.

"This class in particular, is the study of ancient Greece and ancient Rome, known as the Greco-Roman era, where the studies of antiquities is largely centered around the Mediterranean Sea. We will look at specific antiquities from four Greek periods, known as the Geometric Period, the Archaic Period, the Classical Period and the Hellenistic Period. In addition, we will be looking at the influence of Rome in Art under the Republic and Art under the Empire."

Milly was captivated, as Dr. Mercer brought different slides up from those eras, whetting the appetite of the students. She wanted to look at the faces of the other students while Mercer went from picture to picture, but was so drawn to the slides, that she could not take her eyes off of them. Milly sensed a new door had opened to things of antiquity and was in her glory, like a queen on her throne extending her scepter. She felt she had another gift bestowed upon her by her education, bringing her closer to her destiny, empowering her to be painted by wisdom.

Class ended to her regret; she wanted to stay longer. The upperclassmen ascended out of their seats, at which time she followed, and trickled out of the class. Mercer stood by the door as they were dismissed to welcome them back to the school. On her way out, Milly tried to keep her face down, so as not to be noticed, at which time Mercer said, "I have not seen you before, what is your name?"

Milly felt paralyzed and looked up at Mercer's red-framed glasses, "Uh, Milly, Dr. Mercer, but on your roll sheet it has me as 'Mildred.'"

Mercer looked at Milly as if she knew a secret, "Is there any relation to the saint of Springfield, Mildred Virginia Lee?"

Milly felt awkward but glad to know that Mercer had made the connection. "Yes Dr. Mercer, she is my Great Grandmother."

"Remarkable," Dr. Mercer said with her index finger on her chin, "I expect great things out of you Mildred Teschlon."

"Yes mam, I hope so."

Chapter 2

Parker and Milly, having their regular conference at *The Grind*, were enjoying their favorite addiction, as they discussed their first month of classes. In the midst of their conference they suddenly saw something overshadowing them, and realized it was Kaufman; he was doing his "hovering" thing.

"Two of my brilliant students at work, knocking out the latest assignment on Theism I am sure," Kaufman said as he stared at the pair.

"You caught us Professor Kaufman," Parker said with a chuckle.

"Listen, I am glad I found you two here; I need assistance with some old files in the basement of Truman. We are moving everything to a computer and need to get rid of our old files. Is it possible the two of you might be able to work a couple of hours a day? It would be decent pay."

Milly and Parker looked at each other being shocked that Kaufman was asking *them*. Seeing their latent response Kaufman gave them a way out, "You can let me know by tomorrow's class."

Kaufman turned, readying to make his exit, when the young man behind the coffee bar brought him his addiction saying, "Here you are Professor Kaufman, the malt-balls latte with caramel shavings on top."

"Sounds good Professor Kaufman," Parker said.

"What, the opportunity or my latte," asked Kaufman, to which Parker responded, "Both."

"Thank you for the opportunity Professor Kaufman," chimed Milly.

Milly could hardly contain her excitement, "Wow, was that neat or what Park?" They both did a fist pump, as they finished their conference.

Home

Milly could smell her mother's meatloaf cooking, and knew that her dad would be happy; that was one of his favorites. Smells of comfort and the sound of her mother's voice on the phone talking with the florist about the upcoming celebration for Great Grand's work in Springfield, made her all the more happy.

"Hey Mom," Milly said softly, as she walked through the kitchen, grabbing an apple. Her mother waved, gave a wink and pointed at the phone, mouthing with her lips, "florist." Milly confirmed with thumbs up, took a bite of the apple and headed towards her cave.

Opening the door to her treasure trove, seeing her latest projects of antiquities and recent poetry assignments still spread out on her gold colored bedspread, alerted her for the Theism paper deadline. She knew that she had to prepare for Kaufman's assignment. Music turned on in the background, playing her favorite songs softly, gave the sense of activity, as she prepared to do her work.

Knock, knock, knock, she heard at the door. "Come in Mom."

"Hey Sweetie how was your day?"

"It was great; Kaufman wants Parker and I, to assist in getting rid of the old department files; they are now putting them on computers."

Milly's mother congratulated her and then said, "I wanted to remind you of Great Grand's celebration this Saturday in the town square, from 10am – 9 pm. I just finalized all the floral arrangements for the event." Lavern, relieved that the day had almost arrived, added, "Milly, this is going to be the best one yet, the planning committee has assured me. They even have many of the fraternities and sororities involved from the University. Maybe you will see some of your friends there."

"I don't know Mom; most of my friends will be preparing for exams this weekend," Milly said as she motioned to the books on her bedspread.

"Milly, now this is important to the family, and since you are named after Great Grand, we expect you to be there."

"Alright Mom, only for you," Milly said jokingly, "I would prefer to stay in my cave and not come out."

Lavern went to her daughter and hugged her, touching her hair lightly, "Say, do you think you need another trim soon Mill; the ends of your hair are looking a little split."

"Mom, pleeeeeeassseeee."

"Ok, I'm leaving, see you at dinner 7 sharp, love you." Lavern closed the door and her heals could be heard on the wood floor, as she went down the hall back into the kitchen.

Dinner

"I'm home, where is the meatloaf," Daniel Teschlon said as he opened the door, expecting to be met by his wife and daughter. Lavern came and hugged him, as he gave her a light peck on the lips. "I smell it already honey, I cannot wait. It's my favorite."

Lavern, acted flattered as ever, as she did every Thursday; it is meatloaf day in the Teschlon house. "Stop," Lavern said as she patted him on the shoulder. "You know that I will always take care of my Danny Boy and make sure that you are fed good."

They kissed again, and Daniel clapped his hands together, which was the sign that he was going to change out of his business attire and get comfortable, while Lavern started the coffee on the stovetop, for them to have after the meal, when they ate dessert. The smell of the coffee percolating made them like two happy beavers on a tree, making a dam on the water. It did not take much to thrill Mr. and Mrs. Teschlon these days.

"Where's Mill, Hon?" Daniel asked his wife.

"She is in her cave, studying as always."

Milly could hear her dad's footsteps coming down the hall, until they stopped. He opened the door, "Hey Mill, are you going to come out of your cave for dinner?" he said winking.

"Yes Dad, I'll be out of the cave at 7 sharp."

"See you then Mill."

Smells so thick in the atmosphere, you could almost taste them, blended together with the meatloaf and cauliflower mash, covered with sautéed mushrooms drowned in butter. The Teschlon family lived a Ketogenic lifestyle, which is a low carb, high fat diet, where fats eventually are converted into ketones, providing fuel for the organs and the brain. Milly's family has a history of seizures and this diet aids in preventing any onset of symptoms.

Milly quite enjoys the Ketogenic diet; it gives her mental clarity in studying for her subjects, where the ketones in her brain make words leap off the page, almost three-dimensional. As a result, it is easier for her to grasp and comprehend the subject matter in her classes, making her a fast learner.

She has shared the Ketogenic lifestyle with others, giving them vital information, and bringing up the analogy of the "runner's high," to provide them greater understanding. "When people run for a great length of time, their body produces ketones, and only those who have felt this experience know what it means, and easily relate," Milly would say.

Milly, living this lifestyle for many years, felt she had this "runner's high" most of the time, and has greater clarity in studying her subjects. In addition, it helps her deal with the issues of bullying from her past, keeping her mind focused on her future. Before the Ketogenic lifestyle, her depression was nearly unbearable, but she hid it well.

However, once getting on the Ketogenic diet, Milly could tell that the GABA (Gamma-aminobutyric Acid) levels in her brain increased. Knowing that GABA is the brain's calming agent, she believed that the Ketogenic diet helped treat her depression, where she stopped cutting. Most of the time she is in a good mood. The Ketogenic lifestyle, has aided her, in dealing with *the voices* that she needs to overcome. Grateful to her parents for getting the family on the diet years earlier, Milly knew it was a game changer in her life. In her moments of weakness, where her low self-esteem has manifest, and the deranged thought patterns speak to her mind, she has been able to remain calm and talk herself through it.

She could not get to dinner soon, enough, looking to keep her ketone levels high. Coming into the dining room, Milly now felt her brain desiring the food that she was smelling, "Hey, I'm here, let's eat; it all smells good. Are we going to have Keto-Coffee after the meal tonight, with our dessert?" Milly's parents looked at each other and laughed; she asked this nearly every night at dinner.

Teasingly her father responded, "Mill, we will only have it, if you will share some details," which meant sharing what happened through the day.

"Ok dad, you got it," she said as she plopped on the seat, putting her napkin in her lap.

During the course of the meal, the family ate, discussing the weekend's celebration of Great Grand, along with the new venture Milly was pursuing in assisting Kaufman. As her mother and father got up to clear the table and prepare the Keto-Coffee, she heard her mother call from the kitchen, "Hey Mill, you know that we are carrying your grandmother to the event, where she will sit there to talk to people about Great Grand."

Milly loved her grandmother, Virginia, whom everyone lovingly referred to as "Jenny." "Oh yes Mom, I know she looks forward to it each year; it must bring back some fond memories of Great Grand in the old days," she paused, "you know when you were little." She could not resist such a good joke. Milly's mother looked at her with a sharp eye wittingly, and then they all began to laugh.

They walked out to the patio, each with a dessert and a Keto-Coffee, sitting down to enjoy the quiet night. "Oh how I love this time of day," Lavern said. They each were looking into the night sky that was lit up by the stars in the skies, sipping slowly on the aromatic and frothy Keto-Coffee, where they could taste the butter and coconut oil, blended in with their favorite Columbian flavor.

Each of them simultaneously said, "yum." They looked at each other laughing, and rested in the armchairs that cloaked them like a good blanket, where their soul was comforted and their body was renewed. Now for the next day, Milly thought, Kaufman!

Kaufman

The next day Milly and Parker walked into Kaufman's class a bit early to accept the responsibility of clearing out the basement. He gave them the specifics of the room assigned to the Philosophy department, with the key. The other students filed into class, excited for the new lesson that Kaufman had for them, having finished their recent Theism assignment. Philosophy 201 consisted of the complex study of what Milly called "the isms," studying the philosophical opinions of the influence on theism, naturalism and humanism.

Kaufman's first month of teaching introduced the students to the different "isms," and now they were going deeper into each individual one. Sitting on the edge of his desk, he directed the class toward the board, where the word "Theism" was written across the top, in white.

"Theism, the belief in the existence of a God or gods, especially one God as the creator of the universe (all things), Who intervenes on behalf of His creation, sustaining a personal relationship with them," Kaufman said, while holding up a piece of chalk. "The question to you stoics of Philosophy 201, is what say *you*? Can you plausibly relate an ideal expression with one to two words, regarding your text and supplemental readings, as you develop a view on this branch of philosophy." The students sat in their seats pondering on the word, as they combed through their papers that were to be handed in by the end of class.

"Any takers?" Kaufman asked while holding up the chalk in his left hand.

"I believe that there is no God or such thing as gods," said a student sitting on the back row, slouching in his desk, as if to be heard and not seen.

Kaufman held the chalk up, "Mr. Lassiter, I believe you have failed to understand the assignment, because the question put to you was that you go to the board and in one to two words put down your view; there is no strength needed or fortitude provided for those who tend to sit in their seats and slouch down, only to be a fading voice in the universe." The students were now nervous for Lassiter and even more hesitant about stepping up to the plate.

Lassiter rose from his seat, walked to the front in a type of swag as if he was a lion on the prowl, retrieving the chalk from Kaufman. His steps could be heard as he threatened the black board with his presence, loathing the word itself, *Theism*. In all caps underneath he wrote BOLOGNA. Some of the students chuckled, while others sat there staring, not certain of what would happen next. They knew Lassiter had purposely-misspelled baloney and instead put bologna.

Lassiter put the chalk back into Kaufman's hand, as he walked proudly to his desk, holding his head high, like a bully in the playground looking for a fight. He sat down, shifted his weight from side to side as he continued getting his *slouch* right in the desk, and then retreated into his own world, daring anyone who would come near him.

Kaufman paused, while looking out of the window in silence, seemingly to search for a word or two to conjure up in confronting a small rebellion in his class, streaming from one of the most popular guys on campus.

Lassiter was head of the main fraternity, having come from a legacy of many relatives at Strytan, who had more than enough money to fund most of the University's programs. He was arrogant and knew it, not caring what others thought of his little ponzi schemes on campus; he was above the law and could do whatever he liked. Lassiter was over the backroom gambling at Strytan, along with aiding a cheating system for papers in the classes. He was walking on a tightrope but did not mind playing with people's psyches, while doing it.

Kaufman turned his head to the front, as he lifted off of his desk and walked toward the back of the room, where an invisible confrontation was going down, and today was everyone's lucky day to see the battle of wits between their beloved professor and the university bully, where they had front row seats. Milly and Parker eyed each other and, each straightened their spine, to be as observant as possible to watch this showdown.

Sounds amplified, as people shifted in their seats, throats were gulping and students placed their feet on the floor that squeaked underneath.

Eyes were focused on the chalk, as Kaufman kept it firmly in his left hand, and walked down the aisle towards the back. Everyone was suspecting that he was going to Lassiter, and let him have a philosophical butt whipping. Students were eager and anticipating the most brilliant face-off on campus.

"Lassiter, philosophy is the study of the fundamental nature of knowledge, as well as the reality of that knowledge, in our daily lives, arriving at *its* existence not in space, but rather in this world."

Students were stirred up with electricity as they heard and watched what was happening. "Thus, if your only response to the word, Theism, is bologna, then that alone is evidence that you are not sufficient to be in this class. That response delivers no knowledge, as a matter of fact it provides no knowledge at all; but rather it lets us see the back end of a pork's butt, dealing not with the issue at hand of *knowledge*, but rather the fact that this is evidence that knowledge does not exist in your mind on this issue. I am looking for you to give something of more intellect, proving that you are more than capable to answer the question. However, your response has been on the level of someone in junior high-school and elementary, not requiring intellect at all, but rather reveals the insults to your own mind that is being challenged to grow and consider something that has so sufficiently been the crux to which our world thrives in thought, interaction and relationships."

Lassiter, still slouched in his seat, wanted to save face now that he was confronted. "I was MERELY trying to wake the class up. Sorry if this offended you Kaufman."

Kaufman nodded at Lassiter and then continued holding the chalk in his hand, walking to the front of the room, "Who will be brave enough to go places that no one else in this class has gone, a new frontier to see the world as never before, by boldly making a one or two word statement of your view on Theism?"

Heart pounding, restless, Milly was unsure of what was going on with her, and found herself standing up. Her mind was racing as she walked toward Kaufman, wondering, "What in the world am I doing? How did I get up out of my seat and why in the biosphere, am I walking to

Kaufman and moreover, what in the heck am I going to write on the board?"

She smiled at a couple of the students she knew pretty well, and like a swan gliding on the water, glided up to Kaufman, lightly clasping the chalk from his hands, as she could feel all eyes on her, staring, looking, anticipating. Parker was thinking, "How is Mill going to do a recovery on this, from what Lassiter did?"

Her eyes on the board, she found herself picking the eraser up and with calm, erased what Lassiter wrote, thinking, "What on earth am I doing? I have no clue what I am doing." Then she sat the eraser down, keeping her eyes on the blackboard, and ten inches under the word Theism, she wrote in capital letters "PAINTED."

Lassiter was bothered by Milly's boldness and thought, "She has no clue who I am and the influence that I have on this campus." Milly turned from the board, as though she was in her own bubble, where no one else entered, carrying on like an autistic child lost in thought, defeating the foes of their life. Had she gone all these years and not been diagnosed with Asperger Syndrome and was finding out at this moment. Crazy thoughts flooded her head, as she handed the chalk back to Kaufman, seeing but not receiving the stares of others who did not understand what she did. Did she just 'dis' Lassiter in front of the class with Kaufman, or was she insane for even considering getting up at all, and especially having the audacity to erase what Lassiter wrote, even when Kaufman did not.

Parker looked at Milly with his mouth open, as she gracefully sat down into her desk, winking in secret to him, where he then mouthed to her, "What are you doing?" Milly simply gave him thumbs up, to which he thought she had to be out of her mind or high. He knew his friend did not mess with drugs, and so she could not be high, but with that noted, she had to be losing her mind.

Kaufman looked at Milly, examining her for a moment, the calm nature of her person, where there seemed to be a peace, with a light exuding from her inner self. He shifted on his desk towards the area she was seated and asked her, "Milly, that is an interesting word, why do you use *painted*, and how does Theism indicate this particular choice of word to you, shaping your philosophy?"

It seemed as though the students were leaning now to the right, as they still had their backs straight, from what Kaufman did with Lassiter, and this peculiar reaction from Milly caused them all the more intrigue, like a bird trying to fly through a glass door, wanting to get on the other side; so were they.

"Well, Professor Kaufman, *painted* means to cover the surface of an area with decoration, which then becomes a protection to that surface." All ears in the room were peaked to hear what sounded like brilliance being born amongst them, and Kaufman himself, was brought into this place of surreal, where he was watching greatness in front of his eyes.

Milly continued, "Painting, is the means by which you predict and produce on a medium of expression, which requires a brush, where you touch colors to a canvas, in order to bring about a description that has not been seen before." Students were wowed.

She continued, "Michelangelo touched the ceiling of the Sistine Chapel creating a description of Theism that has captivated people for centuries. " The class was stunned, eyes were glued, mouths were opened as oxygen was sparsely used; everyone was holding their breath to see what Milly would say next.

Thoughts flooded her mind, as she realized that the voices of the bullying and self-inflicted rejection were silent. Somehow, she found another voice inside of her speaking, and realized that this was the voice, which she was listening to as she spoke. This voice brought comfort to her soul, like standing under a waterfall.

"Theism," Milly said, "Is the depiction of believing in a God, that pulled out a brush from the heavens, as He dipped it in colors to create. He brought description of what and who He is, on the canvas of each of our lives, this earth, and throughout all time, where He wants to be seen."

Kaufman was blown away, Parker's eyes still wide in disbelief. Milly had a new found respect with the other students, especially the upperclassmen, who gave her a thumbs up and nodded, as a gesture of acceptance.

"What a profound word Milly," Kaufman said as he arose from his desk to pace the front of the room slowly, pondering before he would give his own discourse as to what Milly had spoken, and the relation of Theism to this term "painted," that Milly had introduced.

He spoke softly, at a steady pace that was building up for the big reveal. Watching him was much like witnessing the symphony explosion at the end for the evening's concerto. "Therefore, Theism, according to Milly's view," he paused and continued, "shows us the freedom of expression and creativity that is provided by the Creator, Who has created. Thus, Milly's term, painted, emphasizes that His creation flows with the same didactic pattern of *painting*, where the brush strokes are continually teaching and speaking to us that of moral rectitude, providing the soul with a meal that cannot otherwise be furnished and satisfied by food. But rather, giving the soul that which it longs to do, which is to create, and in turn, the canvas of the heart and mind are both covered and protected, thus we have philosophy."

You could hear the wows and see the heads nodding, as others agreed demonstratively with Kaufman. His watch alarm went off, to which he announced class dismissed, ending with, "We will pick up with this term *painted* and expound upon it at the next class, please be prepared to speak to this point." He looked at Milly and then nodded, as he said, "Good word Milly."

Parker bumped shoulders with her on the way out, "Way to go Mill, man I have never seen you like that, what in the world happened. Its like there's a Milly I've known for the last year and a half, but this is a whole new Milly I've never seen."

She smiled as they exited and said, "I don't know Park, but it felt good."

"Oh, so we are in conference now, and we have not gotten our addiction at *The Grind* yet," he said jokingly. The two of them laughed and headed onward to *The Grind*, to which they enjoyed a new addiction from the coffee bar, and shortly afterward headed to their classes.

"Let's meet up after class, and start Kaufman's project in the basement," Parker said, "And we are going to have to give that a name too," he chuckled.

"Sounds good, see you then."

The Basement

After classes, the two of them met at the basement door in the Truman building. They opened the door, finding the light by the steps. Parker flipped the switch on, and they commenced their journey into the *unknown*. As they walked down, Milly began to get a strange feeling that she had been here before, and immediately she was taken back to her dream.

Her dream had now become a full-blown vision, while she walked down the stairs. She saw the steps in a new way; underneath her feet looked like the stone steps in her dream. Not wanting to tell Parker, she kept it to herself. He was already tilted by her behavior in class today, and this would certainly not help.

Although there was not much light appearing on the steps from the few lights over their descension, Milly was picturing a warm light surrounding them as they continued downward. She was spooked to say the least, and could not help reverting to the possibility of her having Asperger Syndrome, or possibly, something else was occurring, "Maybe it was stress," she thought. She stopped for a moment, blinked her eyes, and everything was back to normal again.

"Hey Mill, are you alright?" A bit worried, Parker was wondering if his friend was having some type of neurological reaction causing her to be a bit off today.

"I'm fine Park, just trying to get my footing."

They headed down the hall and saw huge light bulbs in industrial glass sconces with heavy metal wall attachments, making the hall look like an infinite corridor, the length of the building. They were dawdling at moving forward, until they heard a squeaking noise, at which Milly jumped, and Parker announced, "Ok, if we are going to work down here, we have to get a cat so we can make sure we don't have to put up with rats; I did not sign up for rats."

Milly laughing at her friend's startled reaction brought much peace to his timidity. They began talking about class with Lassiter going off half-cocked, and Kaufman's response to him. Passing ten doors, they arrived at the Philosophy department on the right side of the hall. Milly pulled the golden looking key out of her blazer, put it in the door, hearing it click and pushed it open to enter.

Dust was settling as it floated in the air that was stirred by the breeze that came with the door opening. Sunlight coming through the small window at the top of the room that was about two feet high and ten feet long, hit the dust particles, giving rise to a philosophical atmosphere, as Milly quoted one of her favorite artists.

"*The purpose of art is washing the dust of daily life off of our soul.*" She paused as Parker looked confused, and she responded to his stare, "It's Pablo Picasso, silly."

Parker laughed and said with hesitation, "I thought you were going into your philosophy bubble, where you were in class today."

"Philosophy bubble?" Milly was not sure what Parker meant entirely, although she had a hint.

"Yes Mill; when you went up to the board, you had this great calm about you, and I almost felt like I was watching my little sister play Barbie dolls, as she would take them different places in her dollhouse. The doll never has control and is carried around. That is what it was like watching you; you were just being *carried* to the board, although on your own volition, still it seemed like something else was driving you, and all I know to call it is the Philosophy Bubble."

She pondered on what Parker said digesting his words and then said, "I don't understand it myself. All I know is when I stood up to go the board, I had no clue what I was going to do, and kept talking to myself the whole time, feeling like a crazy person trying to talk myself out of responding to Kaufman's question. So, I just kind of went with it, and I guess the Barbie doll description is a good one; I was in control but felt a little out of control not knowing what would come out of mouth. But once all of the revelation came out about the word painted, it was as though I was hearing it for the first time as the class was. I knew it was somewhere in my soul, but needed the right opportunity for it to be made known."

They heard another squeak in the hall, to which Parker quickly responded, "We have got to tell Kaufman we are bringing a cat to live in this basement, I will not put up with any rats."

The two laughed, and then began the process of clearing out the files from the room. The dusty philosophy coffer was 10 x 20, the room somewhat large, had metal shelves, topped with boxes holding old files. Dust was piled up everywhere, so the two of them knew that this day was about making a plan, to work adequately in getting the files moved.

Milly pulled out her pad and paper, "First things first, is that we are getting some dust cloths and I am bringing my electric handheld vacuum to make it more palatable to work among all this dust. The next thing is that we need to wear clothes that we can get dirty, between the dust and us sweating, we are not going to carry this back to our house."

Parker agreed. They went down each of the aisles to observe the boxes stacked on metal shelves. Inventorying the number of boxes on the last aisle, they saw that there were boxes stacked upon boxes in the middle. This was a project that they could begin tomorrow they thought, and were glad to call it an early day, now knowing fully what they were getting themselves into.

"Ok Mill. Also, if we are going to work a little late, it might be good for us to bring a lantern, in case the sun goes down; we will have more light than the little light here in the room, those bulbs look old." Milly added that to her list, and the two of them left agreeing to return after classes tomorrow.

Milly went home, having dinner with her mother and father, enjoying their Keto-coffee on the back porch. They shared with each other their daily activity, and her parents listened, as she talked about what happened in Kaufman's class, with the showdown he had with Lassiter, and her own small role in readjusting the class' focus to the subject.

"Good for you Mill," said her mother. I am so proud of you; that sounds like something Great Grand would have done.

"Oh Mom please, you are always comparing me to her no matter what I do," Milly replied.

"Listen, your Great Grand was only 22 years old, when she was considered the town hero during the depression, having a notebook for all that they were to do, delegating the tasks in the city, as well as dealing with the bullies of her time. You know it had to be hard to be a young woman then, dealing with the discrimination."

Milly rolled her eyes, "Yes Mom, I know."

Daniel knew his daughter was a bit restless, and touched Milly's arm lightly saying, "Listen to your Mom, this is important to her, you know?"

Milly straightened up, sipped her Keto-coffee, and repented, "Mom I am sorry, I love hearing about Great Grand." She fidgeted, "I guess I feel unworthy, or far from being as great as she was and it makes me nervous at times when I hear you comparing us."

Lavern had a tear in the corner of her eye and responded, "Milly, please dear don't think that; you are as brave as Great Grand and cannot see it. She was so busy during her time with the oddities of her own personality, and what you described today in Kaufman's class, was a lot like the behavior of your Great Grand. She would always repeat, 'I am not my own,' as she would go about her work. That is what I thought of as you shared Parker's description of you being a Barbie doll. I am so proud of you and only want you to believe the best of who you are." Milly leaned forward from her chair, and put her hand on her mother's arm, mouthing the words "Thank you."

The Basement Part II

Milly and Parker met at the basement door the next day, dressed and ready to move files. Parker flipped the light switch, watching his footing as he descended. Milly put her right foot out to step on the first step, and found herself caught up again in a vision, where the steps looked like the stone ones in her dream. The beauty of the ancient stone, and the warm lighting that covered the steps captivated her.

She could hear Parker talking, while she was in the vision. There were two realities in which she found herself, the present and her vision. Sound in her present reality shut off and she could hear someone writing on paper. It was the scribbling of a large pen put to a piece of paper, where the weight of the writer's passion was put into the words. "What is that sound," she asked herself.

She continued down the steps, when she heard Parker snapping his fingers, saying, "Earth to Milly, earth to Milly."

"Sorry Park, I don't know what happened; I just have to get used to being down here," she said.

"You better," he said, "because we are going to be down here a while."

They headed down the hall, to the Philosophy storage, and entered to begin the long arduous process. Handheld vacuum cleaner ready to go, Milly began getting dust off the boxes. Their goal today was first and foremost to dust as much as possible. Parker had a dust cloth, with which he was wiping the shelves, while she did her part with the boxes. Parker laid his phone on the clean shelving and turned on his music, while the two worked away, enjoying his tunes and each other's company.

The work was methodical, starting their dusting at the front part of the room, working towards the back aisle, which also had boxes stacked upon boxes. Sun setting, the afternoon was winding down, as they now depended on the overhead lights and Parker's lantern.

While dusting the last aisle, Milly wanted to move some of the boxes that were stacked upon each other, to get them out of the way, when she realized that they were actually blocking or hiding something. "Hey Park, come here for a minute; I'm curious what's behind these boxes."

"Sure."

The two of them were a small conveyor belt as Milly picked the boxes up and handed them to Parker to stack them on the other side. Box by box they came down, revealing a school desk that looked to be from the early 1920's. "Wow Park, look!"

"What a cool desk," he said, "I wonder how long it has been sitting here?"

She responded with confidence, after having Professor Mercer for antiquities, and said, "First look underneath the desk to see if there are any markings of the manufacturer, or the carpenter. According to the age of this school, it could be as old as 1887. But judging by the desk itself, before we get under it, I would think it has to be before the 1930s."

Impressed with his friend, Parker put his flashlight underneath to look for a manufacturer's plate or the carvings of a carpenter. No plate could be found, but rather there were markings of different symbols, that appeared to be caveman like in nature. "This is odd," he said "because there are definite markings, but what kind they are, I have no clue." Milly got her phone and took a picture, knowing that Mercer would come to her aid.

The desk was a dark stained piece, similar to a drawing table, except that the width and length of the table made it obvious that it was used specifically for writing. On top of the grain, etchings could be made out from someone's writing pressed onto the desk while scribing on paper. In the middle was a circle, where an inkwell most likely was placed.

Looking at the desk, like a little girl looks at a lost kitten, Milly had found something that peaked her interest and passion. She felt the desk represented a combination of philosophy and antiquities. She handed Parker her vacuum, holding her hand out in exchange for his rag asking, "May I?"

"Sure, here you go," he said teasing her, holding the rag out like a carrot to a rabbit.

"Give it here Park, will you," Milly said jostling for the rag.

Carefully and tenderly like a mother wiping soot off of her child's face, she began to wipe the dust off of the desk. "Hand me that water over there, will you Park?" He handed her the water as she dabbed it on the rag. Clutching the cloth, she put it on the desk wiping the dust away to see the treasure underneath, where a brighter color of the dark stain was revealed. "It had been hidden under all this dust," she thought.

Mesmerized in the process, she whispered under her breath, "*The purpose of art is washing the dust of daily life off of our soul.* Pablo Picasso."

"What did you say," Parker asked inquisitively.

"Parker, Pablo Picasso could see the CANVAS and the PAINT BRUSH, he could see THEISM, and he realized what covered the eyes of mankind was the dust of daily life, the distractions of the present age!" Milly was bubbling and overflowing with excitement because her philosophy lesson was coming alive.

He looked at her stupefied, taking in the stupendous revelation, unable to speak for a moment, as he measured his own life against this thought. "Wow Mill, you are right. Things just seem to get in the way, where we don't realize what might be truly happening. Man, that's deep friend."

"Please don't tell anyone that I have shared this with you and keep the subject about this desk between us, until we have a chance to investigate it more and talk to Kaufman." He agreed as she continued wiping the rest of the desk, moving to the individual legs. Under the desk finishing with the legs, she then noticed a chair next to the metal shelving, concealed in the corner. It matched the desk! "Park, grab that chair will you; it goes with the desk."

Parker assisted his friend, realizing she was like a kid in a toy store, and turned up his tunes louder, using her handheld vacuum cleaner on the rest of the room, as she finished dusting the chair.

Milly could no longer hear the music and thought something was wrong with Parker. Standing up, she turned around to check on him, and comprehended that she had been transported to somewhere else either in time, or another dimension.

Suddenly the floor underneath her feet was the ancient stone. The desk and chair were in their original condition, as though they were newly made. A glass inkwell sat on top in the middle of the circle, with a large quill pin. Fresh bluish/black ink was ready to be used. Milly noticed a thin piece of paper on top, walking slowly over to view it, hoping that she might see what was on written on it. Then she saw it! In a beautiful script it read

"Mildred, the door is soon to open, be ready for Wisdom to paint you."

She was stunned, as she stepped back two steps, not realizing she was now running Parker over, when she finally heard him say, "Whoa there cowgirl."

Turning fast to see his face, she was caught off guard, unsure of what just happened. Still clutching the rag in one hand and holding her other hand outward beside her waist, Milly was trying to speak. "Parker, I don't know what," she stopped and was silent.

He looked at her doing a *Kaufman*, but he in all sincerity was concerned about his friend who had been acting a bit differently the last two days. "Are you ok Mill, did you see something? Are you not feeling well?"

She looked at him, giving him the rag, and held her hand out for the vacuum. Milly picked up her bag and motioned that she had to go, putting the rest of her items away. Still surprised, her friend said to her, "Look, did something just happen, I've been caught up in the tunes, and I didn't see what was going on. Are you alright friend?"

Milly nodded her head and replied, "I think I am tired and need to get some rest, I have to get home." The two closed up shop, as they locked the Philosophy storage door and headed back up the steps.

In the Night

Overwhelmed and thoughts racing in her mind, Milly headed back home. She returned to the house by 8:30 pm, walked in, and told her parents that she had a long day. Her dad asked if she at least wanted her Keto-coffee to which she responded, "No thanks, I'll get some in the morning; I just want to go to bed early."

Lavern and Daniel looked at each other and shrugged, as they simultaneously bid her good night, "Sweet dreams Mill."

Opening the door to her cave, she went straight for her bed and lay down, staring at the ceiling. Unsure of what happened in the storage room, she thought that if she kept her hand on her forehead, that her attempt to touch her frontal cortex would bring the answers she needed. Blindly, she reached for her journal on her nightstand, pulled the pen out that had been keeping her place, and began recording.

October 2, 2012: *Odd vision when I walked down into the basement, it reminded me of my dream going down these ancient stone steps, entering a room where there was a desk, chair and a bed. On the desk was a scroll. Each time I have entered the basement in Truman, it's like I am transported into the dream and the basement steps look like the stone steps. Tonight in the basement I found a desk and chair, and as I was wiping the dust off, I stood up to find myself in some other ancient time. It was like I was awake in my dream. The desk and chair that were in the basement were actually the same ones in my dream. While in the vision tonight, I saw a scroll on the desk that had written on it, 'Mildred the door is soon to open, be ready for Wisdom to paint you.' I don't know what is going on, but it's something odd that cannot be explained; in class yesterday I talked about the word painted with Theism.*

Milly placed her pen in the middle of the journal and laid it back down on her nightstand. She was in a safe place, her cave, where she knew nothing extraordinary would occur. Changing into her pajamas, she slipped under the golden covers and the white cotton sheets, where she felt sheltered and drifted off to sleep.

In the night, close to 1 am, a breeze entered into her room. She usually slept with the windows open this time of year, enjoying the fresh wind that had a hint of coolness, lightly blowing past the curtains, that seemed to whisper over her face, hovering like a well-known friend, who visits only in the night to give secrets.

Unbeknownst to her, there was movement in her room while she slept. She dreamed that she was back at the ancient steps, entering the room that was lit up with the desk, chair and bed. She saw herself asleep on the bed and was trying to make sense of it all. She heard a man's voice in the room calling her name, "Mildred." It was a comforting voice that sounded like that of a grandfather bringing peace to the soul. She watched the scene like a movie, as the Mildred that was asleep on the bed awoke to the voice and answered, "I am here, speak." With excitement, she saw what she thought was herself, getting up from the bed and going to the desk, to pick up the quill from the inkwell.

Immediately, the scene shifted and she found herself carried into the heavens where she saw the stars of the universe, hearing what sounded like a heartbeat, quietly beating as she stared at nebulas and stars throughout the heavens. Light was filling the heavens, and she turned to see where it was coming from. Upon her turning she saw a door with a huge bright light coming from behind it. As it opened, more of the light that was contained behind the door began to spill out, causing the stars in the heavens to fade as the brilliance of the light enlarged in the heavens. The same voice that Milly heard in the room calling Mildred on the bed, was now speaking to her, "The door is soon to open Mildred, and My wisdom will be poured out upon you."

Next, Milly was back in the ancient room, seated at the desk, watching her own hand scribe on the ancient paper. Dipping the quill pen in the inkwell, she put the ink to paper, and saw symbols being etched, much like those that were under the desk in the storage room! She could not believe what she was seeing, and then she heard her heart *Thump.... Thump..... thump-thump.*

She could feel the blood coursing through her veins with energy. She was now back in her cave, sleeping soundly under her gold spread and white cotton sheets, which she could feel against her skin. The lightness of the wind touched her nose and cheeks. The coolness she felt, let her know that she was coming out of what had to be a dream. Until, she heard a man's voice, "it is time; she is the chosen one and has to be awakened."

Immediately, she felt the same peace that exuded through her when she was in Kaufman's class talking about the word *painted*, and she recognized that the intimidating thoughts and the voice of rejection was drowned out, as she was captivated entirely with a calm and peace she could not explain. Presently, although her amygdala should be firing off causing her thalamus to release a hormone to go to her adrenals, releasing the fear response because of a man standing over her in her bedroom at night, she was still unafraid.

She realized the man was not alone, as another man asked, "Is she ready Rafael?"

Fearless, in such a surreal moment, all she could think was, "Who in the world is Rafael?" Milly wanted to get up, but it was as though she could not awaken herself. Although she could hear all that was going on around her, she could not get up!

The two men continued to speak while over her, as the wind touched her face. Then she heard Rafael respond to the question. "Tubal, she is ready, *He* has spoken, and the door is soon to open. She has been prepared for this moment, and now she must see."

Milly was thinking to herself, "See what? Why can I not get up out of the bed to see who these men are."

She felt a tusk like round object moving close to her ear. Wondering what kind of crazy thing was going on, she realized a little to late; a loud trumpet sound blasting into her ear, caused Milly to leap out of bed, thinking that it would also wake her mom and dad.

When she came to her feet, she was standing in the midst of what appeared to be like the universe, and saw two men about 9 feet tall, dressed in the most brilliant clothing. One was wearing silvery bluish colored attire that was almost like glass. His face was bright white, with long blond hair flowing down his back. He had a sword on his side, and looked at her, introducing himself, "Mildred, I am Rafael, do not be afraid."

She was mesmerized at the beauty of his entire being; he seemed to be emitting light. The other man with long dark hair and a fair appearance had royal blue apparel. His garment shimmered as different lights from the stars shone upon it. There appeared little stars caught in his suit that would shine and sparkle as he turned. In his hands was a long trumpet made out of an animal horn, layered in beautiful silver. He nodded and said, "I am Tubal."

Flabbergasted, and overcome by the entire occurrence, she found herself possessed with great elation. Never had Milly experienced anything like this. Suspended in space, she was having a conversation with what seemed to be two angels, as she noticed wings that were folded behind their backs. She was unsure what to call them; they looked so much like men, just none she had ever seen on earth.

Rafael continued, "We know that you must have many questions Mildred, but from this point, you have been awakened to see that which is in the spirit. You humans use the term supernatural. The veil between the world as you know it, and the spirit realm has been removed. Strength will be given to you so that you are not frightened by what you see."

Her jaw dropped open, she was speechless.

"Mildred, do you understand what is being spoken to you?" At which she nodded her head, still with her mouth wide open.

Rafael continued, "El Elyon has summoned us to watch over you and battle alongside you for things that are to come shortly. This is the hour that you were prepared for, and now we must train you for the battle."

In disbelief, as she heard everything Rafael was saying, Milly had difficulty comprehending all that was being spoken. "What hour and what battle," she asked.

Tubal looked at Rafael, getting his approval to proceed in educating Milly, Rafael gave him the go ahead, at which Tubal began his discourse. "Did you not know that you have a gift, child? It is a special gift that not many have. Your Great Grandmother had this gift and she was used greatly for battle in the time, of what your nation knows as the Great Depression. She was equipped with the ability to see, where she would receive dreams and visions, recording them in a book. The dreams that you have been having as of late are significant. Most of your dreams, allow you to see yourself. However, the dream that you had this night where you thought you were the one on the bed hearing the voice that was calling Mildred, was actually your Great Grandmother, whose name is Mildred, as well." Milly's jaw dropped again.

Tubal continued, "You have her gifting and as she was trained to see, and to battle, so will you. You saw her get up from the desk and begin to write on the ancient paper. Since you were unable to see what she was writing, you were carried into the heavens, to be mantled in this power, and came back to earth in your dream, sitting at the same desk, where you then put the quill in the ink to begin to write the Ancient Language yourself." She was listening but felt as though she was still dreaming.

Confused, Milly asked, "Is *this* a dream?"

Rafael responded, "No child, this is an actual vision. There is a difference between a vision and a dream, and you have been gifted with both. A vision occurs when you are awake, whereas a dream happens when you are asleep." He then nodded for Tubal to continue the education.

"Mildred, your gifting *to see* has opened you up to the spirit realm, where you will now not only see us, but others like us, whom your world knows as angels."

Milly was excited at the fact that she got at least one thing right, and said to herself, "I knew it."

"You knew what Mildred," asked Tubal.

"You heard that? I was just thinking something in my mind," she responded.

Rafael looked at her and said, "We can hear your thoughts, as well as speak to you with our thoughts."

Blown away by all that was occurring, she looked around as they were suspended in the heavens. Rafael spoke in a resolute tone, like a commander of an army. "Mildred, you will not only see us, but you will also see the hordes of darkness, which El Elyon's Spirit will give you understanding on. You are not alone because His Spirit is upon you and you will know much by Him, as He tells you all things that are to come."

She looked at her hands, hoping that somehow she would be able to see El Elyon's Spirit on her. Rafael implored her to be patient and let her know, that at times she could discern El Elyon's Spirit on her when she would see a special armor.

"Special Armor? What Special Armor and why do I need armor?" Milly inquired.

Rafael brought an unusual mirror in front of him that was almost the color of his silvery blue attire. Animated, it was trimmed in a beautiful gold, with leaves etched in it, appearing to blow upward on the gold trim, making the mirror come alive. He put it in front of Milly, so that her eyes could be opened to the armor of El Elyon.

"Absolutely stunning!" she exclaimed as she beheld the image of herself in the brilliant armor, colored mostly in gold and silver. The helmet on her head was a dazzling gold, trimmed in silver, with an eagle engraved on the side. The breastplate matched the helmet with a shiny gold, accented with silver trimming around the neck, waist and arms, seemingly a thin material. There was an energy inside of it that poured into her own body, giving her strength. "What is this," she asked, as she pointed at the breastplate.

Tubal responded, "This is the power of El Elyon, and His armor on you provides you with supernatural strength."

She continued eyeing the shoes that were a fascinating bronze color, and noticed a special belt around her waist that was the same coloring. On her hip was a sheath with a sword. She pulled the sword out and noticed the bright silver blade with a gold hilt that housed a blue sapphire stone. Milly was caught up and mesmerized, looking at the blade in which she could see her own reflection.

Rafael interjected, "Reach to your back Mildred," at which time she did, and noticed a huge object that was easily undone, as she brought it forward to see a magnificent gold shield trimmed in silver, with an eagle etched on it, same as the helmet and breastplate.

"This armor is amazing, I cannot believe my eyes," she said as she put her hands on the beautiful covering, touching the helmet, and then the breastplate, looking again at the bronzed shoes and belt. "What will I need this sword and shield for?"

Tubal eyed Rafael, and she could tell that between the two of them, Rafael was the one in charge. After getting approval, Tubal continued her education, "Mildred, these will be used against the demons that you will be fighting."

"EXXXCUUUSE ME?" she replied. "Demons!" She had no idea what to think and could not believe what she was hearing. It was difficult enough that she was dealing with seeing angels in the spiritual realm, and now, not only would she be seeing demons, but would be fighting them, as well.

Rafael interjected, "Your Great Grandmother did this in her time, and you will, too."

"My Great Grandmother, I don't understand?" Mildred was confused as to all that was going on, and the fact that her Great Grandmother had all of these extraordinary happenings, as well, brought more bewilderment.

"Mildred," Rafael spoke, "The Great Depression was the spawn of a satanic group of people, and with it came much demonic oppression, releasing hordes of demons into regions throughout the States. In each area, were *chosen ones,* whom were selected to be watchmen. A watchman is someone that is set on a wall, to guard the town and sound the alarm on the enemy, as well as to assist those in the area."

"So you are saying," she paused, "that I am a chosen one, a watchman?"

"Yes," Rafael answered. "The door is about to open in the heavens for the Wisdom of El Elyon to be poured out upon His chosen ones. This Wisdom intimidates your enemy, for it is something he once knew that has become foreign to him. The language you will come to know is a mystery that he cannot hear or see, and torments him." He paused, staring at Milly, seeing her need for bravery, "You will be brave Mildred. When this Wisdom comes to you, you will be brave."

She had to inquire. "What does this Wisdom do?"

"Your term, I believe, is firewall for your computers. This Wisdom is similar; it is a firewall to the attack of demons that are carrying out evil plots, to take over regions. It pushes back the assaults of the hordes of hell, and counteracts the works done by those under its spell. Certain people are given over to its incantation, but it is possible that it can be broken."

"It is time for you to go back to your room. In this vision things seem real, and you might think others can hear and see what you are hearing and seeing, but that is not the case; with you it is your gift. You will be using this gift, as the ancient paper is given to you, where you will gain understanding from the prophet, on what it reads. Wait for what is to come next, and in the meantime, be on guard, for your adversary is ruthless, and desires to kill you. You must resist his mental tactics and do not give ear to his lies, they will weigh heavily on you if you succumb to them."

Suddenly, Milly found herself opening her eyes, seeing the curtains blown by the wind's small breezes, feeling the coolness of it on her face. She sat up in bed, looked at the clock, seeing that it was only 2 am. She thought she had been with Rafael and Tubal for hours, but in reality it was only 30 minutes. She reached for her journal, opened it and wrote:

October 3 2012 2am: *I met them, Rafael and Tubal. I saw the armor. The door will open soon and everything will change. I will understand the Ancient Language, as I meet the Prophet.*

Chapter 3

The stench was like mustard gas on the battlefield. Darkness all around, and heat from the rocks throwing a hot mist into the air, as you heard a continual sizzling making this place all the more loathsome. Through the boiling mist you could see black rock that resembled granite, but what was it? It was a mineral at the core of the earth that had not been seen by man. No human had brought his or her footsteps into this place, for it was far and unreachable, except to a certain species.

Beelzebub walked stalwartly to his cause to make all of mankind's life an utter ruin and misery. He definitely was not human, but rather a *creature*, and was 9 feet high in full length, whenever he wanted to stretch to his full capacity. Mainly though, he seemed to be in a slouch and bended position, which was his normal stance when thinking of some malevolent cause to inflict upon humanity. He loathed mankind and what they stood for; it reminded him to often of El Elyon.

Covered in a soot color all over, his eyes were beady and red, which looked like lasers beaming through the nasty vapor in the underworld. Only the serpent species, known as demons, entered this realm; where their headquarters had been relegated ever since the battle of angels and demons took place in the heavens.

At one time demons took part of the universe and warred continually to claim their territory in space. They wanted Mars and Jupiter, failing to win the war over those biospheres, and were cast down into the earth, where their battle now is over this planet, where they wage war with El Elyon's angels and the humans who enlist in His army. Before mankind, Beelzebub had no concerns of other species from the different planets being enlisted to fight with El Elyon. It was not until they came to the particular biosphere of earth that a species was being conscripted.

Beelzebub found out that it worked both ways though, and took advantage of this system, enlisting humans to aid in the battle he waged against El Elyon. Beelzebub, and the humans that were joined to his plan, formed dark societies. Before the wars over the planets,

Beelzebub was a general in El Elyon's army. However, when he was dissatisfied in his position, wanting more, a darkness manifested in him, like black soot spreading across his entire being; his pride was a cancer spreading in himself and throughout El Elyon's army.

Prior to this disease that took his entire being, he had been beautiful and known as the *Wise One*, where many of the angels noticed the beauty that he brought with him, bringing a presence of El Elyon's nature; he had been painted in Wisdom. He had been feared and respected by all the creatures of the universe. However, when he became hungry for more power, he began to make war against His superior, El Elyon, causing a division in the heavens amongst the angels. It was at this point that he was cast out, so that the spiritual disease would not infect all of the other angels.

Thus, started the sinister evil rule of Beelzebub in the earth, now in his horrid appearance, which he did not see; he still believed himself to be beautiful as before, and acted as if he was better than El Elyon. Delusional and full of arrogance, he was convinced he was the most beautiful creature ever.

Beelzebub was the only one allowed to do his slinky walk, where his shoulders bulged forward as he leaned, intimidating all whom he came upon. All the other creatures had to keep their shoulders hunched lower. To him, he believed that it was the walk of a god. The other serpent species were consigned to walk like an ape, so that they were never taller than he. Shoulders barreling over his body, as if a small house could be carried on his back, made him feel far more superior to the other demons under him.

Serpent species were not serpents in form. They had been given over to the *serpent nature* before creatures stopped speaking on earth; the serpent was the most cunning and wise creature of all. This was the first creature that Beelzebub enlisted to war against El Elyon, and as a result of the curse that was brought upon it, as well as the demons, the nature of the serpent was passed on to Beelzebub and his cohorts. No longer did Beelzebub have the wisdom that he had prior when he was a general under El Elyon; his wisdom was that of this present age.

All the serpent creatures here in the underworld had arms and legs, except they were of a slithery kind, which was slimy to the touch. Just as snakes have different colors, the demons were different colors as well, mostly being dark in nature and some being a reddish brown. However, Beelzebub in all his glory was a mixture, with his body being covered in soot like color and the back of his head and his hands were a reddish brown.

His feet were huge, going out wide in the front, where he had claws on his toes. He used them diligently when climbing the black rock, as he held meetings for the generals and his army. Vladamore was the highest in rank of the generals, ensuring that Beelzebub's orders were carried out. Vladamore was a brownish soot colored demon, a foot shorter than Beelzebub, having reddish brown hands, and a reddish brown tint to his shoulders that he proudly bolstered when in arguments with those who were inferior, when Beelzebub was not around, showing them as trophies in their face, to intimidate them into obedience. In this army, fear was the weapon of choice, used to keep each one in line.

"Gather around generals, commanders, principalities, powers and underlings of the underworld, for there is a war in the heavens over earth. Something is soon to begin." Beelzebub touted in all his arrogance, stationed high on the black rock in the underworld, with hot boiling stench rising up in the midst of the gathering. The claws of his feet were the longest of all, and he esteemed them, as he made sure that his footing would cause all the creatures to see his long claws while he stood. His hands, reddish brown and long, made it easy for the underlings who were in the far back of the crowd, since they were lowest in rank, to see his fingers and his gestures, causing them to understand the intensity of his speech.

"I have seen El Elyon's door opening in the heavens and the angelic host that are gathered all around. The archangel, Michael, is still warring in Israel, while Gabriel is doing battle to get El Elyon's messages through to earth. My dark princes are guarding the portals and gates around the biosphere, to attack as much as possible when they enter into the planet." Beelzebub loved these long speeches; it was the only time that there was silence between the serpent creatures; he made sure of it.

"I have captured another human leader in the Middle East and have him in the palm of my hand, as he works with us, being a new crony to add to our army with the humans." Beelzebub referred to all his human alliances as cronies. "We are ahead of time, I am sure. Our plans are going according to schedule, as the cronies of the different societies launch my brilliant plan, for this is the hour that I change the times on this earth even more, as I have already been changing their laws," Beelzebub said as he held up one finger pointing upwards, and his other hand on his hip, as if this posture gave him a more glorious appearance to the demons.

"My cronies have built the glorious machinations throughout the world, so that nation will turn upon nation, as I interrupt their time line, and bring a great scale assault against the minds of mankind. Our programs have been operating superbly as we have indoctrinated many of their brains with lies, making them slaves to their thoughts, unable to see past their own hand. Moreover, we have poisoned their foods, causing them to be blind to what they are taking into their body, as the increase of disease spreads among them, killing most. With this plague of disease, many will be taken out before they know it." Beelzebub held his head up, with his mouth opened wide, for all to see his jagged teeth, that looked like shark's teeth, releasing a shrill laugh as mustard gas came from his mouth filling the air, causing all the other demons to follow suit. The entire underworld was filled with this hideous laughter.

Then Beelzebub held up his hand and cut the air with it, as if it was a sword. "QUIIIIIET!" All was still as he continued. "We have to work speedily because of what El Elyon will release once the door opens; it can be devastating to our plans. He has His angels and watchmen stationed around the globe, and it is their intent to begin the building of the towers." Beelzebub moved two paces to the left and then four paces to the right, finally coming back to his original spot, as he stood still with hands behind his back. "If this happens in the different areas, we will be overthrown as we were in the heavens and pushed further into confinement. We must not let this happen, but rather we must work to hinder every watchmen in the area, to ensure this does not transpire."

The underlings in the back, stood mostly about three to four feet high, and were jumping up and down, to get a good look at Beelzebub, which actually brought more energy to the group; it seemed like cheers were erupting from the back row. The underlings were different colors, soot, dark brown, reddish-brown, and red. One of the favorites to Vladamore was Serugar, who was at his beck and call, carrying out the latest top-secret assignment. Serugar, who was reddish in color, felt that because he was Vladamore's underling, that he had more power among the group. Usually he was the one up front in the group of underlings, and all around him, did as he. Serugar motioned with his huge hands and long arms that were nearly taller than his four-foot frame, for the underlings to quiet down, as Beelzebub finished his speech.

"We cannot afford another time of the towers, my army. The sound that entered into the earth 2,000 years ago, and other times afterward, where the Ancient Language flooded the earth, bringing utter torment here into the underworld, must not happen again.

"Do not forget the time where all we could do was *claw* with our hands and feet, hearing the Ancient Language all throughout the underworld, as we constantly *gnawe*d on the black rock and whatever we could find to put between our teeth." The demons remembered as Beelzebub referred to the time of terror, and they began to cover their ears, some screaming, as if they were reliving it all over again.

"Finally, my league of the underworld, we have to ensure that the towers do not rise in any area. I am to be immediately informed on this issue, so that we work together to bring mankind down!" Beelzebub finished as the demons cheered and jumped up and down, laughing their shrill laugh and declaring their allegiance to the fight.

Clawing and Gnawing

Later, in a more secluded meeting with one of his generals, Beelzebub, summoned Vladamore to the war room of the underworld. The war room had a huge table in the middle, made of the black rock, with 13 chairs around it, one of which was Beelzebub's chair that was much like a throne. Every creature that entered the war room was to immediately bow and pay homage to Beelzebub, showing their allegiance.

Vladamore entered and bowed, as Beelzebub motioned that he stand and proceed to the table. They both sat in their chairs, with Beelzebub at the head, and Vladamore to his right. On the table lay the blueprints of the war in the different nations and regions of the nations, where extra reinforcements would be needed because of the intelligence that was received of El Elyon's latest advancement.

"Vladamore, my general, I have urgent need in this hour to discuss the specifics on Area 9," which was mostly in the United States of America. The demons had different areas across the globe, and did not call the nations by name most times, but rather used numbers for areas. They did this specifically in order to communicate across their grid and get messages out as soon as possible with the battle plans.

Their communication grid was invisible to the naked eye and could be seen only in the spirit, where it went from the ancient temples in Egypt and those that were built across the earth, in order to effectively carry out their attacks. In addition, they used different forms of media and the dark societies to alert demons that were unable to come to the underworld, because of their battle station. The different forms of media provided battle orders where all the demons would be informed.

Vladamore responded to Beelzebub, "Speak my liege, your general is listening."

Beelzebub continued, "In Area 9, we have seen the activity of Rafael and Tubal, and have been told that a specific human child who is gifted as a Seer and Watchman has been activated into El Elyon's army. This would not be so troubling, had this human child's great grandmother not operated in the same gift to the highest power of wisdom."

Vladamore retorted, "WISDOM!"

Beelzebub spoke softly as if the thick black rock could hear, "Yes my general, El Elyon's Wisdom." To that reply, Vladamore began clawing his hands on the table.

"This cannot be my liege, what must I do?"

"I need you stationed there; they must be preparing for her to guard one of the towers in the area, and we cannot let the tower rise, and release the Ancient Language."

Vladamore grabbed his rod made out of the black rock, put it in his mouth and began gnawing. "This can never happen my liege."

With his beady red eyes Beelzebub said, "If any hint of a tower begins to rise," he leaned in almost to Vladamore's nose as he growled, "I want to hear immediately! Do you hear me well my general?"

"Yes, yes, yes my liege," Vladamore said as he bowed down and exited out of the room.

Quickly, Vladamore assembled his team, and took them to Area 9, where deep underneath the ground they stationed an office. "This will be our war room, as we advance Beelzebub's plan."

Around him were his commanders Tildash and Morder, as well as, his informant, Serugar, who stood by his side. Finally, there was Dadanel and Heradacio, who were what is known as "instigators," that would be used to interact directly with the humans, releasing demonic mental assaults, much like a huge hand grenade going off. Like the shrapnel of a grenade, these two specialists, Dadanel and Heradacio, had their own teams of underlings that assisted in their weapons release, as they used different tactics to destroy an area.

Vladamore looked at each demon stationed in the war room of area 9, and began his speech, aspiring to the level in his own mind of Beelzebub. Looking at each one with his red beady eyes, he spoke, "We are here, my troops, on special assignment and our liege has need of our achievement so that we take down the most crucial weapon stationed against our success. There is great probability of a tower being prepared to rise in this area," he paused as the demons began clawing on the rock around them, covering their ears at the news that was delivered.

"I know, my troops," he retorted, " we cannot allow this tower to rise; if it does it will release the Ancient Language and the Wisdom of El Elyon, which will utterly destroy our plans." They were tormented all the more at this news and each one grabbed for the rock around them and began gnawing on it in pain.

"Do not fear, my troops, because this will not occur; we will ensure it," Vladamore proudly stated, as his chest was lifted up. "We will bring an end to this pitiful plan."

Vladamore looked at the commanders, Tildash and Morder, and began his battle strategy. "I need you two to gather your troops and spy out the area; we are looking for Rafael and Tubal; they have been spotted, and it is necessary for us to find the human with whom they are collaborating."

He turned to look at his instigators, who worked cooperatively with the spirit of Leviathan, ensuring that the messages of satanic nature were released against mankind. "Dadanel and Heradacio, I need your best weapons on this, we cannot assail these people with our normal deployment. I want something much worse, effective in tormenting them into submission, as fast as possible."

The two of them nodded and spoke, "Yes general."

Finally, Vladamore looked at his trusty assistant, Serugar, "You, my loyal underling, will prepare the area with your traps, so that we can set hell's cords up, to release the poisonous venom to flood the city. It is necessary that the area be made ready for my commanders," he looked at Tildash and Morder smiling his horrid smile, and turned back to Serugar, "for all of hell to be released!"

Serugar, hunched in his full position, like a monkey on a tree, with his reddish colored body, holding up his long arm, lifting up his index finger with his long claw exposed, replied, "You have it my general." He laughed and simultaneously began to rub his head, as if petting himself, while thinking of villainous plots for the specific area.

"That is it my troops, now you can leave." The demons left the putrid rock war room, carrying with them the smell of sulfur, as they exited and went to their respective positions, to employ Vladamore's orders.

Out to the Battlefield

Tildash and Morder began their reconnaissance, sending out underlings that would assist in the search for Rafael and Tubal. It was their intent to scour Springfield throughout the night, in order to see the angelic activity, and find "the chosen one." Wherever Rafael and Tubal were, would be the place of *the chosen one.*

Tildash assigned his underlings all throughout the north and east parts of Springfield, while Morder put his underlings in the south and west parts. As most of the town slept, demons, like serpents sliding on their bellies, slithered into the area, creeping into the homes of its inhabitants.

They would pass through the exterior walls of a home, being enveloped by its material, and passing through to the other side. However, there were some homes that had a wall of fire around about them, and in the midst of them was a blazing fire with an Ancient Language overtop of the fire.

Tildash pointed with his reddish fingers and long claws to the houses that had the wall of fire around them, as he spoke to his underlings, "Presently, those dwellings are forbidden, for there abides the Ancient Language. The only tactic, by which the firewall will come down, is for the weapons of Dadanel and Heradacio to bring drudgery to those within, when they come outside of the firewall. If they are successful, we can bring down all the firewalls and invade the homes."

Tildash quieted himself, as he spied. A huge snarl appeared on his face, with a crooked grin, as he spoke, "I have much need to bring them down, my underlings, so that we can ensure that no tower rises in the area." He broke out into a shrill laugh, as the hideous serpent creatures around him, broke out into the same hoot. Even the snakes of the Springfield area, could perceive what was going on in the spirit, and they began to hiss along with the shrill laughter.

Meanwhile, Heradacio and Dadanel were building their weapons, as they created a makeshift arsenal room for storing their artilleries. First they started with, what looked like an ordinary grenade, but inside, was packed with venomous poison which, once released, would go into the areas in which cords of hell were placed. There were different types of cords, other than hell; there were also the cords of the ruling powers.

The cords of hell, come from the gates of hell, and are the most important weapon of the powers of darkness in battle. Once released, they feed poison to the minds of humans, causing delusional thoughts, to be filtered through a person's amygdala, which is the part of the brain for fear conditioning. With the amygdala under hell's control, Vladamore was sure to win this battle. "This would be a swift victory," he thought.

Moreover, the *cords of hell* destroy a person's intellect. They release a slimy film, putting a seal around their victim, where neurons within their body begin suffocating, unable to oxidize properly. Beelzebub hated the intellect given to man and wanted to do all he could to destroy it. If he did not destroy the neurons within a person's mind, belly or spine, then they would be candidates to receive the Wisdom that would come from El Elyon, Who had His own cords.

The other cords of darkness were from the ruling powers, which could be placed into one of three areas in humans, the brain, the spine or the belly. Neurons operated within these areas, and with the cords of a ruling power controlling a person, made them defenseless, where they would become a pawn of that ruling power.

Gradually as Heradacio and Dadanel worked on their weapons, Serugar had his underlings lay out the long cordlike objects that would, in time, come up out of the ground. Like a plant growing vines, these cords would be the branches to come up through the rising gates of hell within the area, polluting Springfield. The gates of hell had opportunity to rise for Beelzebub and the powers of darkness, as the Towers had opportunity to arise for El Elyon.

Cords

Cords are the means by which messages are also transferred to humans. Once a person gave of their being to an entity in the spiritual realm, cords could begin to send them messages. Humans could choose what to give their intellect to, whether it was El Elyon or Beelzebub.

When a human gave their mind over to Beelzebub, the cords of hell had influence over them, feeding them with negative, seductive, prideful, and violent thoughts, as their neurons were suffocated. The slimy ooze from the cords is a magnet to dark matter.

Ruling powers in the heavens, known as Leviathan, Jezebel and Divination, used their cords in a different way. These ruling powers of darkness, worked cooperatively with Beelzebub, getting messages through the grid of what destructive plans to carry out in certain regions, as well as using human pawns in the different regions.

Although Beelzebub had his own cords coming from out of the underworld through the gates of hell, the main purpose of those cords were to send messages to poison the person's spirit and personality with discouragement, depression, oppression and thoughts of death and suicide, as well as maintaining bitterness and offense. However, the cords from the ruling powers of Leviathan, Jezebel and Divination were to go into the victim to control them, where the ruling power would use them as a puppet.

For area 9, Beelzebub had conjured up the plan for all three of these ruling powers to work together. Usually, they worked in pairs, but with the urgency of the towers rising, Beelzebub could not risk anything, and summoned all three to the battlefront. Each spirit worked in a different dynamic than the other spirit, but together, they were the dream team of evil, where the gates of hell could be raised, as the strength of darkness was given to this team, by the souls who were bound to them. The more souls they could deceive and infiltrate, the more power they had.

As much as the underworld did not want a tower of El Elyon to rise, likewise, El Elyon did not want the gates of hell to manifest. It was not that the gates could not be defeated, but rather that it would take much more awakening of His human warriors, to assist with the given weapon of choice to fight this battle, which looked like a whip. The whip was actually the cord of El Elyon. As the enemy had cords, so did El Elyon, but His worked through the warriors enlisted, who were matured through the battle to use them strategically to bring the demonic ruling powers, and the gates of hell down.

Heradacio and Dadanel worked on building their artilleries, storing many weapons, which had all kinds of demonic venomous attacks that would be used in concert with the cords of the enemy. As hell's cords were operative, there was a heightened ability for the three ruling powers to carry out their diabolical attacks controlling humans with the cords they put into them.

Serugar assisted the commanders, by laying the cords out in the underworld at the root of hell's gates deep underground, fastening them much like a hose being joined to a fire hydrant. Like septic tanks filled with slime, hell's ooze would flow from underground and be carried to the top where hell's gates would rise. The slime, in some tanks was a greenish color, while in other tanks there was a clear slime, and then still others a reddish slime. Once the slime went from the tanks through the cords, it would travel above ground, to the present station of a small gate on the rise in the area, known as the gates of hell.

The slime would rise through the individual cords above ground, which then had many smaller cords like seaweed on an ocean reef. At this point, it would be up to Dadanel and Heradacio to ensure that the cords got into the different homes, businesses, and any other facilities, where there would be a constant release of the green, clear, or red slime, and some of places releasing all the colors. This slime was much like gangrene spreading throughout the area, getting on those who would yield to it, as they were zombified and covered in a film.

Other victims, who were susceptible to the cords of the ruling powers, were already given over to the slime that would come from the gates of hell, magnifying the work of the ruling powers, where they had more potency in the region, having hundreds to thousands submitted to their control. Cords from the ruling powers would go into specific areas of the person. The most a ruling power could put into a person was three cords, which was not easily broken.

If Divination were assaulting the person who was zombified, then the cords would be green and go to the belly. If Leviathan were attacking the individual, then the cords would be colorless and go into the mind.

Finally, if Jezebel were attacking, the cords would be red and shape shift into octopus tentacles and go into the person's back.

The cords of each ruling power would come into the person, as they were given over to more of the work of evil, unknowingly, being used as a pawn. The first cord was used to begin to send assignments to get the person to yield, and, if they did, in time a second cord would be placed into in them, causing them to be consumed with the affairs of the ruling power. Finally, when a ruling power was successful enough to get three cords in, the zombified person would totally be a puppet in the hands of the ruling power.

The ruling powers were very territorial and did not like another ruling power controlling a person. Therefore, they were competitive in nature and hideously backstabbing at all costs to get their cords in faster than the other ruling powers.

Once an individual had cords beginning to come into them, an angel from El Elyon was released to go give the person messages to resist the cords and not let the evil power take over. However, if the person resisted El Elyon's message, then the ruling power would take over and they would merely exist as a puppet to that power.

Still, hope was not lost; one of El Elyon's human warriors could have physical interactions with the person that was bound up. If El Elyon's warrior had His cord, they could bind up the ruling power's cords and use their sword, to cut the cords off of the person, loosing their hold.

Therefore, cords in El Elyon's realm were more effective than the cords in Beelzebub's realm. This war against cords was out of reach for many to comprehend, unless they received enlightenment by El Elyon's Spirit. His Spirit was their teacher and translator of all that El Elyon said or did. His Spirit translated the Ancient Language to His warriors, which is why the serpent creatures could not understand; they did not have His Spirit. Although the serpent creatures knew about their cords, and had some knowledge of El Elyon's cords, they did not know everything, and were susceptible to El Elyon's warriors who had great Wisdom.

The war between Light and dark was more intense than ever. Time was getting short on earth, and Beelzebub knew it. Having attacked earth for millennia, it was slowly dying, as Beelzebub's employments against mankind took effect. Creation all around was deteriorating, due to the mind control that many had been under for years, from Beelzebub's cronies in the dark societies. These dark societies existed to bring about the demise of both mankind and the earth, as they assisted Beelzebub in carrying out his heinous plots, being used to corrupt all that was good. As great darkness covered the globe, like the night skies where brilliant lights could be seen, the true light was now shining brightly. These lights were El Elyon's flame around and within people, given over to the Light, who were able to resist the presence of darkness that was taking over.

Many of the dark societies had built ingenious machines and inventions that were used as weapons against other humans, to degrade their ability to think, as well as engineering a slow genocide of the human population through processed foods and plastics. Little did the humans know how much poison was in the processed foods that began to bring a chronic state of different diseases not seen until the 1940's. Moreover, with the engineering of plastics, during the late 1950's, furthered the poisoning of humans, who would use them to drink and eat out of, not realizing the microplastics that were released within the material, would enter their body, and block hormone receptors, making the reality of cancer, brain damage, hyper activity, and attention deficit all the more pronounced in the children, who had grown up on these devilish designed products, to cause humans to ingest more and more particles that would cause their body to turn on itself.

With the evil plots of dark societies in the early 1900's and around World War II, the ingenious conspiracies created a depression in the States, allowing Beelzebub's cronies to be seated on the boards of the big banks, which took many lives and families. However, Beelzebub did not expect things to turn around, and later realized that El Elyon recruited more warriors during the time of great calamity. Towers began rising up in the midst of The Great Depression, with Milly's Great Grandmother, Mildred, being one of the mighty warriors of that time, who knew the Ancient Language to assist in the turnaround that was experienced in such time of oppression. Because of her efforts,

Springfield was saved from the more violent attacks that other areas experienced by the underworld.

Now, it was Milly's time to arise and shine like her Great Grand when, now nearly 70 years later, the Springfield would experience a great assault from Beelzebub due to the threat of the towers rising, releasing the Ancient Language. All was stationed between both El Elyon and His angels, and Beelzebub and his serpent creatures. The battle was for the souls of mankind, and little did Milly know how huge of a part she would play in it.

Milly's house was covered with the firewall, where no intruder of the demonic realm was able to enter. As she lay sleeping, the armor began to appear on her, as the shield that was given her, covered the bedroom window, while she slept. Rafael and Tubal entered, as they spoke El Elyon's plans over her during her sleep. With humans, their spirit stays awake continually, while their body gets rest. Thus, it was more advantageous for El Elyon to get his messages to the enlisted warriors while they slept, where their mind and body could not interfere with the purity of that which was delivered.

"Does she know what is soon to happen Rafael," asked Tubal.

"No," Rafael replied, "the chosen one has no illumination as of yet, to what is to come. We must leave her the next weapon she will use against the serpent creatures, which is the whip, the cord of El Elyon."

Rafael nodded to Tubal to take out the whip, and place it beside Milly, on her bed stand. Tubal pulled forth a bag that had been slung around his neck and arm, carrying different weapons of El Elyon that were to be distributed to those who were chosen. He opened the amber colored bag that had been sealed with a beautiful crimson colored stamp, having eagle's wings on it. As he opened the bag, light came pouring out into the room, flooding it. Reaching his hand into the bag, he pulled out the tightly coiled whip, which was the same amber color as his bag. Fire burned brightly inside of the whip.

Distinguished throughout this brilliant weapon, were keys all throughout, enveloped in the fire. It was beautiful! A whip that looked like a living flame with beautiful gold keys, caused its possessor to walk in greater power to defeat the hordes of darkness, once they were taught by El Elyon's Spirit.

This night, Morder and Tildash, who were outside of Milly's house, were met with a sad plight, not having found *the chosen one*. She was kept hidden under the firewall of El Elyon, and little did they know she was being prepared for the greatness of His power, to overcome their works.

To throw off hell's scent, Rafael and Tubal came out speedily from Milly's house, where their massive wings spread out, lifting them up high into the sky, as they made their way to the angelic war room in the mountains of Montana, at Granite Peak. There the angelic council met, receiving instructions from El Elyon and for Area 9, which included North Dakota and Montana, as well as parts of Canada. Beelzebub had knowledge of the angelic war room, but knew that it was futile to attempt any assault against it, since it was heavily guarded.

Milly, in her room fast asleep, was having another dream about all that was going on this night. El Elyon's Spirit gave her instructions of Beelzebub's plan, as well as the inner workings of Tildash and Morder's reconnaissance work to find her. Moreover, El Elyon's Spirit showed Milly the cords of the enemy that Serugar and the commanders were setting up, as well as the cords of the ruling powers. Further instructions were given about Heradacio and Dadanel's artillery, where Milly saw the demonic grenades and cannonballs being made. The download she received in her sleep was large, giving her further training.

Then, El Elyon gave her wisdom on how to use the special whip she received, where she was strengthened against hell's cords, firmly competent in how to use it adequately against the underworld.

Many deliberations occurred this night, as the plot thickened in the epic battle that was taking place for the souls of mankind.

Chapter 4

Parker and Milly ended their daily classes and headed to *The Grind*, to enjoy another conference with their favorite addiction. The young man behind the coffee bar, served them with a smile saying, "Enjoy your conference, my friends."

Surprised, Milly and Parker looked at him with a *Kaufman*, tilting their heads. Winking at them, he responded, "What? You didn't think I knew of your daily *conferences* on the patio?"

They walked off, unsure of how much he had overheard. "What is up with that?" Parker asked.

Milly laughed, "That my friend, is a good question to which I do not know the answer."

The two sat down, as they noticed both Kaufman and Mercer walking by intensely enveloped in a discussion. Nearly whispering, they carried on, so as to not be heard by anyone who would be passing by. The professors were too preoccupied to notice Parker and Milly.

"Man, things are really weird today Park," Milly said half jokingly, but knew that deep in her subconscious it was honest.

"Yes Mill, I'm not sure what to make of it myself, between the barista boy, as well as Kaufman and Mercer. I feel like they know a secret we do not." It didn't hold Parker's attention long, as he went back to drinking out of his lab experiment coffee cup.

Milly contemplated about sharing her latest dreams and occurrences with Parker, feeling it the opportune time to open up to him. "Park, I have been meaning to share something with you, and I know you are going to think I am a bit weird." Heart beating, sweat beading on her forehead, Parker noticed Milly's anxiety and knew that she was speaking with all seriousness.

"Mill, are you alright; you look so anxious, you can tell me anything, and I won't think you're crazy," Parker said to ease his friend's fears.

Swallowing, she responded, "It's just that I don't know how to explain what is happening, and what I have experienced, without sounding like I'm going insane. I have been troubled at times about these happenings, and with all the strength that I could muster, have tried to keep it to myself, but I feel like I'm going to explode if I don't tell you."

He was intrigued and sitting on the edge of his seat, focused on what she had to say. "Go ahead Mill, I'm listening."

A bit uneasy, she shifted in her seat. Trying to find the right words to grasp for and employ to use, it was important that she relay adequately, without hesitation, and in a manner that would be intellectual, that which she had to share; it would give her story more validity she thought.

"Well, it's like this," she said. "Remember that dream that I had at the beginning of the semester?"

"Yeah, the one with the stone steps and you going into this room with a desk and a chair," Parker said.

"Yes, that's it, and a bed," she responded, to which he quickly nodded.

"Well, since we have started going down to the basement to clean out the old files from the Philosophy department, each time I have entered and walked down the steps, its as though I have been transported into my dream simultaneously, where I see the stone steps, as I walk down." She paused, looked at Parker and saw his eyes begin to get larger. "Can I go on Park, are you alright?"

He nodded as Milly continued. "That's not all, because when we started dusting the room and discovered the desk and the chair, I was taken back into the dream again, where I felt as though I was in another time. Although I know I was in the room with you, it was like I was transported; I was in the dream awake, which was when I accidentally stepped all over your feet." Parker listened, thinking this might be the reason why his friend was spaced out on occasions.

"Is that why, when you have come down the stairs, I had to snap my fingers in front of you, seeing if you are ok?"

She nodded. "Yes, I only pretended to be getting used to the basement, to throw you off, so you wouldn't think I was weird."

"Oh my gosh, Mill!"

"There's more," she said, as she looked at Parker to see if he was ready to hear the rest. He submitted his full attention, so that Milly could continue.

"I have had more dreams since that time, where I was in the room again, and heard a voice calling *Mildred*, thinking the voice was calling me. I then saw what I thought was myself going to the desk to write, and discovered later, it was my Great Grandmother; she had the gift for something I now have, too. I found this out, after I was suddenly lifted into the universe in outer space in a vision, seeing a door opened. I then witnessed a brilliant light and was brought back to the desk, where I began writing this Ancient Language on the paper."

Parker's eyes were huge by this time, as he responded, "Whhhaat?"

"But wait; there is still much more. The Ancient Language I was writing was the exact markings we saw on the bottom of the desk." Parker, completely glued to Milly's story, was a captive audience as she continued. "I was later visited in the night, after I came out of the dream by what I thought were two men, named Rafael and Tubal." She knew that it sounded insane and hardly anyone would believe her, hoping that her friend would not jump to conclusions before hearing her out.

"Oh…my… gosh!" Parker replied. "What! Are you serious girl," he exclaimed.

Milly sipped her drink, placed it in front of her, took a deep breath, and continued. "Park, I know you don't believe me but its true. When I woke up, the two men I discovered were angels. They had these incredible suits on, and their appearance was like none I have ever seen, like being in a fantasy movie. They told me that I was *the chosen one*, who was in training for a battle over the demonic realm in Springfield."

Parker put his hand over his mouth, trying to keep from laughing, "No way Mill," he said as he broke out in laughter spraying her with his addiction. "I'm sorry, I didn't mean to get that on you." Picking up a napkin, he wiped her collar off from where it landed.

He noticed her eyes swelling with water, as she was trying to fight tears. "Hey, did I do something wrong; you weren't serious were you?" Then he noticed a tear running down the left side of her eye, spilling on to her cheek, as she quickly rubbed it off her face.

"Just forget I said anything Parker." She appeared stoic and was not going to let this moment get to her. She thought he would believe her but was finding out how much of a friend he really was, thinking to herself, "If it were him telling me, I would believe him."

"Wait a minute Mill," Parker said trying to make peace, "Look at me. So, you are saying this is for real?" He laid his hand on her shoulder as a gesture of empathy. She was not sure if she could trust him, or if it was him simply wanting the two of them to be at peace. Whatever it was, she knew that she did not want to be *fake*; she detested plasticity over the soul, which is why she loved philosophy and antiquities.

Milly said speedily under her breath, as she leaned into him, so that no others could eavesdrop, "Listen Park, I know you might not understand this, and to be honest I don't understand it myself, and prayed that this would have never happened to me; it feels like a curse at times."

He sat there frozen, unsure of what to say to his friend.

Then Milly, whispering in all seriousness said, "I did not ask for this, and would not wish it upon my worst enemy, who is Dana Dryer." She paused. "All I know is, that things are happening. And to make matters more complex, I find out that the girl in my dream that is awakened on the bed to write on the paper, is my Great Grandmother, whose gifting I keep trying to run from." Milly was irritated at the notable disrespect she received from Parker, in her eyes.

He sat up in his chair, realizing how dismissive he was with her story, and his thoughts were all over the place, as he contemplated the times where he knew something was going on with his friend, thinking *something* had to be the matter. It was all starting to make sense, about her walking down the stairs and being spaced out, and then her quirky behavior in Kaufman's class. "I'm sorry Mill, please forgive me, I should have known you trusted me enough to open up and tell me the truth."

He reached out his hand as a peace offering to shake, "Please Mill, I call a truce."

Eyes dried up, she stared at her friend, who gave her a crazy look with his tongue sticking out, to which she laughed.

"Truce Mill. Please, I believe you," Parker said while he looked at his hand and back to her, for her to take it and shake.

She smiled and reached out her hand, "Truce, my friend, just don't ever do that to me again." He nodded in agreement.

"So what now Mill?" Park asked.

"Well, I feel the need to make the ancient markings on the bottom of the desk known to both Kaufman and Mercer. I believe Kaufman, because he is the one who called us to this task, and then of course Mercer, because she knows antiquities."

In agreement, Parker lifted his lab experiment coffee cup, holding his shoulders back as if celebrating, "Today, let us drink to life and adventure friend! Adventure that pulls us into a dimension of understanding that, which we have not met, and to life, which is the gift given in time, where we celebrate friendship and things that are to come."

"Cheers!" said the young man behind the coffee bar, who was now standing over them. "What are we celebrating?"

Milly and Parker looked out of the corner of their eyes, as she asked, "How long have you been standing there?"

"Long enough, but your secret is safe with me," he said as he put his index finger to his lips, making a sign for keeping quiet. "I won't tell."

Basement Part 3

Milly and Parker stood in front of the basement door, ready to make their regular descension. "Are you ready," Parker asked as his hand was stationed on the door, to open it at Milly's signal.

"Parker, I know this seems so insane, but I don't know if I can continue doing this? I just don't want to feel like I'm losing my mind. If it is real and something is happening to help all of us out here in Springfield, I'm for it." She paused.

"But..." said Parker.

"But if I am going crazy Parker, I don't want to know anymore." She timidly replied, "Ignorance is bliss when it comes to mental insanity."

"Look, I am here, and you can trust that I don't think you're crazy; you are my best friend."

Wanting to break the tension, Parker said, "And if you can see what an awesome guy I am, then I know you're not crazy." She began laughing and punched him on the shoulder, giving him the signal that she was ready. "Now when I open this door, let me go all the way down first before you proceed, and then let me know what you are seeing as you walk down. Don't stop Milly, but continue on to the storage room, and tell me what you see there."

She mouthed in gratefulness, with a slight tear coming from her eyes, "Thank you."

Parker slowly opened the door, looked at her and asked, "Do you see anything yet?" To which she shook her head no. "Ok let me go first, and when I am all the way down then you can start."

"Ok, got it."

Parker went down as he normally did, and once reaching the bottom of the stairs, he turned to look upward at Milly, and replied, "Ok Mill, your turn. Be careful."

Nervous, heart beating fast, breathing patterns increased, Milly called down to her friend, "Ready Parker?" To which he responded yes. Right foot in front; ready to place it on the first step, she took a deep breath, while her hands were positioned on the sides of the door, as if she was plunging into another world. Holding her breath she finally exhaled, as her foot set down on step number one.

Instantaneously, she was taken into the other dimension that either existed before this time, or outside of it. Calling to Parker, hoping that he would hear her and that she could hear him, she stated loudly as if speaking to a person hard of hearing, "Parker do you see me?" Taking deep breaths she was waiting for his response.

"I do Mill, do you see the steps or are you in your dream?"

"I'm in my dream, I'm not scared but feel peace." She was flooded supernaturally like a flask being filled to capacity, with this overwhelming joy, and she found herself giddy like a child again, getting up on Christmas day.

"Can you still hear me Mill?" he asked. She responded back with a joyful yes, happy that she was not alone in this place.

As she walked down the ancient steps that were lit by a beautiful warm glow, she felt like she was in the sun, bathing in more than the light; the Light pierced her soul, and she felt that the Light was alive! "Oh Parker, I wish you could *experience* what I'm experiencing right now."

"Continue walking Mill."

She reached the bottom and moved forward down the corridor of the basement, which to her, appeared as ancient stone walls, with gothic metal lanterns hanging from the ceiling by a chain. They were lit with fire, and she heard the voice calling her, "*Mildred, this way My child, there is much to be done, time is short.*" The hair was standing up on her arms and the back of her neck, as she reached to grab Parker's hand, who immediately clasped his hand into her reach.

"I'm here Mill," he said.

Over the door, where the Philosophy room was, she saw a placard with ancient markings or symbols. The door opened slowly. She walked in, where she saw the desk and chair, and briefly she was curious as to why there was no bed. Amber colored light poured from the ceiling onto the walls, which was the same ancient stone walls she saw in the corridor. On one particular stone within the wall, was a red mark of "X."

Like a vacuum, she was sucked back into their time, seeing herself now standing in a dungy basement room, filled with files and her friend holding her hand. "Parker, Just Wow! I so wish you could see the things that I do. Here, where the desk and chair are, there was a mark on the wall that had a red "X" and I feel we are to look beneath this part of the wall; I believe something is there."

Parker, completely on faith, took his friend's lead, going toward the wall. He began to look for a loose brick; the walls from the floor to four feet high were cement, while it was brick the rest of the way up. He first began to press onto the brick to see if there was one that was loose, to which he discovered two bricks that were stuck together and movable. Stunned and in disbelief, he began to move the two bricks that were stacked, one on top of the other, pulling them out.

"Mill this is crazy," he exclaimed, as he reached his hand in the hole. Fingertips reaching as far as possible, he felt that he was touching old metal, and then distinguished a place on the object to firmly grab a hold of, bringing it out to the light.

A beautiful small tube about 8 inches long, and 4 inches wide, was fashioned in dark wood, that had symbols etched all around. On each end was old metal, now with a green patina. A slim chain reached from one end of the metal part of the tube to the other end. Parker put his hand on one of the metal ends, and turned to open it, "Oh my gosh Mill, you're right!"

He felt a crisp piece of paper as his hand entered the tube. Out of it came a yellowish tinged paper, rolled like a scroll. He handed it to Milly. "What do you make of this Mill?"

Now in ecstasy, she was living in a moment where both worlds existed, the present time and the *other dimension*. Hands shaking, she unrolled the yellow tinged paper, ensuring its preservation, having studied documents in antiquities, as she laid it out on the desk in the room. Now astonished, she saw the same markings from her dream, and let out with a deep breath, "WOW!"

Parker, now excited, realized that if his friend was right about this, and she was, then she was also right about the angels and demons. His mind was unable to comprehend the mysticism of it all; it seemed like a fantasy to him, but he was willing to be open to it.

"Park, we have to take this to Kaufman and Mercer. Moreover, I might share with them my dreams and experiences, so that we can get to the bottom of this particular relic from behind the wall. Somewhere in this universe, someone is leading me on this path, and you are here too, so we are doing this together." Milly's heart beating fast, she said with excitement, "What do you say? Are you in Park?"

"Am I in? How can I not be, angels, demons, relics, Ancient Language, and who knows what else, this is better than all the thriller movies I could watch in a lifetime."

The two laughed softly at first, then in uncontrollable exhilaration were roaring with laughter, hunched over holding their bellies, rationalizing the ridiculous sound of it all, acknowledging that this *craziness* had become their reality.

Time to Meet the Professors

Early the next morning, when they entered Kaufman's class, Parker went to him, updating him that they should meet to discuss their progress in clearing out the basement. Kaufman agreed, and mentioned that it was possible for them to meet in his office later that day.

Parker giving a hint to the mystery of their soon to be talk, said, "Say, Professor Kaufman, it might be advantageous to have Professor Mercer attend, as well."

Unsure of why it would be necessary to bring in another professor, Kaufman probed Parker about the need for Mercer's presence. "And why would we need Professor Mercer? I am intrigued as to your reason."

A bit hesitant Parker spoke, "We found something that will be of great interest to you both," Then he shifted into a boldness, like a CIA agent gathering intelligence, "It will be helpful for Professor Mercer, to address questions regarding our finding."

Kaufman returned with, "Ok, I'll invite Professor Mercer, and we can all meet in my office, and discuss your findings. I must say you have my attention with this mystery Parker, and I look forward to our discussion."

Parker turned and walked back to his desk, winking at Milly. After class the two briefly spoke outside of Truman Hall, and then headed towards their next classes. Milly went up to Antiquities, seeing Professor Mercer, and was met with intrigue, as she was addressed by her, "Milly, I heard about a brief meeting on the findings you and Parker made in the basement, and I must say that I am interested in your discovery. Hopefully, we can make this more than a meeting, and possibly get some extra credit, if you are able to do extended research for this finding."

Milly was stoked and felt high on life, as though she was an archeologist making the discovery of a lifetime. Although, she was unknown, having the attention of her favorite professors was more than enough to satisfy her desire for accomplishment. "Awesome Professor Mercer, I hope we can."

Class ended and she headed towards her mathematics class, Math 201, where she was learning Linear Algebra. She was so pumped for the meeting that was to take place with the professors that she could hardly contain herself while in class. Once class ended, she darted to meet Parker, having to walk through campus, so they could proceed up to Kaufman's office for the meeting.

Walking through the campus, she smelled the aroma of coffee, passing *The Grind*, her peers all around the campus quad, some sitting on the grass like hippies, others sitting at tables going over their latest assignments, and still others standing around listening to the cutting-edge tunes, and carrying on conversations about life at Strytan. You could see the sororities and fraternities preparing for the upcoming homecoming game, and a buzz was in the air, making it electric.

She arrived at Truman Hall, meeting Parker at the front steps. "Shall we?" Parker asked as he held his hand out to head in the direction of the door. Pushing on the thick glass, hearing the door swing open, Milly noticed that her senses were more heightened than normal. She was unsure if this was because of the excitement she had with meeting the professors or if it was an overall sense of wellbeing. Regardless, she loved the bliss of it all and took in the stimuli all around, moving up the stairs to Kaufman's office. Students that she knew from both departments greeted her all the while, as she returned salutations.

Kaufman's Office

Knock, knock, knock Parker knocking on the door to Kaufman's office, stood there with his friend, looking forward to what would transpire.

"Come in Parker and Milly," Kaufman said, waiting on their conference. "Let me ring up to Professor Mercer, and she will come join us."

Kaufman's office was the coolest ever. He had a vintage desk that looked like the size of a dining room table, stacked with books upon books of different philosophers and papers he was grading. His walls were surrounded with bookcases, while his desk was stationed in front of a huge window. You could see across the campus, out to the football field, where players were practicing for the upcoming game.

Two chairs were in front of his desk for guests to sit, as well as a couch on the wall by the door, where the chairs could swivel around for there to be a group discussion. Kaufman extended his hand out for Parker and Milly to sit on the couch, letting them know they would conference in that area. A coffee table sat in front of the couch, where Kaufman had clay coasters painted with different philosophers outlines, to set beverages on. The worn leather caramel colored couch, was from another era, welcoming philosophical minds to entertain discussions in style.

"Awesome," said Milly, as she unzipped her backpack retrieving her phone. Mercer walked in, greeted everyone, and sat down in one of the swivel chairs directly across from Milly.

"Hey Milly, good to see you again, and I have not met your friend yet," Mercer said.

"I'm Parker, Professor Mercer, nice to meet you. Milly has told me so much about your class." Mercer nodded and delighted herself in the intrigue that the two of them had for she and Professor Kaufman.

Kaufman sat down, looked at everyone in his office, and began the conference. "I understand you two have found something while cleaning out the storage room for the department. What is this *thing* that you have found?"

Parker motioned to Milly, since she was the one who was getting dreams and visions, which were related to the find, and did not want to speak on her behalf. Milly cleared her throat, while holding her phone tightly to her chest.

"Well Professors, while Parker and I have been cleaning out the storage, we stumbled upon an old desk that seems to be pretty dated, what I am guessing is before World War II." Kaufman and Mercer looked at each other, impressed with what was being shared.

"In the corner of the room, we found a matching chair, making it a complete set." Mercer was excited and sitting a bit more straight in her seat to hear the rest. "We looked under the desk to find the builder and discovered these particular markings."

Pulling the phone away from her chest, she opened her photo gallery and clicked on the photo with the markings. Mercer's eyes enlarged, as she began to feel drawn into a new adventure, building hopes to this little discovery that would lead to more. Kaufman positioned his glasses, to see the markings.

Mercer held her hand out as if to see the phone and look at the markings more closely, "May I, Milly?"

Milly handed her the phone, "Yes Professor Mercer, you may." Mercer enlarged the photo and her eyes widened behind her red-framed glasses that seemed like a magnifying glass, where her deep golden brown eyes were more pronounced with gold flecks speckled throughout.

"I must say Milly, this is quite a find; it is the ancient language of Pre-Canaanite Hebrew," Mercer stated. "And you say that these markings were under the desk?"

"Yes Professor Mercer."

Kaufman looked at Mercer and asked to see the phone, as he enlarged the pictures to see the treasure that was discovered. "Impressive you two, had I known that a great find like this was down there I would have done it myself."

Parker nodded to Milly to tell them as much as she felt comfortable to share. "There is more," Milly said a bit sheepishly. She had Mercer and Kaufman's attention, as they leaned forward.

Both professors simultaneously looked at each other, then at her, and asked, "There's more Milly?" They eyed each other, seemingly perceptive to some unspoken knowledge.

"Yes Professor Mercer and Professor Kaufman. This is the odd thing, and I don't want you to be weirded out by me when I share this; I assure you I am an ordinary girl and what I am going to share might freak you out."

Kaufman looked at Mercer, as they spoke with their eyes, then to Milly. "Go ahead, we are listening, and we will not judge you. We know you have a brilliant mind and esteem the staff here at Strytan, making every effort to maintain a high GPA."

"Well," Milly paused, "Before you asked us to work in the basement I had a dream, where I was walking down this ancient staircase, winding down to what would seem like a cave." Mercer and Kaufman looked at each other again and then glued their eyes to Milly. "The staircase had a glowing light radiating all around it, and at the bottom I discovered a room that had a desk, chair and bed." Milly looked up, paused as she stared, "The desk and chair in my dream were the exact ones in the Truman Hall basement."

Mercer was straight up in her chair like a peacock getting ready to unfold its massive feathers, fanning their wings with eyes bedecked all over; Milly could feel more than two eyes coming from Mercer, where it seemed as though she had many eyes.

Kaufman shifted to the other side of the chair, as he pondered on what was being said, and daringly asked her, "Is there more to the dream than this; I would dare say that there might be something you are keeping to yourself."

Milly was nervous and tried not to get anxious. She heard the sounds of Kaufman's clock over the window, the players outside across the field calling plays for the homecoming game, gulps in Parker's throat as her friend felt nervous for her, when finally he said, "Milly, just tell them already."

She inhaled slowly then continued. "Ok, here goes. While going down the steps and into the storage room, it seems as though my brain wants to relive my dream. It happens to always be when I enter into the basement." Mercer and Kaufman were more enthralled, as their minds were captivated with Milly's story.

"Each time I walk down the steps, I actually see the ancient steps in my dream. And what is more incredible is that when we discovered the desk and chair, my brain did the same thing, going between my dream and reality, where I remembered the desk and chair." You could hear a pin drop as Milly continued. "To better understand this I have to share my dream. I had a dream before and after we discovered the desk. In the one after we discovered the desk I was writing on a piece of paper, in the Ancient Language." She paused because her neck felt uncomfortable, which usually happens when she felt insecure about others' opinions of her.

Mercer gently leaned forward and encouraged her, "Milly, we are all scholars and intellectuals here, discussing what you have found and the seemingly odd occurrences around your finding. Please understand dear that we do not think you are crazy." She sat back in her chair treating Milly as she would a colleague and said, "Continue please."

"Well, more came yesterday, once I told Parker all that was going on," she stopped, looked at Parker, who seemed to be her backup, chiming in agreement that he knew. "He encouraged me to walk down the steps and be open to the fact that my dream might occur again, and to not resist its purpose, and follow it through until we got into the storage room. I did, and once in the room, I saw the ancient stone, with a red marking of an "X" on the wall, to which Parker investigated that area of the wall, and found two bricks that were attached together, easily pulling out of the wall." Milly looked at Parker to have him tag team with her and jump in to come to her aid.

Parker reached for his backpack unzipping it, "Bottom line Professors, what we believe we have found, is a relic." Mercer nearly leapt out of her chair, trying to keep herself glued to the chair as she waited for Parker's reveal.

He pulled out the ancient looking capsule covered in the markings and handed it to Mercer. "Inside you will find what appears to be a paper rolled almost like a scroll, and on it, is the Ancient Language that is likened to the markings under the desk, as well as the exact symbols in Milly's dream." Milly nodded in agreement and relief, that the truth was out, and finally people could think whatever they wanted; it was no longer a burden for her to keep.

Mercer rolled the remarkable object in her hand admiring it, then opened it up pulling out the paper, to which her eyes enlarged as she looked at Kaufman, showing him, as if he knew something. He nodded at her, giving freedom for her to speak to Milly and Parker, as he stood up, went to the door, looking outside to make sure no one was around, putting his "Do Not Disturb" sign on the knob, locking it, and then was seated back in the swivel chair by the bookcase.

Mercer sat up with her knees close together, as elegant as a princess attending a royal dinner. "Milly, both Professor Kaufman and I have been speaking, and it is good that you are sharing this, so that we can share what we know." Milly and Parker were not expecting this and were surprised to hear what was being said.

Mercer continued, "Both Professor Kaufman and I know about your Great Grandmother, Mildred, and within a small circle here in Springfield, her journals have been released from hiding. In them she shares what went on during the Great Depression. For those who do not believe in the supernatural realm, this would be a bit much, but since you are sharing your dreams, it is necessary for me to share more with you about your Great Grandmother." Milly was sitting on the edge of the couch in disbelief of what she was hearing, nodding for Mercer to continue.

"For the past year," Mercer said, "some of us have been committed to solving the messages she left; many of them are written in the Ancient Language." Milly was stunned; it confirmed her dream!

Mercer paused seeing Milly's response, looked at Kaufman who then nodded for her to continue. "We have discovered, as crazy as it might sound, her writings about dark societies plotting against our nation, possible discussions of demonic inner workings, which is not uncommon when it comes to antiquities."

Professor Kaufman chimed in, "and philosophies."

Professor Mercer took a breath, relieved at Professor Kaufman's interjection and lifted her left hand up to him, to continue. "Milly, we have been talking amongst ourselves, once we found out that you were here at Strytan, and by happenstance in both of our classes, that you would be the one for us to send down into the basement, merely as the beginning of getting to know you, so that we could form a camaraderie, or working relationship, hoping that one day something might happen where you would have knowledge of your Great Grandmother's diaries."

Stunned, Milly sat back onto the couch, putting her hands by her hips, looking at her phone on the coffee table, the relic, her friend, and then Mercer and Kaufman, relieved that she was not going crazy, and overwhelmed at what she was hearing.

Kaufman continued, "We had no clue about the desk and chair downstairs, and certainly not about this relic. To us, this is a sign that we are being steered toward something larger than any of us, and if it is alright with you and we have your permission, we would like to invite you to this group, and see what help we can be to one another; it is our belief from the things that we have been able to decipher from your Great Grandmother's writings, that she was speaking of a time to come, where there would be another attack in this nation, and especially in this area at about this time. There is now a team of people in whom I have utmost respect, that are collaborating on this project. I would like you to attend our meetings, but I do not want you to feel uncomfortable in anyway, should you decide not to come, and of course your friend, Parker is invited."

Parker wanted to break out and do a fist pump with his friend but with restraint, held his emotions back, "Yeah, I would like to come and be a part of whatever you all are doing." He looked at Milly with his big smile and leaned his shoulder into hers, giving her the signal to agree.

Startled, relieved and overwhelmed, Milly responded, "Yes...I would be interested and especially since they have my Great Grand's journals. I had no clue that she had written any of this and that her writings were kept somewhere, being studied. It would be an honor to be with the group and do whatever I can, to help."

Chapter 5

Charged with excitement, the town was celebrating homecoming. Residents and alumni participated in the annual tailgating before the big game. Local restaurants shutdown each year at this time, giving all their support to the school, setting up local kiosks on The Quad. Fans were bedecked in blue, white, and gold as the Strytan Eagles prepared for battle against their opponent.

Streets emptied, neighborhoods quiet, all appeared humdrum outside of the campus, except on Keller Street, where the dream team, to which Kaufman referred, met each week on Friday evening. Parker and Milly pulled up, riding in her baby blue convertible Volkswagen Bug.

Car doors shut, Milly pushed her lock button. The two headed to the front door of the Doctors Mercer. *Knock, knock, knock*. Parker and Milly stood at the door waiting to see all who would be present. The door opened with Professor Mercer's husband, Dr. Alan Mercer, welcoming them. "Hey I'm Alan, Anjali's husband. Welcome to our humble home, find a seat and get your favorite beverage; I have a coffee bar to the right side of the room as soon as you walk in."

Parker motioned for Milly to lead the way, as he took in the scenery of the incredible artwork in the Mercer's home, some of antiquities and others of abstractive collections highlighting the brain, which was Alan's favorite. Parker, studying to be a neurobiologist at Strytan, was taken in with anything that had to deal with the brain.

Milly rounded the corner to enter the room, and saw two seats, where she laid her purse and backpack down for the two of them. Turning, she walked to the coffee bar and found the barista boy from The Grind there! He smiled and asked her, "What is your addiction Mill?"

"Wow," she said, "I had no clue that you were here at Kaufman's and Mercer's meeting." Parker walked up alongside her and conveyed his amazement, as he too was now able to connect the dots, regarding the barista boy's canny behavior around them.

The young man smiled, held out his hand, and said, my official name is "Anthony, but you can call me Tony." Parker and Milly shook his hand, laughing as they discovered Tony was more than a barista boy, and actually had a life outside of the coffee shop. "I'm majoring in physics at Strytan and am in my junior year. While studying anti-matter and dark matter, I was led to the library for some late nights, seeing both Kaufman and Mercer in a conference room. Eventually with peaked curiosity, I lingered by and introduced myself. I shared with them what I was studying, as well the *odd things* I noticed, and one thing led to another where I am here for my second meeting."

"Odd," Milly asked.

"We can talk about it more at *The Grind*, sometime when you guys are there. Let's go ahead and get seated for the meeting." Tony directed them to their seats, as everyone began to take their place, with Kaufman standing in front of the group of about twelve.

He welcomed the members, "Good evening everyone." Clasping his hands he continued, "It is a marvelous night to be meeting; most of Springfield is tied up in homecoming. There was no rush hour traffic, I am sure, for any of you to get here, since you were headed away from the University." The group broke out in small chuckles.

"We have two new guests joining us tonight, whom some of you might know, are Milly Teschlon and Parker Harbin." He reached his hand out, giving attention to the two of them, to which Milly and Parker held their hands up and said hello.

"Many of you might not realize that Milly Teschlon, is the great granddaughter of Mildred Virginia Lee; Milly's name is actually Mildred Lee Teschlon." You could hear a couple of wows as some of those present were learning of it for the first time, acting as though greatness was in the midst of them.

Milly felt like a small celebrity, and although they were not her fans, but definitely fans of her grandmother's writings, she shared the joy of it vicariously.

Kaufman continued, as he addressed the relic that both she and Parker found. "Something new has come to light for our group; as of yesterday we have discovered, through Parker and Milly's work in our basement at Truman Hall, that a relic containing an old document was found. The relic has the same ancient letters as in Mrs. Mildred Lee's journals." Again, you could hear the wows and gasps, as the group became filled with exhilaration; it was like static electricity all throughout the room. Individuals looked at each other giving nods, eager to find out what the new discovery would bring.

Kaufman motioned for Professor Mercer and her husband to join him, as they stood up, she began to speak. "I am delighted to have all of you here tonight; with this new piece of information, we believe that more answers will come to light; it could possibly be a key of some sort, bringing us closer to the puzzle we have been trying to solve with Mrs. Mildred's diaries."

Professor Mercer held the canister up that contained the ancient document, saying, "From my initial investigation, it seems as though this document was much older than Strytan itself, and placed in the building once it was built."

"We will do an ongoing examination to find out the exact time in which it was written, and see what speculations we can achieve, in finding out the name of the author. In the meantime, I am going to reproduce the document by drawing an identical match and copying, for each of you to have individually, so that you can research in your spare time. Please do not share this with others but keep this to yourselves." The group nodded in agreement.

Mercer looked at her husband, Alan, at which time he spoke. "There is something specific that I want you all to consider as we look at this new found document. With what we have discovered thus far, we believe there will be some attacks against the central nervous system, and if you have any insight, I ask that you please contact me directly." Parker sat up in his seat, excited at the possibility of working with Dr. Alan Mercer, since he was majoring in neurobiology.

Lights turned off and projector screen down; Kaufman began a slide show, giving attention to certain pages of Mrs. Mildred Lee's diary. "Ok, this first slide has a drawing of a sun on the horizon, unsure if it is setting or rising. In the sky, there appears to be a drawing of a grid structure. Underneath the ground, is a hidden cavern, with huge barrels and hoses that come out, leading up to the ground." You could hear the slide shuffle in the projector. "Next slide, here is a picture of a whip, with keys throughout it, written in an Ancient Language." Milly lit up, wanting to blurt out her knowledge, but knew that she needed to wait and talk to Kaufman alone.

"Slide three, here is what appears to be radio waves coming from the skies and hitting across the globe, and a big clock, with the time showing 3:33." Kaufman stopped for a minute, looked across the room. "That's it for my part tonight. We will do a coffee break, where everyone can meet our newest members, and resume as we discuss our findings from last week's meeting, breaking up into our respective groups."

Milly looked at Parker as she raised her eyebrows with wonder, letting him know her approval of the meeting thus far. They got up and began to move about the room, as others greeted them, introducing themselves.

Tony came up, and leaned in, whispering, "I guess you already know me, see you at *The Grind*, if you know what I mean." Milly smiled and Parker did the "dude's handshake," pulling Tony to himself as they bumped shoulders.

The Diaries

People hushed, movement was stilled, as Milly's eyes were on the dining room table where three old books were stacked. Her feet, drawn like a magnet pulling metal, stepped towards the table. Latex gloves lay beside the books with special tweezers to turn the pages. Her eyes widened as she found her hands reaching out and picking up the latex gloves. The group's eyes were on her, as you could hear the slight breaths taken by the individuals gathered.

She looked at an old distinguished looking gentleman, who then handed her the tweezers and said, "Milly, it is time for you to see your Great Grandmother's journals." She was grateful for his kindness, unsure of who he was, but still he was seemingly familiar to her soul. His plump face and round glasses resting on his nose, comforted her soul, as he looked like a wise man smiling.

"Thank you sir," Milly replied.

Gently, she picked up the first book, opened the hard cover, and began to look at the brilliant pages unaffected by the years, not growing old with time. They seemed durable and sturdy as she handled them, which was a mystery to her. "These have to be special papers," she thought.

Then she heard a voice speaking to her in the midst of all that was going on, "These are My papers, which I have given to Mildred, your Great Grandmother. She was able to see, at a time when others could not, and saved many lives." The hair on the back of her neck stood up, and she looked up to see if others could hear. No one made mention of anything, and all had returned to their conversations, while she turned the pages with the utmost care.

Thoughts flooded her, "Oh I wish I would have known her well." Her Great Grandmother died two days after she was born. "She was not much older than me when she wrote this. How lonely she must have felt, when pouring out from her soul, the Ancient Language that flowed like liquid, causing her own tongue to be a pen, etching that which was eternal upon that which was mortal." She did not know where that thought came from and continued turning the pages.

Throughout the book, pages were filled with the Ancient Language, and others scripts, along with drawings. Very few pages had English, but the ones that did, were philosophical at best, seeming like gibberish on first pass. She knew why the team was assembled, because it would take more than brilliant minds to decipher this. However, with the new relic she and Parker discovered, maybe it was a *key* of sorts, like a legend on a map that would provide answers to these riddles.

"My dear," said the gentleman, "are you alright?" His face was kind, one you would want to see each morning when you walk outside of the house, to greet you and splash you with happiness. Joy was all around him and in him, like a fragrance in a bottle, ready to be doused on each passerby.

She replied, "I'm sorry, have we met Sir? I feel like I have seen you before."

"I would hope so, Ms. Milly, if you are attending Strytan; I am William Peyton, a Professor of Theology." He smiled, and held his hand out.

"Right," Milly said with a grin, "I have seen you at The Grind on occasion, where Parker and I frequent."

"Yes Ms. Milly, and I assume you have met Anthony, who makes everyone's favorite addictions?"

Hearing his name, he could not resist jumping into the conversation, "If you need a coffee, I am the man," he said laughing.

Milly and Professor Peyton laughed, which made her feel quite at ease among this group of intellects. They were on one big scavenger hunt, and her Great Grand was the one to thank. Had it not been for her, Milly would have never met all these amazing people.

She took the gloves off and sat at the table as the rest of the meeting proceeded. Kaufman and the Doctors Mercer broke everyone into three groups. Alan Mercer's group was working on the neurobiological attacks that were expected, and Professors Kaufman and Mercer's groups continued working on solving the mystery of the journals, with the newfound legend from the relic. The meeting proceeded, as details were wrapped up, until the next Friday.

Parker and Milly left, getting into her Bug, as she went to drop him off at the School. Streets were filled with partygoers reveling Strytan's win. Meanwhile, Parker and Milly were celebrating their newfound friends and the most thrilling adventure a college student could ask for. They were high in all their glory, knowing that great things were around the corner.

"Was that not awesome Mill? Man oh man that had to be the best time I've ever had! I will be working with Dr. Alan Mercer on a neurobiological attack! Who would have ever known?" Parker elated, was like a balloon in the heavens and wasn't coming down anytime soon.

Pulling up into the parking lot, they saw Tony, and called out to him, "Hey, see you Monday Tony." He did thumbs up and headed to his dorm. Milly bid Parker goodnight, and headed home.

Walking in, her parents were still up, waiting to hear the details for the evening; they knew that she was working on a *project* with Parker and some others at the university. "How was it dear," asked her mother.

"It was absolutely awesome!" Milly's eyes twinkled with excitement, where she was abounding in expectancy, and both her mom and dad became happy, not knowing exactly why, other than Milly was contagious.

"Wow Mill, that is great," said her dad. "Details please."

Milly knew that she was limited on what she could say; she did not want to give it away about her Great Grandmother's journals. She needed time before she could share all the details. Moreover, she knew that once she shared about that, she would also have to reveal her dreams and supernatural encounters, which she was definitely not sharing anytime soon, concerned her parents might think her schizophrenic.

"We are still in the beginning stages, but it has both the Doctors Mercer, Kaufman, and another professor from Strytan, as well as, of all things, the Barista Boy, whose name is Tony. I'm going to have to teach him how to make Keto-Coffee," she said laughing.

They could tell Milly was overcharged with excitement and knew it best to let her get to her cave and wind down for the evening. They were safe in their home, feeling comfortable in the cool of the night, not realizing that outside, Morder had stationed his troops to keep an eye on their house. There was no way the demons could enter, but the comings and goings of Milly were noted, especially when she connected with Doctors Mercer and Kaufman, attending the same meeting; Vladamore had his suspicions about them; he could see the light emanating from within them.

Bitterness and Lying Serpents

Vladamore called his commanders, instigators and Serugar, moving forward with his devilish plans to attack Springfield. With Kaufman's dream team now meeting regularly, they were a threat to darkness; the group knew that there was underlying revelation to Ms. Mildred's journals, of a deliberate assault against Springfield, and there was no time to waste. Now, with the relic found, they would be able to speed things up.

Since the meeting at the Doctors Mercer, a small tower was spotted at the Quad of Strytan, and no more time could be wasted in ensuring its complete failure. The gates of hell were slowly rising up, as well, and the race was on.

"Come here my commanders, instigators, and underling, time is growing short." Vladamore reached out his reddish hands, slowly motioning to those relegated to him, glorying in his own claws, as well as his evil plot. "We have to speed up the process; news has been received from Beelzebub that he will be arriving sometime soon, as the timeline of earth is interrupted. Mankind thinks that he is lord of this earth, when instead Beelzebub is ruler, which will be made known to all shortly."

Vladamore looked at Tildash and Morder, giving them orders. "I need the cords of slime operative this week, pumping our poison out of hell itself, so that the ruling powers can begin to attach their lethal cords to the humans, releasing all the manipulations of hell against their precious city. I will not be mocked, and will have Springfield in the palm of my hand," he said as he clutched his hand, long claws extending out to his palm, laughing with a putrid smoke filling the air.

Tildash and Morder agreed, and Morder filled Vladamore in on what he believed was brewing at the Doctors Mercer, with Kaufman and the possibility of Milly being the chosen one. Once Vladamore heard the report, he knew that they were on the right track at taking down those who were a threat to the gates of hell.

Responding to Morder, Vladamore continued, "They are the ones you say that are emanating the light?" He was plotting his evil plan. "How are their homes; are they protected by the wall of fire?" Morder responded that they were, at which Vladamore knew he had to work with the humans already given to the ruling powers, in order to bring distraction and offense against the Doctors Mercer, Kaufman and Milly. These particular assaults, if successful, would get them out of the place of safety where they would no longer be surrounded by a firewall and covered in the Ancient Language.

Looking at Dadanel and Heradacio, Vladamore instructed them to release their artillery throughout the city so that the cords of hell could be firmly laid, as the gates got larger. The grotesque grenades were filled with the venom of bitterness that would pass to those susceptible to it, making them nearly defenseless to the lying serpents that would be released through the larger artillery, much like cannonballs, which were filled with serpents. Lying serpents were one of the most used tactics with the venomous grenades, as a synergistic effect, causing human emotions to run amok.

As serpents in the natural realm, these serpents in the cannonball were varied colors, with each color having its own purpose. The orange colored snakes would whisper lies of the enemy to the person's flesh nature, bringing in seductions of the present age. Yellow serpents spoke the complaints of a person's situation, over and over, causing them to agree with the lies and speak them out loud. The red colored snakes brought lies of the enemy through anger, whispering lies to them, in order to get a person enraged. Brownish snakes brought discouragement and disappointment, in order to pull the soul into depression and oppression, leaving a cloak of heaviness upon them. Black snakes operated with witchcraft and spoke to a person's soul about acts of past rebellion, or tempting the person to rebel presently. Purple snakes constantly spoke deceptive words, trying to bring division between a person and others. Finally, green snakes whispered lies of money and greed, getting the person insanely hungry for a lifestyle beyond their means, bankrupting them emotionally and relationally with their family.

Sometimes, one or more snakes would be on a person, who was given over to the venom from the grenade of bitterness released. The snakes had hooks coming out of their mouths, where they would hook onto areas of bitterness in the soul. Since the soul is comprised of the heart and mind, snakes would put a hook either into the heart or the mind, and wrap around the person's neck. Sometimes, a person might have three different snakes, with some hooks in the mind and others in the heart.

Only the armor that Milly wore could be used to come against these lying serpents to set people free of their lies, using her sword to cut them off. Moreover, the person that had these serpents would have to come to the knowledge of their bitterness, in order to be set free, so that they would no longer be susceptible to the same attack. Milly, the Doctors Mercer and Kaufman were their targets, and since they did not have any vulnerability to the grenades, the underlings had to use others, who were already given over to the ruling powers' influence. Leviathan, Jezebel and Divination would send assaults against the minds of their zombified puppets, having them become a distraction to their targets, to bring offense. If there were no *offense*, there would be no opportunity for the enemy's assault to prosper.

"Serugar, you know what you must do," Vladamore insisted to him regarding the quick deployment of his plan.

"Yes my general, I do." Serugar replied.

At the University

The week was already started at Strytan, as Milly, Parker and Tony headed to their classes, meeting up at The Grind earlier than usual, touching base with one another, excited about what Friday would bring. Milly knew that she had to meet with Kaufman and Mercer to tell them about the whip she had received, which meant she would have to tell them about the angels, and what they spoke.

Tony waved from the coffee bar, as Milly and Parker walked in, and then gave the two thumbs up. Once they went to the counter, he did a fist pump with Parker, and asked them, "So are you going to have your addiction now or later?" They informed him that their stop was to say hey and check on him, and that later after Philosophy they would get their addiction.

"Later troops," Tony said.

As they were getting ready to exit the building, Lassiter walked in, looking strangely at Milly, giving her a *go to hell* look. She felt, what was like knives, penetrating her chest and shivered, as the stare itself released something against her soul. What, she did not know.

Parker nudged her on the shoulder, "What was that?"

"I have no clue, but obviously something is up with Lassiter. He is not the happiest camper on campus, that is for sure," Milly replied.

She felt a little out of sorts after Lassiter's stare, unable to figure out what the problem was. Headed to the second floor, they entered Kaufman's class, in full knowledge it would be eventful and inspiring. She needed inspiration after that insane stare from Lassiter, and his rude delivery.

Time came for class to begin, and Lassiter opened the door, strolling to his seat, giving the same stare to Kaufman, like a walking time bomb ready to explode. Kaufman put his index finger around his collar, to shake off the eerie stare as if it had some power over him. Milly noticed the struggle and turned to see what was occurring, and caught Lassiter's eyes as he glared at her again, and then back at Kaufman.

"Surely something is up," she thought.

She realized that she was becoming irritated with Lassiter's moods and verbal vomits that continually followed from him like a hurricane wherever he went. Taking a deep breath, she did not want to lose her cool, and instead focused on class to hear the lesson for the day.

Kaufman addressed the group with the quote prompted by Robert Burns, in his poem, "*To A Mouse*." Pacing slowly across the room, he delivered the well-known quote that comes from the famous line. "*The best-laid plans of mice and men often go awry. No matter how carefully a project is planned, something may still go wrong with it*." He paused, looked around the class, and asked, "Are there any takers on the ideations of this quote, other than the obvious?"

Parker expected Milly to do her brilliant *thing*, but her *thing* was not happening this morning; she was off. Moreover, Kaufman was tussling with his neckline, and he seemed out of sorts, as well. Wanting to break the observable tension, Parker lifted his hand.

Glad to find the welcomed relief, Kaufman called on him, while walking slowly to his desk. "Yes Parker, what say you?"

"Professor Kaufman, as you stated, *the obvious,* is that we make plans but regardless, things can interrupt our plans."

Kaufman listening said, "Continue Parker."

"Also, the mice have a plan to go after *the cheese*, and so symbolically, its intent is to find that which it desires. On the other hand, with man, *we think* we know what we want and desire, but sometimes the interruptions that come our way, steer us towards truth, in the midst of the plans going awry. Therefore, regardless of what happens, the main point is that through it all, we learn truth." Parker paused and said, "Burns was speaking to the point of vanity and not to let vanity guide you. Therefore, if we can be flexible or open minded, when things go awry, there is no room for vanity."

Kaufman and Milly pondered on the depth of what Parker was saying, and suddenly the Spirit of El Elyon began to move upon Milly, speaking to her of what was going on with Lassiter, and that it related to the saying from today's study, where demons were trying to get both Milly and Kaufman offended, and given over to vanity. Lassiter was merely their unwitting puppet to move her and Kaufman to that aim. She raised her hand to continue the thought.

Kaufman, relieved to see more participation responded, "Yes Milly."

"Professor Kaufman, there is much opportunity in life, for us to fall into traps, like a mouse going for the cheese. What I mean by traps, are the distractions that lead us towards the area of vanity, which is the wisdom of this present age. Areas in which we feel offended for not understanding someone's gesture or stare." Now, she had Lassiter's attention.

She continued her discourse while smiling, "We have to choose not to let the vanity of this present age be a disruption to the world that we live in that is far beyond the reach of the simple minded, which was why the mouse was brought in. The mouse represents the small minded, people dwelling on things to put in their belly, to get them through the day. However, the distinction between mice and men is, that men have the opportunity for a much higher wisdom, if they do not allow their appetite to be controlled by their belly, which represents this present age, the distractions."

Parker was into what Milly was saying, as well as Kaufman. Professor Kaufman was notably grateful for Parker and Milly's viewpoint, and felt the chokehold around his neck being broken, uncertain of what it was. Unexpectedly, Milly's eyes were opened up to the supernatural realm, and when she looked at Lassiter for a brief moment, she saw cords being sent to his mind that were like colorless power cords, with a liquid being pumped into his brain, emitting a yellowish stench.

El Elyon's Spirit showed Milly, that Lassiter had three cords of the spirit of Leviathan, which caused something to appear over his mind. There were seven heads of dogs that would shape shift into dragons. When they were dogs, they would snarl and growl at Milly. However, when the heads were dragons, they would release fire. It was blowing her mind at what she was seeing. She realized that Lassiter was given over to this demon, and it's intent was to attack her and Kaufman, to get them to become offended with the vanity of this present age!

It did not matter what Lassiter did or thought, but rather what she and Kaufman did and thought. She continued on after clearing her throat. "If we are not careful, those who are simple minded and given to the wisdom of this present age, can become a distraction by their ill gotten behaviors, hoping to spread its disease to us like gangrene."

On his feet, and his eyes wide open, Kaufman understood. "Yes, Milly and Parker, I see what the two of you are saying, and it's brilliant." He paced across the room, with a slow walk, thinking, pondering, looking out the window, and then, revelation! "Those who walk above simple mindedness are not guided by the appetites of this world nor led into the mazes of the mice, who are unable to see beyond their belly, thinking they know truth. Rather, man has an opportunity to choose whether or not to let his belly guide him, for the possibility of something greater to occur. Wisdom beyond our present reality is given to those who do not faint."

The seven heads over Lassiter were snarling and growling, as Leviathan knew that its cords of manipulation were not going to work on Milly or Kaufman. Bitterness was not able to settle in on either of them, as they instead chose to look past the vanity of Lassiter's behavior, and look for the higher achievement of solving the mystery to which they were committed, a Wisdom that was much higher.

Kaufman, Milly and Parker smiled, as a glow emanated around all three, where it seemed like an amber colored light was shining forth. Simultaneously, Milly saw a light shining from her backpack, which was the whip. The keys within began to move all throughout, making it alive, when suddenly the Ancient Language began speaking to her mind, and she received the translation. She took out a paper and wrote quickly.

"The whip has the keys to lock and unlock, wielding it has much authority over darkness, as you bind the cords of the enemy, and see My Sword cut them completely off, rendering the demon powerless. Use it well, as I instruct you. Not only will others be spared of its attack, but also the one given over to it, can be set free if they are willing."

Milly was amazed to know that this whip had more power than she ever realized, to which she knew she had to inform Kaufman and Mercer. Time was of the essence and she could feel the urgency of the hour. Without thinking, Milly stood to her feet, and in all nervousness, was afraid of what others might think, and the possibility of Kaufman's reprisal for her behavior.

However, to her astonishment, everyone seemed to be frozen like a statue, as Milly looked across the room, Kaufman's finger was pointed out as if to make a statement and his mouth open. Parker was leaning forward on his desk and his eyes looked still. Everyone else was frozen in time, when suddenly she thought to look at her watch. The second hand was stopped, and then she heard El Elyon speaking.

"Mildred, use My whip to bind the cords over Lassiter and speak to the seven heads telling them that they are bound and cannot speak while in your presence."

With courage, she pulled the whip out of her backpack and walked towards Lassiter, standing three feet away; she flicked her wrist and released it, seeing it wrap around the three cords over Lassiter's mind, binding the seven heads. The dogs were now yelping, as the whip tormented them. She opened her mouth and got in their faces and said, "I bind you, and you will not speak in my presence, and in the authority of this Sword that is on me." She took the sword from the sheath, as it appeared at her side, "I will cut your cords in time." The dogs began yelping even louder and immediately disappeared. She walked back to her desk, sat down and then time commenced, as Kaufman gave out the next assignment. Class dismissed and she and Parker headed to *The Grind*.

"Parker, you will not believe what I just did," Milly said with some trepidation in sharing, but knew that she had to tell him.

"What Mill?"

"We have to go to *The Grind* and I will tell you there."

Chapter 6

Milly found herself in a battle as she was wrestling with a demon. Her armor on, whip and sword at her side, she knew that she was prepared for *such a time as this*. Instinctively, she pulled out the whip, which was lit up with an amber colored glow, displaying brilliant gold keys throughout. The keys had a weighty sound; when Milly would flick the whip, the heaviness of the keys clanking throughout could be heard. *Clank* sounded the keys at the thrusting of the whip.

Milly had the demon bound up, its beady red eyes stared at her, and it screamed a shrill sound, like that of a siren, releasing the sound of its torment throughout the atmosphere.

"I bind you demon, be quiet, by the authority of this Sword. And with this Sword, I cut off your demonic assignments and command you to go to the wilderness," Milly said without thought. She had no clue what the wilderness was, just that she was to say it. The demon was sucked into a singularity, like a black hole in the supernatural realm, as her whip loosed it, coming back to her side.

Uncertain of what was happening, she found herself standing in the heavens among the nebulas and stars, when she saw Rafael and Tubal before her. Arms at their sides, shoulders pulled back, and glimmering in all their glory with a brilliant shine of the heavens, she was exhilarated to see them.

"I see you are learning quickly Milly, as El Elyon's Spirit has led you in how to use the whip and wield the Sword." Rafael said.

She looked at the armor all over her body, and eyed the whip attached to her hip on the left, and then put both hands on the hilt of her sword to the right. "I don't understand what is going on, but I can feel the Sword, as though it is alive."

"You are right," said Rafael, "because you and the Sword are one; it is alive, and you feel what the Sword feels, acting instinctively to do what the Sword speaks to you."

"You mean the Sword is speaking to me?" She paused, touching the hilt, then unsnapping its sheathe, she pulled out the beautiful sword that had a silver blade, looking at the sapphire stone encased in it. It was resonating with a vibrating movement that was releasing both sound and light. "Wow, it *is* alive!"

Tubal looked at Rafael with insistence that they had to continue Milly's education on the tools that she had been given. Rafael gave his permission for Tubal to continue the education. "Milly, El Elyon's armor is unique; each piece of it is alive, and is a part of you now. The Sword is distinctive and is the most powerful weapon against the demons you fight. Although you were dreaming just now, it was very real what you experienced. A demon was allowed to enter your dream, in order that El Elyon could train you on how to defend against the attacks, with His keys in the whip, and with His Sword."

She looked at Tubal, confused about the singularity that opened up to take the demon in, and the word she used on where to send it. "What is *the wilderness*?"

"The wilderness is the prison for demons, where they roam in an arid place, either waiting to return to a person, who has let down their guard, from which they came, or until El Elyon brings judgment upon them." He looked into her eyes that were now a brilliant green, signifying her heightened ability to see in the spirit. Eyes on earth had a certain color, but in the spirit realm, when scales were removed off of someone's eyes, the color was more brilliant and pronounced. Humans had no clue at the eye's ability to perceive up to 10 million colors, and it was not until they were spiritually able to see, that their eyes were able to make the distinctions, which were denoted by the changes in the color of their iris.

Tubal, seeing the beautiful green color of Milly's eyes spoke, "Veils have been removed from your eyes, as you have overcome this demon, and you will see more in the spirit. Each time you overcome an attack, your eyesight becomes more pure, giving you strength to see beyond your prior ability, as you see further in the spirit and also the future."

"The future?" Milly asked in shock.

"Yes Milly, like your Great Grandmother, you too are a watchman and a seer, walking in a prophetic gifting, where El Elyon's Spirit is training you in all manner, especially to see spiritually and into the future. Like your Great Grandmother, you will be able to see and know the Ancient Language, as well as to war against demons. The Sword will guide you, as you are one with it. Trust the Words it speaks, and open your mouth, and it will be filled supernaturally."

Tubal finished, to which Rafael began, "Time is drawing short for this battle, and we have to inform you of the recent workings of Beelzebub's demons in the region." Milly listened, as though it was natural to hear this type of conversation and even more so to be speaking with angels. She had no clue how this felt *normal* to her, other than the Sword at her side was now one with her, and she understood what the Sword knew.

Rafael continued his detailed update, "Beelzebub's general, Vladamore, has brought his team here to Springfield. Presently, he has his commanders looking for the chosen one, which is you. They have determined that you are that vessel chosen by El Elyon and are now targeting you and those who were at the meeting for your Great Grandmother's journals. Kaufman, Anjali and Alan, have been chosen to work with you, just as Parker, Anthony and the others at that meeting. When you all met, the Tower of El Elyon began to emerge in the midst of Springfield in the spirit. Your eyes will be open to see the tower and the power it carries."

Milly was mesmerized and wanted to know more.

Rafael looked into her deep green eyes, as light emanated from his. "When El Elyon's tower is established and His door opens in the heavens, the light that will pour out will be such a powerful Wisdom, encapsulating the region, going to His warriors who are ready to receive extraordinary supernatural power. The tower not only effects that which is above ground, but it is like a plant taking root, and releases a fire throughout the ground, shaking the underworld, that reaches to the root system of the gates of hell, in order to uproot it, tear it down and destroy it."

This seemed as though it would be too much for her to comprehend, but Milly was like a sponge, as she continued to listen to Rafael.

"Vladamore has his instigators, who are the demons making artillery, building and storing grenades that release a venomous poison, which is that of bitterness. When the poison touches mankind, if they have any offense, the venom will ooze into their heart and mind, and provide areas, for which hooks can be latched to from their next weapon. After the grenades are released, they will send huge balls, much like your cannon balls, except there will be hundreds of lying serpents stored in each one, looking to attach to the human's soul who has hooks.

Once released, the different lying serpents will attach to the hearts and minds of its victims. That is why Lassiter behaved with such vile, to distract you and Professor Kaufman. Vladamore wanted the two of you to become bitter, hoping the grenade would be effective. However, El Elyon opened your eyes to see the ruling power of Leviathan over Lassiter, revealing the seven heads that were operating and controlling him."

Eyes as big as golf balls, Milly was blown away as she received understanding. "Wow, so that is what I was dealing with, Leviathan?"

"Yes," said Rafael. "Moreover, there are two other ruling powers, who are stationed over your region with Leviathan, which are Jezebel and Divination. Vladamore is soon to invade the area with massive hysteria and chaos, turning everyone on one another, as he releases the grenades, and then the cannonballs. All of this is to be a distraction to his real agenda, which is to set up the cords of hell from the underworld that release a slime of oppression across the region, bringing great discouragement, hopelessness and depression, with much heaviness, during the global attack that is to take place. If this happens, then it will be easy for the ruling powers to attach their own cords to those individuals who are defenseless against these attacks, with Leviathan's cords attaching to the mind, which you witnessed with Lassiter; three cords of the ruling power in a human, make them its puppet."

Milly's education was stellar, with what Rafael and Tubal were teaching her. She felt as though she was in a university for spiritual warfare in the supernatural, and was nearly at a senior level.

Rafael continued. "The cords of Jezebel will look and sound like octopus tentacles in the spine of a person. Moreover, the cords of Divination will go into the belly and be a greenish color. It is necessary for you to assist those whom El Elyon leads you to; their soul is willing to be set free of the oppression. If three cords are in the human and they choose not to be set free, then the actual ruling power will send a demon to possess them, bringing the demon from the wilderness, as the dark matter in the earth increases, being drawn to them. Demons who are imprisoned in the wilderness are looking for a human host to inhabit. Therefore, although you just sent one into the wilderness, if you and the team do not move fast, many might be released by Beelzebub and enter human hosts."

Shocked, Milly's mouth was open wide, and she was trying not to be overwhelmed. Rafael and Tubal could see her disconcertion with all that was being put on her, and Tubal continued to set her at ease. "Be at peace Milly; anxiety is a thief of the Wisdom of El Elyon. You walk in a measure of it now, but it will increase gradually, and even more, when the door is opened in the heavens. All of you together, can send these demonic troops fleeing."

Tubal paused to let Milly soak in all the information just given her. "Milly, be confident that you are ready for this and you are not alone; you have El Elyon's Spirit and His Sword guiding you. Now your eyes will be open to see all the serpents that will be released with Vladamore's assaults, but you must walk in confidence that you can fight this, and equip others, who will soon have their eyes opened, too."

Rafael looked into her eyes, when she felt strength and resoluteness fill her entire being. He informed her of what she would need to do next. "Tell Dr. Alan that he is on the right course with a neurobiological assault, and that the relic will reveal more, as it is a key to your Great Grandmother's writings. When you meet with Professor Kaufman and Professor Mercer, tell them of this conversation, about your whip, and that there is a Prophet, whom Pastor Reginald Fielding knows. He is in the group, and will direct you. El Elyon will be speaking to those on the team, as well as giving them dreams about specific assignments, as His tower continues to rise in the area, which will bring the Ancient Language into Springfield, bringing torment to all of hell. Be of good courage and stay the course."

Speechless, Milly could only thank them for their message, and comforting words for the battle, bidding them farewell until their next meeting. Silently in the night, her vision ended, and she awoke moving back into the dimension of her present reality.

Truth Be Told

Alone, facing the stairs into the Truman building, Milly had to let Kaufman and Mercer in on the details of her supernatural encounters, as well as her knowledge of the whip that was in her Great Grandmother's journal. Milly had arranged the meeting that Kaufman and Mercer agreed to. She ascended the steps up the west end of the building, breathing deeply with butterflies in her stomach.

The door was open, with her two favorite professors sitting there in conversation. Professor Kaufman saw her at the door, and asked her to join both he and Mercer. He sat at his desk, while she and Mercer sat on the other side, which was a relief; she did not want to feel she was at a counseling session.

"So what brings us here today Milly," asked Kaufman.

"I need to share some *things* with you." She waited for their signal to continue, and they both nodded to receive the news. "First, about my Great Grandmother's journal and the whip, and next, about odd occurrences that I've experienced."

Mercer looked at Milly and said, "Please Milly, continue."

"About the whip, in my Great Grandmother's journal, I have been given one." She hesitated, waiting for questions, as they came pouring out by both professors.

Mercer straightened herself in the chair, and positioned her eye frames, "Where on earth did you find this?"

Kaufman leaned forward with his elbows on the desk, "Who gave it to you?"

"That is what I thought you would ask, which leads me to the second thing, which is my supernatural encounters," she said. "I began seeing things, first with dreams, and then later, I saw things with my own eyes, like an open vision." Unsure of what to say next, Kaufman was rolling his hand for her to continue, like a maestro in front of a symphony wanting to hear the composition.

"Well, this is the thing, its not only what I saw, but who I saw."

Mercer wanting to get to the bottom of it prodded Milly, "Go on, Milly tell us, we will keep an open mind." Mercer had an extra antenna that could sense what someone was about to say, and with her interactions, provided the leverage for them to do so.

"I've seen and talked with angels." She blurted it out as if to get it out of her mouth like spitting out bad medicine. It wasn't as painful as she thought; whether or not they believed her was the least of her worries; she was tired of carrying the knowledge of it around, like dead weight. Now it was off of her and out in the open.

Kaufman pushed away from his desk a bit, as he sat up and stared at the books across his library, while Mercer was straightening her skirt and doing her royal position of sitting, indicating that Milly was being taken seriously, this was a good sign.

Mercer then responded, "I believe you Milly, without a doubt." She looked at Kaufman, as if giving him the nudge with her look to follow suit.

Instead, Kaufman got up walked around the desk past Milly, and was still perusing his top shelf of books, eyeing one in particular. "Here it is," he said, "*Saint Thomas Aquinas*, as much of a philosopher as he was a theologian." Mercer knew well of Saint Thomas Aquinas and was excited to feel like a student under Kaufman for the moment, to hear the wisdom he would give.

"Oh wow," Milly said.

Holding the book, looking at its spine, then the cover, Kaufman spoke, "*Summa Thelogica*, which I am sure Professor William Peyton, whom you met the other night, is very knowledgeable about."

Milly had never heard the term, *Summa Thelogica*. "What is it," she asked.

"*Summa Thelogica*, is the writing of Saint Thomas Aquinas, who was an Italian philosopher, as well as a theologian, from 1225 A.D. to 1274 A.D. Founder of the Thomistic school of philosophy and theology, which is named after him, where he disputed the questions and commentaries of Aristotle. It is also the reference point of philosophy and theology for the Catholic church."

Milly was excited, because she knew that Kaufman had a point, and hopefully his aim was to prove her own sanity. Both she and Mercer were like kids in a candy store, waiting for what delicious treat would be served by Kaufman next.

"Thomas Aquinas addressed the ontological arguments of his day, by using five arguments for God's existence. His first four arguments, known as *The Cosmological Arguments*, deal with Motion, Causation, Contingency and Degrees. This series of arguments provided him, with what he believed to be the evidentiary facts about the universe itself."

Walking back to his desk and standing in front of the window, with the book opened, he continued. "With Thomas Aquinas' argument of degrees, he fashioned that 'properties come in degrees, thus, in order for there to be degrees of perfection, there must be something perfect against which everything else is measured,' signifying that God was the top of that perfection."

"The closest thing to that perfection in his eyes was the next degree, which was angels, identifying that with them, there was no matter or form, like a body that we have. Rather, he saw them as pure substantial forms, being pure with no mixture. Since they were not formed in bodies, their substance of spirit comes from the pinnacle thought of, Who is God. As a result, he determined that each angel is the only angel of their kind; each one being its own species."

Milly didn't understand exactly what was being said, when Kaufman saw her confused look and responded it to it with, "Humans are of a species, that of Homo Sapiens. Whereas, angels have no species; they did not evolve from anything other than God, thus, each one had to be its own species."

Milly then understood, nodded and responded, "Got you. Wow!"

Milly felt a bit intimidated listening to this, while Mercer was already very familiar with the philosopher/theologian.

Professor Kaufman got to the bottom line, "Milly, what he did for philosophy in his day, broke the rules off of the substance of a being, and opened a new way of thinking for philosophy as we know it today." He paused, closed the book, and laid it on his desk, pushing it towards her. "So yes, I believe in angels."

She gave a sigh of relief. "Thank God, oh I don't mean that in a crude way, I'm sorry; I mean Thank God!" The professors were laughing, seeing the opportunity to lead into her discussion about the supernatural experiences she had.

Milly smiled and began to share, "The first time I saw them, Rafael and Tubal, I thought I was in a dream, but they said that I was in a vision, and taught me the difference between them. Then they handed me a whip like the one in the journal, which lights up with an amber glow, having keys float inside of it, that I can hear at times clanking when I use it."

"So, you have used this whip," Kaufman asked.

"Yes, as a matter of fact yesterday with Lassiter in your class."

"Did I miss the class? I don't recall you pulling out a whip," Kaufman said.

"That's the thing; I use it only when it lights up, as well as the Sword that I have been given, which cannot be seen by natural eyes, because, I guess like Thomas Aquinas is saying, its substance is pure and not material form. The Sword talks to me with radio and light waves I believe, telling me what to do and when to do it. When the whip lit up yesterday, you and everyone else in the class were all frozen."

"What? You mean I was still?" Kaufman and Mercer were amazed at what they were hearing from Milly.

"Yes, it was like the substantive part of me in that instance, which I guess was my spirit, was in tune to the whip and the Sword, and in that moment time stood still, and I moved amongst you."

They were awestruck, and now Kaufman had his arm resting on the desk, feet on the floor under his desk feeling like they were stuck in glue; he didn't want to move. This was deeper than anything he had ever heard, as well as Mercer, who had read much through her study of antiquities.

"I found myself walking to Lassiter," Milly said, "Because he had seven heads over the top of his that were mad dogs snarling at both you and me, during class. They would shape shift into dragons' heads and then go back to dogs. I took the whip out and wrapped it around the three cords that were going into his mind from the seven heads, and bound them up, commanding them to not speak in my presence."

The professors were floored, Kaufman's elbow on the desk, now resting his chin on it, trying to allow his brain to process. Mercer was sitting at an angle in her seat, like in a movie theater, back far enough to get a better view, trying not to hurt her neck.

"After I threatened those snarling dogs, they began yelping and vanished. It was then that I raised my hand in your class to speak about the subject of mice and men. That demon made me feel horrible before class, from that insane behavior Lassiter dished out at me when in *The Grind*, and then I noticed him walking into class with the same attitude."

"Yes, I remember that; he gave me a stare that was very disturbing," Kaufman added.

"After I did all that to Lassiter with the whip, I saw the vice grip of the demon loosed off of us. The angels said that You, Professor Mercer, Doctor Mercer, myself, as well as everyone at the meeting were on hell's target list. The demons wanted to get us offended, so that we would be susceptible to the attacks they are bringing soon with grenade like objects in the spirit realm that release bitterness, in order to allow lying serpents to attack us. Rafael told me that the main demon we are dealing with, whom he called Vladamore, was building the gates of hell up in the region, to release attacks with three ruling powers he called, Leviathan, Jezebel and Divination. He said we had to overcome them, and that the relic was a key to my Great Grandmother's journals and that the pastor in the group would know of a Prophet, to send us to for the answers."

The professors were completely blown away; you would have thought they were on the front seat of a roller coaster ride at a theme park, coming to a stop.

Stunned with his eyes focused on Milly, then looking at Professor Mercer, Kaufman said, "Pastor Reginald Fielding, yes, he is in our group."

Mercer chimed in, "Yes, I believe he has been telling me for some years about some Prophet in the area."

Kaufman, still ruminating on everything, stood up, gripped his belt, rubbed his right hand through his hair, as if to regain his composure. "This is a lot to take in Milly, and I cannot imagine what all you have gone through to obtain, as well as comprehend all of this knowledge; and with this information, it seems as though you have a gift to see the spirits, both good and bad."

"Yes Professor, that is right."

Milly, forgetting to inform them of Dr. Alan, quickly wanted to tell Mercer what Rafael had said, "Also, Professor Mercer, Rafael said to tell your husband that he is right about a neurobiological attack that is coming."

The War is On!

Vladamore's plans were delayed, causing him more frustration. He was beyond mad, in full rage, and began to vomit out his unrelenting irritations to his team. "Tildash and Morder, I need deeper penetration into El Elyon's camp, where the chosen one is hidden. Something is occurring where El Elyon's warriors are releasing the Ancient Language and battling the gates of hell. Our cords will not be effective in releasing the slime of the underworld to bring confusion and chaos, and reach to the idols of the souls of mankind, if we do not stop them from *seeking* the Ancient Language."

Vladamore was like a hornets nest stirred up, he could not stop pacing back and forth, staring at his team with his beady red eyes, while he thrust his horrid nose in their faces. Slime oozed out of his nose, dripping nearly over his top lip. The slime was the fuel source for all the creatures of hell; it was the same slime that was placed in the gigantic tanks to be distributed throughout Springfield. This substance sustained all of hell. It was their fuel and their food, keeping them constantly paranoid on every turn, intimidating and driven by fear.

His claws into the rock wall, feverishly making claw marks, showed that Vladamore was out of control. Sweeping his rod into his teeth, gnawing on the black stone was revealing his wrath, soon to be taken out on all around, until his anger was pacified. "Heradacio and Dadanel, have you not yet had success against the chosen one and those in her group?" In fear of retribution, the two demons hunched over and lifted their demonic hands up to their chins, letting their hands hang with their claws exposed, ready to defend against Vladamore, as they shook their head no, while in fear and trembling.

"You imbeciles! Work harder in pulling the weapons out of your artillery to fight them NOW!" In full tyrannical rage, Vladamore spewed out at his loyal underling, "Serugar, stop playing with these humans and do what ever is necessary to release the underlings against others in their vicinity so that they will be racked with chaos and confusion, leading them to give into fear or offense, but preferably BOTH! Also, if there is a weakness of pride within them, use all your tactics to exploit it."

Vladamore's team scampered out of his presence to begin their conquest over El Elyon's warriors, to prove their talents. Any means necessary had to be used in bringing utter chaos against the chosen one and the others; the tower of El Elyon was rising slowly in the Quad at Strytan. It was difficult for the demons to move back and forth as freely through the area; being around the tower tormented them. Therefore, they had to ingest more slime from hell, in order to keep them preoccupied with their tasks, so that the enlargement of the tower would not hinder them. The battle must go on.

Heradacio and Dadanel sent out troops to gather more intelligence on the weapons that could be identified on El Elyon's warriors, as well as determining who had His full armor. El Elyon's warriors were fierce to deal with, and especially those in full armor; they had greater strength to walk in the power of His Wisdom, which was like poison to hell. The Ancient Language was torment; those who walked in Wisdom with the Ancient Language could not be defeated, and were like a roaring lion against the demons, overcoming them on every turn.

Vladamore knew that they had to be stopped, and right now was the pinnacle point before El Elyon's warriors found out how powerful they were.

El Elyon used those who looked foolish in man's eyes, not considered mighty, fast or strong. Rather, He chose to use those who seemed weak; it was in those, that humility resided. The secret to El Elyon's warrior's ability to overcome the serpent creatures was not in how great they thought they were, but rather in their humility, knowing they were nothing without Him.

Pride was the enemy to strength, in El Elyon's warriors. Thus, all the demons knew what they had to do in order to lure the chosen one and the others into a state of pride or offense, so that Vladamore's plan could proceed, and the Ancient Language would be hindered from being spoken.

The Basement Part IV

While walking down to the basement, and in her dream trance, Milly was speaking the Ancient Language. At the bottom of the steps she came to, and began speaking with Parker about it.

She and Parker learned one word written on the ancient relic; Mercer had already given them their copy of it. In bold red letters, next to the symbols of the Ancient Language, was scribed ***tĕshuw`ah*** which they found out was pronounced ***tesh·ü·ä'***. Beside the word was written, "VICTORY," signifying that El Elyon's warriors would have victory over the serpent creatures and hades.

Milly then entered back into the dream on the way to the storage room, and found herself in a vision, as she saw the door opening in the heavens, and again spoke out in the Ancient Language, both she and Parker had chills on their arms and the backs of their neck. Immediately, she was given the English interpretation of what was said. Parker wrote down the interpretation in her journal, recording it for the group.

She and Parker were assured that they were learning El Elyon's battle plan against the gates of hell. The relic had proven very useful, and brought more of an advantage; which would be known, once they could met with the Prophet, that Pastor Reginald Fielding was connecting them to. After Milly's conference with Kaufman and Mercer, the professors moved promptly, getting a meeting with him before Friday.

Today was the day that Milly, Kaufman, the Doctors Mercer, Pastor Reginald and Parker would be meeting with the Prophet. Classes could not end fast enough, as she set high hopes on the small gathering to take place over at his house. "How does a prophet look like," she thought, never having seen one herself.

This was new to Milly and at times made her uncomfortable. Like a fish out of water, desiring to have legs to walk on dry land, she was that fish, hoping she would grow legs soon enough to manage the course of direction in which she was going. Having her Great Grandmother's memory to live up to, she felt inadequate and, at times, grew weary. Now with the added assault from Vladamore's camp, she was in need of some supernatural charge, and in her mind, meeting the Prophet would hopefully provide that.

She and Parker rode in her bug, while the Doctors Mercer and Kaufman travelled in the car in front. Pastor Reginald was already at the house, waiting on their arrival, and getting there could not come too soon for Milly.

The group traveled about twelve miles out of town, unsure of what the Prophet's house would look like. Soon, they arrived at a picturesque site, with a pond, green-rolling hills, and a fenced in property of about 3 acres, to a ranch style house. A white haired man, whom Pastor

Reginald was talking with, was watering the trees and flowers in the garden.

"Surely this is not the Prophet," thought Milly, not realizing she was saying it out loud to Parker.

"Uh, well you don't know Mill, it could be," he interjected.

She looked at him, realizing she said it out loud, and said, "This is all out of my comfort zone Park, and it might take more than a minute to get used to all of this."

The two got out and joined the rest of the group, as the Doctors Mercer and Kaufman introduced themselves. Walking up, Parker held out his hand, "I'm Parker, Sir," to which they shook.

Then reflexively Milly held out her hand. "I'm…" Milly said, before being interrupted gently, by the white haired man.

"I know who are, Milly," said the Prophet.

Awkward, not knowing what else to say, Milly stood and looked around at the garden.

The white haired man sensed the notable discomfort, "I'm Robert Edwards, nice to meet you all," he said in a thick Welsh accent, as he looked at the group. He patted Parker on the shoulder, and looked at Milly, "You can call me Robert, no formalities here please."

His voice was like warmed butter on a hot piece of bread, that seemed to drip down into the pores, saturating it with yumminess. Robert's voice had a calming quality with his motherland, giving Milly peace and comfort. Everyone entered the house, stepping into the front sitting room that was rather spacious. Modestly decorated, his house kept in theme with the outside of the property, having furniture from the 1970s with variations of wood added into all the arm pieces of the chairs and sofa. Old coffee table, topped with coffee cups and a steaming hot pot of coffee, moved everyone past formalities and into deep discussions, regarding the reason why they were gathered.

"I suppose you want to tell me that the reason you are here is because you found an ancient relic," Robert said as he looked at Parker and Milly, winking showing them that he was in the know.

Kaufman, Doctors Mercer and Pastor Reginald were in awe, wondering if anyone had prepped Robert before their meeting. "No, no one has told me anything," he paused and smiled, "we prophets have a sixth sense of knowing what is going on before it happens." Parker and Milly were sipping their coffee while speaking to each other with their eyes, communicating how AWESOME it was to be in the presence of such uniqueness.

Robert fit the bill of uniqueness, with his 6 foot 3 inch frame, like a pillar in a room, each time he stood. He wore humble clothing that would make you think he grew up as a farmer, yet he spoke with a thick Welsh accent. His parents moved to Springfield from Wales when he was eight years old, settling down in the area, making it their home.

After their passing, Robert continued to stay on at their property, having inherited it. He medicated his grief by keeping the grounds up, since his father, William, said it always reminded him of Wales. Eventually, grief turned into healing, and led to a passion.

Water colored paintings of Wales done by his mother, Sarah, hung in homemade frames around the room. Robert looked at the group, and observing Milly, asked her to get up and open the drawer to the table, to which she was seated nearby. Milly made sure she was at the right piece of furniture, to which he nodded. She pulled out the first drawer, looking at only one piece of paper that was folded up, being careful not to open it.

"Please get what you see Milly and bring it here to Professor Kaufman."

Walking with the piece of paper, like a butler carrying a message on a silver tray, Milly handed it over to Kaufman still folded. Kaufman looked at Milly, thanking her for the paper, and holding it between his thumb and index finger like a prize, he looked at Robert, "What am I looking for?"

"Well Professor Kaufman," Robert said with his thick Welsh accent, "open it up and read it aloud to the group, please."

Unfolding the quadruple fold, Professor Kaufman began to read from the top. "Date: June 20, 2008, there is a war coming to Springfield where heaven and hell will battle for the souls of mankind. El Elyon will bring forth mighty warriors in this time, as they come together though kindred spirits, lit ablaze with a flame from an Ancient Language that speaks from eternity." Kaufman paused and swallowed, as the others stopped sipping their coffee, placing their cups on the table, captivated by the words.

Kaufman continued, "These people will be sent to you, seeking out the Prophet, who has news on an ancient relic, that will be the key to the diaries of Mildred Lee. Her Great Granddaughter, will be gifted like she, and come search you out with a pastor, doctor, two professors and another student. When they arrive, you will see those who have been prepared before they were in their mother's womb, for that which is to wage war in the supernatural in Springfield, as strength is brought to them from El Elyon with gifting beyond measure to bring victory to the area in a time of great darkness." He paused, wiped the sweat from his head, and looked at Robert.

"Continue Lad," said Robert.

Hands trembling lightly, clearing his throat, Kaufman read, "You will know the Ancient Language that you are to interpret, as the relic is given to you, showing the architecture of My victory, preparing for the door in the heavens to be opened so that My Wisdom is poured out."

All were quiet in the room, while sips could be heard from Robert taking in his coffee. The Doctors Mercer, Kaufman and Parker all had their mouths open while Milly sipped her coffee, so it would not be so obvious at how stretched she was in this moment; she fiddled when she was nervous and the coffee cup kept her busy.

"What?" Parker was shaking his head, as if in total disbelief, unsure of what to say next.

"Wow," said Kaufman, while putting the paper on the coffee table.

Pastor Reginald slapped his knee, "By gonnit, you have surely done figured this one Robert, why should I be surprised, and yet I still am."

Anjali, gently picking up the paper and pushing back her red glasses, putting her eyes to it, as if to assure herself of the folded letter's authenticity, held it up to her husband, "Alan, it is legitimate."

Doctor Alan, befuddled having never experienced this before, looked at Robert, who was still drinking his coffee, "How Robert, how did you do this?"

Robert knew that the questions would be coming from all sides, "Some call it intuition," he said, which sounded all the more mysterious with his thick Welsh accent. "However, others call it *the gift*, but I like to call it what it is, which is prophecy."

"Where is the relic, I would like to see it?" His accent made requests all the more amplified; you felt you were in a time capsule hearing the voice of wisdom speak to you.

Professor Mercer pulled out the relic, which housed the document, and gently handed it to Robert, who then grasped it firmly. He turned it over in his hands, seeing the carvings all over, whispering under his breath, "What a mighty fine work this is." Strength entered his hands as he continued to touch it, like a living being, bringing energy to his person; the relic charged him with excitement, knowing that it existed, and even more so, of the group of people who brought it to him.

Pop, you could hear the metal sound echoing off of the wood container, once Robert twisted it open. Long fingers reaching in, he pulled the document out. Glasses now pulled up from the neck chain on which neatly lay on his shoulder, he used them to look at the Ancient Language. "Yes," he said, "Oh my, yes, this is good," he looked up smiled, winked and said, "All of you are going to enjoy this one," and continued reading the document.

The others were looking at one another during his perusing of the document, and then back at Robert with excitement; all were curious as to what the result would be from their inquiry. Doctors Mercer and Professor Kaufman were on the edge of their seats, while Milly felt a magnet pulling her to the back of the chair. Parker still in shock, trying to process it all, was halfway between reality and fantasy in his mind, comprehending all that was going on.

"Well, the results are in my new friends; these are particular passages out of the Hebrew scriptures giving emphasis to major things, one of which will interest you Dr. Alan, about the coming neurobiological warfare in the spiritual realm."

Dr. Alan was in awe, "I knew it," he said.

"The other scriptures reveal the towers that are rising here in Springfield and the torment of hell that will result, as they continue to arise. One tower is in the midst of us now, but it is *His* intent," Robert said while pointing his finger upward, "for there to be many. The warfare you are experiencing right now individually, is a result of one tower rising up. But once the tower continues to rise and your individual giftings manifest, other warfare will come. Beelzebub wants nothing more than to take the towers down because of the torment hell experienced over 2,000 years ago."

The group was still awestruck and speechless. Robert continued, "Take these scriptures that I give you with this relic, and use it as a key to Ms. Mildred Lee's diaries, where you will see detailed depictions of the neurobiological attack, as well as the demon's grid system that will be used." Kaufman slapped his knee; he knew exactly what Robert was referring to.

"You all are being prepared for a larger battle than you can imagine. Many are called but few are chosen; not many can handle all that will be required, in order to endure what is coming. You fine people have specifically been prepared throughout your life, and your unique gifting will be of special service for this hour. We saw great victory when such a battle took this whole nation, during the 1930's, at which time Mildred Lee rose up. This present day battle is much worse, but together you all will conquer." Robert stared at all the faces with their mouths wide open, and their eyes nearly glazed over not knowing what hit them.

"That's it Lads and Lassies. Other than what I told you, I have no more until next week, when we will meet at the same time and same place, to discuss the gates and cords of hell."

Kaufman, rubbing his hands on his knees, finally stood up and clasped his hands together, "Thank you so much Robert for your time." Looking at Pastor Reginald he extended further gratitude, "Thank you too, Pastor Fielding for the pleasure of meeting up with this..." he paused waiting for the right word, "... this prophet."

Chapter 7

Anticipation for Friday's night meeting stirred up the young ones of the group, as Milly, Parker and Tony were having an experimental addiction, recently concocted, *coconut pie* with a twist of Keto Coffee; Tony added coconut oil and butter to the mix. Milly was in heaven, making yummy sounds after every sip.

Parker, staring at her with each sound, became a little irritated, and in jest spurted out, "enough already Mill, we know its good."

"Sorry Park, but I have to say, Tony, this is uttttterly amazing!"

Tony, proud of his latest lab experiment added, "I had to put the right velocity of spin on it, giving it a greater foam, where the air bubbles of butter would pop while inside of your mouth."

"They do," she replied, with another *yum* given under her breath. Parker cut his eyes to her, as she laughed and put her finger to his shoulder as if to push him, "Look, I cannot help it Park, and you are just going to have to get over it. Maybe when the oil and butter starts going to *your* brain, raising your GABA levels, you will chill out and relax."

Parker was a little on edge, and shared with Milly and Tony that he did not sleep last night because he kept hearing something outside of his window, followed by an awful dream.

"Oh wow Park, why didn't you tell me?"

"I'm telling you now, which is why I believe the meeting tonight cannot come soon enough." He took a sip of his drink and began his story. "I was asleep for about four hours, when I heard something calling to me from outside of the window, like a woman's voice who was beckoning to me to open the window and let her in." Milly and Tony put their drinks down and looked at Parker with a more serious look.

"Go on Park, we're listening," Milly said.

"I told the woman that she was to get away from my window, and in no way in hades, was I going to open it up, so that she could come in. After that I went back to sleep and dreamt of this beautiful faired skin lady with long black hair. Green smoke came out of her mouth each time she spoke. She got me to look into her eyes, and they began to turn this blackish color with green swirls in the midst of them."

Parker with gusto standing up made motions with his hands to convey the dream. "Suddenly," hands flailing behind his head, "cords came out of the back of her head, and towards my belly."

He now was holding an imaginary sword in his hand, as he spoke. "Next thing I know, a sword is in my hand, and I hold it up to her cords and say 'I cut your cords Divination, go to the wilderness, by the power of this Sword.'"

Parker looked at them both as they sat there staring at him while finishing his animated description. Bluntly he said, "That's it."

"Wow Park, that's some serious stuff Man," Tony said.

Milly joined in, "That was one of the ruling powers that the angel Rafael told me about; the three ruling powers are Leviathan, Jezebel and Divination. Rafael said that all of them were being unleashed by Vladamore, against Springfield, and especially against those who are in the group."

Relieved somewhat, Parker was glad to find out what he was experiencing was not uncommon for the group. As a result, he knew that the group had to get ready, and prepare for the spiritual warfare that was coming. "This stuff is serious man, I had no clue how bad it was Mill, until I experienced it myself. But the incredible thing was, that I had this armor on like you have described, where I pulled the sword out and cut the cords of that devilish woman."

They ended their conference at *The Grind*, as they turned their focus to the rest of their schedule for the day, where later they planned to meet up and ride over to the Doctors Mercer in Milly's Bug.

Meet and Greet

Now at the Doctors Mercer, Milly, Parker and Tony arrived, ready to get into the house, excited for what they thought would be a long meeting of great substance, where the group would make sure progress. Chairs out, Milly, Tony and Parker put their backpacks in a row, ready to take on the events for the evening. They each went to meet the other members, still uncertain of some names, as well as their profession. Milly remembered Pastor Reginald Fielding, since she was just with him at the Prophet's house the day before.

"Hey Pastor Reginald, so nice to see you again. I look forward to next week's meeting with Robert."

Pastor Reginald, with his warm-hearted grin, reached out to shake Milly's hand. "Nice to see you Ms. Milly." Eating a piece of coffee cake, he held the plate still, looked into Milly's eyes and said, "You know... it is a wonderful thing what your Great Grandmother did. And according to Robert, *you* will do much more."

Not knowing how to respond, she found herself saying, "Well, I hope I can live up to that." This was a test of all tests; all she wanted to do was to run and hide, not desiring to be seen or have any extra attention brought upon her. "I'm going to get some coffee," she responded, "thank you."

When she turned around, in front of her was both the Theology professor and the local priest. Professor Peyton stopped her momentarily, "Hey Milly, have you met Father Jonathan Sanderson, who is a Greek Orthodox Priest at Saint Timothy Cathedral?"

Looking at the distinguished dark gentleman, dressed in black regalia, she could not help but think of the movie, *The Matrix*, and the fact that Neo was sporting a similar outfit to Father Sanderson. "Nice to meet you Father Sanderson, I'm..."

Before she could finish, he interrupted her with, "I know who you are Milly."

"Oh, have we met before, I apologize."

"You were much younger, about 16 years old. I was in the ice cream shop with some from our congregation." She was trying to place him, as Father Sanderson continued, "You worked behind the counter at that time." She could not believe that he remembered her working there.

"However, I was not a priest at that time, it would not be until two years later that I went into the priesthood." She stared at him and his attire, at which time, he could not resist saying, "I know, I look like Neo right, just a darker version," he ended with a chuckle.

She let out a laugh, as did Professor Peyton. "I'm so glad you said that, because that is exactly what I was thinking."

Father Sanderson replied, "Most young people have made mention of that to me. I do not take it personally but rather find it to be an alluring icebreaker that puts people at ease."

Tony popped his head into the discussion, feeling the great harmony of the trio enjoying a good laugh while in conversation. "You're right Milly, I totally see *Matrix* happening right here."

Father Sanderson looked at Tony, greeting him again, "Hey Anthony, so good to see you here, as well as at mass early this morning."

Milly did not realize that Tony went to Father Sanderson's church, and learned a little more about the Barista Boy. She and Parker felt that Tony would be a regular on the *team* with them, at Strytan. "Wow Tony, so you go to mass at Saint Timothy Cathedral?"

"Yes Milly, I've been going a while; my parents took me as a young child and it just stuck, you know what I mean?"

She nodded, and then Kaufman stood in front of the group welcoming them to the evening's meeting, as they congregated and took their seats. "Welcome everyone, it is good to see you back here, ready and willing to work as speedily as possible on this puzzle. Tonight should prove to be a success as we share that which Robert Edwards revealed yesterday, while looking at the Relic."

Kaufman nodded to Professor Mercer. She would hand out the copies of the relic documents along with another sheet, to those who did not have them yet, which included the information on the ancient texts given to them by Robert.

Kaufman resumed his introduction, "What each of you have, is the reproduced copy of the relic document, detailing the Ancient Language, which appears to be in a spiral, going clockwise. As the ancient letters go in a spiral more towards the inside, they appear smaller. With this said, I will now bring up Professor Mercer, Anjali, who will use her expertise to assist in the deciphering of the document, along with the new found information from Robert." Holding his hand out to Mercer to take the floor, he went back to his seat.

Like a swan on a lake, she glided from the wall and stood in front of the group. "Hello everyone, it cannot be said enough, how grateful Alan and I are that you have chosen to participate with us and Professor Kaufman on this scavenger hunt. What we are discovering though, as of yesterday, is that, this is definitely more than a scavenger hunt. Look at the document of the relic, and you can see the ancient Hebrew letters that are pre-Canaanite, as well as some Aramaic letters. The Hebrew letters changed once in Babylon, and the actual original letters look more like caveman drawings. On the other handout you will see that there are 22 different symbols, one representing each Hebrew letter. One ancient text in the relic that is addressed is in Aramaic, and the other in Hebrew." Mercer paused to see if the group was following along.

"These same symbols are in Mildred Lee's diaries, along with another surprising twist we discovered in her journals, of the Coptic language interspersed throughout. The Coptic language comes from the word Aigyptos, which means Egyptian. Thus, Coptic is not only used to refer to a specific Church, out of the roots of Egypt, but refers to the Egyptian Christian Church at large. All through Mildred's diaries you see the Coptic cross, which is tattooed on many in the faith. We will get to the reasoning we believe is behind the Coptic use, momentarily."

You could see the intrigue on everyone's face, clueless to what the Coptic language was anyway. Mercer continued her talk, "On the top of the relic document, we see the Hebrew word in pre-Canaanite symbols, as well as written in our English letters of ***tĕshuw`ah*** which is pronounced ***tesh·ü·ä',*** which means "victory." From our discussions with Robert Edwards concerning the relic, we have discovered Aramaic and Hebrew texts, which have connections, with Ms. Mildred's diaries, in both providing us with the description as to her pictures of the grid, and Alan's expectation of the neurobiological warfare, which I will let him get into."

Parker was lit up like a kid in candy store with anything having to do with the topic of *neurobiological*. He could not wait to hear Dr. Alan speak. Professor Mercer introduced her husband, "without further ado, I give you my husband, Dr. Alan Mercer." Applause could be heard from the small crowd, as though he would be the main speaker for the night.

"Please, I'm no celebrity here, we are all a team; each member here is as important as the other. What I want to speak on, is the area Professor Kaufman shared last time with the diary relating to some type of grid." He paused, put up a slide on the wall from the projector, and continued, "We have looked at the Aramaic and Hebrew text from the relic that Robert has given us, which actually comes from the book of Daniel and Psalms. Thanks to Robert, who understood the means by which the letters were rolled together, that which was hidden is made known."

Highlighting the circular pattern in the form of a clock, where the Aramaic and Hebrew letters swirled around, Alan pointed out the beginning of the Daniel text, and then the beginning of the Psalm text. "The specific text in Daniel provides information to the coming neurobiological attack, affecting all of the central nervous system. This attack will come in different measures, as we first see the grid's use as part of the release that will take place. I have discussed this with my wife, and Professor Kaufman and they are in agreement with my speculations."

The next slide shuffled into place, which was the picture from Mildred's diary, of the grid structure in the sky, with a sun on the horizon and barrels underneath the ground, having hoses hooked up to them, piping something above ground. "This my friends," Alan said as he pointed toward the grid, "is the communication protocol the enemy will use to infiltrate the central nervous system, which we will call CNS from here out. Once it enters into the CNS through frequencies of both radio waves and light waves, which we believe to be dark matter, then those who are unprotected will be vulnerable to having their brains altered in different areas, including, but not limited to, forms of brainwashing, brain damage, hyper activity disorder, insane thoughts implanted in the mind, and dementia." The group was shocked.

He continued as if there was no element of surprise in his information or sharing. "If you remember the third slide that Professor Kaufman brought up in the last meeting, there was what appeared to be radio and light waves, along with a clock at 3:33. For those who remember, two weeks ago there was a lightning storm that occurred at 3:33 in the morning, causing the clock at Styron to be stopped permanently to 3:33." Light gasps could be heard.

"It does not stop there," Alan said; "in time, there will be a joint operation on this same grid, to ... please understand I am in all seriousness when I say this..." the group was waiting, wondering what he would say next, "to have our timeline interrupted by what could possibly be another parallel universe, affecting our history in the minds of mankind."

Confused, Father Sanderson raised his hand, "Please Alan, can you explain this?"

"Yes, the particular text that brought us this information in the relic, matching Mildred's diary was the Aramaic in Daniel 7:25. It is interesting to note that from Daniel 2:4, through Daniel 7, Aramaic is used and the rest of the book is in Hebrew."

"Oddly enough, in Daniel 2:4 there is a reference to the Chaldeans speaking to King Nebuchadnezzar in Aramaic, asking about the dream he had, in order to interpret it. Thus, from Daniel 2:4, we see the distribution of dreams given to the wise men in the ancient days that could interpret the dreams. Therefore, we also see this linking to Mildred's diaries (journals) that are full of dreams that she drew.

In Daniel we see the translated text:

"And he shall speak words against the Most High, and shall wear out the saints of the Most High; and he shall think to change the seasons and the law; and they shall be given into his hand until a time and times and half a time." Daniel 7:25 [vi]

Alan motioned to Anjali so that she would continue. "Thank you Alan." She stood in elegance, looking at the group, "If you notice the word, *time,* here in Daniel 7:25, written three times, is actually Aramaic, which is the language that evolved from Hebrew in the 6th century B.C. Think of it like this; both Hebrew and Aramaic are different languages of the same family; they both are from the Northwest Semitic dialect, because pre-Canaanite came from the Northwest Semitic."

"The Aramaic word for *time* here, is ***'iddân*** pronounced ***id-dawn'*** meaning, 'a set time.' Technically, it means 'a year, and then time.'"[vii]

Mercer looked up for a moment to see if the others were following along, and continued, "When we look at the Hebrew letters that compose this word from the relation of Aramaic to Hebrew, it provides more understanding and gives us more clues. Remember, we will be looking at these Aramaic letters now from the pre-Canaanite Hebrew letters; both evolved from Northwest Semitic. Each symbol has meaning, and when you put them all together, it gives you a word picture. Are you all still with me?" Everyone nodded. "The fact that the word *time* is written three times here in the ancient relic and, on the clock drawn in Mildred's diaries, the time there is 3:33, we believe there is a connection. Especially since, like Alan mentioned, two weeks ago during a storm, the clock at Strytan has remained on 3:33."

"Here, the three ancient symbols derive from the Hebrew letters Ayin, Dalet and Nun. Ayin is the ancient symbol of an eye, meaning to see, know and experience. Dalet is the ancient symbol of a door meaning to enter and pathway. Finally, Nun is the ancient symbol of a fish swimming through water meaning, life and activity. Therefore, when you put all three of these Hebrew letters together, you have the word picture of SEEING AND EXPERINCING THE PATHWAY YOU HAVE ENTERED THAT BRINGS THE ACTIVITY."

It was silent. Everyone staring, some with their coffee up to their mouths, and others resting their pen on paper, were speechless. Tony chimed in, "Uh, Professor Mercer, can you please repeat that word picture; I want to write it down."

"Sure Tony, the word picture," all were ready with pen waiting, "is, *seeing and experiencing the pathway you have entered that brings the activity.*" Wows were going off in the room, like fireworks on the fourth of July. You felt joy and wisdom rising up in the group, expecting someone to get up and shout, "now that is cool!" No one did, but you could tell by the energy in the room that they wanted to.

"Can I proceed," all heads nodded as everyone sat up in their seat. "Therefore, the *pathway,* we believe," she said as she looked at her husband and Kaufman, "is that there are demons bringing activity into our time, through their grid system, for this neurobiological attack, to both hack our brains, as well as interrupt our time line, from what we are postulating at the moment, is a parallel universe." People were hushed, as they could not believe what they were hearing.

"We can see this more as we look at one other word in Daniel 7:25, which is used for *'wear out'* that comes from the Aramaic word ***bĕla'***, pronounced ***bel·ä'*** meaning, 'to afflict and wear out.'[viii] Its ancient Hebrew symbols evolve from Bet, Lamed and Aleph. Bet is the ancient symbol of a tent meaning, tent, house and household, Lamed is the ancient symbol of a cattle goad, which looks like a shepherd's staff with a prick in the curvature, meaning, 'tongue, control and authority.' Finally, Aleph is the ancient symbol of an ox meaning, strength, beginning and first. These three symbols form the word picture THE HOUSE THAT BRINGS ITS TONGUE TO CONTROL OTHERS BY ANOTHER STRENGTH. This strength, we believe, has to do with Ms. Mildred's vision of underground tanks or barrels pumping something to the surface, which we speculate has to deal with the neurobiological attack, that is to be released."

Milly raised her hand, remembering the part that she wrote down in her journal while in an open vision in the basement. Knowing that she had to read the interpretation that was given.

"Yes Milly," said Mercer.

"I was given a message in the Ancient Language and the interpretation was given to me. Parker and I recorded it in my journal, which I believe was meant to be read at this moment. May I?"

"Yes Milly, by all means share," said Mercer.

Milly opened her journal to the entry and began reading. "Tell my warriors to listen to the news that I bring them about the Neurobiological attack, which is very real and is found in the book of

Daniel. Their minds have to be guarded against the wiles of Beelzebub." Milly closed her journal and sat back down.

Kaufman jumped up to the front to join in, relieving everyone's concerns, as he interjected. "Listen, as preposterous as this sounds, I truly believe we cannot rule this out. With the advancements of technology, and one particular advancement with science and singularities, as well as anti-matter and dark matter…"

Tony shouted out, "PRINA."

Kaufman nodded his head, "Yes, as Tony mentioned PRINA, which is the *Physics and Research of Intellectual Neurological Advancement,* is a possible contender for this hypothesis. PRINA is a gathering of many nations' top physicists who have now made it possible for a singularity to be created, of which we have been studying Roger Penrose's Twister Theory. Although intended for being used to study outer space, we believe PRINA is a *front,* as well as being funded, by the dark societies whose intent is to interrupt our timeline with this new machine, known as a particle accelerator, both opening the parallel universe, and releasing dark matter into our dimension."

Kaufman looked at Alan, and then to Anjali, where he was given the signal to proceed. "We," he said, motioning between all three of them, "have deliberated this with much angst and time, talking to some of the best physicists we know, and they have not discounted our hypothesis. As a result, we are not throwing it out, until, like in medicine, it can be ruled out."

Anjali stepped up to tag team on the topic. "We are in the belief of the hypothesis because of Mildred's diaries, which have Coptic writings in them as well. The Coptic writings seem to refer to a particular grid that can be affected by a singularity. Because the Coptic language is derived from Egypt, it is believed that there were some monks from centuries ago, who saw the grid that the demons tapped into from the pyramids, and they were possibly seeing interruptions of some sort, what kind we do not know, but something, where Mildred seems to be telling the story of what they witnessed, which would provide ample opportunity in our day, for this very same activity to occur on a larger scale through PRINA and the pyramids."

Interrupting, Parker could not help himself, interposing, "Now, are we talking about aliens or demons?" He paused. "I'm not sure about any of this, but I want to be certain what we are referring to here; when you bring in monks from Egypt many years ago, I cannot help but think of aliens."

Alan and Kaufman motioned to Anjali who was the expert. "Parker, that is a good question, thank you for the clarification. What you and I believe today is aliens, is actually what the Coptic Egyptians, centuries ago, believed and depicted as demons. From the Coptic writings and some of the pictures in Mildred's journals, we think that she was relaying the information from centuries ago in Egypt, of something they knew that would happen in our time. We still have experts studying some of the pages we have sent for confirmation. Hopefully, we will hear from them this week."

"So there are no aliens then," Parker asked.

Professor Mercer pondered on her words, to make sure she gave clarification to her thoughts. "In my opinion," she emphasized, "I would call an alien a demon; they are one in the same. The media has created forms of these creatures, for us to accept them, by which we have been brainwashed, through sci-fi movies such as *E.T.*, *Close Encounters,* and *Contact,* for the purpose of making us receptive to their presence, when instead, we do not realize that we have been brainwashed all along; they are malevolent creatures."

Alan stepped in, "May I add to that Dear?"

"By all means."

"The controls and manipulations by these brilliant but malevolent beings, what some call aliens and what we know to be demons, is that they have been using everything imaginable to unravel our minds. The CNS attack has been prepared for centuries, as they have invaded our food supply with poison, our water system with mind-altering chemicals, recently plastics where microplastics infiltrate our foods and drinks, and of course our media that have encrypted messages making us slaves to their system. From Mildred's diaries and the relic, we believe that there are towers, that are rising up in our area, which we will get into greater detail in our next meeting, that will be a barrier or firewall, against all these demonic attacks." The group was still, as they pondered the weighty news.

Kaufman walked up, took a breath, clasped his hands and looked around, "Well, let us take a break, then get into our respective groups. When your group is finished, you are welcome to leave until next week. Again, thank you all for your involvement."

Slowly getting up from their chairs and still processing all that was said, people were filing towards the coffee bar, grabbing a coffee or water. The Doctors Mercer were religious on using stainless steel or glass, so every time they had guests, everything they served with beverages and food, was in a stainless steel or glass container.

After the intense meeting, Parker and Tony piled into Milly's Bug, and headed back to Strytan.

Parker, still unable to wrap his mind around aliens being demons, asked, "Do you believe all that with the aliens really being demons."

Milly spoke in confidence after having dreams and encounters, "I cannot help but believe it Park."

Tony added his two cents, "Parker, to be honest, I never felt like aliens were good and always felt that they were evil. I totally buy what Kaufman and Mercer are saying, dude."

They rounded the corner to the main street of Springfield, where the old downtown area had eagles' wings painted along the street, leading straight into the university. This night, the eagles' wings were glowing with a certain liquid essence, covered with blue shimmer. The wings looked to be made of organic elements of matter flying on the road.

"Wow, this is awesome," said Tony.

"What in the world," Milly commented.

"Now this is something crazy here, guys," Parker added.

The three then saw where the liquid essence was coming from. Straight ahead, stood a crystal tower in a majestic swirl, rising up in the middle of the campus. Within, burned a mesmerizing blue flame, where blue liquid lava poured out, covering parts of Springfield.

They were charged up in the car, being filled with excitement beyond all measure, as Tony stood up, while Milly's convertible top was back, shouting out as they drove up the street. "Woo Hoo!" Others were looking at them as if they had lost their mind. The three of them could not figure out how anyone could remain calm in the presence of such a marvelous display of light, color and drama.

Stopped at the front of campus, they were in awe, as they got out of the car and stood. Others came around them as if nothing was happening, acting like it was an ordinary Friday night; they were clueless and unable to see into the supernatural.

Getting out of the Bug, Milly, Parker and Tony, lifted their faces upwards, as they stood in awe of this majestic, unexplainable feat that was towering over them literally, providing the most spectacular light show they had ever witnessed. Captivated and spellbound, they stood quietly, while others gathered around, trying to figure out what they were staring at.

The Demons Boiled!

The demons were boiling at the news of the tower, beginning to hear the Ancient Language rising up, like a pot on the stovetop that was simmering. Vladamore was hideously foaming at the mouth while putrid brown foam came out of both his mouth and nostrils, where those nearby would be spewed upon for certain. Tildash wanted to keep his distance, as well as did Morder, knowing that their reconnaissance proved a big failure, having allowed the tower to get to this height.

In an uproar, Vladamore foamed out from his mouth at the group, spewing on them, "You reckless maggots, what have you done now, is it too difficult for you to keep an eye on the little girl and all of her friends?" Foam spewed on Serugar who, unfortunately, would bear the force of his brute. Dadanel and Heradacio were hunched over like feigned wolves caught in a trap, trembling at the likes of Vladamore.

Vladamore, with great evil intent, released the sound that was captured by one of Serugar's underlings, recorded in what is called a *voice trap*, which looks much like a conk shell, being black, covered in a tar-like substance. "Do you hear that?" Releasing the vile contraption from a bag, having his own ears covered, Vladamore had the group listen to the Ancient Language from the voice trap. The sound caused the group to writhe in pain, like a woman in labor, where they then gnashed their teeth, and began clawing the rock walls in torment.

All were trying to cover their ears from the repelling sound that made their innards want to bust out, and pulses of implosions oscillated through their serpent creature heads. It was unbearable.

"Please master," begged Serugar, "turn the voice trap off."

Vladamore put the voice trap back in its container, and got his beady red eyes up in the group's face, with foam still coming out of his grotesque nose, oozing with the slime, mixing to form the most gagging smell and sight. "Your job, is to get the cords ready, and to have all your artillery in position for a great assault; we cannot afford for the tower to get bigger. The sound of the Ancient Language will increase in volume as the tower rises, and people will begin to have dreams and visions! This will gain more recruits for El Elyon's army, which cannot be permitted. Beelzebub will destroy us if he hears of this news, we must work quickly to undo it!"

Pacing back and forth, looking around the room as if to grasp a brilliant idea, Vladamore stopped in his footsteps, held his long arm up, with his claws spread out like a canopy over his body, "We will implement the three ruling powers assault now with greater intensity, as we release a pulse of the radio waves along with the dark matter, to seep into the neurons of humans from the slime, through the cords of the underworld, causing all their understanding to be distorted when they talk to one another. Then they will be more susceptible to the cords of Leviathan, Jezebel and Divination. All of our cords from both the tanks of the underground, releasing the slime, and the ruling powers (enmeshing cords into the bodies of their victims) must be released with the ferocity of hell, so that the humans know our gates are in the midst of their precious city! They cannot know the Ancient Language, lest it spread across the earth! El Elyon will begin to raise another tower shortly. If this continues we are done for!"

The serpent creatures stood frozen like statues as they waited for Vladamore to commission them out, so that they could carry out their assignments. "Move on, my troops! Soon, Beelzebub will be here, and I will not fail my lord, as the best general he has appointed in the underworld." Vladamore, in a festive evil laugh, began to declare, "We will forge ahead with the blackness that took our hearts, and look for our moment to strike; the gates of hell will rise! Offend them, cause their minds to be deceived with twisted speech, and let them be empty of compassion!"

Making Contact

Vladamore's troops exited the conference area, as he walked slowly to his magic ball, which operated by sorcery and witchcraft, much like a crystal ball. The size of small kitchen table, the huge black ball levitated inside of the room, as he began speaking to it. "Rise up loyal ruling powers, and come to hear what I have to say. It is time to advance."

A black smoke began blowing within it, as it swirled like a whirlwind and vanished. Vladamore could see the three ruling powers, Leviathan, Jezebel and Divination that were in the *first heavens*. Their work in the first heavens was to back up the plans of Beelzebub over regions and territories. Whereas, ruling powers over nations, were called *princes* who operated in the *second heavens*, fighting to hinder the movement of El Elyon's angels.

Usually, El Elyon sent His archangels or high level ranking creatures to battle the demonic princes, as El Elyon's hosts worked in concert with the recruits of His army on earth. Little did Milly and the others know, how effective their spiritual warfare affected the area, with their words dampening the assault of the ruling powers in both the first and second heavens, as the Ancient Language continued to increase in the atmosphere. Jezebel, Leviathan and Divination in the first heavens, were not as successful with their goal of positioning their cords within more victims, and the princes in the second heavens were not as effective in wrestling with El Elyon's angels.

El Elyon's recruits had great authority, especially when they worked together. Their unity hindered the ruling powers on a magnified scale.

The Friday meetings, without the group's knowledge, made the strategy of the demonic princes ineffective against restraining El Elyon's hosts.

The first tower of El Elyon, now rising, strengthened those in the group, like Parker, who also was receiving dreams and warring in the spirit, as the Ancient Language was released. Because of the group's work, and other recruits throughout Springfield, the demonic princes would continue to be unsuccessful, incapable of stopping El Elyon's angels from entering through the guarded gates into earth, to assist in the battle for the souls of mankind.

Demonic Control

El Elyon battled Beelzebub in an ancient clash before mankind was seen on earth. A stepping-stone of all that there is in existence, the heavens, became the corridor of all that was to come throughout the universe as the first epic battle was won. Beelzebub and his cohorts were cast out of the third heaven, El Elyon's domain, onto earth. Filled with evil intent, Beelzebub began to spread his darkness as a spiritual cancer covering the earth, setting up his ruling powers, in both the first and second heavens. The princes guarded the gates and nations in the second heavens, while the ruling powers in the first heavens fortified their demonic cords, to control regions with their diabolical plans.

Beelzebub's instructions were clear, to hinder each angelic entity from passing through the second and first heavens. He did not want them getting through to assist El Elyon's recruits in the earth. Had it not been for El Elyon's Spirit, the humans would not have the strength or wherewithal to fight against the serpent creatures, and striking the kingdom of darkness. Humans' efforts aided the angelic hosts of El Elyon to fight effectively as they could then enter the gates, and assist them in warring against the serpent creatures and ruling powers.

Vladamore knew that the humans of El Elyon were gaining more might, and as a result, the cords of both hell and the ruling powers were hindered. They had to act fast. "Greetings of darkness, great ruling powers, Leviathan, Jezebel and Divination, it is time for our strategy to be laid out. In order to succeed, in an expedient manner, we have to traumatize the area with the hordes of hell."

Leviathan, like a large red dragon, used its seven heads, as each one spoke a message to Vladamore. The first head said, "We are here for the battle," while the second and third head responded, "Time is short." Next, the fourth head looked at the fifth saying, "Will you tell him what you told me," to which the fifth head replied, as it looked at Vladamore, "We have to work cooperatively with all of our cords to overthrow El Elyon's tower." The sixth head roared and shape shifted into a snarling dog, growling. Finally, the seventh head breathed fire out of its mouth in a raging fit.

Jezebel, like a huge octopus, still had a beautiful appearance, long dark hair flowing over her shoulders, a slim figure with a fuchsia dress, from which her tentacles came spreading out from underneath like an area rug. Although her arms looked like that of a human, her tentacles were obviously squid like in nature, which were the cords that she would put in the spines of her victims, sucking all life out of them, leaving them zombified and brainwashed by her control and manipulations. She did not care what gender she used; her preference was men; to her they were worse than the women whom she controlled.

Finally, Divination, in her dark green dress, looked like a witch, as snakes came out from under her garment, like a puddle of water circling around her. She was always ready to send her divining snakes against her victims to distract them, so that she could put the cords from the back of her head into their bellies, delivering messages to the neurons within the stomach, where she would control their speech. Her victims spoke deceptive words, oozing greenish smoke. Divination had greenish smoke swirling in her eyes, and coming from her nose and mouth. She motioned to Vladamore to continue. "We are ready, speak."

"I have sent my troops out with artillery, so that we can release our weapons of offense and bitterness against the area, as well as to set up the cords of slime so that the lying serpents released, are effective against the souls of humans. We will be ready for your cords, to assist us and control those whom you overtake, to hinder El Elyon's recruits in everyway stopping the tower from rising. We have to destroy the tower now, so that the Ancient Language will not flow out."

Vladamore lifted his right hand in front of his face, as if clutching something inside of it. Suddenly, a holograph of Milly appeared. "This is the chosen one, and we have reason to think that she and her cohorts are working with the journals of Mildred Lee."

The ruling powers made a shrill sound, like that of a siren. They knew Milly's Great Grandmother well; she assisted in El Elyon's towers rising in the area many decades earlier, where hell was devastated. Because of Mildred, hell was unable to withstand the release of the Ancient Language, and El Elyon's power in both the human recruits and His angelic hosts.

Leviathan's heads shape shifted into snarling dogs that growled with a devilish sound, while Jezebel's eyes turned red and her tentacles shot up around her like an upside down skirt as she screamed. Divination was tormented remembering the defeat, and hissed like a snake, black slimy serpent tongue out of her mouth, hissing while gruesome smoke came out of her nostrils.

The ruling powers were tormented with the thoughts of a happening similar to the time of Milly's Great Grandmother, and were appeased momentarily by Vladamore, as he spoke, "There is still time for us to release the darkness of hell against them, so that our gates will rise and overcome the advancement of the towers springing forth. Be assured, I will get you your victory; I am the best general that Beelzebub has!" Their torment shrills now turned into a repugnant sound of laughter, as they cheered in agreement with Vladamore's assault.

"Beelzebub will be arriving to the area shortly, and it is necessary for us to prove that our darkness cannot be outdone. Take heed to my words and do not let your guard down." With his claws lifted up again, pointing to them with confidence, he spoke. "Block all of El Elyon's angelic hosts. But especially, dismantle the human recruits, by using the zombies under your influence to war against their minds and emotions. We all know the best-laid plan against them is to work through offense and twisting their ability to understand what is spoken."

Divination began to laugh with her hissing tongue still moving while dark green smoke flowed out of her mouth like a small river looking for an end. Leviathan's heads, now in the form of dragons, were lifted up as each one opened its' mouth releasing fire. Finally, Jezebel looked as though she was cuddling her long tentacles, knowing that they would be reaching more human hosts soon, whom she would control.

Vladamore, peering into the magic ball, lifted up his gnarly hand as the hologram of Milly still floated within it, and then with a hideous shrieking laugh, he clutched his fist as if crushing her. "This will be the end of her, you know her weakness, which is her insecurity from being traumatized when we urged others to bully her. Use that trauma and fear, as your strength through your zombies, and we will win the battle!"

Dark smoke began to swirl again in the magic ball, as the meeting ended between Vladamore and the ruling powers. Turning around with a crooked smile, he spoke to himself as if two people. "We have her now great general, look to how you will be hailed as Beelzebub sees your dark work." He bowed to his own words in a congratulatory way, like a person receiving a prize, making it seem that his mind was the most brilliant in the underworld.

Chapter 8

Back at the Prophet's house, Milly and Parker exited her vehicle, where she walked with trepidation towards Robert's front door.

Parker, noticing her behavior, couldn't remain quiet. "Milly, what is going on with you?"

"I get so nervous coming here, because when Robert looks into my eyes, I feel like my soul is naked or something and he can see all kinds of things going on inside of me." She didn't understand it and the best words she could use to describe it were "a piercing of the soul, like heart surgery."

"Come on Mill, it isn't that bad, let's go see what cool thing we will discover today. I know the Doctors Mercer and Kaufman are already inside, with Pastor Reginald."

After knocking, the door was opened by Robert, who greeted them with a subtle grin, sensing Milly's anxiety. "Welcome again, coffee is on the table, make yourself at home."

The group was seated around Robert's table, with the cinnamon scent filling the room, climbing through Milly's nostrils as her hippocampus retrieved memories about Christmas. She longed to be sitting near a Christmas tree, which would be soon, since it was already nearing the end of October.

Robert, shutting the door behind them, said with his Welsh accent, "Looking forward to Christmas, aye?"

Milly turned swiftly and peered into his eyes. She felt a singularity of her soul opened up, to where he could reach in and pull out the pain that needed to be removed. "Milly, Christmas always has good memories of gifts. What more could you ask for from El Elyon during Christmas, knowing that He has put so many gifts in you Lassie." Her eyes were big as she listened on.

Robert continued, "Could it be that your soul needs healing, where all doubt and unbelief of who you are in this life is removed. That is a gift from Him, to aid you in overcoming the trauma of your past, so that you can live in today and dream for tomorrow."

Breath taken away, she envisioned herself on a surgeon's table. Soul laid bare, for the instrument that would do the cutting, to divide between her soul and spirit, removing the tumors of fear, doubt and unbelief from her heart. The locusts that had been buzzing in her mind from the past bullying she had from Dana Dryer were sucked out of her memories.

As she was still, Robert spoke, "What a pleasant gift to us all, to have any pain removed; we are all in need of good gifts, wouldn't you say?"

Leaning into her presence, he whispered ever so lightly, "All is well Milly Teschlon, be at peace," and then he winked, as though it was a secret between the two of them.

Milly had insecurities that stemmed from the bullying she endured during middle school and high school from one particular girl, Dana Dryer, who many affectionately referred to as DD. She could not understand how anyone could be affectionate at all towards the girl that harassed and emotionally abused her all throughout school, keeping her in utter torment, to where she felt at one time, that she did not want to live.

Between the constant bullying on campus, as well as social media, Milly's emotional state, especially in her sophomore year of high school, was very fragile. Her parent's thought she was shy and did not want to be around others, when instead she had been in her room, cutting her arms with whatever instrument she could find. The volume of her pain from the constant taunts and public displays of humiliation left her defenseless against the stares of others, as the amygdala in her brain fired up, sending her into panic attacks. She would have to go to the restroom frequently to calm down.

Milly hid it well, wearing long sleeves, no matter how unrelenting her parents were for her to wear something normal. She put on a good front, and at times, had a mask that she would discover later, would be the film that covered her until it was broken off in her senior year.

Remembering it so well, with the smell of cinnamon in the air, it was Christmas Eve years ago, where she was having Keto-Coffee with her parents, when she immediately felt an overwhelming peace, and wanted to retire early for the evening, and go to bed. Getting up from her communion with her parents, she walked upstairs, stepping into another dimension for a brief moment as her feet hit the landing. Eyes opened in the spirit, she saw a thick reddish film covering her body and her mouth. Unafraid of what she perceived, immediately a bright light appeared, like lightning breaking all around her, at which point she noticed that the film was gone.

She laid down, too tired to consider all that went on, and then in her dreams, she saw a bright figure standing in front of her, pouring out an iridescent liquid that covered her from her head to her toes, where she heard, "You are sealed." It's funny how she forgot all of that until she walked into Robert's house smelling the cinnamon that triggered the memory. She knew that the amygdala was the place in the brain, of fear conditioning, as well as reward reinforcement, and was highly activated by stares, and the sensory avenues of smell and touch. The smell of cinnamon, being so potent, must have triggered the rewards reinforcement she received that night, when the oppression of bullying was completely broken years ago.

However, the damage that it did to her soul was still an issue, and she knew that she had to get over it. She was tired of feeling, at times, like a walking wound, hiding it from others who could not see the real Milly. But, Robert could see.

Robert motioned to the armchair for Milly to sit. Pushing the coffee cup filled to the top, towards her. He smiled with a gentle look in his eyes, to which she felt bathed in the same iridescent liquid that she did the day the film was removed from her years before. Picking it up, she pulled the saucer and cup to her chest, where she picked up the cup of coffee taking in the aroma, and then she took a sip, realizing that Robert had made her a Keto Coffee. With surprise, she looked at him and mouthed "thank you," to which he nodded.

Looking at the group, Robert spoke. "Right, are we ready to get started; there is much to be covered at this meeting." All heads nodded, as people sipped his delicious coffee, taking in the ambiance of peacefulness to the point that it could be called blissful.

"Let us put our attention on the relic, as we consider first what we saw with Daniel 7:25 about the wearing out of El Elyon's people in a specific time. As you have shown me Mildred Lee's diaries, I agree as to the specifics of the time 3:33 on both the drawing and the recent storm that took place at Strytan, halting the clock permanently on 3:33."

Kaufman looked intently at Robert, taking notes on his I Pad. He pulled up the saved files on both the relic and Mildred's diaries. Robert noticed Kaufman's files and, while towering over Kaufman's chair, put his finger on the file of the relic, enlarging it.

Looking at the group, large body bent over while pointing to Kaufman's screen, Robert carried on. "There it is. There, do you see it," he asked as he pointed to the ancient Hebrew word from the text.

Curious as to what Robert was speaking on, they listened, "The towers of El Elyon, will be our main discussion today." Kaufman looked up to Robert's countenance, seeing the excitement on his face like a kid at Christmas, sensing that something huge was to be shared. Professor Mercer, giddy, was like a horse about to leap out of the gate. Robert had all of their attention as he began the session.

"Yes, the towers of El Elyon, is seen in the ancient Hebrew in the text of Psalm 48. Here in the relic, the revealing of it starts specifically from verse 12 and then goes backwards to verses 4-6. This pattern is not happenstance, which I will get to in a minute. First, we saw the Aramaic language with Daniel 7:25 on the outer part of the clockwise picture, and as the spiral goes inward and gets smaller, it begins with the ancient Hebrew in Psalm 48:12, then 4-6."

Robert, holding up his yellow legal pad, read from the thoughts that were scribbled with black ink. He was a walking thesaurus ready to pour out of his treasury of knowledge and wisdom.

"*Walk about Zion, and go round about her: tell the towers thereof.*"[ix] With buoyancy in his voice, he lifted his hands, like a giant tower himself. In his Welsh accent he looked at Professor Mercer knowing her enthusiasm for the ancient Hebrew, "Anjali, you will like this one for sure." He paced the floor slowly as if musing before letting out the Hebrew word, treating it like a diamond ready to be displayed in a showcase.

"*Tower*, here in the ancient Hebrew text, is the word ***migdâl*** pronounced ***mig-dawl'*** meaning, 'a tower, by analogy it is a rostrum. Figuratively it is a pyramidal bed of flowers, as well as meaning a castle.' This comes from the Hebrew root word ***gâdal*** pronounced ***gaw-dal'*** meaning, 'to be large, as in body, mind, to exceed, be excellent," arms raised up he kept going, "To wax greater, make greater, nourish up, promote, be proudly spoken and tower."[x]

Smiling as he moved about the room like a Sunflower jutting out in a garden, he spoke. "The connection we see with the tower in Psalm 48 is that El Elyon's tower has a direct affect on His Army, as they are strengthened in their body and minds, to be exceedingly great while nourished by the Ancient Language in order to SPEAK it, where they themselves become a tower." The group was stunned as Robert carried on.

"Many might not understand, that when we see the pyramidal bed of flowers with the Hebrew word for towers, that it is actually referring to the brain, and the neurons within it. This is illuminated much more deeply in Song of Solomon, revealing that the amygdala is protected from the brainwashing of this present age, in order that Wisdom from above can speak to our mind. For those who are able to resist the demonic assaults," he said almost spitting, "your brain will be the most brilliant brain that earth has ever seen, which we will see why, shortly." He grinned as he saw the eyes of those in the group, widening the more he kept speaking.

"It is not a coincidence that the word *amygdala* sounds similar to the Hebrew word for tower, ***migdâl***. El Elyon's tower is directly linked to the amygdala in our brain, shielding it from the central nervous system attack. As you might know, the amygdala is the place of fear conditioning, as well as reward reinforcement, housing both traumatic memories and/or incredibly good memories; it is the place of great emotion. The common triggers for the amygdala are emotional faces, which we can consider through the *emojis* on our phone; but for us it is the stares that we get from others. With the fiendish plans of Beelzebub, he is certain to come against the mental states of mankind in order to distort our perceptions of others, making us paranoid on every end, as he has his cronies operating in the media through emotional faces in movies, as well as the news, which is no longer informative but rather startling, using it as a vehicle to attack mankind's amygdala."

Robert paused, hoping not to lose their attention, knowing that the information he was giving could be overwhelming, at the least. "The other thing that triggers the amygdala, setting off a panic attack with the sympathetic nervous system, is the senses, with mainly the senses of smell and touch being directly linked to its operation. Therefore, another assignment planned by hell, will be to release assaults through our senses, via smell or touch, triggering any traumatic circumstances in our life. This was actually used by the dark societies in Operation Chaos Butterfly, brainwashing their victims, so that they would be easily triggered to assassinate someone. One minute, they would be a loving person, however, after experiencing a certain smell, touch, as well as, sound or visual cue, could trigger the amygdala, changing their personality.

"You and I will have the most brilliant minds of the time with the Tower rising, as it releases the Ancient Language; not only will it protect our amygdala, but also, it will open up neural pathways in the brain, where we are able to use 70-80% more of our faculties."

Anjali, Alan and Kaufman were speechless, while Milly ruminated on the idea as she sipped her drink. Parker was astounded, grabbing his head, as if he could feel the neurons waking up and firing, providing him truth. He could not help but shout, "Wow!"

Robert smiled and continued, "The revealing of the power of the *Ancient Language* in El Elyon's people, is seen through the Hebrew letters for the word Towers. Anjali, would you do the honors," Robert asked, as he handed her the scribble of the ancient Hebrew on his yellow legal pad.

"Thank you Robert, and yes."

He motioned for her to stand in front of the group, encouraging her in the gift she had been given. Upright in front of the small gathering, she adjusted her glasses. Immediately, her eyes widened as she looked intently at the ancient letters. Under her breath she said, "Oh my."

Looking up with excitement she could hardly contain herself. "You are not going to believe this." They were all ears. "The Hebrew letters for the word *tower* are Mem, Gamil, Dalet and Lamed." She paused and tried to pace herself, so as not to be overly excited. "Mem is the ancient Hebrew symbol for water meaning, massive or chaos, as well as indicating flooding. Gamil is the ancient symbol of a camel, meaning to lift up or pride. Dalet is the ancient symbol of a door meaning to enter or pathway. Lamed is the ancient symbol of a cattle goad meaning tongue, control and authority." Feeling as if time stopped, she glanced up from the page. Her brain turning with huge revelation, she was like a river waiting to gush out.

"Are you ready," she asked. To which everyone nodded profusely.

"The word picture for *towers*, is, THE MASSIVE FLOODING FORTH BY THE OPENING OF THE DOOR THAT YOU ENTER, GIVING YOU THE TONGUE OF AUTHORITY AND CONTROL!" Like a cheerleader for a brief moment, Mercer let loose and shouted "Woo hoo!"

The group was excited, because of her excitement, but not fully understanding why. Robert's eyes were dancing as he waited for the revelation to hit them. Milly put her coffee down, leaning forward, light bulbs going off in her mind. Parker, with an inquisitive stare raised one eyebrow, as both Kaufman and Alan sat back for the moment taking the word picture in.

"It means," said Mercer, "that the tower is connected to a door, and when the tower is to a certain height, the door will be opened, where we will be flooded with this massive authority of Wisdom, giving our tongue even more power against the hordes of hell."

You could see the "ah ha" moments people were having, as they too got the revelation and sat up straighter, wanting to know more.

Kaufman looked at Milly, and then pulled up the file of Mildred's diaries, specifically showing a huge door opening in outer space. "May I, Anjali," he asked wanting to interject his thoughts.

"Absolutely Norman, please."

Milly was not used to Professors Kaufman and Mercer going by their first name, still adjusting to the change. Kaufman enlarged the file of the door, and began to speak. "The other night I had a dream of a door opening in the universe, and a voice in the dream mentioned Mildred's diaries and said, ask Milly." Motioning to Milly he said, "I remember you telling Anjali and I about your dream with the open door."

She stared at the group, finding herself as a peer with her own professors. Mind you, they were the professors whom she enormously respected. "Yes Professor Kaufman, in my dream, I was carried up into the universe where a door was opening with this brilliant light coming from behind it, when I heard a voice say that Wisdom would be poured out soon. Afterwards, two angels, Rafael and Tubal were there to meet me, giving me instructions on the armor, and the whip, as well."

Robert, brimming over with joy, slapped his knee, "There it is Lassie! The gifts He has given you to take down hell itself! I love it!" She smiled, feeling warmth in her chest, and took another sip of her Keto-Coffee.

Robert pulled on the gift within her, "Milly, tell us about that whip and what the angels said to you."

Milly asked Kaufman to pull up the picture from her Great Grandmother's diaries. Picking up his I Pad, she pointed at the special detail given to the whip. "You see the whip coiled up here, with small things dispersed throughout, these are actually keys within it. Before I get into more about the whip, I want to mention that I have seen my special armor, discovering later, where *time* seems to stand still; I have already mentioned some of this to Professor Kaufman and Professor Mercer."

Robert jumped in, to expound on the amygdala and genius faculties of the brain, with Milly's experience of *time* standing still. "Right Lassie, you see the reason that time stood still while you operated in the spirit realm, was because your brain was on a different level of operation, receiving the Ancient Language, which exists outside of time. I like to call it *eternity time*. When you are operating on that level, your brain and heart, which comprises your soul, along with your spirit, accelerate to the speed of light, causing everything else to seem frozen. You might not realize that your true body is frozen, while you are actually in your spiritual body, but your soul is in sync with it. When you come out of eternity time, you step back into time itself, where you re-enter your body."

Kaufman desired to understand the difference between that and Einstein's theory and asked Robert, "so what is the difference between eternity time, and space time?"

Hands on his knees, Robert stretched in his seat and continued. "The difference is, that in Einstein's theory of general relativity, which we know as space time, is *effected* by the *matter* within space; there is cause and effect. Thus, earth's existence is warping the space-time continuum, and light is actually bent, effecting time, as we know it on earth, where what we conceive of as normal, goes by the measure of our clock. Eternity time is outside of space-time because light is not bent but rather perfect and unaffected by matter. It would be as though space-time was on the sea level of the earth, and eternity-time was on the mountaintop."

Kaufman, still confused, was doing his Kaufman stare, to which Robert explained away, "It can best be described by this. Time accelerates the further you are away from the earth at ground level, actually going faster on a high mountain. Likewise, when our bodies stay grounded, it does not mean that our spirits are; they operate in a different continuum much like being on the mountaintop, if we are sensitive to it."

Still confused, Kaufman needed more. "Can you give any more details, Robert?"

"Absolutely Norman, and you will be enlightened by this one Lad. Scientists made two clocks exactly alike. One clock they put inside of a building that was at sea level, and the second clock they took to a high mountain peak. Before separating the two clocks, they made sure they were in sync. Days later when they took the clock back down from the mountain and brought it to the clock that had been at ground level, they discovered that the clock on the mountain had actually sped up. It accelerated because of the decreased influence of the space-time continuum on it. It is like that with us.

"The difference with space-time and eternity time can be seen when the tower began to rise here in Springfield. The tower provides us the influence of a mountaintop experience, as it is lifting our minds up to the door that is opening, where our eyes are focused on things above and not on things of this earth, whereby we enter the door; we enter Wisdom."

"Time is being squeezed and stretched by the gravitational waves from the tower, which are creating a cosmic window to be opened up in time. Because of the squeezing of space, in that window matter does not exist, making the space-time effect is irrelevant; and you know why," Robert asked while staring at Kaufman.

"It is because the Light from the beginning, what many call the Big Bang, is presently squeezing into our time through the open door with the tower that is rising, making it possible for those of us, who are pulled into its influence to operate outside of the natural time, and space time."

Milly was blown away at the understanding she received from Robert's explanation. She and the others had their mouths wide open. She looked at Robert and he nodded for her to continue.

She took a deep breath and spoke. "The keys in the whip are keys of a supernatural Kingdom. You and I are used to seeing keys on a key ring, but that is not how it is in the supernatural; instead, they are within the whip. When I am to use the whip, it lights up to an amber color. A liquid fiery essence moves throughout, making it seem alive. I know what to do with the whip, because the Sword, that is part of my armor through vibrations of light waves and sound waves, speaks to my mind telling me what to do. Usually, when I use it, I see cords of demons, especially from the ruling powers.

"The Sword instructs me to use the whip in order to bind the cords of the ruling powers. I speak the words as directed, while binding the cords of the dark powers. It is like my tongue is taken over in that moment, fully given to the Ancient Language."

Kaufman robustly stated, "Milly Teschlon, its Wisdom!" Unable to sit after such excitement, he paced the floor as if speaking to his own class. Pausing, seeing pictures of Wales all over the room, he then looked at Milly stating, "You remember, when in class we discussed King Solomon's quote, which differentiated between wisdom on earth and Wisdom from above."

She eagerly nodded. "Yes, I do Professor Kaufman!"

"This door opening in the heavens, that you have described from your dream, and now from your Great Grandmother's diaries, must be the same door that opened up in her time, to cause Springfield to survive great devastation, and moreover prosper, while all throughout the nation people died and were in the midst of famine." He looked at Robert, as he sat down, showing his eagerness to know more, "So in reference to *this tower*, which can potentially turn into more towers, according to Psalm 48, it goes higher, which in time causes a door to open in the heavens of El Elyon, because we have entered a new time, known as eternity time?"

"YES LAD! You are correct! I am willing to bet that even Milly and her friend Parker over there have already seen the display of the tower at Strytan." Robert's face beamed as he looked towards the two.

Like children caught taking cookies out of the cookie jar, they slightly nodded. Parker spoke up, "Man, you should have seen it!"

Excited, he could not sit down. "After last Friday's meeting, the eagles' wings on Main Street looked as though they were alive and moving, with a liquid blue lava, like that of a blue opal. When we pulled up to The Quad at Strytan, there standing in the middle of campus, was a huge crystal tower with hot blue liquid lava bursting forth. People thought we were crazy. They couldn't see it, thinking we had lost our minds, making a big deal about nothing."

"Wow" said Alan, as his wife and Kaufman sat speechless.

Professor Mercer, intrigued asked, "Can you see it now at Strytan?"

"No, not all the time Professor Mercer," Parker said, "Just last Friday was the only time so far. I don't know why we only saw it then."

"Other than..." Milly joined in, "other than, when we saw the tower, it was right after the meeting, and most likely because we were all coming together at the Mercers, looking to get Wisdom about the

Ancient Language. There must be a correlation of us seeing in the spirit when we *seek* to know the Ancient Language. The only thought I have is that we obtain Wisdom from the tower, which pulls on the Wisdom from above! Our hunger to know the Ancient Language is a connection with the tower and the open door."

Robert smiled as he watched all the gifts of the individuals come together like a symphony to play the ancient sound that desperately wanted to be heard. Now they were joining together like an army ready for battle, delighting in the weapons that had been handed to them from the Ancient One.

"So what about the rest of the text from Psalm 48," Alan asked, as he looked intently at Robert.

"Glad you asked Alan, let me preface this, with the fact that I am going to go through a few Hebrew words with the letters, and will not be repeating the same ones we have discussed, but will merely give you the meaning. I do not want you to be overwhelmed, just remember that this is the only time we will look at the ancient Hebrew letters."

The group nodded and knew that they would press in for what would be a brief moment in order to comprehend the revelation of it all.

"Let's move forward to find out why this text is put backwards. Now we are referring to 8 verses earlier than the prior, by looking at verses 4-6. Remember we first looked at verse 12. Are you with me?" They all nodded.

"First of all, when we look at the variation *numerically*, we see the number 12. Then going back to verse 4 for the next text, we have to go back 8 lines. This is easy math so hang in there," Robert said smiling.

"Each of these numbers, 12,8 and 4 are a variant of 4. Moreover, if we look at 12 divided by 4, we have the number three. In addition, three numbers are represented here. Whenever you see 3 in a pattern, there is representation of power, which here the power is through El Elyon. Interestingly enough, 33 actually means wings, so 3:33 means wings of power in fullness, which is the lifting up in the spirit realm to the open door.

"What Mildred must have known, was that the wings in the supernatural realm, depicted throughout her diaries, are the lifting up into the heavens, where El Elyon's warriors to obtain Wisdom. These wings are the strength and power of El Elyon's Spirit on His army. The fact that the wings, painted on Main Street were painted many years ago in her time, I believe it is actually a sign of what happened then. We know that Strytan was built before the Great Depression, and it is my suspicion that, whoever put this relic in the wall, knew what would come both in Mildred's time and ours. Strytan was built in 1887, and most likely a door opened at that time, as well. Many things happen in cycles, where times of opportunity occur because of a door that is opening in the spirit. The door that is presently opening now, is that of Wisdom in the heavenlies, which works in concert with the tower."

Holding his yellow legal notepad up, Robert continued. "Let us now focus on the next three lines of text in Psalm 48, looking at the ancient Hebrew to understand the potency of the towers and the terror that it brings to all the serpent creatures and ruling powers."

*"**4** For, lo, the kings were assembled, they passed by together.*

***5** They saw it, and so they marveled; they were troubled, and hasted away.*

***6** Fear took hold upon them there, and pain, as of a woman in travail."*[xi]

"Here, in line 4 of Psalm 48, we see that the kings assembled and passed together. Kings, here in Hebrew, is the word ***melek*** pronounced ***meh'-lek*** meaning, a king, and comes from the Hebrew root word, ***mâlak*** pronounced ***maw-lak'*** meaning, to reign, to ascend the throne, consult, be king or queen, and rule."[xii]

Looking at Professor Mercer, he handed off his yellow pad with the ancient letters written down, asking her to do the ancient symbols and the word picture. Delighted to assist, she pulled the notepad up to her face, and spoke to the group. "The Hebrew letters that compose the word *kings* are Mem, Lamed and Kaph. Mem as we saw earlier, means massive or chaos, as well as indicating flooding. Lamed means tongue, control and authority, while Kaph is the ancient symbol of the palm of a hand meaning, to cover, open and allow. Therefore, the word picture for kings in this specific context, since the kings are negative here, is, THE TONGUE THAT FLOODS FORTH WITH CHAOS TO COVER."

"What?" Parker exclaimed as he put his hand on his forehead, flabbergasted by it all. So much confirmation was coming to his brain about the CNS attack, as the word picture was revealed.

Alan saw the confirmation as well, on the CNS attack, which would be the chaos that would come. The chaos would come through some type of frequency, which could be considered a tongue. Enthusiastic because of the confirmation he blurted out, "That tongue that floods forth with chaos to cover, is the demonic attack that will hit the grids in the area, sending frequencies to the brains to fill people with chaotic mental assaults, affecting their mental state as well as sending signals of pain throughout the body."

Parker looked at Alan agreeing wholeheartedly replying, "I see it, too!"

Robert affirmed Alan, "You are right Alan, and more than ever, as we look at these kings, we see that the kings represent RULING powers and princes; the Hebrew word king means to rule. Thus, the kings referred to here are the ruling powers and princes in both the first and second heavens, which we are fighting as the towers rise.

"The towers give us more power in the tongue of El Elyon, which is represented by the blue flame within the crystal tower. The blue flame is the purest flame that burns, having no toxins in it, representing a pure power. This blue flame will actually be triggering our neurons and become a spiritual substance, feeding us the Ancient Language. Many do not understand that in the spirit realm there is food, but the food is *language*. Thus, the cords of the ruling powers or of Vladamore from the underground, releasing slime which covers a person with film, can be the substance of a person's spirit, which is fed by the tongue of hell, bringing chaos."

"On the other hand, for those whose amygdala and spirit are connected to the tower, they are fed a strength of the blue flame, which looks similar to a fiery blue opal. It strengthens your spirit, even when your body and flesh are weak, the strength that it gives to you for spiritual warfare is unmatched and cannot be beaten by the hordes of hell. Thus, it is important to resist the attacks of the slime of the enemy.

Your spiritual sustenance comes from the blue flame of El Elyon's tower, releasing the Ancient Language, giving you constant downloads in your mind of Wisdom and talents that are within you."

Seeing the need for a coffee break so the group could process the present download of revelation, Robert offered a small rest, "Let us take a small break and fellowship over some macadamia nut cinnamon bread with my homemade butter, getting another cup of coffee if you like. Slowly getting up, Milly and Parker looked at each other; speaking volumes with their eyes, of the intensity of depth they were at, with this *scavenger hunt.*

Alan and Anjali got up, nodding to each other to enjoy the special bread, while Kaufman sat quietly on the couch meditating. Robert invited the group into his kitchen, where cinnamon continued to fill the air, as he pulled the loaf of bread out of the warm oven.

"Yum," said Milly, "one of my favorite Keto delights!"

Robert smiled at her, "Milly, the Keto diet is good for your brain and your spirit; it is much like the blue flame, burning pure energy, releasing ketones in your liver to be distributed through your blood stream going to your brain, where you are running on a purer energy than glucose. Your parents were very wise to get you on the diet."

Second Wind

Back at the coffee table in the sitting room, the group took a breather, getting their second wind for the rest of the news on the ancient relic. They had no clue the depth to which they would be getting into about the relic this night, and the small reprieve was welcomed so that they could mentally rest, in order to wrap up the evening.

Yellow legal pad in his grip, Robert picked up where he left off. "In line 5 of the Psalm 48 text, we see the reference about the kings going about marveling, and then suddenly their marvel turns into angst, where they then become *troubled* and are *hasted away.*" Pausing and looking at the group to mentally prepare them for more training he said, "We will get into some Hebrew words in this line and the one to follow, and will be done, hang in there Lads and Lassies."

"*Marveled* here in the text, is from the Hebrew word ***tâmahh*** pronounced ***taw-mah'*** meaning, 'to be in consternation, marvel, amazed and astonished.'[xiii] This is a primitive root word. The Hebrew letters are Tav, Mem and Hey. Tav is a new one for us, and is the ancient symbol of a cross or an "X" meaning, sign, seal, mark and covenant. Again Mem means massive or chaos, and indicates flooding. Hey is the ancient symbol of a stick man holding its arms up worshipping and means to reveal. Therefore, the word picture for marveled is THE MARK THAT SEALS, FLOODS FORTH IS REVEALED."

He paused to let it sink into their hearing, like water trickling, to find the lowest place it can reach. The words from Robert's lips were finding their way into their souls, as it trickled in their ears, passing through the synapses in their brains, firing off in great measure with the Ancient Language oozing from the tower towards them. Then it trickled down to their soul. Like a hand massaging the heart memories of when they were back in their mother's womb, bringing depths of learning that they could not comprehend until now. They understood!

Milly thought, "Man, His words are deep, I hope I can survive this knowledge."

Parker, with his inquisitive stare was quiet; Kaufman did his head tilt, giving the Kaufman *philosophical contemplation stare*. Alan and Anjali, still taking in the supernatural logic, let their brains do its mapping within their neuron groupings.

"Whether we know it or not, we in this group are all marked and sealed by El Elyon, which is exactly why Wisdom flows to us from the tower. This is depicted in quantum field theory as we look at a vacuum being opened, where zero-point energy can flow. I believe if you look closely, in your Great Grandmother's diaries she refers to the time she spent with Nikola Tesla, and the discovery of this energy, but that is for another visit after this battle is fought."

The group's eyes looked as though they were on a roller coaster, trying to take in this revelation, and especially looking forward to the time they could see when Mildred Lee connected with Tesla. Robert continued, "Zero-point energy is an unlimited energy supply that exists in a vacuum. Scientists are studying, on how to contain and harness it.

This zero-point energy is a good example of the power of Wisdom from El Elyon, and His mark upon us. His power exists in a vacuum that we know as Wisdom, which is made accessible to us by the mark by which we are sealed. We are able to harness His energy, because of His mark.

"The open door in the universe, gives a high level of strength to the tower and other towers that will rise, which then flows to those who are marked by El Elyon. Those who are marked have their minds protected from the CNS attacks, but are also able to receive downloads of Wisdom, through what some might analogize as this zero-point energy.

"As we see that zero-point energy is a power force, which exists that scientists are working to harness. The difficulty scientists have is in harnessing and containing the power. Like zero-point energy, the power force of Wisdom, can only be harnessed by The Ancient Language, and only flows to those who are marked. Those who are marked become containers of this power. Beelzebub knows that those who are marked by El Elyon will receive supernatural Wisdom. We will walk in a greater knowledge and understanding, which is Wisdom, in order to tap into a power that is beyond the powers of darkness."

Just Breathe

Noticing those in the group were overwhelmed, Robert redirected the conversation. "We need to look at the Hebrew letters and meaning for the words *troubled* and *hasted away*. Will you do the honors Anjali," Robert asked. He knew that he had to give them a breather, and having Anjali get up to do the word picture would provide ample time. It would be a while before the group truly understood all that was occurring. Robert believed that their spirit would comprehend it all during the nighttime while sleeping.

"Sure Robert," Anjali said, as she inhaled. Picking up his yellow notepad, she cleared her throat. "*Troubled* from Psalm 48, line 5, is the Hebrew word ***bâhal*** pronounced ***baw-hal'*** meaning, to tremble inwardly, suddenly alarmed or agitated, hasten anxiously, speedily, trouble and vex."[xiv] She stopped and looked at Robert.

"Continue Anjali, by adding the next Hebrew word hasten, and then do all the ancient symbols together for both words. This will provide a more accurate word picture, giving a greater depiction of the horror that the towers inflict upon the serpent creatures."

Professor Mercer agreed and continued. "The next Hebrew word in the Psalm 48 line 5 text is, *hasten away*, which is ***châphaz*** pronounced ***khaw-faz'*** meaning, 'to hasten away, to start up suddenly, to make fear and to make haste.'[xv] The Hebrew letters that form *troubled* are Bet, Hey and Lamed. The Hebrew letters that form the Hebrew word, *hasten away,* are Chet, Pey and Zayin.

"Bet is the ancient symbol of a tent meaning, tent, house, household and family. Hey means, to reveal, and Lamed means, tongue, control and authority. Next, Chet is the ancient symbol of a fence or inner chamber meaning, to separate and secret place. Pey is the ancient symbol of a mouth meaning, word, open and speak. Finally, Zayin is the ancient symbol of a weapon meaning, to cut or cut off."

Anjali felt elation bubbling up in her soul, as she was now ready to do the word pictures for the two words. "Therefore, the word picture is, THE HOUSE IS REVEALED, AS THE TONGUE COMES TO SEPARATE, SPEAKING WORDS THAT ARE WEAPONS USED TO CUT AND CUT OFF!" She wanted to run, jump, shout and scream, but instead, restrained herself and cleared her throat.

"Is that not crazy," Parker said, as he was trying to wrap his head around it. "Now, say that again, Professor Mercer."

"Yes, the word picture for *troubled* and *hasten away* is The house is revealed, as the tongue comes to separate, speaking words that are weapons used to cut and to cut off." She caught her breath and finally could not restrain herself and shouted, "Woo hoo!"

Robert laughed, getting joy out of Anjali's excitement and seeing the room animated at the joy of the revelation. She revealed her revelation to the group, "The way into a house is through the door, so the fact that the door is opening up in the heavens, means that the Wisdom that is in that house, is coming to us through a special tongue (the Ancient Language), as it separates us in our soul (heart and mind), where we now speak words that are a weapon to cut, just like Milly taking care of

Lassiter's ruling power of Leviathan! We are a weapon, like a sword that cuts the kingdom of darkness with the Ancient Language, as we now go into their house, using the Ancient Language to destroy them!"

Milly wanted to jump and shout with Professor Mercer and was taken back by the fact that she could be so animated, unlike her demeanor in class. Robert stood back up, reaching for his yellow pad, continuing the meeting. "We are nearly through and I know it has been a long evening, since it is nearly 9pm, and there is a bit more that needs to be covered before you leave."

Everyone was still, as Robert continued with the last line of the text. "Now, we are to the last line of the relic, which spirals at a much smaller size, making the emphasis of that line like an exclamation mark, as we reach deeper to pull out its meaning. The last text of Psalm 48, line 6 refers to the fear that seizes the ruling powers, bringing them such pain that it is compared to a woman in labor. So let us start with the first word fear, which in Hebrew is ***ra'ad*** pronounced ***rah'-ad*** meaning, 'to shudder and trembling.'[xvi] *Pain* here, is the Hebrew word ***chîyl*** pronounced ***kheel*** meaning, 'pain, pang and sorrow.'[xvii] Finally, the last word that we will examine in the text is referring to the woman in labor/travail. The Hebrew word for this is ***yâlad*** pronounced ***yaw-lad'*** meaning, travail.[xviii] And this is where we finally look at all the Hebrew letters that compose these words."

"Take a breath, Lads and Lassies, and get ready for the revelation to come, these are our last Hebrew letters," Robert said, preparing them. "The Hebrew letters for fear are Resh, Ayin and Dalet. Next, the Hebrew letters for pain are Chet, Yood and Lamed. Finally, the Hebrew letters for travail are Yood, Lamed and Dalet. So let us look at the letters and then do the word picture. We have done most of these letters already except Resh and Yood. Resh is the ancient symbol of a man's face meaning, head, highest and person. Ayin is the ancient symbol of an eye meaning, to see, know and experience. Dalet we know is the door meaning to enter and pathway. Chet means secret place or separate. Yood is the ancient symbol of an arm at work meaning, works, make and deed. Lamed means tongue, control and authority. We have another Yood for works, make and deed. Again, there is another Lamed for tongue, control and authority, and finally another Dalet, which is the door, meaning to enter and pathway."

"Are you wanting to know the word picture for all three of these words put together?"

"Yes," shouted Parker.

"The word picture is, *experiencing what happens as the door opens where in your head/mind, the tongue comes to separate doing a mighty work, bringing the works of authority from the open door to you.*" He paused to let them soak in the deeper meaning of it all, before he ended the night.

"So, what are you saying Robert," asked Parker.

"Lad, I'm saying that as you and I experience the power of Wisdom from above because of the open door, that the Ancient Language, which is the Ancient tongue, is actually a weapon against the demons terrorizing their entire person.

"When demons experience the Ancient Language from us, they feel a weapon cutting them within their mind, because of their dark deeds. It utterly destroys them, like an atomic bomb, making it unbearable for them to endure its judgment"

"Demons experience the open door but it is utter pain. This is why the demons are so violent at fighting us on the issue of the towers. Where the towers are, the Ancient tongue, soon to be made known, revealing the Ancient Language, which is a weapon like radiation seeping through the area, touching all in the spirit realm. This is a spiritual battle, not a war between flesh and blood; we wrestle not against flesh and blood, but against ruling powers of darkness and principalities and rulers in the heavenlies."

Chapter 9

Taking their usual break at *The Grind*, Milly and Parker now had Tony joining them for their daily conference. The three of them created their own support group, which they dubbed, *The Ancient Language Seekers.* Now in conference, each one was enjoying a new addiction that Tony concocted, calling it, "turtle pie."

Milly and Parker felt as though they were cramming for exams, from all that they learned at Robert's house the night before, and needed to unwind before the meeting tonight. This time at their conference, Parker was relaxed experiencing the yumminess of Tony's latest lab experiment, as he too, decided to go Keto, having butter and coconut oil added to his coffee, with Stevia. Parker wanted to take advantage of all he could, after hearing Robert mention the benefits of Keto to Milly. He too, wanted to make sure his brain was operating at the most optimum level.

Tony looked at them asking, "Are you two pretty much through with the basement?"

Parker responded, "Yes, we only have one more week and that is it. Every time we leave there, I feel like I have to dust off; it still keeps piling up all around us ready to greet us when we come back, so much so that I feel like dust."

Curious as to Milly's supernatural encounters, Tony had to know. "Say Milly, do you still have open visions while in the basement?"

"Actually, not really. Since discovering the relic, they have ceased; it was as though the visions were to lead me to its location. However, since that time, my supernatural encounters are all throughout the day, everywhere I go, when I least expect it. I see demonic attacks against individuals, and sometimes lying serpents attached to people. Also, I see a mustard colored stench coming out of the mouths of people who are bitter, to which the Sword has me speak things over them underneath my breath. In addition, I see those who are susceptible to the cords of the ruling powers that are being put into, either their brain, spine or belly, where the Sword, will at times, instruct me to bind them once I step into another dimension where time, as we know it, stands still. I am sure Kaufman will have me share what Robert taught us yesterday on what is actually occurring in those moments."

She was glad to share this freely. Meeting at Robert's the night before, caused weights to be lifted off, where there was a greater calm in her soul. Simply remembering the reddish film that had been removed off of her years earlier and understanding why, gave her great assurance as to what she had always felt was going on. Milly's knowledge about spiritual matters increased, realizing that the reddish film was connected with the underground tanks of the enemy that were illustrated in her Great Grandmother's diaries. She had learned so much in a short amount of time that she felt she should be a triple major, with Philosophy, Antiquities and Spiritual Warfare, if there was such a degree.

"Guys, you are not going to believe what just came to my mind," Milly said, like a light blub was going off in her neurons.

"What," asked Tony, "Do you think your brain is operating more succinctly because of my latest concoction," he said joking.

She responded in jest, as she cut her eyes to him, "Tony, that's good, but no. Nice try though." With a more serious tone, Milly continued, "I believe what we all are experiencing in the supernatural realm, is Wisdom from the Ancient language, flowing from the tower. No sooner had she said it, than she saw the crystal tower appear in The Quad towering over them.

"Oh my gosh! Look guys! Do you see that?"

Parker and Tony began turning. A piercing trumpet sound was heard off in the distance. Upon turning, Parker and Tony saw the majestic tower. It was a crystal structure, swirling around like a staircase to the heavens. Sunlight hit the crystal, causing a prism of colors to dance around it, while blue lava, the color of fiery blue opal, oscillated throughout, looking as though it was coming from the ground, like an oil rig drilling for oil. The group was captivated and unable to stop peering. Others around them were blind to what was occurring, since their eyes were dull to the spirit realm.

Each of them longed to hear the trumpet again; it had the most piercing sound, reverberating through their soul, lighting it ablaze with knowledge and truth. After a few minutes, the tower vanished. Stunned at its appearance and the sound of the trumpet, along with what it did to their minds, they were speechless momentarily but extraordinarily refreshed; feeling veils lifted off of their faces, where they were able to see more clearly into the spirit.

Translucent waves from the tower poured over them, like an iridescent clear liquid, seeping through the atmosphere. Suddenly, an "X" appeared on each of their foreheads, marking them with the fiery blue flame.

"This must be the seal or mark," Milly said, "that Robert was referring to. It is given to those who are connected to the tower by the Ancient Language." She paused, deep in thought, and then exclaimed, "Wisdom must pour out on those who have this mark!"

Synapses firing on overload in Tony's mind caused him to perceive his studies in physics as never before. "Dude, I don't know how much more of this I can stand, but I am totally thrilled."

Parker wanting to see if he could touch the mark and was feeling around for it with his fingers. He was sure that the presence of the mark on his forehead was there, as he looked at the other two, "Man, this is some crazy stuff here."

Trying not to be the spoiler, Milly spoke up from hearing her cellphone alarm go off. "I hate to break it to you guys, but we have to go to class, and be ready to meet up later to go to the Doctors Mercer."

"Sounds good Mill," said Parker. "I have no clue how we can get through the day without constantly thinking about this mark that is on our forehead."

The group got up from the table and saw professors Kaufman and Mercer coming from the Library. To their surprise, they saw the mark beaming brightly on Kaufman and Mercer's foreheads of the ancient Tav, as well. Kaufman looked at Milly, and pointed to his forehead, as if motioning to her that he could see their marks as well.

"Let's go talk to them a minute, before we jut to class," said Milly.

Scurrying up to the professors, trying to contain their excitement, Milly inquired, "Did you see the tower and hear the trumpet?"

"Yes," said Mercer, "which is why we nearly came running out of the Library. We were uncertain if there was a tornado siren going off, or if it was the band preparing for tonight's game. Once we arrived at the glass doors, we saw the ancient crystal tower with the fiery blue lava. I never knew how incredible the tower looked until now. It was then, upon its appearance, that I immediately noticed that we were marked."

Kaufman knew this would be a topic of discussion for the night. "We will have a lot to share tonight, between this and Robert's meeting yesterday. I am hopeful that it will prove to be a most stupendous meeting. We will see you a bit later."

Saying their goodbyes, each student went to their respective classes, as the professors returned to their classrooms. The smell of frankincense permeated the atmosphere throughout the campus. A scent similar to that of fire lifted the soul, of one who could inhale its warmth, filling the chest with a burning flame, where wings took the soul in flight, to a supernatural experience of joy and elation.

Kaufman, Mercer, Tony, Parker and Milly were emotionally and mentally high, as they walked in an extraordinary rest throughout the remainder of the day. Even so, the day could not end soon enough for them, so that they could get to the meeting.

Only Time Will Tell

Like a battery with too much power in it, the group was overcharged, unsure if they could discharge the pent up excitement flowing within. Each person was filled with revelation and enthusiasm, eager to share. The meeting would provide a means by which they could distribute all that was within their brains, as their thoughts bounced around like Tigger in Winnie the Pooh.

"Welcome everyone," said Kaufman, "let's get started." It was easy to sense his excitement about the night, as he ruminated on Robert's meeting the day before, along with the recent occurrence today at Strytan. Milly, Parker, Tony, Professors Mercer and Kaufman could not see the marks at the moment, but would be sharing about what occurred.

Kaufman began with introductions, and then had Mercer share the ancient Hebrew symbols used in the Psalm 48:12 and 4-6 texts, which they learned the night before from Robert. Milly gave her witness to the armor she had used, along with the whip in her Great Grandmother's diaries. Moreover, she provided them with Robert's depiction of time standing still, describing space-time and eternity-time.

Parker shared the experience that he, Milly and Tony had, after the last meeting, with the tower in The Quad at Strytan, as well as depicting today's experience of the tower and the mark. "Man, you should have seen the marks on all of our foreheads, when we saw the tower and heard the trumpet, it was insane!"

As they moved throughout the evening, and went into Mildred's diaries again, comparing it to the relic, it was evident to all that the tower was a firewall against planned demonic attacks. The connection between the Ancient Language and the tower mesmerized each person, after hearing what Robert taught the smaller group the day before.

Their need to move forward into *battle mode* was ramped up like an aircraft carrier in the water ready to deploy its jets. All their eyes were opened up to the supernatural realm where each now saw the demonic assaults, as well as the hosts of El Elyon. All of this kept them buzzing with stories during the coffee break, sharing experiences, like kids talking about their Christmas presents after Christmas break in school.

Father Sanderson also shared of the exorcisms he had done in the past as compared to now, where he had seen demonic entities in some measure, but never to the degree that he saw now. He was doing "deliverance" soon, with another congregant, who was a young lady Milly's age, and asked if she would be interested in attending.

Milly, curious as to the *word* asked, "What is *deliverance* Father Sanderson?"

"Milly, it is nothing to be concerned about; it is where someone is demonically oppressed and in need of a priest to help them become set free of that oppression." He considered what she had already shared with the group, and asked her, "When you see things such as cords in the spirit realm, what do you do?"

"I do what the Sword tells me, which is to bind them and cut them off, so that the person is set free," she said with confidence.

"Well, that is deliverance," Father Sanderson said.

"Oh wow, I had no clue that was deliverance. Then yes, I would be glad to attend the deliverance meeting you are leading."

"Great, it is Tuesday of next week at 7pm, I'll see you then Milly Teschlon," he said smiling.

Shortly after the coffee break, it was time to get back from the small recess, and meet in the large group again. It had been determined that, with all the work that was to be done, that the three small groups could meet aside from the larger meeting, on other occasions.

Tony pulled out his small notebook and thumbed through it. Unaware, he raised his hand slowly while eying his notes.

Kaufman noticed and asked, "Yes Tony, is there something you want to share?"

Caught off guard, Tony realized what was going on, accidentally raising his hand while reading his notes. "Yes Professor Kaufman, I do. May I come to the front and share with the group about an area of my studies that keeps coming to mind, as it relates to all that we are experiencing?"

Kaufman assured him of the freedom for the entire group to share. It was not about one person; each person was a key player. Tony stepped up front, moving his bangs out of his eyes, as he stood with most of his weight on his right leg. His lean tall body appeared like a tree in winter, waiting for leaves to blossom. He was tall and lean, reaching about 6' 2". A brilliant mind, and humble appearance, he would catch everyone off guard, with revelation that would shake the core of their soul.

"Good evening everyone, I have been considering Robert's discussions with the smaller group yesterday on *eternity-time*, and then today's encounter with the tower, as we saw iridescent waves coming towards us, marking us once its presence was upon us, with an Ancient Tav, like a fiery blue opal. In considering all of that, I had a dream last week, where a note I wrote down a year ago from my quantum physics class kept leaping out at me like a holograph illustration within the universe. I know the purpose of it was to get my attention." He saw everyone perk up, and continued his thoughts.

"It came to me about Louis De Broglie, who we will get into a bit of discussion on. He was a French physicist, who won a Nobel Prize in 1929. Believe it or not, when he submitted his thesis in 1924 to the University of Paris, most of the science community could not comprehend his thesis, and almost failed him for his degree. However, before doing that they took his thesis to Einstein. After Einstein reviewed De Broglie's thesis, he stated, that '*it was the first glimmer of light in the worst of our physics enigmas that he should get the award of his degree.*'" Tony stopped briefly, asking Kaufman if he could use the dry-erase board to explain De Broglie's theory.

"By the way, his name is pronounced like De-Broy, although you might see me spell it D...e...B...r...o...g...l...i...e," he said while erasing the other material on the whiteboard.

"De Broglie's theory for quantum mechanics is called *Wave-Particle Duality*. Many physicists have looked at light before he presented his theory, seeing it mainly as a wave, and at times denoting the particular particles of that wave, which are photons. They described it as being an all or nothing display, that it would either be light waves or light particles, which was determined by the circumstances, but never both a wave and a particle."

Tony did a drawing of two lines that were perpendicular to each other going up vertically. The line on the left, had two slots opened in the middle part of it, and the line on the right was continuous without interruption. "Now De Broglie believed that light was both a wave and a particle simultaneously, proving Einstein's theory on light waves through his Wave-Particle Duality Theory by using electrons. He stated all particles were transported by waves. When he sent the electron particles through the first vertical line on the left, it would pass through the two slots, to the second line, as a wave and not a particle. Normally, one would think, two slots in the first vertical pass would land 2 rows on the back line or back wall.

"In other words, how in the world did five rows end up on this back line, when there is only two slots by which electrons could pass through? It was proven that the electron passed through, operating as both waves and particles."

The group looked at Tony inquisitively, still trying to grasp De Broglie's theory. Milly perked up, realizing she knew where Tony was going, based on her recent spiritual experiences. Kaufman pondered on prior philosophers, realizing that through Tony's discussion of De Broglie's theory, he was able to see the connection of the human *mindset* with matter; literally it was mind over matter; De Broglie believed that all matter had this wave-particle duality.

Tony continued, "To better understand this theory, it is necessary for me to bring up the term 'realism', which means that concepts exist independent of the observer. In other words, something does not have to be real to *you,* to actually be real. For example, I am real, and because many other people do not know that I am real, does not mean that I do not exist." Heads nodded, as the group understood this term much easier than the prior.

"Looking at Wave-Particle Duality, not only does it have *realism*, but it has what is known as *determinism*, too." Tony did not want to lose the group's attention, in explaining something so simple that seemed complex. He looked around at the group again, to see if everyone was with him. He noticed Kaufman's posture and his excitement; realism and determinism were as much philosophical terms as they were scientific terms.

"Determinism in physics is a bit different than philosophy; in philosophy, determinism points to the fact that everything is determined outside of our will and control. However, in science we see it mainly as a causal determinism, that events, in a given paradigm are bound to causality because, their prior states determine it. It is basically cause and effect. If A happens then B is the result."

"What I like best about realism and determinism, as it relates to De Broglie's theory, is that he takes a combination of determinism from both science and philosophy, *in my opinion.* Therefore, by understanding realism and determinism we can view his thoughts. He states that the positions of the momenta of a particle are *hidden* variables from the observer, where we cannot see it. In other words, we cannot see how electrons are moving around us in this room, but they are. The fact that we cannot see them does not mean that they do not exist; they are hidden from our view.

"The emphasis here is, on the observer *not knowing the precise value* of an object. Once you or I try to measure and give value to an object by looking at it, then it disturbs the true value of that object. The power that comes from our thoughts as we scrutinize the electron changes its value because of the influence we have on it.

The group was blown away by the fact that their thoughts on what they looked at affected the value of an object. This was stretching beyond measure, and they knew they had to hang in there to get the understanding as to the power of the Ancient Language that they carried.

Tony continued, "The act of measuring the object by your eyes and opinions sends brain waves out to the object, actually causing a condition to exist of the object, bringing into reality an actual event, where the object's value to the viewer's perspective or lens is made known.

"For example, let's say there is a box and we have no clue of what is inside of the box. *Realism* says that no matter what we think is in the box, what is actually in there is real and exists. *Determinism* says that the value of what is in the box is greater than we can imagine, and in order for it to keep its value, we don't need to look at it. However, once we look at what is inside of the box, it becomes what we think! Literally, it is Mind creating the Matter! What we think matters!"

"We do not realize that our value system is driven by an internal clock, determining all the events and circumstances in our lives; shaping time as we know it. I have heard the saying, some need to see to believe, but it is believing that causes you to see."

Parker totally confused said, "What?"

"Let me make it easier. As we look at the tower that some of us have witnessed at Strytan, and the door in the heavens that some have dreamed about, as well as in Mildred Lee's diaries, our internal clock, which is eternity-time, changes our lens."

"According to De Broglie's Wave-Particle Duality, it is inferred that, not only do photons and electrons have the ability to shift between the two forms of either wave or particle, but that ALL MATTER is able to do this very thing. 'His conjecture with this theory was based on an *INTERNAL CLOCK*, which he believed existed in the electron. The internal clock in the electron, he believed, constituted part of the mechanism by which a pilot wave guides a particle." He wanted to jump up and down, because the revelation in his mind was off the charts. "In other words, *the clock* is the guide of the particle; the clock is the WAVE!"

Professor Mercer gasped, "Oh my," as her husband Alan exclaimed, "What!" They got it and were chomping at the bit for Tony to teach more.

"The clock in the diary stopped on 3:33, as did the clock at Strytan, a few weeks ago, stopping on the exact time. Are you still with me," Tony asked.

"Yes," said Kaufman, "I think I know where you are going."

"You mentioned earlier, Robert's depiction of Eternity-Time, as well as Milly's personal experience of time being frozen. Moreover, when we saw the Tower today, I saw an iridescent wave hitting us, which then opened our eyes to see a mark of an "X," the ancient symbol for Tav, on our foreheads."

"We are with you," said Alan, "go on."

"Well, what if the wave we are experiencing is another *internal clock* operating amongst us, which was revealed in Mildred Lee's diaries, and connects to the relic, where the same internal clock, releasing Wisdom, is from the Light of when the Big Bang occurred."

Wows were rippling through the room, as people were slow to speak, and the room was silent for over two minutes before anyone uttered a word.

Kaufman, who had been leaning upon the wall, stood up and walked over to the dry erase board, as he stared at the drawing, looking at the picture of the light wave on the initial pass of the first vertical line, passing through the two slots, onto the back wall of the last vertical line. "You know Tony, I can see this, and add more to it from a philosophical perspective, may I?"

Tony, happy to have assistance, was agreeable. "You may, by all means Professor Kaufman."

"By the way Tony, I am very impressed with this thought," Kaufman stated as he began his suppositions. Kaufman was excited about the revelation he had received and could not wait to lend his explanation in more practical terms to Wave-Particle Duality. "As we look at the Wave-Particle Duality Theory, think of it like this. There is a racecar driver in a car. The particle is the car and the wave is the racecar driver. Both of them exist. It is the racecar driver (the wave) that causes the racecar (the particle) to move."

The group nodded glad that they could grasp the simple analogy, as Kaufman continued. "Therefore, the true value is given to that which is hidden and cannot be seen, which is the wave, the racecar driver; it is what drives the wave, the car. Thus, since the Big Bang, Light has been driven into our time, but what we do not realize is, that it is the VALUE of the wave hidden inside of the light wave, which is also the *internal clock*, that is bringing the Light into our time. The wave is hidden and exists, and if we see it in its unhidden form, then it has the value that we give it. Thus, our opinion matters.

"The Light therefore is the particle, and hidden within the Light that is the driving force of that Light, is the Ancient Language! The Light is driven and guided by the Ancient Language, which gives us power!

"The Ancient Language, I believe is the wave (race car driver) inside of the Light (racecar). Thus, the way, which we perceive, *or view* the Ancient Language, determines the outcome we see. As a result, our minds have to be purified from the wisdom of this present age, in order to receive the Wisdom from above, which causes us to see with purity the value of the Ancient Language, and know its power!"

Kaufman did his pace as he usually did in class, looking around the room, at the abstract brain displays of Alan's passion knowing that the Ancient Language protected their minds. "Moreover, this CNS attack by the hordes of hell, will release both sound and dark light waves from the grid it has set up, which is on a different frequency, of course, than the tower. This is the epic battle of Light and darkness, from the beginning of time, where there are two frequencies of lights fighting to control the world! Those who are on the frequency of the pure Light, which we will refer to as Wisdom, by the open door in the heavens and the tower at The Quad, are marked by that Wisdom and frequency, where they are completely protected from the frequencies coming off the grid of darkness."

People were agreeing with an "ah," and throwing in their "yes's." The eyes of those in the group, revealed their comprehension of revelation.

"Let's go further; pure light, a fiery flame for instance, does not cast a shadow, therefore light and darkness cannot co-exist; darkness is unreceptive to the light and cannot overpower the light, but rather light pierces the darkness, like a laser beam. The Ancient Language in us is guiding us, as it does the Light, destroying Beelzebub's works,"

Still pacing, trying not to lose their comprehension, he slowly went on, pointing to Tony's drawing. "What if the first vertical line with the two slots represents time, where the particles are passing through, as Tony said, from the Big Bang, and is reaching those who are driven in their mind by this *internal clock* of something that is infinitely larger than us all."

In a softer tone, Kaufman looked at the different eyes staring back at him, "This very night has been pre-determined, and by all the prior-occurrences of Mildred Lee, being Milly's Great Grandmother, of me needing the basement files cleaned, where the relic was." He stood still. "Of Professor Mercer teaching antiquities, and so forth. Something has happened that is supernatural. And why?

"Because, we have not *tried* to measure the Light, but simply sought the Ancient Language that speaks of that measurement of Light to our mind, revealing the complexities of it to our heart, as we are willing to listen, and like the blue flame, be pure in our thoughts, so that we can receive the power of that Light, which intimidates all of hell! Thus, we see the TRUE VALUE of the Light!"

Milly jumped up and shouted, "That is why the demons fear us!"

Father Sanderson yelled, "Yes!"

Anjali followed suit in her excitement, "Agreed, because demons cannot stand the frequency of the Ancient Language, which is the driving force of the pure Light, releasing the particles of Wisdom in the atmosphere."

"Yes! Yes! Yes!" Kaufman exclaimed emphatically.

Kaufman summarized the meeting, as he stated, "The Ancient Language is the pilot wave of what we are experiencing in the supernatural, guiding us into Wisdom from Eternity-Time, which is our internal clock. 3:33 means we have been lifted on the wings of eagles before all of time itself, and been given Wisdom from that which is not of this earth."

All were mesmerized, amazed, and stared in awe. They had come to grasp that they were becoming the wall of fire because each of them individually had the Light. In Springfield, they would work together cooperatively with the towers, protecting the city from hell.

On the Way Home

Milly dropped Parker and Tony off at Strytan and headed home. They all had hoped to see the tower again, but since seeing it earlier in the day, the group wasn't totally disappointed. Humming to the tunes on her player, she began feeling odd. Her hands were sweating, head nauseous, she could not figure out what in the world was going on.

Worried and anxious, she pulled off the side of the road. Her body was fighting itself; everything inside of her frame felt antagonistic. She was lethargic, and processing what was happening, without freaking out, and with the little strength she had, Milly picked up her cell phone.

"Oh no!" She thought; "I cannot dial!"

She had no strength! Her soul anxious and her thoughts going a million miles an hour, did not help the fact that her body was not responding. She closed her eyes, hunched over the steering wheel so she could breathe and think; too weak to open her mouth.

"El Elyon, what is going on," she thought

Suddenly, she felt like vomiting when, at about 10 mph, a huge glob shot out of her mouth like a projectile, landing in her hand. She had a horrible gag reflex, and her immediate thought was, "oooh, yuck, what is this? Gross!"

She was starting to feel back to normal again, and found herself staring at a glob in diameter, the size of a coffee cup. It was not total mucus but more globbish in nature, similar to the texture of a jellyfish, mostly translucent with a hint of whitish tinge throughout. "Don't stare," she thought, as she opened the door and flicked her wrist to get the grossness off of her hand.

Instantly, she saw in the spirit realm, the blue fiery lava, streaming through the air, coming into her mouth. She saw the flame filling her belly area, and felt as though she could run the New York Marathon; Milly was ready to put running shoes on with a newfound strength.

"What just happened, El Elyon," Milly asked.

She saw the warrior armor appear. Glistens of light were like lasers leaping off of the metal, similar to a diamond shining brightly, reflecting the light. Unable to figure out what was occurring with her armor, she saw the sword appear on her side, reverberating a sound to her heart and mind, instructing her to pull it from the sheath.

The Sword connected to her mind, "You have been set free from the spirit of fear, that was within your belly, roosting like an owl taking over an eagle's nest."

"What," asked Milly, as she tried to understand how fear took root in her, and of all places her belly.

The Sword continued, "When an owl sees an eagle's nest, which can be up to 9 feet wide, it tries to intimidate the eagle, and settle in its nest if the eagle will let it. Owls are as territorial as eagles are. The owl represents the wisdom of this present age, which is that of darkness. The eagle represents the Wisdom from El Elyon, which is from eternity. It has much more strength then the wisdom from this age."

Milly, still listening had to ask, "why my belly?"

"Your belly is the place of your spirit, like the womb of a mother houses a baby, the belly is the womb of your spirit. Likewise, many spirits that attack mankind go to the area of the belly, which is different than the oppression of the ruling powers. The belly is your nest."

Floored, Milly understood what happened; the fear of the present age had taken a hold of her, driving her at times, in great angst under the opinions of others. It made her feel as though she wanted to fit in, when instead, the Sword informed her, that she was born to stand out! Like her great grandmother, she had to walk into her destiny in order to help others.

Hands now trembling, she was still clutching the Sword, which supernaturally continued to open her ability to understand its great power. The trembling spread throughout her entire being like fire burning in her bones; she was a living volcano.

The Sword continued teaching her, "When you come to know the Wisdom from above, it floods you mightily and drives out the wisdom of this present age, which is fear based. That is what you are experiencing now, and why you are trembling; you are feeling the Sword's power."

She felt as though she was holding on to dear life, and time around her was frozen. Only those who were in the spirit would be able to see all that Milly was experiencing.

"The coming assaults on the minds of mankind are fear based, and each of my warriors, have to be delivered of this oppression. You are free Milly, now walk in the peace of Wisdom; it is the foundation of all that there is in El Elyon's Kingdom, bringing the eternal Light that overcomes the hordes of hell."

Milly wanted to jump out of her car and shout, she wanted to call Parker, and she really wanted to tell her parents, but all she could do was sit there in her Bug, dwelling on the euphoric feeling that encapsulated her entire presence, as though she was in a cocoon of the blue lava.

The Watchers

Little did Milly know, Serugar and the other demonic serpent creatures, as well as Beelzebub's "watcher," were all observing. Before Beelzebub was kicked out of the third heaven, he had watchers, which he turned against El Elyon. However, the loyal watchers could not be turned. The watchers of Beelzebub, guarded all of his comings and goings, as well as watched those who were a constant threat to the plans of darkness. They were not sent against ordinary threats, but high level menaces, which could do extraordinary damage against his dark kingdom.

Constugard was the watcher assigned to Milly, and was deployed by Beelzebub the day before, to prepare for his arrival in Springfield, and apprise him of threats in the area. Constugard hunched over, much like a huge gargoyle on an old cathedral, stared at Milly, loathing her every breath, fuming, with mustard colored stench coming out of his nostrils, as he saw her filled with more of the blue flame from the tower, where he then saw her mouth releasing the Ancient Language.

Torment filled his entire being. Fire surged in his head, amplifying the sound of the Ancient Language that spoke his demise. Constugard writhed in pain, he began clawing the old stone of the building, on which he was sitting, an old Ancient Gatehouse meeting place, that welcomed the dark creatures; they were the darkest of societies, the diplomats of hell itself, cloaked in forms of light, deceiving all who would come near them.

The Ancient Gatehouse, a conscripted crony of Beelzebub, appeared to be in the light of El Elyon, but the light that they were cohorts with, was darkness. Dark light is a false front for those whose eyes are not spiritually opened. They are blind to the reality of the false light, not seeing the deception that ensnared them like a noose around their neck.

Only the spiritually blind are taken higher in the organization before they realize it is a covert operation for hell's fury against mankind. When it is revealed to the deceived of the false one they serve, they are provided dark powers of sorcery and witchcraft, mastering the dark arts.

Beelzebub's watchers were always drawn to the locations of the dark societies, because the ritualistic practices provided strength to the gates of hell, where the slime from the underworld was released easily, providing a portal for demons to go in and out. For Springfield, this Ancient Gatehouse was the front that Vladamore was using for the gates of hell to arise.

Windows covered in a dingy, vintage green curtain with ruffles, let those who pass by, know that the place most likely had not come into the 21st century. A four-story building, built of a thick stone, with a gothic appearance, like an old world church from Europe, which did not quite fit into the town's scheme.

The man who began The Ancient Gatehouse in Springfield, Clovis Knight, was the Great Grandfather of the present Dean of Faculty at Strytan, Bobby Knight. Bobby was a man of unruly character, masking his true self to others while at Strytan, fooling many to believe he was the savior of the town, when he was working with Beelzebub's spell book and tactics, in taking complete control of the city. His position at Strytan was a stepping-stone to the highest place he wanted to rule, which was being Provost or President of the entire university.

Bobby knew that the highest place of control was not mayor; that position could be bought if necessary. Rather, the highest position was the place in which young minds could be shaped and molded, by the brainwashing schemes of hell itself, if a dark leader was in control. He was presently head of the local Ancient Gatehouse. Because of the recent activities, this night, Bobby was in the building. Since the gates of hell were rising up, with the threat of the tower, and from what he heard, more towers to come, Bobby was spending most of his time at The Ancient Gatehouse outside of Strytan.

The watcher, Constugard, sent a message to Bobby, who was conjuring a spell in the basement, obtaining the next plans of Beelzebub for the area. In the midst of Bobby's conjuring, where demonic spirits began speaking, Constugard opened a portal of communication, calling Bobby to come up and see what was befalling.

"Dark servant," Constugard communicated to Bobby's mind, "come quickly and see the vile thing we have to tolerate, until we have rid ourselves of this loathsome life."

Bobby ran up, feet banging the old wooden steps that had been beaten and worn down from the many decades of use. *Stomp, stomp, stomp.* You could hear the wooden soles of Bobby's Italian shoes stomping as he ran up. He was at the highest rank, the 33rd level of the watchers, which is what the members of The Ancient Gatehouse were called.

Bobby's hands were stained with blood. Not paying attention, he used them to move the nasty green curtain, leaving bloodstains on its edge. "What is it Constugard, I am here."

"Look across the way, darkened heart," which is what some demons called the cronies, "at the vile creature, whose name is Milly Teschlon.

"She attends your university. Her powers of El Elyon are increasing and we must do what we can, to rid Springfield of her, lest the gates of hell be hindered and not prevail."

Bobby opened his mouth, exposing his teeth, tinged with dark stains, revealing blood on the inside of his lip. With his disgusting long swollen tongue, he licked his lips, and replied, "I know her well. My stomach sickens each time I see her on campus. She is nothing but a puny speed bump that can be handled immediately. I will do it, let Beelzebub know that all is well, and we pledge our allegiance to hell."

Constugard began to laugh with a shrieking sound that filled up the building, dancing off of the rafters throughout the stonework. The inside of The Ancient Gatehouse was a corridor to the abominations of the underworld. Constugard's power would remain strong by reclining here for the evening.

Bobby let loose of the curtain, seeing a drop of blood on his pant cuff's and new Italian shoes. "Not now!" he exclaimed. "I have to get the stain out before returning home." You could hear his shoes loudly against the floor as he moved from the front, through the main room, and down the steps. Scuffling sounds could be heard from the basement, where Bobby had left the door open, and a small amount of light peered from underneath, throwing shadows on the wall. The sound and shadows unveiled the seditious nature of his soul, and all of those caught up in the dark magic.

The angelic host of El Elyon, Rafael and Tubal, guarded Milly, catching the eye of Constugard, as he discovered all was not well for the gates of hell.

Let's Go Home

Eyes still on her steering wheel, Milly was trying to make sense of everything, but she was still in ecstasy over what occurred. Nothing could ever make her get used to the supernatural; she did not want to take it for granted, and was made alive by all that had happened since all the spiritual things began occurring.

She turned the engine on and drove home. Peace consumed her soul, oozing out of every fiber of her being. Music blasting out of her convertible Bug, she laughed and sung along, being a one-woman show for Springfield that evening. Colors were more brilliant, sounds amplified, and smells were heightened. She was a walking poster child for the transition of ordinary into hero.

Happy to get home, she came bouncing into the house, seeing her mom and dad were on the back patio, with their Keto-Coffee.

"Hey there happy girl," said her mother.

"Well did Santa arrive early this year," her father asked.

Laughing, she poured her coffee into the blender, putting in her tablespoon of butter, and then a tablespoon of coconut oil. She reached for the Stevia liquid toffee essence, and put 4 drops into her concoction. "Just making my addiction folks, nothing new!"

"Oh yes there is something new," said her mother, "but I will not complain because I like this *new thing*."

Milly had a smile from ear to ear, and they were certain that she had met someone at Strytan, wondering if it was the Barista boy that was now hanging out with her and Parker.

Daniel stared suspiciously into her eyes teasing her saying, "Oh, so is there a beau?"

"Gosh! No Dad!"

"Well, ok, just wondering what is making you so happy.

She poured her drink in her favorite coffee cup, that she bought form the bookstore, carrying it outside to the porch, where they could all sit down. Her parents were so excited by her excitement that they had come into the kitchen to meet her. Then they all walked out to the porch, sitting down in their favorite chairs, grabbing blankets.

"Look guys, I am just finally really happy with my life, for like the first time. I mean really, really, happy." Snuggled under her blanket, and the fire pit burning, she sipped on her Keto-Coffee, acknowledging how awesome the fire was, her parents' smiles, and the sounds of the nighttime, the stars shining, and simply life! Everything, everywhere was beautiful to Milly Teschlon this night, how could it not be?

Chapter 10

Strytan was buzzing with energy, with midterm exams long gone; students were now gearing up for Thanksgiving. Fall had fully set in, while the campus was covered with young people wearing their favorite sweatshirts. Hot drinks in nearly every hand, the holiday cheer was already spreading, as the upcoming break was the topic of discussion.

The *Ancient Language Seekers* were in conference at *The Grind*, sharing war stories of their freshman year, laughing at Tony's list of concoctions, and Parker's new found ketone buzz from the Ketogenic diet.

Cheers were being toasted between them, holding their lab experiment coffee cups, filled with their addictions, congratulating each other on their mid-term success. For a brief moment they were living life as normal as possible, before getting back into spiritual warfare mode. They knew that they were not created to battle all the time and their souls needed reprieve. This is where the importance of fellowship did them good, as they shared the details of their day, giving life more meaning.

With their eyes and ears, they took in all the action on campus, enjoying their time sipping on their addictions. Great memories were in the making. "Life could not get better," Milly thought while daydreaming.

Each one of them was thankful to be involved in the supernatural, which was underneath the radar to the rest of the community. Their work would most likely go unnoticed, as they did that which others could not even fathom.

"Wow, what a day," said Milly. She was looking at the clear blue sky, sipping on her Banana Cream addiction, hoping the moment would last forever.

A sound was heard off in the distance, like a roaring thunder, to which the three of them looked around, trying to figure out where the storm was rolling in. No cloud could be seen anywhere, which confused them as to why they were hearing the thunder, when suddenly they spotted the mark upon their foreheads, as the fiery blue opal colored Tav appeared.

Tony perked up, like a physicist ready to run to his lab, stating, "*That internal clock* of eternity within us, is speaking. I believe the thunder we hear is from that dimension and not our own."

Parker was interested in what Tony was getting at and responded, "How so?"

"When do you hear thunder," Tony asked.

Both Milly and Parker replied, "When there's lightning."

Tony replied, "Exactly! You hear thunder when there is lightning... because the heat of the lightning expands the air, creating space in the atmosphere that, once empty suddenly fills with air, making the sound we know as thunder."

Parker shook his head and replied, "That is crazy. So you mean to tell me, that the heat of lightning enlarges the space it enters, creating a vacuum, which is then filled with air?"

"Yep, you got it," Tony stated. "With that said, it is my speculation that the marks appearing on our foreheads, are always visible to us, when we hear a sound of some sort from another dimension, which relates to the tower." Milly and Parker understood and agreed, chiming in with a "yes," and an "ok."

"With the internal clock of eternity-time going off inside of us, because of our connection with the tower," Tony said, "we see increased frequency of spiritual activity. Therefore, I suspect that as we get more power from the tower and the Ancient Language, more spiritual matters will be revealed to us."

They kept staring at the luminescent fiery blue mark of the Tav on their foreheads. While sitting there, they heard the ticking of a clock. *Tic tock, tic tock*, they heard, looking around to see where the noise was coming from. The sound grew louder and louder, amplified in their ears, blowing their mind.

Tony was shaking his head back and forth mumbling to himself, "Man! Guys this is huge; the dimension of eternity-time overrules space-time as we know it, which is why the clock here at Strytan went out a few weeks ago. It allows us to see from the dimension of eternity." He looked at Milly, "This is what your Great Grandmother knew Milly."

"Oh wow, Tony!" she exclaimed. Uncertain of what else the clock was revealing, she inquired, "With that said, what do you think the clock is saying to us."

Time seemed frozen as the students on The Quad were still, which gave them the signal that something was about to happen.

Tick tock, tick tock, the sound grew louder and louder, until they felt pulled into the middle of a huge clock. Then, without warning, the huge crystal tower materialized in front of their eyes. They were unsure if it was a holograph coming into view, and curiosity drew them near. Stepping closer to the tower, they could see that within the structure there was blue liquid lava carrying ancient Hebrew symbols, erupting into the atmosphere.

Reaching her hand out slowly, Milly touched it. The texture under her fingertips was that of fine crystal, only thicker. It was surging with energy that gave life and strength to those who were near it. Tony was mesmerized trying to use his studies to understand it better, while Parker was taken back with the immensity of it all.

"Hey guys, this is real," said Parker.

"Do you see the ancient symbols," Milly asked.

"Yes. Look, do you see the intensity of the surge of lava coming from the ground? It is reverberating an energy throughout the crystal," Tony solicited.

Suddenly, a fiery blue whirlwind wisped around them, as blue lava began infusing them with the Ancient Language, encircled them. Everyone else was frozen in their tracks, while Milly, Parker and Tony were lifted up in the blue whirlwind, five feet off of the ground, having pure strength fill their bodies. The cells in their bodies pulsed with life, and they shouted like triumphant warriors in battle. Armor appeared on them. The brilliant shine of the gold and silver cladding of their armor reflected the tower, gleaming in the light of the tower itself, when they were able to behold something that looked like the ancient relic.

A voice came to their soul and spirit, speaking from the midst of the tower, while the ancient relic was opened, and a scroll unrolled. "This is the *Ancient Language* of My towers. I will not only raise more towers as in Psalm 48, but I will make you, My bold warriors, a tower of terror to hell. Demons will tremble and fear you, because of the Ancient Language that fills you. Trust and know the armor that you have been given is for use against the hordes of hell."

Still lifted in the air, strengthened by the power of the blue lava and the Ancient Language, they were immediately pierced by a bright white light, where the ancient letters leapt off of the scroll and went into their belly like a sword, penetrating flesh.

Blue lightning could be seen throughout their body, like blood coursing through veins, as they were filled in their heart and mind, releasing the Ancient Language as they opened their mouths. The marks on their foreheads shone all the brighter, and within the palms of their hands were blue fiery Tav marks, like jewels deposited within them of the fiery blue flame.

The voice spoke again, with each syllable reverberating throughout their bodies. "Your hands have been given My power, which brings ruin to the gates of hell, burning the demons with torture. You are ready for greater combat; you are My army!"

Then, their spirit was brought back into their bodies, which was still at *The Grind*, their meeting place. Time was normal again. Looking at their feet and hands, feeling their forehead, and staring at each other, was a sight to see; they were overwhelmed and, regardless of their ability to comprehend, they were ecstatic, unable to be quiet.

"OH MY GOSH!" Milly exclaimed; she wanted to run to Kaufman and Mercer to see if they saw anything.

"This is freaky crazy!" Parker hollered. He was still was trying to process last week's meeting and this just topped the cake.

"Unbelievable," shouted Tony.

The Dark Side

They were caught up in their discussion of the armor and the transaction of the light into their belly, with the blue lightning, when quickly, a dark cloud rolled in from out of nowhere. Stench filled the air, and the group's eyes were opened to the spiritual realm. They could see mustard colored gas, floating like a rope seven feet high, streaming throughout the campus.

Literally smelling the stench, gave them a sickening feeling. They then saw from where the stench was coming, the office of Administration, where Dean of Faculty, Bobby Knight, was now walking out. Cords in his spine, like tentacles of an octopus, let them know that the ruling power Jezebel was operating.

An alluring woman was floating behind him, as her squid like tentacles poured from underneath, like an octopus in the ocean, looking for prey to bring into its mouth. The upper part of her was like a woman. Her slender body and long dark hair distracted the observer from looking deeper. However, once closer, it was easy to distinguish that underneath the dress was something that wasn't human.

Dean Knight headed towards the group, who were clueless as to the reason why. His eyes shape shifted into red beady eyes, glaring straight at Milly. If looks could kill, this one would; it was pure evil.

"What in the world," Milly asked.

Tony and Parker both stood taller putting themselves in front of Milly, as her personal bodyguards, against this spiritual attack. Parker, very protective of his friend, stepped forward to break Dean Knight's momentum; Knight was an unstoppable train barreling his way towards them.

"May I help you Dean?" He said, letting Dean Knight know that his behavior would not be tolerated.

"My discussion is not with you Parker," he said glaring at Milly, "I mean to take up a little talk, with Mildred Teschlon." His teeth, stained with darkness all over, were demonic looking. The stains did not come from coffee or tobacco, but rather it looked to be the stain of hell. Darkness was written all over of his soul. Like someone taking a cigar and blowing smoke under the skin, whirls were caught between his flesh and his soul, making him creepier.

Milly stepped between the two guys, letting herself be seen, and addressed the Dean boldly, "What is it that you want to have a little talk about?" She was feisty and filled with a spitfire attitude; knowing that she was not dealing with a person, but rather a spirit. "I am more than happy to address you Dean Knight."

Every time Knight's lips moved, Jezebel's lips moved too; she was puppeting him. A human was not talking to them, but instead a ruling power.

Time froze again. The group was in armor, weapons on their side. Milly's rope lit up, she flicked it, binding the tentacles of Jezebel that were reaching from Jezebel into Knight's spine.

"I bind you Jezebel, in the authority of this Sword, and you will not speak to me; I do not speak to devils!"

The Jezebel spirit was throwing a temper tantrum, like a two-year old unable to get their way in the supermarket checkout line, wanting candy. Her fit was a drama of its on, tentacles flying around from underneath her skirt, face contorting and eyes turning red.

As she manifested to the group, Knight began to have similar reactions. His face contorted, where the left side moved upward, as the right side of his face moved downward. It was as though someone had their hands on his cheeks moving them. They realized that the blue flame from Tony's hands was being released, as he held them out, causing the mouth of Knight to be bound up from speaking as Jezebel's puppet.

Knight was a dark knight of Beelzebub, and operated in the spirit realm, as well. He was not pleased with the confrontation, realizing that Milly, Parker and Tony were a force to be reckoned with.

Knowing that she would not tolerate Jezebel's workings through Knight, Milly responded, "I will not tolerate Jezebel nor her puppets speaking to me. I am not intimidated by you or that ruling power, and will not back down from what El Elyon has called me to do."

Knight snarled like an animal about to growl, replying, "You wait Mildred Teschlon! You and your group will experience hell, as we attack you all on all fronts. This is only the beginning of what I am about to do, and more is soon to come. You will fall into the snare of your enemy, as well as your two friends."

Time then returned, unfrozen, and Knight swiftly storming off, like a bully leaving a playground fight, knew he had been defeated. The group turned to one another and did high fives as they did their first team face-off with the enemy.

Pumped, Parker belted out, "Boy, did that feel good!"

The group felt they could run, with the euphoria they were feeling from both the tower, and after overcoming the darkness in Dean Knight.

"Wait a minute," said Milly. "Dean Knight is hooked up with the Ancient Gatehouse, which is where I pulled over, across the street, on my way home the other night. The fact that he came raging towards me today means that he knows what happened to me.

"What happened?" asked Parker.

"Well, its really crazy. It happened right after I dropped you two off after the meeting. I was driving back home, and began feeling horrible, with this sinking feeling in the pit of my stomach that I was going to die." She was reliving the moment, using her hands and moving about, recalling the incident.

"Everything within my body was turning on itself, is the only way that I know to describe it. I pulled off the road, and tried to call my mother, wanting to say goodbye, in case I was dying. But it was insane; my hand was too weak to dial. I was hunched over the steering wheel, when then I felt like vomiting, and a huge globbish *thing* came out of mouth. It was like a force was driving it out of me. Then, it landed in my hand, which was totally disgusting." She shook her head again and shuddered thinking about it.

"Afterwards, I saw the blue flame come into my mouth and downward into my belly when an Ancient voice spoke, telling me that a spirit of fear had been driven out of my belly, comparing it to an owl getting into an eagle's nest."

"Wow," Tony exclaimed. Trying not to interrupt he said, "Go on Milly."

"The voice said that demons worked with fear and the wisdom of this present age against the minds of mankind, and that all of us were being freed of this oppression. The eagle represents the Wisdom from above from the Ancient door being opened. It is the strength we feel from the tower."

"Mill, that is some kind of crazy there! But also, it is totally awesome!" Parker exclaimed.

"I couldn't move for a while, in utter awe at what I was experiencing. I wanted to call you both or text you, but I was so high from the experience and how I felt, that I went home and relaxed with my parents in silence as we drank our evening coffee."

"That is something else Milly," Tony stated, as he connected the dots. "So if you are saying that it happened across from the Gatehouse that night, then most likely Dean Knight was inside. I know from my past encounters, I remember creepy feelings I would always get passing by that place. It's not just the dingy green curtains that totally do not go with the building. The whole thing just creeps me out. Moreover, I have heard stories about that place, and Ralph Massinger's dad got out of The Ancient Gatehouse five years ago, refusing to talk about what happened. All I know is that Mr. Massinger told Ralph to stay away from that place."

Parker remembered his own encounters about The Ancient Gatehouse as Tony spoke. "You are completely right Man. I remember my freshmen year here at Strytan, when I was up late with a bunch of the guys, and we were messing around daring each other to go around that place because of all the stories we had heard from the locals."

"A group of us walked to the back of The Ancient Gatehouse, and it sounded like someone was screaming from the basement. We tried to look in through the basement windows, but they were covered up by black film. One of the guys in the group banged on the door to get someone's attention, and a nasty old man came out, telling us to get away from there if we knew what was good for us. We asked him what was going on and he said they were watching a movie. I never believed him though."

Milly and Tony took in Parker's story and knew that things did not add up with the local Gatehouse, and from all accounts with Dean Knight's behavior, since he was the president of The Ancient Gatehouse, their suspicion was correct.

"He must have seen you Milly," Tony said, "And if he is able to see in the spirit realm, then probably, he observed what you saw with the blue flame. Moreover, when you think about the gates of hell rising in the area, what better place for them to be than The Ancient Gatehouse?"

The group agreed, and because of their suspicion, each one peered over their shoulders, seeing if anyone was listening in. They went their separate ways to class; Tony had much to do with his physics studies and both Parker and Milly had a heavy philosophy paper to finish.

The Underworld

Vladamore, unrelenting, got up in the faces of his leaders, spewing foam on them, while castigating them for not utilizing their skills and efforts, to inform them, things were getting worse. The tactics that were employed to stop Milly and the group members were not working. The human cronies that the demons were working with had not successfully carried out their assignments. Vladamore, listing the failings against those in The Ancient Language Seekers group, was fuming.

Knight's task should have been an easy one, taking out Milly with the spirit of Jezebel. Since Parker and Tony were with her, and they all received more power from the Ancient Language, it failed.

Serena, a practicing witch in the area, attending St. Timothy's Cathedral, was sent to bring division into the Church, as well as bring offense to Father Sanderson's soul. Her plans failed, as El Elyon gave a warning to Father Sanderson through a dream, where he had 'prayed up,' according to him, in order to overcome the attack.

Lassiter, still oppressed by Leviathan, was manifesting against Kaufman, requesting private meetings about his grade, using his parents' status at the university as leverage to tempt Kaufman into giving him a good grade. This tactic did not prosper; Kaufman, a man of character, would not be moved to doing things underhandedly.

Both the Doctors Mercer were verbally attacked, as a woman came out of the grocery store hurling insults about their community work, and that they were in it for the show, stating they were insincere and busy bodies, needing to stay in their own lane. All those outside the store could hear the insults. Her assignment was to sow lies of doubt and unbelief, where they would question their efforts, trying to get them to look for the wisdom of this present age, but it did not prosper.

Many more assignments took place with others in the group, but on every turn each attack failed. Vladamore, now foaming at the mouth, wanted to make someone pay; with Beelzebub on the way, he was surely to get a railing in front of the underworld.

"If you worthless maggots cannot do what you are asked to, then it is time for me to demote you and look for others to take your place." Vladamore still in a tirade, paced back and forth, getting in their faces with his beady red eyes, threatening them with his presence.

"We are here for the purpose of our dark liege, who has devoted himself entirely for our welfare, in taking out the human cohorts of El Elyon. The rest of them, we can easily sway and brainwash further, through the continued media messages, and the polarity that is about to be released by the physicists who are on our side, to open up the parallel universe, that will make zombies out of many, being nothing but a source of existence for us to use for our purposes."

Vladamore paused, standing in the middle of the group against the putrefied rock oozing dark liquid, and proclaimed with determination, as he lifted his nasty hand and fanned out his long claws, "They all are merely batteries! Their existence is nothing! The human souls must be put into prison, so that we can use their bodies."

He knew Beelzebub's ultimate plan was to use the humans as hosts, discarding them once they had fulfilled his purpose. "We have to attack them in greater measure before the release of the global assault from the grid, lest they be protected from its plan by the tower and the Ancient Language."

"Prepare the cords of hell, as we continue to pour out the slime across Springfield, ready for when PRINA releases the global attack." Vladamore touted.

The serpent creatures were stationed directly underneath The Ancient Gatehouse, where their cords reached up from the underworld to the basement, releasing slime that would feed and strengthen the gates of hell, influencing those in membership and others in the area.

Green, red and clear colored slime pumped from the tanks into the cords, filling them to capacity. The substance moved to the smaller cords, like wires in the main entry part of the building, slowly distributing slime throughout the city. In the spirit realm, it was easily detected, and El Elyon's angelic hosts, Rafael and Tubal, were keeping watch, seeing Constugard on top of the Gatehouse, while the gates of hell continued to rise.

Turn the Battle at the Gate!

Rafael scrutinized the workings of the underworld while spying out The Gatehouse, seeing the gates of hell rise, as the torture of the souls of mankind screamed and moaned behind it. The gates were of the horrid evil black rock that oozed black sludge, looking to be 20 feet high and 40 feet long. The gates were shut, holding back the souls of mankind, where all behind them were red roots of an evil looking tree hooked up to each soul. Thousands upon thousands of roots reached from the tree, tormenting the souls that they were attached to it.

Rafael heard the most horrid of sounds coming from behind the gates, of the souls already bound to eternal damnation, unable to escape. They cried in continued agony, as hands reached through the wretched gates, souls believing that they could be pulled out.

Rafael hated the miserable sounds; yet it reminded him of those who still had hope and had not been met with this fate. He was committed to fight for the souls of mankind. Tubal watched on as well, feeling the angst that Rafael did, realizing the battle had become more detrimental for Area 9.

Rafael still looking at the gates said with resoluteness, "All hope is lost for the souls behind those gates, Tubal. But there are souls still in Springfield that have not reached this fate, so we must fight."

Rafael had to get word to the other angels in Area 9, who knew the achievement of the tower rising in Springfield. The angels hoped that mankind could turn this battle at the gate, not allowing evil to spill over and spew its venom in the region, protecting Springfield from hell's fury.

Tubal agreed, declaring, "With El Elyon's warriors in Springfield, much hope still stands for mankind! We must get word back to the Angelic Council!"

The two angels took to flight towards Granite Peak, where El Elyon's hosts held Council for the region. Swiftly, like missiles blasting off to the heavens, Rafael and Tubal glided, arriving at the angelic war room for Area 9.

Granite rock covered the outside of Granite Peak, living up to its expectations for spectators. However, inside was much different; a gleaming crystal palatial war room was hidden from man's sight, and the entire underworld. Rafael and Tubal walked in, where the height of the space towered over a thousand feet high. The palatial war room was made out of crystal that was alive with colors skipping throughout, as light coming from within the angelic hosts shone upon it, when they were present. Angelic Hosts of El Elyon constantly glimmered in the brightness of the Light, a pure substance of His hope.

El Elyon created the angelic beings, and put His Light within each one, causing the brightness of that light to shine to all around them. Like moving stars ushered to earth, the angels served His purpose. Rafael's garments of bluish silver matched the palatial grand war room, as it reflected the colors and light all the more, bouncing off of the crystal.

A winding crystal staircase without steps, like a highway ascending to the heavens, had much activity as heavenly hosts were coming and going. The entrance was at the peak of the mountain, where angels would ascend and descend, going through the cavern's wall located at the peak, since their structure was that of spirit. They would enter and exit from the crystal highway, being welcomed and sent forth with the strength of El Elyon that permeated the palatial crystal war room.

Granite Peak was considered a *high place*, which had been taken by the angelic host, dedicated solely to El Elyon. High places were important, because they were the strongholds of the areas; a place of authority that was highly treasured by both El Elyon's angels and Beelzebub's demons.

Beelzebub sought the high places in regions, nations and in places of ruling and reigning, as kings and heads of state; he wanted every HIGH PLACE. Therefore, when El Elyon's hosts took this high place in 1 A.D., it devastated the underworld; it was the highest place for Area 9.

The presence of El Elyon was all over His hosts who carried the pure blue flame within. The power of the blue flame was well known to Beelzebub; he, at one time was the main keeper of the blue flame. Beelzebub had been head watcher and protector of El Elyon and the flame. However, once evil entered his heart, the blue flame was quickly taken out of him, and he was completely given over to the dark nature, where he then made it his mission to destroy the flame.

With the blue flame, came the Ancient Language, where the voice of the Ancient One could be heard. This is what Beelzebub hated most; it not only tormented him with his demise that was to come, but also reminded him constantly of what he had lost. Beelzebub knew the power of this Wisdom and had to stop it at all cost.

Tonight We Fight!

Angels gathered round Rafael and Tubal, who entered the war room, giving honor to them; they were El Elyon's head angels in Area 9. Their wisdom was unmatched in battle for the region, and their devotion to mankind was evident through the compassion they walked in of El Elyon.

Compassion was a mystery for the angelic host, and they were intrigued when observing it. They were eager to catch glimpses of El Elyon's sentiments through those angels who carried more of the blue flame, who were able to feel His empathy for mankind. Rafael and

Tubal had much of the blue flame and were able to feel El Elyon's compassion towards Milly and the other members of the team.

"Hello legions of El Elyon," Rafael said as he entered the palatial war room. Angels could be seen all over, like a tidal wave coming upon the mountain, their presence was everywhere, many on the spiral staircase, others on the different levels within the great war room, like tiers on a cake towering up, where they were provided more standing room, so they could observe the discussions happening at the war table, which they called ***lâcham***, pronounced ***law-kham'*** meaning ***to fight.***

"Hoorah, we are ready to fight," were the cheers that echoed throughout the grand room. All the angelic hosts were ablaze with fire. Although the hosts did not have gender, from a human's perspective they looked male or female. They had been waiting for this night, surmising that something great was occurring with the tower that was rising, and now slowly causing others to arise throughout Area 9. Springfield now, was not the only one in the region with a tower, and this was great news.

Angelic hosts of many colors were all around, wearing beautiful garments, as they glimmered like stars, shining the light of the blue flame within. A jubilee was taking place, as they gathered around in hope and expectancy. They were ready to hear from Rafael and Tubal, knowing that it would be an urgent message to send them out to fight.

A striking massive table made out of a cobalt blue sapphire, stood in the middle, as it spread in a great expanse like the wings of an airplane. The table's name was ***lâcham***. That was the name, spoken devotedly by all the angels, denoting its importance.

Lâcham had come from the same substance that composed the sapphire pavement of El Elyon's dwelling. The intensity of the heat of the blue flame constantly flowed through Him, as His feet were grounded on the sapphire pavement, increasing the energy level within the precious jewel, causing white lightning to be fragmented throughout. This table to the angels was the presence of El Elyon, and told them how to fight!

It was on the main level, the stage for the palatial crystal war room. Head angels gathered around ***lâcham***, with two angels from each section of the area, standing side by side at the table. Altogether, there were over 100 sections in Area 9, accommodating 200 angels who stood at the large sapphire table, discussing the battle plan.

The other hosts listened, as they stood on different tiers that were open to the happenings of the war room. Each time the council would convene, there was electricity in the air. Much like warriors at a fireside before the battle. Tonight with discussions at ***lâcham***, there was a bonfire amongst them in their presence. When the hosts met together, their presence became a blue flame. The Ancient Language was immense within them, and as they spoke with one another only in the Ancient Language.

The crystal palatial war room, in all appearances, seemed like the tower in Springfield, because the angels within were lit with the blue flame, as they were ignited in the thought of the great battle that was to come. This energy was that of the Life of El Elyon burning, like fuel in a jet, the war room was a fuel tank for their, soon to be, combat with the hordes of darkness. They were grateful for the moments of camaraderie. Tonight was special, because the angels had been waiting for decades for this particular time.

With arms raised, greeting the hosts, Rafael burned brightly as he hailed the group. "Hello my fellow messengers of El Elyon!"

Cheers erupted all throughout the war room, as the heads of the sections pounded their hands on the large sapphire table, showing their allegiance to El Elyon. Their agreement with El Elyon's plans created white lightning in ***lâcham***, as they struck their fists on it. Other angels standing on the tiers, as well as around the room, threw their right hand up with their sword in its sheath, proving their devotion to El Elyon's plan, shouting, "We fight for the Ancient One!"

Lightning flashed throughout, rippling across the crystal expanse, as El Elyon responded to the angelic hosts. He was always present, and spoke through His lightning and thunder.

Rafael continued, "I have come to speak on behalf of Section 33 of Area 9, where the tower is rising speedily in Springfield, and we hope to see another one spring forth soon." Cheers erupted amongst them, as angels looked forward to the battle, tasting the victory that was soon to come.

Rafael held his hands up, to which the hosts hushed. The blue flame enlarged the more that he spoke, revealing the compassion of El Elyon resident within him. All were captivated as they observed.

"We have seen these brave warriors that are willing to lose their life for El Elyon, who have heard the Ancient Language from the towers, and they have been successful in engaging in the spirit, with the armor and weapons of El Elyon, fighting ruling powers, demons and dark principalities." By this time, Rafael's speech had the angels wanting to take flight and lunge into battle, because they were witnessing El Elyon's hope in mankind, as Rafael spoke.

He then put the question out to the other area leaders, "How many other towers are rising in our midst, angelic leaders?"

Fawna was ready to speak. A beautiful female angelic messenger, captivating in appearance, with piercing eyes of bright green, and lovely dark tannish skin, sparkling almost like copper. Hair, a deep dark brown, rolled in waves down her back and over her shoulders. Her garment, a beautiful crysolite, matched the color of her eyes.

"May I speak Rafael, for I have good news to bring," Fawna asked.

"Yes, of course Commander." All the heads at the table addressed each other as commander, except for when it came to Rafael, whom they addressed as general.

"Thank you General," she said as she nodded to Rafael. "It is with great news that I bring about Sasawatch that is in Canada, that this week a tower has begun to arise, and we have El Elyon's warriors there that have their armor and weapons, ready to fight." Cheers erupted again, angels were being charged like a battery, plugged up to the excitement of the blue flame of El Elyon, as Lightning distributed throughout the place, giving them more strength.

Mishal leaned forward to the table, looking at Rafael, asking, "May I also speak, General?"

"Yes Commander, you may."

Mishal, whose color was a deep dark brown, stood at 9 feet high. His large shoulders bulged from the rich colored red garment trimmed in gold that sparkled like rubies all over. It was striking against his skin, and made his glimmering caramel colored eyes, all the more pronounced, which was intimidating to demons. He could send any demon fleeing at the sight of him. He had many victories under his belt, and his weapon of choice, looked like a machete, that would also function much like a boomerang, when he sent it off into a far distance to destroy demons, returning safely each time to his hands.

"Yes Rafael, we too have experienced a tower rising in Riverton, Montana. The warriors of El Elyon have been operating in their armor and with their weapons, and are receiving the power of the Ancient Language, as well. They are marked with the blue flame, and are moving quickly to divert Beelzebub's plans."

Angels could not contain their jubilation over the warriors in this decade that were working with El Elyon. For in years past, many were called to war but very few were chosen; they were not willing to count the cost, to put the souls of mankind above themselves.

Rafael lifted his hands to quiet the hosts down, which took waving his arms up and down three times. He did not want to interrupt their cheers, but the battle plans had to be laid out. They hushed, as they waited for his lead. "Yes, the warriors of El Elyon in this generation are most unique and were born for such a time as this, for this purpose to fight with us." He knew they wanted to cheer, but holding his hand up, they knew he had more to say.

"We have seen the watchers doing their menacing work, assisting Beelzebub's generals to broaden the gates of hell, which are being established in the dark society, The Ancient Gatehouse, where each one is being flooded with the slime of hell to release into the cities. Once this is done, we have to be ready to avert this plan; it is then when their artillery of the lying serpents will be released, causing people to become more susceptible to the ruling powers of the area."

He continued, and lifted his head, as he spoke to the angels up high on the tiers, letting them know that they too were in on the meeting. "The warriors of El Elyon are working cooperatively against the ruling powers, and resisting hell's tactics, giving us more chance to overcome Beelzebub's strategies and destroy the gates of hell," to which Rafael let his hand drop, giving notice to the hosts that they could cheer.

Erupting like a lightning storm, cheers and El Elyon's lightning, electrified the palatial crystal war room, charging the angelic hosts all the more. It was time for El Elyon's hosts and warriors to turn the battle at the gate, for this particular night the angels would fight in greater measure, battling not only the ruling powers, but also the princes in the air, so that more of El Elyon's hosts could enter into the first heaven.

Rafael nodded to Tubal to speak. Tubal motioned with his hands to the great angelic audience, lifting them, so they could hear the urgency in his voice. "We have information about the humans bound up under Beelzebub, who have been used to work with the demonic grid, in order to interrupt the timeline, by breaking into a parallel universe. We must work expediently to shield those whom we can, in order to protect them from the attack against their central nervous system. Beelzebub's plan is to use the humans as batteries in this parallel universe, where demons will hook them up to cords sending them thoughts they believe to be real, when instead the cords of hell will be feeding their mind and robbing them of the use of that which El Elyon designed for His Wisdom."

The angelic hosts immediately turned to anger vexed upon hearing the news. Much was to be done quickly, to prepare El Elyon's warriors, and disrupt hell's plan. This was a faceoff between the power of darkness and the power of Light.

Tubal raised his hand, to which the hosts listened. "We must fight this night with El Elyon's might, knowing that hell's fury will soon be put to flight! Be hopeful and expectant as we go forth into battle, strengthening the hands of the weak mortal, who clings to life dearly, not wanting to let go, knowing that time here passes quickly for them, as many souls are still going to hell's gates, and it is up to us and the human warriors to stand for truth, as the Ancient Language leads us."

Immediately, the angels exploded again into cheers, knowing that this battle would be remembered in the time of mankind, as a momentous occasion, in order to turn things around. The meeting came to an end as Rafael lifted his hand, and spoke the mantra that all the angelic hosts speak.

"El Elyon be with you!"

The hosts shouted back, "El Elyon be with you!"

A Fast Exit

The angelic hosts were ready and fully charged to go into battle. Their exit from the crystal war room was volcanic, like erupting lava, as they gushed out with speed, to the different sections of Area 9. Their garments were beautiful, covered by brilliant armor, shielding them from demonic fire. The angels warred with their weapons, while many times the demons would use demonic fire, which they called fiery darts. Demons would also use demonic fire against the warriors of El Elyon, who had the shield.

The hosts of the 100 sections rushed off across Area 9; it would be this area that would affect the whole world. The last time a battle was this great, Area 9 rose up for the occasion, which was seen with Mildred Lee, the Great Grandmother of Milly.

Rafael and Tubal, landed firmly in Milly's bedroom, where she was getting ready to go meet Father Sanderson for the deliverance that was to take place tonight. Surprised at their appearing, she replied, "What are you two doing here?"

She knew that if El Elyon's angels were present that something was hugely amiss. She noticed they shone all the brighter, as their person was outlined by the blue flame surrounding them. It shone within one foot from all around them, outlining their form.

"Wow, you two are shining brightly, where have you been?"

Rafael responded, "We have met with the angelic council of Area 9, after seeing Constugard, the demonic watcher over The Ancient Gatehouse. The gates of hell are rising and Vladamore is releasing the slime with his cords, because he is threatened with the tower here in

Springfield, which is now causing other towers in Area 9 to arise, with other bold warriors of El Elyon."

Milly was elated and wanted to jump up and down. This was news to her ears.

Rafael brought her to reality, quickly saying, "Do not get too excited Milly Teschlon; there is still more battle to fight. The group has to know that the central nervous system attack is coming sooner, which is why we have to work more quickly, being prepared for its release, which will make human batteries out of many souls, who are not prepared. If the tower rises up here fully, then this area will be shielded under El Elyon and hell will not prevail."

Tubal could sense Milly's doubt, and El Elyon's compassion burned in him, letting him know that she needed encouragement. "Milly, do not be discouraged or disappointed, for El Elyon has chosen you and prophesied that you would be used for this particular battle. Each warrior is hand picked by Him, and He only picks the bravest. Be brave and courageous Milly, you will fight with us, even as you do deliverance with Father Sanderson, do not think that this is all happenstance." She was comforted by Tubal's encouragement.

Her armor appeared, with her weapons, to which Rafael pointed to the shield on her back, "Get the shield from your back Milly, and I will show you how to use it."

Reaching behind her, she pulled the large beautiful shield from her back, and drew it in front of her face. Rafael positioned it, as he lifted her arm higher and further out, showing her the warrior's stance against the fiery darts.

"This is important Milly; the demons have fiery darts that they release against those who have shields. These darts are one of their main weapons against the angels and those with El Elyon's shield, and has a devastating blow if it hits you. For you humans, it causes exhaustion in the battle, to where you are in your own strength outside of Him. You have to be in union with the Ancient Language that is in you, and listen to the Sword, especially against this assault so that you will be able to overcome. El Elyon has faith in you Milly, as well as Tubal and I, and we are certain that you will be one of the finest warriors in your time."

Tears began to roll down her cheeks, feeling the largeness of the hour upon her soul, where all of mankind was weighing in the balance in Springfield, Area 9 and the entire world, for she and her group members to fight.

"Be of good courage Milly Teschlon," said Tubal again, as he put his hand on her shoulder, "You will be brave and courageous and cause many of El Elyon's warriors to fight! The victory is not to the strongest or the fastest, for El Elyon uses the weakest that have been delivered by Him of the torment of hell, because those are the ones most dependent and loyal. Know that you can not lean on your own understanding, but the Ancient Language in you will lead and guide you, along with the Sword."

As she dried the tears off of her face, Rafael and Tubal disappeared. She looked in the mirror, straightening her makeup that was smeared. Her eyes began to sparkle, where she then saw a blue flame light up within her pupil. She then spoke softly to her reflection, "Milly, you can do this, you were born to fight!"

Chapter 11

The evening for Milly was just starting as she nervously headed to see Father Sanderson. She was clueless as to what an *exorcism* would entail. Personal experience from her own encounters with spiritual warfare provided some basis, but she was lacking in knowledge and understanding with what Father Sanderson termed as "deliverance."

Father Sanderson was of the Greek Orthodox Church and not the Roman Catholic. The Greek and Roman Catholic churches split during the rule of Charlemagne, at his crowning, causing deterioration between the two. The split occurred in 1054 A.D., where the Greek Orthodox Church became the Eastern Church, severing all ties with the Roman Catholic Church, all the way from the Emperor to the Pope, on down.

Roman Catholics look at the Pope as one who is infallible, whereas the Greek Orthodox does not. Father Sanderson had his own beliefs about the Pope at large, and they were not in favor of the Pope's character. From the information that he had gathered, his belief was that there were many connections with the Pope and dark societies, making him overly cautious to the true nature of what was taking place. He knew that there were many good Roman Catholics who had no knowledge of what was going on in different areas of the Vatican, and he would rather err on the side of caution, staying far away from the Western Catholic Church.

The Green Carpet

Milly walked to the side of the old church, built in the early 1900s, due to the influx of the Greek Orthodox influence sweeping across the North. The old building was beautiful, with an appearance of an antediluvian stone, brownish hue with rust tints throughout, cut in huge blocks, which made the building appear resplendent. The carved woodwork around the windows captured the skill of the craftsman from the age.

Milly was more than impressed each time she walked through Springfield, and caught eye of Saint Timothy's Cathedral, each time she passed. She loved reading the placard at times, when no one was looking; it's writing was a magnet to her soul.

It read: *Saint Timothy Cathedral, built in 1902, by the hands of the Greek Orthodox Church, heralding a message that is timeless, with the breath given to Saint Timothy, who rightly divided the Word, training many into such a stewardship of Wisdom only provided in truth, through the Ancient Language.*

Then she realized why she was so drawn to it; it ended with THE ANCIENT LANGUAGE! Why had she not seen it before; other than she was simply drawn to the placard. Her Great Grandmother had a placard, as well, which is why she must not have paid as much attention to this one on Saint Timothy Cathedral. However, interestingly enough, it was only a block from her Great Grandmother's placard.

Milly opened the doors, feeling that time was of the essence, with Rafael and Tubal's meeting this night. The evening was only beginning according to them, and much needed to take place to stop hell.

She could not wait to see Father Sanderson and was eager to welcome a familiar face. She felt that she would be more grounded spiritually, in seeing someone else from the team to learn more on El Elyon's anointing.

Her hand on the ironwork of the huge dark stained wooden doors made of maple, she stopped to take in the exquisiteness. The carvings of grapes trailing from the top to the bottom of the door stunned her, and she could not take her eyes off of it; it was beautiful. Such detail, artwork and labor given to the door and the building had to whet the appetites of those who would pass by, speculating the great opulence within.

Her hand felt the heavy metal iron underneath her palm and fingers, as she gave the handle a good tug. There was weight to everything with this building, the door, the stone, and now to see what was inside.

Upon entering she saw three stone steps, leading up to the back hallway covered in a twine-like green carpet. She was not very fond of green, and especially the green carpets that they had in the old bank building offices, but this green was different.

One would think it was as aged as the building, being such a different carpet, one that she had never seen. There was a fine twill combed together of different hues of green, and a bit of caramel splashed throughout, creating an ambiance with the stone walls on the inside, where you almost felt carried back in time to even the *ancient time*. It was hard to explain, but regardless, she was enthused and wanted to see more of what she could, before meeting Father Sanderson.

Green carpet, like the floor cloth of the ancient world, was the pathway leading throughout the entire administrative part of the building, and into other backrooms that were used for counseling and small group gatherings. Her heart was pulled to explore and she did not know why, when she entered another dimension and saw the building in its original form, where a stone pathway was the original flooring.

Milly followed it as it led her to a room. Then, hearing the voice of Father Sanderson pulled her back into reality, at his calling, "Milly, I see you made it. And you are exactly at the door to where we are meeting."

Eyes opened to see what the room was, she saw no identity given to the room, only that a beautiful Gaelic arch in multi tiers was the frame for the dark stained door. Breathtaking was the only word she had for Saint Timothy's Cathedral. She knew more would be revealed in time, and continued to enter the room, where Father Sanderson caught her up to speed with the evening's session with the young female congregant.

"Milly, it is nearly time for the young lady to come for the exorcism session and I need to fill you in on a few matters before she arrives. First, I have already told her you would be coming and she agreed that your presence was welcomed, as well as your input, should you see something spiritually that will be of service to her freedom."

Father Sanderson was delighted to see her inquisitive eyes, and knew she had more questions than there was time to answer. "Listen Milly, I want you to be at peace and comfortable with what will take place, and you must understand that no matter what you see, know that you are armored in El Elyon, and nothing can by any means harm you. Do not have conversations with demons; rather take authority over them with the weapons you have been given."

She was excited, unsure of what would come, and looked forward to the evening's accomplishments. Milly felt comfortable with Father Sanderson, and trusted that things would go according to how they should be.

"One more thing Milly, this young lady says she knows you, and although she has dealt with shame in her past, she has a history of drug abuse, as well as having been molested when she was younger by a family member. She has not shared this story with her family for fear of reprisal but rather has only divulged this evil committed against her, to me recently during confession one day. Whatever is spoken within the walls of this room stays here and cannot be communicated to anyone else, can I have your word on that," he asked.

"Absolutely."

She did not know who this young lady was and felt bad that she was unable to help her earlier when they knew each other, hearing the horror she had to endure of molestation, and being bound up to drugs troubled Milly. Like a golfer getting a Mulligan, a do-over, Milly was ready to clear her conscience of the inability to see it years earlier, and could not wait to assist this nameless friend.

Milly saw in the Spirit as Father Sanderson prepared the room for the night. He had brilliant gold armor on, with a red and purple sash about his waist. The sword on his side was burning in an amber colored flame, and had wisps of fire that would fling off, as he used it. It was twice as large as the one on her side. The fiery amber Sword was massive! He unsheathed it as he spoke, and took authority.

"In the Name of this Sword, every demon in hell is bound and unable to operate in this meeting." He then opened a book of the Greek Orthodox exorcisms and read from it, anointing himself, as well as her, and the room, doing the motion of the cross in front of him. Afterwards, a knock came to the door, with his secretary announcing the young lady's entrance.

Milly could not wait! Who was the young lady?

"Father Sanderson," Theresa, his secretary, said lightly, "Dana Dryer is here for the scheduled meeting."

"What!" Milly thought while shouting inside of her own brain. "Dana Dryer, DD!" DD was not her friend; in fact it was the girl that bullied her all through middle school and high school. How could Father Sanderson ever think that they were friends, and what is crazier is how could DD agree to her attending if she knew how she treated Milly all those years.

Milly immediately became angry and wondered why Father Sanderson had not made her aware of whom the young lady was. She wanted to give DD a piece of her mind at what she had put her through all those years that led to her cutting and depression, as well as low self-esteem. Parker's voice filled Milly's head as she heard herself saying, "This is some kind of crazy here."

A slender figure entered the room, almost anemic, at 5'6" tall, long blond hair going over her shoulders and down her back. She wore a plaid skirt with stockings underneath, and brown penny loafers. Her navy sweater looked as though it came from Ireland; they had such beautifully knitted tops.

DD looked as though she had not matured from high school, seeming to be stuck, even having mannerisms that she did four years ago, not showing much maturity. She whispered a bit sheepishly, unlike her normal self, as she said, "Hello Milly, I bet you never expected to see me in close quarters, and especially here."

Milly's heated anger turned into pity as she saw the shell of a life standing before her, of a soul barely holding on to life by a rope, ready to let go at any moment. She could sense the assignment of hell over DD. With the blue flame burning within Milly, she found herself having compassion for someone who had once been her enemy.

The flame enlarged, as she heard El Elyon say, "Mildred, love your enemies."

Her heart was pierced with great conviction, and thoughts flooded her heart and mind. Tears seeped from Milly's eyes, as she watched herself lean forward hugging DD, assuring her that all was well between them.

Milly's mouth opened, as she watched herself speaking to DD, almost like a person divided in two, where her soul and spirit had been split, allowing her spirit to take over, speaking on behalf of the heart of El Elyon. A reservoir of compassion surprised her as it spilled out of her soul, like a drink offering onto DD, seemingly refreshing Dana a bit and giving her hope.

"I am so sorry Dana, I had no clue that you had been through all that you had. If I would have known..."she paused.

Dana shook her head, sobbing uncontrollably, "You couldn't have known, I would not let you, nor anyone else for that matter." Dana reached out for Milly's hands grabbing them. "I knew there was something different about you Milly, and that you could somehow see. I *had* to keep *you* of all people, at bay, so you would not know the spiritual disease I experienced, causing blackness in my heart. Please forgive me for the awful way I treated you. Those that hurt the most hurt others."

By this time both Dana and Milly were sobbing, with their tears falling on the green carpet. Father Sanderson, encouraged by what he was seeing, took the box of tissues and placed one in each of the hands of the two ladies who were now hugging.

It lasted for ten minutes, as Milly and Dana wept and embraced. Milly felt a huge release within her soul, the last cord where the enemy could oppress her over any hurts, and replied back to Dana, whispering, "I forgive you. But I also ask you to forgive me for not being brave enough back then to love you regardless of your pain."

They both stepped back regaining their composure, taking deep breaths and patting their eyes, knowing that something would soon take place this night to deliver Dana. She would be set free from the torment of her soul.

Father Sanderson looked at them with a huge smile and asked, "Are we ready to begin, Ladies?" Milly looked at Dana waiting for her response, letting her know that she was ready.

Inhaling deeply, Dana replied, "Yes Father Sanderson, I am."

He began the meeting by opening the Book and reading a prayer over Dana, as he anointed her with holy anointing oil from a jar, that he retrieved from a unique wooden box, that Milly saw had an olive tree carved into it, glowing an amber color. There was also Greek writing around the box, glowing in fiery opal blue.

Suddenly, after Father Sanderson anointed Dana, Milly could see in the spirit. She watched Him in his armor, and with the weapons of El Elyon, taking authority over the demons that were controlling Dana. The first thing he instructed her to do was to forgive her perpetrator, who was her father.

Milly's stomach turned at the thought of Dana's dad molesting her. She had known him for many years and would see him often when she walked by the lumberyard, where he worked. He seemed rather harsh to all in his presence, except for Milly, to whom he would smile at eerily. It always gave her the creeps and now she knew why! He molested his daughter more than once, too much to count! "Gross!" she screamed in her head.

Milly watched in the spirit, as Dana held these heavy iron chains, wearing iron fetters on her feet. The bondage she was in was great. Dana wailed in pain, as she opened her lips and screamed, "I forgive you Dad!" Milly's heart sank as she watched the pure agony of hell's release, which had gripped Dana's heart, keeping it in prison for all these years.

Suddenly, she saw lightning enter the room in the spirit, from El Elyon's dwelling, as it shattered both the chains and the fetters that had been on Dana setting her free!

Milly saw bronze colored shoes placed on Dana's feet superimposed over her penny loafers, and wondered what it was. Immediately she heard El Elyon say, "This is my peace Milly; I have shod Dana's feet with My peace; that which she has never known. This is what I put on My warriors as they come into the power of My Sword."

Mesmerized at all that was occurring, it was like watching an action thriller movie, packed on every turn with a complex plot. Milly was caught within the moment. Something began to sicken her, as she heard an animal growling out of Dana's belly, to which El Elyon told Milly, "This is rage, and it has a stronghold on her heart."

Milly watched as Dana's body shook and trembled, being unnerved at observing her own hand trembling out of control, wondering what was going on.

Then Milly saw what it was in the spirit, as a huge snarling dog was over Dana's body puppeting her. Cords were attached on her feet, her head and her hands. This was mind blowing to observe, however, Milly remained calm as the blue flame continued burning within giving her assurance and peace.

Dana asked, "What is going on with my body; why are my hands shaking?" After she asked, they shook all the more violently when her body was lifted four feet in the air. Suspended above the floor. Father Sanderson was not moved by what he saw, but read out of the Book, as the deliverance continued. He remained calm and unmoved, being at peace.

Dana's body then moved across the room suspended in the air, as she was turned over, being carried by some invisible force, screaming out in terror, "God, please help me! God help me!" She wanted the event to end; she had never experienced the supernatural and was unsure as to what all was going on.

Immediately, the shoes of bronze on her feet lit up, to which she calmed down, and like a rag doll, was turned around face downward, and brought gently to the floor where her knees were bent under her stomach, as if praying. Within the walls of the room a loud voice thundered, "REPENT!"

Dana began to tremble in a different manner, not shaking in violence, rather her hands trembled as if in fear, and she repented of her anger and rage, acknowledging that it was demonic in nature. Within a flash of her confessing and repenting, the blue flame began to come within her head and move throughout her spine removing the cords. Then she asked for more freedom, knowing that the there had to be a huge stronghold from her addictions. "I want more freedom!"

No sooner had Dana spoken the words than Milly saw greenish colored cords coming out of her belly. Divination manifested in front of her eyes standing in front of Dana, as if to fight Father Sanderson.

"She is mine," said the stunning lady, whose eyes swirled with a green color. Greenish smoke came out of her nostrils as if to fumigate the room with her stench and catch everyone under its spell.

Dana was weary and laid down on the sleigh couch in the room, which was seven feet long almost looking as if it were a bed. She was unable to understand all that was occurring and only knew that her desire was to be set free of all that controlled her. This divination spirit was a ruling power in the region, operating through many avenues, one of which was drug use.

Because of Dana's prior history with drug abuse and addictions, having dabbled in opioids, but mainly into marijuana, she had opened a door. The cords were firmly in her belly and pulling on her, not giving up without a fight.

Dana's belly lifted up in the air, to which the rest of her body was being pulled. Milly could not believe her eyes again. Dana began renouncing the use of drugs and repented for giving her soul over to it, at which time Father Sanderson stepped up.

"Not here divination, I will take care of you!" exclaimed Father Sanderson, as he held up the Sword and read out of the Book. Immediately, his Sword came across the cords that were in Dana's belly, and cut them off, as he sent the spirit, screaming, into the wilderness commanding it to loose Dana.

Dana's body sunk back down into the couch, and she cried all the more, with laughter now coming out of her mouth, "I am set free! Oh My, I feel it!" Leaping up to her feet, she was doing a little dance, as if back in school.

Milly, overcome by the joy that Dana was now experiencing from the deliverance that Father Sanderson was able to bring her, did not know what to think. The whole occurrence was more than her mind could comprehend, and going between the two different dimensions, as she saw what was taking place, made her wish that she had known this years earlier. She wished badly that she could have helped ease Dana's pain.

"You could not have known Mildred," said El Elyon, who was now speaking to each person present. El Elyon was speaking to Dana things in which she had not known, where He was present throughout her life, and that nothing went unnoticed by Him. He let her know how much she mattered. To Father Sanderson, El Elyon was speaking of things that were to come for Dana and Mildred together, to which He wanted him to release the prophecy to them.

"May I speak to you both ladies," asked Father Sanderson.

It was absolutely fine for him to speak to her, Milly thought, as she looked with intrigue while Dana nodded her head in agreement. Side by side they stood. In a small seam in the upper pocket of his garment, was a tiny green colored glass crucible of anointing oil, holding a special blend of fragrances he made.

He looked at them and anointed each one's forehead with the oil, as the aroma of the cassia, frankincense, myrrh, spikenard and cinnamon lifted up at the bottle's opening and off their foreheads, climbing through their nostrils and up to their brain. The oil was steeped in the abundance of smell, overtaking their senses, triggering their amygdala with the reward reinforcement of the power of El Elyon given to them.

"You two ladies will become best of friends, as El Elyon uses you to walk in a way that is less traveled, working together for the good of those in your generation, especially for women, to show them the power and strength that is given to those who lean not on themselves but walk in the difficult path."

The words leapt from his lips, into their hearts and minds, as their souls ruminated on the breadth of what was spoken, knowing that all could not be comprehended now, but that in time, things would make sense.

Friends

Father Sanderson showed the two young women to the door, getting them through the administrative corridor without a fuss; he knew that prying eyes and ears might be around. As they exited out of the side door, he bid them goodnight saying, "You two be careful and know that El Elyon has given you a precious gift of friendship. Do not take it lightly; you two will do great things for young women in Springfield, and especially at Strytan."

Still overtaken by the entire experience, their mouths could not move and they nodded in agreement, when he then locked the door to the small cathedral. They walked towards their car, Milly towards her Bug and Dana's sedan that was parked next to it.

"Milly, I am so grateful you were here tonight because there were so many times I wanted to tell you. I knew that I was taking out my rage and anger on you. You did not deserve it."

She assured Dana that all was well and that she was glad to be present this night in the midst of something that was so personal, making Dana vulnerable to trust that Milly would not tell. "Your secret is safe with me Dana, never worry about that."

Dana looked full of life now, as if she had undergone a makeover. Prior to the meeting, the oppression had become too much, to where she was no longer able to function under the bondage of all that held her down. Tonight's deliverance was a lifesaver, giving her hope for the future. The breath of life oozed through her pores as energy strengthened her from El Elyon.

The thought came to Dana about the women's meeting that was taking place in the spring semester at Strytan. She was one year ahead of Milly, having begun earlier on her college courses. She wanted to get out of home as soon as possible, to get away from her perpetrator.

"Say Milly, I believe the prophecy Father Sanderson gave us, has to do with the women's meeting that is taking place next semester. We are having speakers come from all the departments for spring orientation for both the benefit of potential students, as well as those already in attendance at Strytan. I am looking for a keynote speaker for the last night, which is a Sunday evening, to wrap up the entire conference. Would you be interested by any chance?"

Milly was floored; here she was talking like best friends with the girl that had bullied her all through school, and now she was being asked to be a keynote speaker for the spring Women's Conference at Strytan. What more could happen this night, she thought.

"Yes, of course Dana, I would be honored to do the engagement. Send me the date and time, and I will put it on my calendar!" She was elated, feeling like a bank teller promoted to branch manager. The two hugged and exchanged numbers. There was no telling where this friendship would take them.

In the back of Milly's mind, it occurred to her that Tony and Dana should meet; it was just a crazy thought. "Hey Dana, one last thing, I don't know if you know Tony at *The Grind*, but I think you two should get to know each other. Check out his insane concoctions, and ask for a Keto Addiction, when you see him next."

"Wow Milly, it's funny that you mention that; I just formally introduced myself to him last week after seeing him here for years, and had this sense that I had known him from some time way before. I will do that; it is confirmation that you shared it."

Remembering

The two said their goodbyes and got into their vehicles, when it came to Milly's remembrance about the vision she had in Saint Timothy's Cathedral. She wanted to see if she could catch Father Sanderson quickly before his leaving, and jumped out of her Bug to run back to the door.

Relieved to see him coming out of the side exit, she called out, "Father Sanderson, I wanted to ask you something."

She stepped up to him, thanking him for inviting her to the meeting as she conveyed her gratitude for helping her to get to know Dana better. It was as if he knew of their history in middle school and high school.

"Yes," he said, "things are not always what they seem."

She nodded and then changed the subject to another topic of discussion, "Listen, the oddest thing happened as I walked into the Cathedral tonight."

"Oh," he asked.

"Yes, when I stepped up to the green carpet I was caught in a vision, of walking down a corridor of ancient stone. There was stone on the floors as well as the walls, and it led me to a door, which I did not realize until later, was the room where we met."

He was surprised and taken back, thinking that the only reason El Elyon led him to invite Milly was so that the two young ladies could be set free from the past. Father Sanderson was pleasantly surprised to find out El Elyon had more in mind.

"You did Milly? So what did you see?"

"While you were doing the deliverance, I could see in the spirit, watching you with your armor and the Sword of El Elyon cutting the cords of the demons that were attacking Dana."

Father Sanderson knew Milly could see well, but did not realize how well. Although he could not see into the spirit all the time like Milly could, he was able to sense all that was needed to be done, as it came to his "gut" as well as his past training and experience. He heard El Elyon better than he knew, in what many called "a still small voice."

He was in awe of Milly's ability to *see*, and now this with the Cathedral and her going into a vision, especially in that room, made him want to hear more. "Did you see anything else as the deliverance was taking place?"

"Yes, for a moment I saw the holy oil you had, and the particular wooden box that it was in."

"Oh yes, that bottle and box were made at the time of the building of the Cathedral. What about it?"

"It was beautiful," she replied, "with the olive tree, and the Greek writing across the box. The only thing is, the tree and writing were lit up, leaping out to me."

A bit confused, he looked at Milly and said, "there is no writing on the box, and there is no olive tree on it either; it is a plain wooden box that was made to hold the oil."

Like an energy rush to her brain, she felt her ketones kicking up, crossing the blood brain barrier, as her excitement level went through the roof of her head, "What!" she exclaimed.

"Yes Milly, there is nothing on the box; it is just a plain box."

"May I see it again Father Sanderson," she asked.

He unlocked the door, as they entered in and went down the corridor. Only this time she did not see the ancient rock on the floor. They entered the room, and went over to the cabinet that housed the box containing the oil. Father Sanderson opened the door to it and pulled out the box, which was more adorning than Milly remembered before.

"Wow, that is beautiful!" She exclaimed while seeing the Greek words light up a fiery opal blue across the outside. The Olive tree that she thought was carved at first was instead a three-dimensional rendering of a tree, outlined in an amber color.

Father Sanderson could not get over Milly's enthusiasm at a simple brown box that had an ordinary appearance, although what was inside of it was of great value. "What is it that you see Milly?"

"It's these Greek words in the appearance of a fiery blue opal, and a three dimensional rendering of an olive tree outlined in an amber bronze color."

Perplexed, he turned the box around in his hands, wondering if his eyes would be opened, too, to see what Milly saw. Instead, he knew that he had to lean on her gift and ask her to write down what it was that she saw. "Can you draw and write down what you see."

"Sure, let me get a notebook from my backpack."

She took paper out, laid it down gently on the desk in the room, realizing that she was now going into a vision, and her paper looked like that of the ancient one in her dreams before, where her Great Grandmother would write. Suddenly, she realized she was seeing her

Great Grandmother, Mildred, in the room sitting at the desk, giving a prophecy for Springfield in the Ancient Language.

"Oh my!" She shouted as she was caught in the vision.

"What do you see Milly," Father Sanderson asked.

"My Great Grandmother in this room, at a desk, like the one in the basement of Truman, writing in the Ancient Language, and then I see an older man with her like a priest dressed similar to you, who is instructing her about the Ancient Language. I see her writing his name on the paper, which is Father Augustine Castellanos."

She continued, "Also, I see the same Greek letters that are on the outside of the wood box, being written on the paper."

"What does it say Milly? Can you read them?"

"Yes, it is like the Greek letters keeping going back and forth into English. It says '*kai humeis chrisma echete apo tou hagiou kai oidate panta.*'" After speaking it she wrote it down, unsure of what it meant. Handing it to Father Sanderson, she waited on his response.

"I'm undone at the accuracy of your ability to see in the spirit realm," he said, "but also, I believe you are a Seer, which is someone who operates in prophecy, and sees visions of things even to come. What you wrote here in Greek Milly, was 1 John 2:20 which says 'But ye have an unction from the Holy One and ye know all things.'"

"Wow, I had no clue," she responded.

"Yes, and you know what is even more credible to your ability to see?"

She shook her head clueless, "no."

He continued, "Father Augustine Castellanos was the first priest of Saint Timothy's Cathedral, and from what you have described, it seemed as though he and your great Grandmother had a connection, where he equipped her in the gifts she was given by El Elyon. Do you know if she attended Saint Timothy's Cathedral?"

"I have no clue but will definitely ask my parents."

"Moreover, the floors here are stone, we simply put the carpet in years ago, to keep people from hurting themselves on the floor. Because of needing something special for the stone floor, we ordered the carpet out of Wales, from a special company that does a wool carpet blend, making it more protective of both the stone, and those who walk on it."

"Wow, wow, wow," Milly said profusely, "and wow again!"

"The other thing that keeps coming to my mind Father Sanderson, is that if it is possible that Father Castellanos might be the one who wrote the relic and put it in Strytan. Did he have any connections with the University?"

"As a matter of fact, he did," Father Sanderson, replied. "He was on the board and sat on the department boards as an advisory council member to both the Philosophy and History departments at Truman. In fact, he was the one that named Truman Hall, which he said represents the TRUE MAN."

"Father Castellanos always said, that if man had the *right philosophy* and the *truth* of history, that he would be a TRUE MAN. He was the one that recommended putting the English department in there, as well, because he believed all three departments worked together for the good of the soul. That once man knew truth and the wisdom of it, that he then needed to write about it."

Both Father Sanderson and Milly stood in awe, as Milly connected the dots, now realizing why her Great Grandmother was under Castellanos' tutelage; she was taking history and philosophy as inspired by him, and writing the Ancient Language! "OH MY GOSH!" Milly shouted, "I am walking in the exact footsteps of My Great Grandmother."

The two of them were in shock, looking at each other, and then the oil, to which Milly replied, "We have to use that oil, it will be of great use later. There is something with that bottle in particular. Can we use it when necessary?"

"Yes Milly, we can do that. Simply let me know in advance, and I will come get it."

Father Sanderson told Milly that he had to stay and finish one last thing before leaving for the evening. He wanted to do his own research and see if he could discover more before Friday's meeting.

She didn't want to leave, but knew that class would come early and she needed to get home. The neurons in her belly were speaking to her brain, as she heard El Elyon confirming all that occurred within the small span of time that she experienced at Saint Timothy tonight. A greater confidence burned through her, as if she was branded by the Greek words, and the vision she had. Thoughts of how effective the group would be against the gates of hell, rolled up within her soul, like waves crashing onshore as the evening tide rolled in.

"All of this has been planned," she thought, while walking out of the room and down the corridor. She bent down to feel the wool carpet that was so beautifully woven and then pressed on it, to feel the stone floor beneath. "I wonder," she thought, "if this was the actual corridor I saw in the basement of TRUMAN!"

She gasped, turned around and saw the building in its original state, realizing that it was! Her vision was of Saint Timothy's Cathedral and her Great Grandmother as a little girl learning the Ancient Language at a very young age, under Father Augustine Castellanos. "Oh my gosh! This is the vision! The reason that Truman is the way it is, with the Philosophy, History and English departments, is because both Father Castellanos and her Great Grandmother knew what was to come! He was the one that placed the old desk in Truman Hall, knowing that one day Mildred Lee's Great Granddaughter would follow in the same footsteps.

Chapter 12

Dean Knight stumbled through the administrative office door, mumbling under his breath what Constugard had told him the night before. The administrative assistant, unable to make out what he was saying, asked, "Dean Knight is everything alright?"

"Yes Julie, I am talking to myself, so never mind me and what I am doing. But call Professor Norman Kaufman, letting him know that I want to see him ASAP!" It was obvious that Knight was in a hissy fit early this morning, and Julie knew all to well how sensitive she had to be when he was in his *mood*.

"Yes Dean Knight, I will."

Knight walked into his personal office, looking at the papers piled on the side of his desk, quaking within his body, knowing the papers were the files of *those* in the group. He despised and hated them all, Milly, Parker, Tony, Professor Kaufman, Professor Mercer and Professor Peyton. Determined to make their life a living hell at Strytan, it was his goal to dismantle their efforts.

Knock, knock, knock. Julie was at the door, dreading the thought of opening it; she could not stand working for Knight and wished he had never become Dean of Faculty. His heart was not into the work, but rather he seemed like a washed up Politician, looking to save his career on whatever platform would tolerate him.

"Yes Julie, what is it? Hurry, I want Kaufman in here now!"

"Dean Knight, that is why I am knocking; he is here to meet with you."

Embarrassed a bit, he replied, "Well, let him in then."

Professor Kaufman already knew what was transpiring, having been given a dream by El Elyon of the sinister plot that Knight was scheming up with the demonic realm. He had known Knight was the president of The Ancient Gatehouse, but was uncertain as to their workings. In the dream, El Elyon informed Kaufman of the dark deeds at the local Gatehouse and with its members. It turned his stomach at what he saw, knowing that what he would be dealing with in this meeting would not be human. No human could commit the evils that Knight had.

Kaufman walked calmly into the room, unmoved by the negative energy of the pit of hell coming from Knight, and then asked, "You want to see me Dean Knight?"

"Yes, as a matter of a fact I do. I have good word that you have been getting with some of your students and other faculty once a week, conspiring against Springfield and Strytan."

"Wait a minute Dean Knight, where are you getting your information; there is no such conspiracy going on, and if anything, we are meeting together based on the studies of history and philosophy, from findings we have recently discovered, to ensure just the opposite." Kaufman knew it was a trap and that Dean Knight was fishing around for information.

"I hope you check your sources again. Your information is unreliable and speculative," Kaufman said, as he looked Knight eye to eye, unflinching. His eyes then moved to Knight's desk, where the stack of files lay.

Kaufman pointed to the files, "So are those all *the people* you have identified in this conjecture of yours?"

Dean Knight realized he was caught and contemplated about what he should say, knowing he had very little time to foil all their efforts. While looking at the darkness of his own heart from which to respond, Kaufman's eyes were opened in the spiritual realm, when he then saw three tentacles going into Knight's spine, along with an alluring looking woman lifted up behind his back.

El Elyon spoke to Kaufman, "This is the spirit of Jezebel, and it is very controlling and manipulative. Its purpose is to intimidate you, get you on the defense, or have you feel sorry for it. You must be wise to its ways and not allow the messages that it sends through Dean Knight to set into your soul, lest it look for any fear, in which to drive you mad."

Kaufman saw his own armor, a gleaming bright silver, almost like that of a mirror that reflected light all over the room. In the rays of light bursting forth, he saw angels stationed as a battalion ready for battle, should Jezebel do anything to harm Kaufman. It was as though the light rays opened his eyes to see the angels, and in confidence he remained silent, until El Elyon had given him direction on what to say.

Time froze, and this time Dean Knight remained still. He usually was able to operate in the spirit realm for the dark side, but since he was consumed with many distractions due to the failings of his plot, he was unable to see in the spirit. Kaufman's hands lit up, where he looked at the blue fire, like a jewel in each palm, as he heard El Elyon say, "Hold your hands toward Jezebel, for this is the time of her torment."

Kaufman held his hands forward, at which time Jezebel manifested all the more, while the blue flame released the Ancient Language into her mind, tormenting her. Her hair turned into a bed of snakes like Medusa, moving towards Kaufman attempting to bite him. The octopus tentacles under her dress began jiggling around and moving, revealing that the Ancient Language's torment was working in nullifying her attack personally against him.

Out of his mouth came the words, "Your rule in this region will come to an end shortly."

Although her mouth was shut, she sent thoughts to his mind, trying to intimidate him as to what her plans were against each group member, looking for the deepest fear hidden within each one. Whether it was health, finances, marriage or children, her intent was to get Vladamore and his team to carry out the attack of lying serpents and release the slime, to weigh the team members down with the distractions of this present age, so she could drive her fears into their souls, like spears being thrown in battle.

Her messages were like spears, and once they hit their target, they sent her opponents in fear for their life, where the amygdala, the place of fear conditioning in the brain, was over stimulated, releasing thoughts from the subconscious that were primal in nature, for man to survive, inducing terror of immediate life threats, making her victim paralyzed.

Then she would use her tentacles on her victim's heads, putting each tentacle on the brain of her prey, laying them on the frontal cortex, the place of executory functioning, which was the area of the brain used as a weapon against her assault. She did not want any interruption in the mental assaults of her victims, keeping them defenseless and unable to fight back. The pressure of this assault on the mind of a person was obvious, like a vice grip squeezing the head.

However, she was unable to reach her tentacles towards Kaufman, and her eyes turned red while the stench of reddish smoke came out of her ears. The angels standing on guard in the room unsheathed their swords ready to fight the ruling power, should she attack Kaufman.

They were huge and of all different tones of color, wearing beautiful armor, some a brilliant gold, others a bronze and still others silver. They were over 9 feet tall, with an intimidating stature and presence against the powers of darkness. Looking at Kaufman they nodded, to which El Elyon directed him, by lighting up the whip at his side that had the keys within.

Kaufman took the whip and flicked it around Jezebel's cords in Knight's spine and said, "I bind you in the authority of this Sword, and I command you to not speak, nor use your tentacles on the campus of Strytan."

The angels quickly put their swords up and as Kaufman came back to real-time, where Knight was standing before him, he exited the meeting with, "I ask respectfully, that you not call me back to your office Dean Knight, unless there is good reason, such as a matter about my teaching or classes. Goodbye."

Door now shut, Knight stood still, when Jezebel began to feed him messages of terror to what she was going to do to him and his family, if he did not obey. He bent over in a fetal position in the corner of the room, saying over and over again, "No, please no, I will do it." Simultaneously, Constugard communicated to Knight through the Black Ball in the basement of The Gatehouse, which was connected to Knight's soul. All the members had a cord from the Black Ball to their soul, where demons would send messages from the Gates of Hell.

Constugard did not know patience, and with Beelzebub on the way soon, more terror was inflicted on Knight's soul, as he said, "You call this an Ancient Gatehouse? What a ridiculous fool you are, thinking that you are doing anything. If you do not follow through with dismantling their plans, then I will dismantle you!"

Memories of trauma, that had been stored up in Knight's hippocampus, were released, like a Tsunami of terror overtaking his mind, where he then pleaded for Constugard to stop. These memories made Knight defenseless to saying no to Beelzebub decades ago when finding out what The Ancient Gatehouse was all about.

Growing up under his father, he had no clue as to the Gatehouse's purpose, until he was sixteen years old and brought in as an early initiate. Legacies were permitted to enter early. Once in, everything seemed normal, like a men's club that met once a week, having laughter and talking about life, along with reading these quotes out of the handbook. He never knew what went on in the basement, until he was eighteen, at which time, the torment of his father's abuse while growing up, was a hook in his soul, by which demons could torment him into obedience.

Heart rebellious and full of anger, made him a prime target for The Ancient Gatehouse; he would be a good puppet for the ruling powers. There was no thought as to whom would be president once his father died of an untimely death that spooked the whole town. He was found outside of the city in the woods, with his skull crushed and all of his limbs broken. Although the sheriff conducted an investigation, it was closed, finding no conclusive evidence, other than ritualistic markings all over his body, with DNA sampling, identifying that the DNA found was not anything of this world.

Knight was heavy into the darkness, not yielding to the many occasions that El Elyon sent messengers of Wisdom to him, to persuade him. However, his mind was already made, and it was his life's mission to do whatever Beelzebub needed.

Moving Ahead

Thursday night, it was time again to meet at the Prophet's house, although they addressed him by his first name to others, within the Ancient Language Seeker's Club, Robert was known as *the Prophet*.

They each had their addiction, enjoying it outside on the patio at *The Grind*. Milly, Parker and Tony, leisured in the brief moment before they went to their respective classes, taking in all that their senses allowed.

Tony made mention of a young lady, who was a junior at Strytan and member of the congregation at St. Timothy's Cathedral, whom he had come to know recently; they had seen each other before but never had formally been introduced. He was looking forward to their coffee date this evening, while Parker and Milly would be at the Prophet's house.

"So what is her name," Milly asked.

"I believe you know her; she said you two were friends. Her name is Dana Dryer."

"Yes, I love her," Milly giggled "and am happy you two have met."

Tony was excited he had a place to hangout on Thursday evenings, trying not to be to jealous of Milly and Parker's meetings with the Prophet. "Well, at least I'll have a place to hangout now on Thursday evenings," he said jokingly.

Parker stretched out his hand, saying, "Listen, I had no clue I would have such favor in going to the Prophet's house, but you know its all about connections." He flipped up the collar on his shirt and put his sunglasses on, acting cool.

Milly laughed and replied, "Yes, you have connections alright; your connection is called Milly!"

They all laughed while finishing up their drinks. Out of the corner of their eye they saw professors Mercer, Peyton and Kaufman walking from the Library, towards Truman Hall. Seeing that no one was around The Ancient Language Seekers, the professors walked up to them. The group could tell that Kaufman had something pressing that he wanted to share, and turned to a more serious tone.

"Hey guys, so glad you three are here," said Kaufman. They waited to see what his news would be. "I want to tell you that Dean Knight is doing all that he can to come against all of those in the group, to which I am sure like myself, you have already experienced." The group nodded.

Parker replied, "If you only knew."

Kaufman continued, "Right, I am sure if it was anything like my encounter yesterday, that you saw in the spirit right away that he is being controlled by Jezebel."

"That is the truth," Parker shouted, and then looked around, putting his hand over his mouth, hoping that it was not too obtuse.

Mercer chimed in, "I think it is important for us to not be alone all the time on campus, in case he tries to corner one of us. Moreover, if he asks you to come to his office, I think it is necessary for you to ask for a letter of intent regarding the meeting, keeping as many hurdles in front of him, before he brings you in."

Professor Peyton ended the meeting with the saying, "Wise as a serpent and gentle as a dove."

They all agreed, and then each one went their way. Dean Knight had been staring out of his window while the group met. Anger seeped from his skin, like a mustard colored orange mix of putrid stench, smelling like a sewer. He loathed the individuals and hated it all entirely when they came together as a group.

Reaching into his pocket for a small black ball, he rubbed it and tried to conjure up Constugard. "Constugard, are you there watcher, I have need of your dark skills." Knight waited as he looked intently for the demon's appearing.

"Yes, what is it watchman? What do you need?" Constugard was eager to answer Knight, since they desired the same outcome, which was for Beelzebub to be satisfied with their work.

"In about 2 hours the team members that are here at Strytan will be going to their particular assignments, one of which tonight is the Prophet's house. I was able to go in the spirit, while they met, and overheard their conversation. If you can station a demonic assault against their going, it would further our efforts for the plan."

Constugard made noises as if he were thinking, and then began a deep shrieking laugh, replying, "I know exactly what to do, leave it to me Dark Knight." On occasion, Constugard called Bobby Knight, Dark Knight; that is what he was known as to Beelzebub. Although a crony, he was still looked at as powerful, in the 33rd level of The Ancient

Gatehouse, the men were made warlocks, and worked with other warlocks and witches over regions.

Bobby had his list of dark conspirators, who did black magic, and texted the ones necessary to send as many assaults as possible in Springfield, knowing the hour that was upon them of Beelzebub's coming. He was eager to have him boast of his dark deeds, imagining already his name being mentioned among the hordes of hell.

"Hell would respect him now," he thought.

Constugard called Vladamore, allowing his team to assist on the effort, to take out the group headed to the Prophet's house. Their plans were to take over one of the 18-wheeler trucks on the country road in route, and get the driver distracted or sleepy so that he would veer off and hit their vehicles. In two vehicles, the Doctors Mercer and Kaufman rode in one vehicle, while Milly and Parker rode in her Bug. On the back road, Farmer's Plot Road, to the Prophet's house, a huge 18-wheeler in front of them began to swerve.

Professor Mercer was concerned that the big truck might swerve too much, where the driver would lose control. Seeing her anxiety, her husband laid his palm down on the horn. Milly and Parker were concerned and wondered what was going on in front of them, as they followed the Doctors Mercer and Kaufman.

Inside of the 18-wheeler, the older man driving had many issues of anger and guilt, to which Vladamore's militia demons, Heradacio and Dadanel released a grenade, with stench smells going up in the spirit, filling the cab of the truck. The driver then became angry with Alan blowing his horn, taking it personally.

Following that, Heradacio let out a cannonball of lying serpents, of which three attached to him, one on his head, and two others on his heart. Hooks pulling on the issues of his past caused him to be all the more fired up at Alan blowing the horn, to which he began swerving on purpose, scaring them all the more.

This poor soul had so many wounds from his past that he was a walking time bomb ready to explode. He rolled down the window and began giving the group the bird as he slurred words, unintelligible to make out, but letting the group know that he was mad.

Seeing the assault, Professor Mercer said, "This is a spiritual attack, we must see in the spirit."

Professor Kaufman and Alan agreed, to which they all began to speak in the Ancient Language. Blue fire came out of their mouth, moving upon the truck driver. Uncertain of what the fire would do, they knew that something would come and move this hindrance out of the way.

Milly and Parker saw the blue fire coming out of the vehicle in front of them, and immediately followed suit speaking in the Ancient Language, remembering that Robert told them of its potent powers. As the entire group spoke in the Ancient Language, while behind the 18-wheeler, the blue flame formed a whirlwind around the man, releasing a hot fire that burned the snakes up, pulling them from the man's soul.

The man began to come to his senses, realizing how carried away he had gotten with road rage, that he knew he had to get off the road and cool off. His wife had told him many times over of how he would get in rages on the road, but he had no clue why; he couldn't see into the spirit, of the lying serpents that would speak to him while in those altercations, in order to realize the demonic realm was attacking. He always took it to a personal issue with his character, never realizing it was a spiritual issue influencing his behavior.

He began to weep, knowing that he had given into the horrid behavior that he so deeply loathed. It was insane to him that he allowed himself to get so easily bothered, returning to this type of conduct. The two vehicles passed by slowly with the group inside, to which, in passing, they saw him weeping in his truck, knowing that somehow the power of the Ancient Language persuaded him to stop.

Constugard knew instantaneously that the plot did not work, having the underlings reporting the details to him. He was racked by pain, as if the Ancient Language was already released, and began to use Latin words like a madman cursing at something. "Beelzebub will never let me live this down!" he said fuming, crouched over the Gatehouse, waiting and looking out for his liege's arrival. "He will be arriving soon. The gates of hell have to enlarge!"

Rattled by the warfare, each of them looked forward to the wisdom that Robert would bring this evening, as they arrived safely at his house. Seeing *him* brought each of them a sense of comfort, like pulling up for a Sunday evening to spend time with *Pop Pop*. Front yard covered with a variety of mums, purple, orange, yellow and crimson, made his house all the more inviting and festive.

They could not wait to get inside, like children getting off of a bus to head home. Each one had their designated place in the front sitting room, where they would drink coffee; it had become a welcomed tradition. Robert made each of them a Keto-Coffee, telling them, "El Elyon told me what happened to you on the way."

He made these particular drinks, for their brain recovery. The coconut oil medium chain triglyceride, he said, would cross the blood brain barrier and bring more calm to their mind, as well as stirring their intellect.

"So tell me what happened."

Parker and Alan, tag teamed from the two different perspectives of each vehicle, each one animated while the group continued sipping on their drink. They gave each other a high five after talking about what El Elyon did with the blue flame and the Ancient Language, thrilled at the fact that the truck driver came to his senses.

"It's interesting that you two chose to speak; today is about your giftings and what El Elyon has planned for the group, as it relates to the Central Nervous System attack, I believe what you, Alan, call CNS. Also Parker, it is not happenstance that you are in this group; your major is neurobiology." Robert tilted his head down a bit, while throwing his eyes up at the two men who were still standing and eager to hear what he had to say.

"You can sit down if you like Lads, and enjoy your drink; you will need it for what I am about to share. Also, get your recorder out; you will want to record this."

With another high-five, the two men sat down and looked at one another, sensing that the information Robert would provide would be more than stimulating for their brainier minds. Alan shuffled through his briefcase and pulled out his mini recorder, pressing the red button to record. Milly enjoyed seeing Parker so animated with Alan, as well as taking in Professor Mercer's facial expressions during their story, making it all the more enjoyable.

Robert stood up and walked to the fireplace; stoking the fire in the warm hearth, he paused, and then clapped his hands, "Let us begin."

The group was sitting up at attention, Milly and Parker in the chairs, and the Doctors Mercer and Kaufman on the old twill couch. A fire blazing and drinks in hand could not make this a better meet, at least not just yet.

"PRINA, as you know is a top physicists brain child of the dark societies. It is true that there are physicists in there who have no clue of what is going on. But all in all, there are many contributors inside of PRINA, some of the greatest minds in the world, that have created a particle accelerator, not only for looking into the research of dark matter that results from particles colliding, but also as a means to harm mankind."

Like moviegoers at a show, they were listening and quiet, wanting to hear each line. Cups lifted up to their mouths, their ears were wide open and oriented towards his speaking, to capture every word that came out of Robert's mouth.

"PRINA has a planned date, this coming week, in which they intend to charge up the particle accelerator and create more anti matter that will be a magnet for dark matter. Many have speculated, that PRINA will attempt to create a singularity, opening up a parallel universe where they will altar time here."

Hushed, no one in the group said a word as they listened. "This parallel universe has a correlation with what many have already experienced, as what is known as the Mandela Effect. Of course, the powers of darkness created this and announced it to the world."

He paused and educated them on the requirement of El Elyon, making the dark powers openly reveal their plots. "What El Elyon did to Beelzebub and his army, after taking the blue flame from him, is to require that they announce their assaults to the world. Beelzebub is limited, where as El Elyon is not."

"When they announce their demonic assaults to the world, most of the time, it is not obvious at what they plan to do; many times they speak in code through different military operations that are carried out, airplanes that crash, boats that sink or go missing, etc. Cryptic messages are buried within each happening, relaying the assault and intention of their plans within."

"On the other hand, the grid that they have is for purposes of communicating to one another, as well as carrying out their plans. It works with the Egyptian pyramids, connecting with the other pyramids across the world."

"I bet you did not know that there is a pyramid in Ohio, did you?" They shook their head acknowledging their obliviousness to the pyramid. "The grid is used for both sending messages as well as carrying out attacks against humans. With the Coptic writings in Mildred Lee's journals, there is information about the CNS assault, which cross references with the ancient relic's Aramaic writing of the book of Daniel."

"I digress and do not mean to get off on a tangent. Let me return to the matter at hand, about a *parallel universe* and the Mandela Effect; these two have common components and interrelation. First, the parallel universe is not what most people think, like a parallel earth, but rather, it is an opening in the universe by the powers of darkness, that have worked swiftly for thousands of years, working with quantum computers and engineering, to create a *matrix*, putting human souls that are vulnerable, into a deep sleep, where they then come to perceive differently about things in the earth, than they *really* are." He paused and stated briefly, "They are put in an alternate state of mind, hijacking their soul to be bound to a different time and timeline."

Parker looked perplexed to which Robert responded. "For example, what if you went to see a movie and afterwards wanted to watch it time and time again, and because you liked it so much, you decide to buy it. Now, let's say you watched that movie over forty times and after having done so, I would speculate that you would know most of the important lines, by that time." He paused and then asked the group, "Right?"

They nodded in agreement.

"Now, if your brain was susceptible to this CNS attack, your orientation of what you believe, known as self schema would be changed, causing your entire perception to be different. Self-schema is the composition of all your memories that are constantly telling you, who you are."

"But this is the thing; there is not only a self-schema, but also a *universe schema*, where the universe has its own reality, according to what others perceive about it. For those that are vulnerable to the CNS attack, both their self-schema and universe schema change. Little by little, they wake up each morning, believing they are who they believe themselves to be, and that the universe is as it should be, making it a self-fulfilling prophecy.

"Little by little through this attack, things change daily, where in time, people do not know who they are, nor what the universe is, allowing Beelzebub's interruptions, where changing the times and laws is easier, because our minds become dismantled."

The group was stunned and alarmed at the thought that something like this could occur. Alan was on the edge of his seat, while Parker buried his face in his hands, trying to fathom how something on so large of a scale could happen across the globe.

Robert went on with the discussion, looking at Milly, "Back in your Great Grandmother's day, the accelerator was not ready and instead, Beelzebub used the grid for brainwashing, working on a smaller scale of this universe-schema, and Springfield was protected because of Mildred." He stood tall in front of the fireplace, leaning his elbow on the mantle, as he waited for his prior sentences to sink into the minds of those present.

"The particle accelerator's purpose is to open a singularity to another parallel universe, which is analogous to, a rice field of the souls of mankind, where demons make them living batteries. Sounds like the movie, *The Matrix*, right?"

Everyone could not believe what he or she was hearing come from Robert's mouth. It was as if they stepped into a Sci-fi movie. He knew that it was overwhelming, which is why he had Alan record the meeting, knowing that the group would have to revisit the information again.

"When they start the singularity, it will open a parallel universe. If your brain is susceptible to this attack, there will be a connection established to your soul and the other universe, which will appear to your mind to be this exact earth, with the same time and the same people. However, sadly it is all a show, that is being pumped into the brains of those that are sucked into its deception."

Parker's mouth was opened as Robert spoke. "I see you are getting it Parker, it's a huge one Lad." Parker nodded.

"This parallel universe is all a smokescreen to what really is happening. Rather, it is a rice field for the souls of mankind, in which they become zombified into a state of existence providing demons more time, to which they think they can delay their doom. Demons believe that the only way they can avoid judgment day with El Elyon, is to keep mankind alive forever, imprisoning the souls they transport to the other universe, sucking out the soul's energy, like Jezebel and her tentacles suck life out of the brain."

"If your brain is not protected when this singularity is opened up, you will believe a new story line, same story, just a little change, not to much, at least right now, in order to make you believe that you are in the same universe, when in reality, your mind is somewhere else. They mesh another stream of thought, feeding you another earth, while you are coexisting in your present life as a zombie. Our universe has been experiencing what is known as a Beta Test over the last few years, in what is called the Mandela Effect, preparing for the big 'crossover' of the souls of mankind.

Alan asked, "So Robert, you are saying that, the timeline that their soul sees in the parallel universe is communicated to their brain here in this universe, all the while believing that this universe is really where they are."

"Yes Lad, you have it!" Robert exclaimed.

"Now, back to that movie that I mentioned earlier, where you know every line. The way in which they are testing the effect of the parallel universe on our souls with the Mandela effect, is by changing one line here and there on the popular movies, to get us to think that the lines have always been how they are, seeing if everyone will buy into it. Those whose brains have been protected from the Beta Test are awake and still have the traces of memories to know the original lines of the movie."

Alan spoke up, "Yes, I have heard of the Mandela Effect and was not sure how that would play in, as well as the parallel universe."

"Right Alan, many believe and remember Nelson Mandela dying in 1991 in prison, and people witness to the fact that they saw the funeral on television, having details etched in their mind. However, according to what we know as of 2012 he is still alive."

Professor Mercer, wowed by Robert's explanation, picked up her notebook, and feverishly searched through it. It was a large bulky brown three-ring binder that she carried everywhere. Filled with dates and what happened during different times in history. She created it while in high school, and continued on through her major, and now her profession. She looked in the year 1991, let her index finger scroll down the page, and there it was. Written in her notebook, in her handwriting *July 23, 1991 Nelson Mandela died and a nation grieves its great loss.*

Eyes bigger than golf balls, she held her notebook up; she was perplexed and alarmed, "It's here! He did die! Why is it that he is alive again? How could that be? If he died in 1991 how could he be alive now in 2012?"

Notebook opened on the table, everyone's head leaned in, as if looking at a treasure map, wanting to see the location of the treasure. Her handwriting from 1991 was their treasure, and seeing her insertion inside of the three-ring binder made them a believer.

Robert told them that it was very good that they were recording the meeting, letting them know that once the parallel universe was opened up, that the actual timeline here on earth could be interrupted in which they would attempt to change the time, which would then affect things such as Professor Mercer's notebook and would not be recorded.

"What can we do about this," asked Alan, and how much has changed during this Beta test that we know of."

"To answer your question about the Beta Test, much was done. Changes are evidenced in popular movies, with the movie lines and titles, as well as branding names for products, and scriptures in the Bible, one of which is about the Lion laying down with the Lamb. In addition, other big changes are people who were believed dead, such as Mandela, and a few other well-known people. It is larger than you realize, and is only the beginning."

Alarmed at all that he was hearing, Alan asked, "What can be done about this?"

"Until we shut down the weapon that is being used at PRINA to open the singularity, the Ancient Language is our tool; it enters the airways and breaks down the polarity of the atmosphere, making it more difficult for their particle accelerator to work. This is another reason why Beelzebub and all the demons hate the Ancient Language; it hinders their plans. With the towers in the area rising up, the release of the Ancient Language increases, causing the demons to writhe in pain; their grid is shut down and inoperable!"

"Their weapon is made from the slime of hell, which is seen through the dark society, The Ancient Gatehouse, that was built on the idea of workers with ancient stone, building gatehouses. We can see this in history, with their slime in the building of the tower of Babel, in the ancient days. Where it is written, *'And they said one to another, Go to, let us make brick, and burn them thoroughly. And they had brick for stone, and slime had they for morter.'"*[xix]

"*Slime* here in Hebrew is ***chêmâr*** pronounced ***khay-mawr'*** and the root word from which it comes means trouble. However, what is more telling is the Hebrew letters that compose it, revealing the word picture of this attack; they are Chet, Mem and Resh. Chet means, secret place and separate. Mem means massive or chaos, as well as indicating flooding. Resh means, head, highest and person. Therefore, the word picture for slime is, BEING SEPARATED IN THE SECRET PLACE BY

THE CHAOS THAT COMES INTO YOUR PERSON MASSIVELY LIKE A FLOOD."

Parker shook his head, raised his hand, "What! Can you repeat that?"

"Yes," Robert said. "It means that you are separated within in your heart, by the chaos that has flooded your person. This is the slime of the enemy, that built the towers of Babel, and it is the same element used for the particle accelerator, which is to flood every human mind with chaos."

Robert emphasized, "Understand, your weapon to fight this *is* The Ancient Language."

"Wow," exclaimed Milly, who was surging with excitement at the thought of the power of the Ancient Language.

Robert looked at them, to make the point. "You said that while you were driving over here, that the 18-wheeler was being driven by a man who was in rage. However, what changed the situation? When you opened your mouth and all of you began to speak the Ancient Language, the blue flame from the tower that was within you, flowed out and was sent to that driver's mind, breaking the assignment of demonic strongholds, speaking to him at the time. You, lads and lassies, have become towers!"

Kaufman sat there trying to rationalize the spiritual matter. Robert knew he was wrestling with the thought and turned to him. "Professor Kaufman, you teach philosophy which, on all accounts, is as mysterious a subject matter as science is at times. Things are organic when it comes to the subject of philosophy and is always evolving. Yes?"

"Yes Robert, they are."

"Very well, do you consider Benjamin Franklin somewhat of a philosopher himself, as well as the scientist and statesman that he was?"

"Yes Robert, I do."

"Franklin said *'Progress is impossible without change, and those who cannot change their minds, cannot change anything. When it becomes more difficult to suffer than change - then you will change. When you're finished changing, you're finished."* *Benjamin Franklin*

"Benjamin Franklin knew that all things changed with our thoughts, as we accelerated from the Bronze Age into the Industrial Revolution. Likewise, he knew that the application of this *change* would be most astutely applied to our mind, which is constantly learning."

Kaufman was getting it! "Yes, I see Robert!"

Eager to share the revelation, he asked Robert if he could expound on the thought to the group, to which Robert chuckled and responded, "Why yes Lad, please do!"

Milly and Parker felt they were in the best philosophy class ever, with Kaufman sharing his new found revelation to them. They were tucked back in their seats, like kids listening to a Christmas story, with the warm fire burning. Steaming hot drinks now in their bellies, they listened.

"What Robert is sharing with us, is that all advancements that we have seen in the universe always evolve out of *the need to change*, and the emphasis here is on the word *need*. A need manifests in our lives, as we encounter difficulty. Without difficulty we would not need anything.

"Correct Robert?"

"Yes Lad," Robert responded.

Kaufman returned back to his revelation, "Technology is always the engine of every invention, but once we begin to advance into a new era, we basically dream ourselves out of the old one, and into the new; the resources that are within our soul show up when we know our need. The need for the new technology advances us from one era to another. But you have to know in that era, that you have a need, which then reveals the technology that is waiting to be invented!"

"What! That is C.R.A.Z.Y, crazy!" Parker was beside himself.

Kaufman went on. "You cannot advance into a new era, without knowing the need you have for that advancement. Likewise, because of these CNS attacks, we see that the prior warnings from the Coptic monks about the demonic grid, reveals that they knew advancements *would come* in time, for the need they saw back then. They knew the enemy was interrupting the airwaves, and wrote it down, so that people in our era, having and realizing the need, would then dream the solution, which we now know is The Ancient Language!"

Kaufman wanted to shout and dance; he was like a boy in high school at the Spring Dance, as he held his hands up and turned around in the small space in which he was standing, shouting, "Woo Hoo!"

The whole group broke out in laughter, with Milly first chuckling, having her hand over her mouth. Parker, with both hands covering his mouth was caught up in the moment, too. Finally, Alan bent over to his knees, couldn't stop snorting while he laughed, and Anjali grabbing her belly had a laugh so deep within her soul, that it was not even heard. You could tell she was laughing but the volume was locked up in her soul.

Robert was up on his feet clapping at the profound revelation Kaufman shared with the group, reveling over the gift that had manifest of Wisdom, knowing that the Ancient Language was being poured out more, as the door in the heavens surely was opening up. They were under an open heaven of Wisdom, feeling caught up in the rapture of each thought conveyed, that they did not want the moment to end.

Kaufman finally got a hold of himself, and sat down, hands on his knees while his back was against the couch, still soaking in the truth he discovered.

"Now that ladies and gents," Robert said, "is why the hordes of hell are mad; you have *the mother of inventions*, so to speak, that will thwart their plans, which is the Wisdom from above, with the release of an Ancient Language that is more potent than time itself; existing outside of time. You do not now how to speak it, but the part of your brain that the blue flame operates in, causes you to trust El Elyon's purpose, as you yield to speaking a language you do not know, which in time, is interpreted to you from El Elyon's Spirit."

"In the texts we examined in the last meeting, with Psalm 48:12 and 4-6, we saw the terror that the Ancient Language brings against ruling powers and principalities. This will be the firewall to protect Springfield. You are seeing the advancement of the tower at Strytan and have been marked by it, as a tower yourself. Moreover, there is another tower rising right outside of town, which will defeat the gates of hell all the more at The Ancient Gatehouse."

"The Ancient Gatehouse was started by Beelzebub for the sole purpose of planting the gates of hell in regions. However, the towers of El Elyon will defeat hell's gates."

"I might add one last thing before you go; El Elyon has given us another weapon, which is our diet. When we are fueled by ketones, instead of glucose, we do not have as many toxins in our body, and the ketones in our blood stream create metabolic pathways of good genetic expression, while turning off the bad genes. In addition, ketones pass the blood-brain barrier, providing greater clarity of mind and focus, so that you are able to do all that El Elyon requires of you for His tasks.

"Beelzebub knows of this diet and the power it has to change lives, which is why he infiltrated our food products through dark societies and people in high places, creating processed foods, GMO products, as well as plastics within most others. It is necessary for you to be at an optimal level in functioning as a tower of El Elyon, which is the symbol of a watchman. This comes from the game of chess, when the rook in the past, used to be called the tower. The tower is the symbol of a watchman. I ask you to consider changes in your lifestyle if you have not already made them and talk to your doctor about the diet, should you decide to get on it."

Milly shared how it had changed her life; she had an epileptic seizure when very young, and the doctor recommended to her parents about placing her on the diet, to which the family has stayed on since. The group took in the information, and then everyone got up, ready to leave.

Bidding them farewell from the door, Robert waved saying, "Be careful watchmen and know that things are always changing, but are we ready for that change?"

Chapter 13 The Chapter of Dreams

The night active, with angelic hosts dispersed throughout Springfield fighting the hordes of hell, was a sight to those who could see. Hell was releasing the slime of chaos and evil from the different tanks, red, green and clear slime, oozed through the cords. Activity was heightened at The Ancient Gatehouse, as Bobby Knight and the other Gatehouse members met, performing all kinds of diabolical and evil rituals, where the sounds of torment and laughter, bled from the building into the atmosphere, in the midnight hour.

Knight, and the other members were employing their black magic. The gates of hell were swelling up, like an inflatable air balloon, used for activities at a birthday party. Only this was nothing to play with. As the gates of hell enlarged, the moaning and groaning of the souls captured within, shrill voices ripping through the air, heard by those awake in the spirit.

Clever Gadget

El Elyon had other plans for the members of the group this night, giving them assignments and instructions in their sleep. Dreams poured out upon their minds, like a simulation in their soul, believable as reality itself. With each dream simulation, the person's senses were awakened stirring up the amygdala, as well as the mirror neurons, making their interaction with the dream three-dimensional.

Dr. Alan Mercer was asleep in the bed with his wife Anjali, who had drifted off an hour before him. Face turned toward the window, he felt the slight chill of the night creep through the windowsill that he had not yet fixed. He and Anjali lived in an older home, and had not gotten around to changing out all their windows.

As the chill came over his face, he became aware of the sensations he was experiencing in the dream simulation he was now in. El Elyon lifted him over Springfield, showing Alan, Beelzebub's grid over the town. It was a fiery red holographic grid, where messages traveled through it, similar to how Milly described the keys in the whip. Except, the messages traveling through the grid were shaped like darts.

El Elyon pulled out one of the darts and broke the tip off, exposing a black stench, releasing a sulfur smell that was to attack the nervous system. Then, El Elyon brought up a holograph of a brain, demonstrating what happens once the dart hits a person's mind. Toxins ooze into the brain, reaching the frontal cortex and the amygdala, shutting down the hippocampus. If the person became stressed they could have a seizure.

El Elyon demonstrated the inner workings of Beelzebub's plan with the grid releasing the fiery darts, and then took Alan to Strytan where the tower was rising. He wanted to show Alan the effect that the tower had on the brain, as well as its ability to overcome Beelzebub's darts.

In The Quad where the majestic crystal tower stood, the same holograph representing a person's brain was suspended in front. The blue flame shot across the atmosphere and encircled the brain, like a helmet tightly fit on a football player's head. El Elyon reached for the dart in Beelzebub's grid and broke it open to release the stench, to which the blue flame totally destroyed it. Alan was mesmerized by the power of El Elyon's blue flame against the dark evil of Beelzebub.

El Elyon gave Alan the coordinates in the city, to which he would bring a particular device that Alan had been working on over the last ten years, which he dubbed, *The Rock*. The name stuck, since it was the name of his first pet dog, a brown colored Chesapeake Bay Retriever, which looked like a rock when it lay down on the ground.

Years ago, in the middle of medical school, the idea of the contraption popped into his head, when he had sketched it out briefly, saving for a later date. After being out of his medical residency three years, he was given more clarity in creating the apparatus, uncertain as to the full potential of its performance at the time. He was compelled to create it this year, when within his soul, there was a drive to hurry up with its completion, feeling that he must have it finished by July.

Dr. Mercer tested *The Rock* briefly at the end of July, when lightning storms came into Springfield, curious as to its success. Two particular storm systems came through Springfield with increased amounts of lightning strikes, capturing the attention of many meteorologists nationwide. It broke history records, for all the states, labeling Springfield as *God's Lightning Rod.*

Alan tested it not only to see if the gadget would interfere with the storm, but also the specially designed antennas around it were able to send out light wave frequencies. He stood in the path of the device, certain that it would send light waves towards his mind, and sure enough it happened!

The waves released in the atmosphere moved towards him from the antenna, increasing the use of the neurons in his brain, spine and stomach, as well as creating new neural pathways in his brain. He tested his mental capacity picking up on seismic activities in the ground during the storms occurrence, where he had a heightened sense of the atmosphere.

After the experience, he pulled up the recordings of seismic activity in the area and found an exact match to his own discoveries. The fact that the frequency of light waves heightened his mental capacity showed him that the blue flame could do much more for the group during the CNS attack, where they could dismantle the frequency of darkness meant to harm the citizens of Springfield.

El Elyon gave him the inspiration and was ready for it to be used in concert with the tower this coming week during the battle. The device would scramble the polarity of Beelzebub's grid, dismantling its workings. The Ancient Language would then be able to reach to the slime that hell was discharging from its cords, incinerating the devilish ooze. The interesting thing was that Parker was in Alan's dream, letting him know that Parker was to assist.

Science Fair Project

Meanwhile, Parker was given a similar dream, where he was assisting Alan. Very humble, Parker was filled with much gifting when it came to the brain, and for this dream simulation to be occurring gave him much elation.

The neurobiological science experiment he did, as a junior in high school, came back to his memory. A brainiac to the core, one would not know by looking at him; he appeared like one of the guys who was, "the cool guy." Being cool and a brainiac did not go together at times, so Parker had two different personalities that he would take on, according to what hat he was wearing at the time.

His high school science experiment was brilliant, as he stupefied the judges, demonstrating the art and power of brainwaves. His subjects were given thoughts to think on for a week that were written on a worksheet, listing positive things that could happen, such as, getting much needed money, having a promotion at work, being thrown a celebration, and so forth.

In addition, he had another group that was given a worksheet on negative things such as, losing their money, losing their job and being put on social media as a horrible person. After a week of looking at their respective worksheets, the subjects came to a clinic, where the doctor allowed Parker to have a nurse assist him in using the EEG (electroencephalogram) to measure the subjects' brainwaves.

While the EEG was attached and being performed, Parker read off the list, the thoughts he had them think on for the week, and then followed it up with the other sheet, which they were not given. His findings were interesting; the ones who had the positive thoughts had stronger brain wave function, while being read the good sheet, and maintained that consistent function even when the negative sheet was read.

On the other hand, those who were given the negative sheet to focus on all week had 30 percent less brainwave activity during the EEG, while being read both sheets. It was then that Parker discovered the power of thoughts and what it does to a person's brain. Little did he know that El Elyon gave him the experiment years ago, which led him to study neurobiology.

In the dream, El Elyon showed Parker the necessity to identify thoughts given to him from the ruling power of Divination attacking him in an earlier dream. Parker felt the intensity of fear in his amygdala that was short-circuiting his ability to process in the frontal lobe effectively and pull on good thoughts. El Elyon instructed Parker that the blue flame would assist in protecting the mind, along with the Ancient Language; the two were one.

Next, El Elyon showed Parker the battle that they would be in, as he and the group would overcome the demons of hell. It was crazy; blue fire came out of their brains in a wave pattern, annihilating the red, green and colorless slime, where it had no effect on them.

EL Elyon put emphasis on the group's thoughts being placed on a favorable outcome from the power of the Ancient Language. As their focus stayed fixed on that, they would not be moved by the activities manifested through others being used by Beelzebub's demons. There would be so much demonic activity that the group would have to be laser focused on the Ancient Language, in order to overcome.

Parker knew his role in Friday's meeting would entail shifting the group's focus to the favorable outcome, where their face would be set like flint in the heat of battle. He felt like William Wallace in Brave Heart, preparing a speech in his heart.

Ancient Cavern

Meanwhile, Professor Mercer lay in her bed, sound asleep, where the simulation given to her by El Elyon, placed her in an ancient cavern, huge in height. Stalactites covered the enormous ceiling, appearing as transparent crystal, branching from the cathedral like ceiling, distributing light throughout.

Within the middle of the cavern she saw El Elyon's ancient cobalt blue sapphire table ***lâcham*** that had shards of lightning shooting within. She would see ghost like images of the angelic hosts coming into view, then fading out, as she saw the revelry of the last meeting, knowing that the victory would be at hand for mankind's welfare. She could hear the speech of Tubal and Rafael, as the angelic hosts then joined in with shouts.

El Elyon then spoke to Anjali, "The lightning you see, is the power of My Ancient Language that, when distributed throughout the atmosphere, will proclaim hell's defeat, which will make them shrink in fear, crushing their black magic.

"Dean Knight and the members of The Ancient Gatehouse have committed abominable acts in darkness that feed the gates of hell. I need you Anjali, to open the Ancient Relic, repeating the Ancient

Language of Psalm 45:12 and 4-6, while Alan carries out My plans with the device I gifted him to create. What you see here in this majestic cave is a foretaste of the power of My Spirit that will be unleashed through the airwaves to interrupt hell's scheme. Like the lightning, My Spirit will be all over Springfield upsetting hell's folly, dismantling its assignments."

Overcome with the angels' meeting, Anjali wanted to get a closer look at the table and touch it. She had always been a curious person, even as a little girl, to where she felt drawn to find out what things were and what they meant. Consumed with thoughts of the blue sapphire table, El Elyon allowed her to walk near. One foot in front of the other, she edged to the table, reaching out her hand.

Slowly, the tips of the fingers on her right hand reached toward the table, fanned out, seemingly putting her hand in water. She felt the tip of her pinky slightly touch the table. Its touch was unlike anything she had known, as the sapphire felt alive with energy. She quickly laid down the rest of her fingers, where her palm was face down on the table.

Lightning shot across the great sapphire table, and she heard *His* voice, El Elyon's! "This is the voice from My throne, where I walk on the sapphire pavement, to where I send My agreement of the Ancient Language. You will know My voice as it is within My table, so it will also be in you; you will hear Me clearly and speak what I say when the time comes."

A Generational Curse

Kaufman, asleep in the reclining chair, had graded papers all night long. Still having an assignment lay on his belly in the middle of being critiqued, his eyes closed and he snored lightly. Within a few seconds, he entered into the simulated dream that El Elyon gave him.

Entering into an entirely new universe, from a distance while hovering in the sky, he saw there was hardly any light because of the smog that covered the horizon. Sun, blocked by the smog, kept it from shining, dinginess coating the ground, everything looked a dingy greyish-brown color. Rice fields and factories were all over the region, where much activity seemed to be taking place.

Coming in for a closer look he realized that the supposed rice fields he saw, were instead fields of the souls of mankind from all different ages, harvesting the energy of the souls in its captivity, where they were bound to the murky water in which they were entrenched that kept them asleep. People did not realize how much energy their soul exerted, and the demons considered it much like a battery for their use. However, El Elyon gave more of His energy to the souls of mankind as they came into His army, providing them with unlimited power. Hell could not tolerate any more recruits for El Elyon, posing as a threat to their plans.

Kaufman saw a singularity opening up over the sky, as the hideous creature Beelzebub entered, making gruesome sounds like snarling dogs that turned into eerie laughter. Each sound turned Kaufman's stomach, and he wondered what was occurring.

Norman was grieved and ready to come out of the simulation. However, peace came to his soul as El Elyon spoke, "I need you to see Norman, be brave, you are protected in My blue flame, invisible to the eyes of *this* world."

Kaufman held his breath and agreed to proceed, seeing bronze shoes over his feet that brought him a weighty assurance of his protection. El Elyon was with him, as he continued to keep his eyes open to see what he could; this information, although grotesque, was pertinent nonetheless.

Looking around, in between what looked like rice fields, were old factories, with a putrid smoke coming from them that filled the air, creating the smog that covered the horizon. Kaufman was brought closer to the factory, where he was taken through the exhaust area, and led down the pipe like a person on a slip and slide at a water park. He landed in a small cargo holder, much like a trough in which coals were put into, hooked to a line of other containers on wheels, going about a track laid throughout the factory.

Now, sitting in the cargo holder, El Elyon reminded him that he was still invisible to the creatures in this realm, and He needed him to see hell's workings. He watched as different underling demons worked profusely putting rocks into the troughs, feeding the *factory like* building with the rocks for the fire, which produced sludge like material for the contraptions that were hooked to the minds of those in the rice fields.

He went to the place, from which the rock was reaped, and ended up at the wall of the rock itself. It was the blackest black he had ever seen, made of substance that wasn't natural, oozing with what looked like black blood. The rock was making sounds of groaning as the underlings had a pickax, putting all their effort into breaking it into pieces.

The rock was put into the troughs, stationed on the track, and carried to a hot burning fire, like lava from a volcano. When entering the heat of the fire, the rock's structure was broken down into a liquid form, which was then placed into titanium looking containers, with a huge metal cord coming from it.

Kaufman followed the cord as he went through the walls of the building, in the air, hovering over the pathway, following it out to the brown murky water that housed thousands of souls. Heads lifted above the water, the souls keeping their mouth exposed to the dingy environment, were asleep.

A metal gadget, like a helmet, was upon each soul; tubes attached to it, seemed to feed the soul. The black ooze of the rock that had been melted down was being fed into the minds of the souls in the rice field. Demons went about the rice field, like watchmen at a prison, making sure the souls were monitored.

Being hooked up to the contraptions, the souls were making different emotional faces, joy on some, terror on others, while still the majority had no expression. Over each head, was a holographic screen, showing what was being fed and played within the mind of the soul. It was apparent that the soul was convinced that it was on earth, and going about their day, seeing the changes that had taken place with the Mandela effect, thinking that it was normal.

At times, you could see a soul resisting, to which one of the demons monitoring would notice, and jump on top of the metal contraption over the soul's head, turning up the amount of black sludge that would go into their brain.

In the back of the spine of each of the souls, were three huge cords hooked up, pulling on the energy of the soul. Inside of their nose, was a feeding tube contraption, where something like greyish slop went into them, feeding them substance into their soulish belly, so they would be given over to the appetites of the world they were in. The illusions given to the souls were worldly, making them crave the things of the present age, unable to recognize that it was an illusion. Kaufman was disgusted and in disbelief at what he saw occurring.

El Elyon spoke, "When you were young, I brought you into the study of philosophy, so that you could be a voice of truth and reason to others about truth, knowing a Wisdom beyond yourself, discerning between the dark wisdom and that which is truth. These people represent those who are being fed a false wisdom, but these souls that you see here, are caught between two paradigms, as their actual soul is here, being fed in the soulish realm, a substance to keep their soul asleep."

"Man is composed of body, soul and spirit. You are used to seeing the body and the spirit, as you have been made awake to the things of the spirit. Here, you are seeing the soulish realm and the souls of man, those who are asleep to what is going on."

Kaufman was mortified, not realizing that a soul could be caught in what appeared to be a purgatory. "What is this, and what does this mean?" He was panicking now, seeing that things were more critical than he realized.

El Elyon moved upon Kaufman through the shoes that he wore, releasing peace throughout his soul, as energy flowed upward, causing him to not be given over to the things of the soul, so he could hear what needed to be said. "I have brought you here, Norman, to show you things that are happening on a small scale. But soon, this will happen on a much larger scale, because Beelzebub means to bring more souls over to this place.

"The Mandela Effect is occurring to the souls that are captured in this parallel universe, and in mild form, is happening to those who are soon to be brought here. A singularity will be opened, to crossover the souls who are susceptible to the demonic powers operating on the grid. Once the darts are released from the grid and the toxin seeps into the mind, the soul can then be separated to this place by being put to sleep, wherein, they are in a constant dream state, being fed whatever the black sludge feeds it."

El Elyon continued, "It is necessary for you to see the critical nature of what is at stake in order for the towers to continue to rise. All of you will be like the rook on a chessboard, which was originally a tower. You will become towers with My Ancient Language, to help these souls. Towers are not only rising up in Springfield, but all across Area 9, where now, other men and women, and young people, are inspired by the sacrifice of your group, as angels have shown them your endeavors and spiritual battles against darkness."

"How does the soul become so deceived," Kaufman asked.

"As you see the holographic screens over the souls of mankind here, it represents the visions that are within their minds, being fed by the dark slime from the rock of hell. The slime, in the other world that you know, has souls bound up in the lusts of the world, the enticements of the pride of life, and the lust of the flesh, to where they have been overcome in their soul, to the point that their soul will be brought here at the time of the singularity."

"Likewise, I feed those who are Mine, with the blue flame, giving them the Ancient Language, where I give both the vision and the interpretation of it, so that they can understand what I speak; I am doing that with you now. My angels carry my messages with the blue flame, releasing the messages to my warriors to encourage them."

Kaufman was beside himself, and wrestled against feeling hopeless. El Elyon knew the inner conflict and spoke. "There is still hope Norman, especially in your area, and even for some of these souls."

"How can that be," he asked.

"Milly has been given a special anointing oil, to cover the minds of mankind, so that they will not be given over to the deception of this other world, and even some of the souls that are caught here, can be awakened and brought back, should they win the battle of the mind. The special anointing that she has can wake them up."

Kaufman, more at ease with what he saw and where things could end up, was strengthened in the hope of El Elyon. The blue flame came into his belly, causing his soul to be refreshed.

"You have all been brought together for such a time as this."

Kaufman still lay in his chair, fast asleep, snoring to the point that the loudness woke him up. He moved his glasses lying on his belly on the papers, and grabbed his laptop to write the dream down.

A Deep Dream State

Milly, in her cave, a treasure trove of mementos that meant the world to her was in a deep sleep. Covers, half way off while the window was slightly opened, bringing in the coolness of the night to brush on her skin, kept her in this deep state. Her navy and white striped pajamas, made of organic cotton, caused her to feel like she was at the beach on holiday while she slept. She was spoiled since finding organic fabrics thinking that it contributed to her feeling better over all.

The meeting at Robert's house had pulled on every fiber and neuron of her body, making her drift off to sleep faster than normal. She was caught up in the mood of the evening having come home from the meeting, and climbed into her pajamas to get to bed right away. Her parents offered her dinner but knew that she was tired, so put a plate in the fridge for a late snack, should she get hungry.

Wind slightly blowing through the thin curtains lifting them up, was like a breath of heaven coming upon her soul, refreshing her in her sleep. She could sense its presence, wishing at the same time that she could go deeper into the Ancient Language, as she lay asleep. Although she was in the REM state of her sleep and should be in a deep sleep, even at this stage, she could still pull on the sensations she felt in reality, taking them with her into her dream.

Her dream states were always deeper than most people, and seemed real each time. Although she had not been in a *dream simulation* by El Elyon, this would be a new door of adventure waiting for her. This was the next level of her Seer gifting, where she would see things in a greater way in the dream state, opening her gifting up to stay at this level of simulation from here on out.

She was taken into a colorful world, where the sky was a rich blue, birds chirping and the sound of laughter filling the air, while she was lifted high above Springfield. She wondered what time she was in, sensing that this had been an idyllic time. Seeing her old elementary school, and then being carried over the middle and high schools, she could see children running and playing about, as if life could not be better.

She saw the ice-cream shop that she had worked at, seeing people come out with huge cones of ice cream, licking it, with the flavor on the tip of their tongue. There was busyness in the street, where no bad thing could enter, but only that of joy, laughter and goodness, with everyone out as if it there were a county fair occurring. There was a buzz around the town, where expectation seeped through the souls of the people.

Milly lifted higher, was brought to the Clock at Strytan, known as Tisdale Clock, named after its creator Ernest Tisdale, in 1890. It was the crown of the campus, and was what everyone pointed to, when sending postcards to others, showing the crown jewel of Springfield, making them envious to attend.

Milly was lifted up to the clock that was 70 feet high, towering over The Quad. At the clock's face she was able to reach her hand out and touch it, seeing the short hand on 3 and the long hand motioned to 33. She was in the present time in her dream thinking prior, that the time had to be during her Great Grandmother's day. Within the clock she saw a light appearing, where there was a brick room on the other side, housing the gadgetry of the great invention.

She went through the wall, inside of the brick room, seeing the inner chamber, feeling as though she was looking at the heart of Springfield. Within the walls on the inside, a light came ablaze in a blue flame with Greek letters, which turned into English letters.

"kai humeis chrisma echete apo tou hagiou kai oidate panta."

She heard El Elyon's voice, "But ye have an unction from the Holy One and ye know all things." It pierced her soul, as a lightning spear shot through her entire being, touching every fiber of her person. Her soul, spirit and body were affected by the power of these Words that she remembered hearing while at Saint Timothy's Cathedral.

"This, Milly," Said El Elyon, "is how my servant Saint Timothy was, much like your Great Grandmother, and others who have carried around a sacred anointing, with an unction from the Holy One. It is these to whom I give great Wisdom, as I open the door in the heavens to cause them to know all things."

She was overtaken by the words being spoken from El Elyon, that it felt like waves were crashing over her soul. The Greek letters lit up, bounding off of the wall, leaping within her soul, infusing the essence of truth within.

El Elyon continued, as Greek words and their pronunciation appeared before her eyes in the fiery blue opal color. "*Unction* in Greek is ***chrîsma*** pronounced ***khris'-mah*** and means, a smearing, a special endowment, an anointing and an unction." She could see the heavens now, as she was in the universe, having the stars pierce her soul with the voice of their light.

Then she saw the door, as it opened wide. From behind it the light that came out was the purest light she had ever seen, painting her in the unction of Wisdom, in which she would carry a special anointing for the battle. "With this unction," said the voice of El Elyon, "you will KNOW ALL THINGS."

Again, she felt waves of light rushing over her body, as she was suspended in front of the open door in the heavens, being poured upon by brilliant luminescent oil which covered her entire body, glimmering the brightness of its beauty like jewels covered all over her, as the stars shone.

The voice of El Elyon continued as Greek words and their pronunciation appeared before her, "*Know*, in Greek is ***eídō*** pronounced ***i'-do*** meaning to see, perceive and understand. You have been smeared by the unction to see! You will see the souls of mankind that are longing to be set free, as you have seen the children and the people here in your vision of Springfield. These souls have need of your gift."

Suddenly, the blue flame of El Elyon filled her and she felt a measure of the emotions He had for these people. Her heart was flooded with emotions that she could not fathom, as the neurons in her brain, belly and spine were awakened to experience a greater knowing of His compassion for the souls of mankind.

Suspended in the midst of space, it was like a tsunami of light hit her soul, as her body bent backward from the power of the unction released to her, for her to see. Although it could not be seen, it was as though El Elyon's hand had her suspended in His palm, cupping her small frame within to give her strength to endure the emotion.

Tears streamed down her face, as she wailed, feeling waves of love for the souls she saw, knowing that their plight would be devastating if she did not act. Wailing, she cried out, "El Elyon, I cannot take this, this emotion of your purity and of your love is more than I can bear, I feel that I am going to burst."

His heart went out for her, as she felt His emotions, even for her, by the power of the light that was released. She was kept in the palm of His hand, invisible to her own eyes, until suddenly she saw Him, and his appearing was BEAUTIFUL! His face was pure light, and about Him was radiant light in different colors with the brightness of the white. So piercing was His beauty that she did not want to awaken from this dream. She was safe in this place and wanted her entire existence to stay here.

More tears poured from her eyes, as she sobbed even more, being pierced by the purity of this Wisdom, where truth was made known to her about EVERYTHING! SHE KNEW ALL THAT THERE WAS!

She could not describe it, but it was as though every neuron and fiber of her being, worked in full capacity, where she had use of her entire brain, understanding all there was about every science, mathematical equation, and depths of literature written in ages past. It was as though her soul was connected to the universe and all its infinite Wisdom in this one moment. She was in *ETERNITY-TIME*! She was eternal, and she felt, outside of time itself, infinite to the rest of all that there was.

Then in the palm of His hand, she found herself now lifted up back to the Tisdale clock at Strytan. She was within the brick walls, and there she found the wooden box that had the oil, from Saint Timothy's Cathedral, where she saw within it the exact oil that had been poured out on her.

The voice of El Elyon continued to speak, "Milly, the oil that is at Saint Timothy, is a sacred oil that I have brought for such a time as this. It is the same oil created by Father Augustine Castellanos, and was given to him by Me. He created that many years ago, knowing that this time would come, where the souls of man would be in the grasp of hell, needing an anointing of My Wisdom to be released."

She listened intently, holding onto every Word that came out of El Elyon's mouth, wanting more Wisdom to cover her person.

"You will release many from the stupor that they are in presently, as they are bound up in the darkness of the wisdom of this present age, not realizing that it has numbed their soul to true Wisdom. You Milly, carry this unction within you of truth, and the power of that Wisdom of truth causes the darkness to be defeated in the minds of mankind."

She wept, feeling unworthy and unable to do what El Elyon had set out for her. Her body collapsed on the wooden floor of the clock room, where she was still hidden within the brick walls, as she wailed, "I cannot do this, I am not the chosen one for this assignment."

El Elyon breathed on her, which felt like the wind from her window, coming into her room, as He spoke tenderly to her, "You have passed the test of becoming worthy for this unction, when I sent you to face your enemy, seeing if you would use the Wisdom I have given you for even the one that has hurt you the most."

Crying profusely, while gasping in between the tears to get the words out, she spoke, "Oh my! El Elyon, I had no clue that was a test! How did you know that I would pass it?"

The wind, gently blowing on her face while she was fast asleep, felt like His breath upon her face, like a mother blowing over her infant's face lightly to calm them down. Her tears began to dry up as she spoke again, "How did you know that I would pass?"

"Milly, I know all things, and I have chosen you from the beginning, knowing that your Great Grandmother would do many things, and that within her lineage, you would come forth, as a chosen vessel to be a Wise One."

El Elyon was silent while Milly soaked in the moment, letting her gather her thoughts, having experienced an overwhelming amount of emotions and knowledge this night. It seemed as though the two of them were still in the moment, waiting for the other one to speak first. When suddenly, He brought her back to the face of the clock, where she saw the time was, again on 3:33.

"Milly, 33 means unction, anointing, it means that now is the time for what I have purposed against the gates of hell, to bring the souls of mankind into true Wisdom."

She pondered on all that was spoken and that had occurred, when she was brought into the vision of seeing the parallel universe, to which she screamed in horror, "What is this El Elyon?"

"This is where many souls presently are, and I have shown your professor, Norman Kaufman, this place to which Beelzebub plans to send many souls from Springfield, when the grid comes into operation by the powers of darkness. Each of the team members have a gift and are given great care over that gift, so that they walk in what I have called them to do, to save the souls of those in Springfield, where they are not brought into this parallel universe."

She listened on, being joined by Rafael and Tubal. Seeing them there gave her great comfort. "Rafael and Tubal will fight with you as the parallel universe is opened, to not only keep the souls of mankind from crossing over, but to also bring others who are captive, back."

"You mean there is hope for them El Elyon," she asked.

Tubal looked with great compassion on Milly, as Rafael appeared stoic, not letting the thoughts of danger, to Milly, be expressed on his countenance. "We are here with you," said Rafael.

Tubal touched Milly on her shoulder, assuring her of their presence, "We are dedicated to serving you Milly, and will not leave your side for this assignment. We have been waiting for this time."

Milly, trying to look for El Elyon's face, put her gaze all over the room, to which she heard, "The moment will come in time, where many souls that are caught on the other side, will be awakened out of sleep, from the darkness of the wisdom of the present age, to know eternity-time, escaping the clutches of Beelzebub. Moreover, those whom you saw at the beginning of your dream in Springfield are the very souls that are bound up in the parallel universe that you will help Me bring back."

"Oh my gosh!" exclaimed Milly. "All those souls? I don't know them all, who are they?" She started crying again at the thought of the souls that were captured on the other side.

"These are not people in Springfield that you know, but rather souls from other areas in Area 9, who are bound up in the harvesting of minds in the parallel universe, wanting to cross back over from the stirrings I have already placed within them. There is an inkling of light, and all we need is a small light to make it bigger."

"These people are bound up to drugs, others to the dark wisdom, others still to witchcraft and others to addictions of other forms. None of these truly know that their soul is completely bound up in that harvesting field of the parallel universe, but with the Wisdom that you carry, as the opening occurs, Rafael and Tubal will take you over for the window of time that is afforded, to anoint the heads of as many as you can, bringing more souls back to reality."

She was timid, unsure of how many she could save in the short span of time, bringing them back into this reality.

"Be at peace Milly, you will be shown before it happens, as I bring you more Wisdom to know the truth of what is to come and what will be."

The dream state ended, as she woke up from her sleep, turning on the light, feeling the wind on her face, and reaching for her journal. She thought on all that had happened and wrote down what was spoken, ending the entry with her own thought, "What will come of all of this?

A time to be remembered and not taken lightly, knowing that Wisdom is always smearing me with love! An emotion beyond measure!"

Chapter 14

Let the Day Begin

Much had gone on in the night while the group was asleep; everything was being prepared, before daylight broke forth in the east. While the members of the group had dreams, including Father Sanderson, Professor Peyton and Tony, the angelic activity against the hordes of hell, were ramped up.

Angels, all over Area 9 were fighting for the safety of mankind, knowing that El Elyon's warriors were receiving their assignments, while the angelic hosts diligently fought through the night. Receiving the assignments for El Elyon's warriors was a great struggle; the messages that were coming from the third heaven, into the second heaven, were making it in by fierce battle.

Demonic princes guarded the gates in the second heavens, and were working overtime, bombarded with waves of angelic beings, who were coming through with the assignments. The princes knew the value of the assignments, and wrestled with the angels, trying to rip the messages out of their hands, knowing that they were for El Elyon's warriors. The assignments from El Elyon would devastate hell if released.

The Message

When El Elyon sent forth His assignments, He did so in messages that would be given in a dream simulation. For his chosen angelic messengers, each was given an individual warrior's assignment, which was placed in a beautiful container similar to a jewelry box. Each unique container signified the importance of the dream simulation being delivered in each message, as the box was especially made for the individual person.

El Elyon put great thought into everything. His thoughts towards individuals are more than all the sand on the seashore, which is so unfathomable to even the most genius of minds. Because of his zealous thoughts that continuously go towards His warriors, He was scrupulous with the detail of each message, ensuring that not only the dream simulation was perfect, but also that the vessel in which it was to be carried, was met with the same excellence.

Milly's message was contained in a silver box, bedecked in carvings of the Ancient Language all around. On the top were sapphires, diamonds and amethysts around the edges, framing a huge blue sapphire. Within the box was a red velvety fabric upon which was a stone, a large pumpkin orange diamond about 14 carats. The stone was the message, encasing the assignment and gift.

Whereas, Kaufman's message was enclosed in a wooden box, that was both organic looking and alive with rings of fire intricately carved within, like the rings of a tree. The interior of his box was a deep caramel colored velvety fabric where, laid upon it, was an emerald stone, appearing to be 20 carats large.

Each warrior had meticulously crafted boxes for their individual message. Seeing the boxes carried in beautiful sacs that looked like liquid lava alerted those who saw. Demonic princes instantly knew what the angels carried, as they came to the portal of the second heaven. Irate, the princes fought the angels on every end to stop the messages from getting through; they knew the importance of the dream simulation.

Dream simulation messages are entirely different than the dreams given by El Elyon's Spirit. El Elyon's Spirit gives dreams to His warriors to warn them of what is to come, as well as speak to them. Whereas, these dream simulation messages were actual gifts sent from El Elyon in the third heaven, being locked within the dream simulation.

Thus, each individual that received their message through the angelic host was given an assignment to protect Area 9. The gift was encompassed within the middle of the dream simulation. The angel, upon arriving with the message, would place the spiritual stone upon the warrior's forehead, which then dropped the assignment and gift within their soul, as their dream simulation was performed within their heart and mind. Like playing a virtual reality game, the dream simulation was as real to the soul, as the fabric of his or her own life. Once experienced, it was woven into their minds.

Rafael and Tubal, along with other leaders, were warring against the demonic princes, transporting the messengers of El Elyon through the portals. Demonic princes were a terror; they were given the prestigious title from Beelzebub once they all had been removed from the third heaven and the blue flame taken away from them. These were the most ruthless of wicked powers that there were.

The princes, normally about 9 feet tall, were covered in the darkness of space, blending in with the second heavens like the universe blanketing them. Fighting them was no easy feat; usually a wrestling match with a prince could take almost 21 days in human time, delaying the message. The angelic messengers had been sent out many days before the dream simulation finally reached each individual warrior. Most of the angels had been warring against the princes for 17 days, which is why the angelic leaders of Area 9 had to aid in battle.

Tubal and Rafael, wearing their armor, used their shields against the fiery darts, as they fought against each prince and his demonic army. The other leaders of Area 9, Fawna and Meshal assisted, using all their weapons to overcome the brutal assault. In the sphere between the first and second heavens, the battle was a gruesome sight, as some of the angelic hosts cut asunder the demonic army, where bloody screams were released. Sounds like hell in the heavenly atmosphere, were the most eerie happenings of all; whatever was going on there affected earth.

The wrestling in the heavens was like watching a WWE (World Wrestling Entertainment) wrestling match, except on a grander scale, which was definitely not for entertainment. Angels grabbing demons, and demons gripping angels, trying to steal the messages, had been an intense occurrence for such a long time, that it could not be determined, which angel was wrestling which demon. Like a swarm of birds filling the air, the angels and demons maintained a constant battle over Area 9.

"Watch the sacs," Rafael said to Tubal. "We must not let them be taken!"

The beautiful sacs shone with such richness of color, burning brightly, while encasing the message. Waves of light emanated from the sacs, showing the greatness of the message contained within that was constantly speaking.

The Message Created

These messages were absolutely unfathomable. Before placing the message in the box, El Elyon brought it gently to His mouth, speaking within the precious stone, giving it the entirety of the dream simulation. Then holding His hands up and clasping them, the stone pressed in the palm of His hand, was given the deposit of the gift.

The precious stones carrying this treasure within were a resemblance of the value of the message and the gift. The intricacy of the entire process demonstrated the particular endeavor the third heaven was committed to. This was usually the buzz in the heavens before the angelic messengers were sent out.

Every angel wanted the honor and privilege of carrying the message to one of the warriors. Before an angel was chosen, for a great length of time they prepared for the battle with the demonic princes, knowing that the message had to be protected and delivered to the warrior with success. A special region in the third heaven was set aside for training the angels for this task. All inner workings of this commission was treated most special, and coveted by all.

With the fierce battle going on this night in Area 9, the angelic hosts of El Elyon broke the power of the demonic princes and their armies. The most prestigious assignments were released, more than the 21st century had seen to this point. Thus, proving the most formidable assignments were being deposited in El Elyon's warriors, for the protecting of the hearts and minds of mankind from the singularity that would open the parallel universe.

PRINA

While things were happening late in the midnight hour in Area 9, Beelzebub's cronies at PRINA were at work, in Geneva, Switzerland, where it was 7 am. The heads of PRINA, were some of the most brilliant minds known in the earth, but most used their gift for darkness, with the perversion of Beelzebub controlling them. These cronies were assisting the powers of darkness, in opening the parallel universe to imprison the souls of mankind, putting them to sleep with the Mandela Effect, as well as attacking their souls with antimatter and dark matter. The reason behind creating the particle accelerator was an absolute debauchery of their profession.

Dr. Mandess Surija was the lead physicist, having graduated in India at Zurafis University. Beelzebub referred to Dr. Surija, as *Mandess Madness.* A fragile looking man in his early 50s, deep olive skin, dark brown eyes, and thin hair parted on the side, did not make him appear as a threat to the whole world. Yet, he was. One of the most sinister hearts given over to the dark magic, through the Illuminati, caused him to be a weapon for Beelzebub.

Appearances were always deceptive when it came to him; he could care less about anything and anyone, other than his prized possession at PRINA, the Hadron Collider (HC), which was the world's largest and most powerful particle accelerator. He had been on the board of PRINA, since early 2000, and conspired with the powers of darkness to bring him to the forefront, knowing that he would yield to their purpose. Things happened, and in time, he was Chief Physicist Engineer (CPE).

PRINA's hadron collider was up and working by the end of 2010, and being put to use for experiments in 2011. The small use of time that was afforded them with the HC, allowed them to tinker with things of the past, as revealed in the ancient relic, with the Aramaic text from the book of Daniel, where there would be an interruption within the space-time continuum, opening portals for demonic activity which would influence people. As changes were made here and there, the Mandela Effect resulted, causing those who were awake in their soul to wonder what was occurring. They knew that they were not crazy, but did not have an explanation as to what was going on.

However, the initial tinkering was just a beta-test for what was coming this next week, which would be the opening of the parallel universe. Dr. Mandess was not turning back and had worked with Beelzebub for years for this one moment in time.

On the other hand, PRINA had brought scientific benefits to the physics arena, having scientists study subatomic particles on a grander scale, not yet completed. Those innocent physicists dedicated to their studies, were ignorant of the schemes of Dr. Mandess and his cohorts, who were instead planning to rule and ruin the world.

One of these innocent physicists, Dr. Merrill Turnipseed, a young brilliant brainchild, now in his mid thirties, had the main project of splitting atoms to look closely at the energy within, which he titled *The Brainchild*. Turnipseed was clueless to the evil plot of Mandess. To him, next week meant opportunity for his projects to be carried out.

He needed his most recent request for the project *Brainchild* to be signed off by Mandess, and was in route to his office. The walk to Mandess' office gave him opportunity to pop in on the other scientists, prying into their work. Sidestepping to different offices while on his way, he would check in on what others were doing. His personality and mind made him one of the most popular physicists; not only was he brilliant, but he was kind, wanting to encourage others in their genius, too.

Turnipseed was pumped after looking at Dr. Kellog's work with quarks, which instigated excitement for the upcoming collider's activation, where he was eager to see Kellog's findings. Quarks were such a wonderful thing, he thought, "colored charged particles inside of neutrons and protons, giving life more meaning!"

Daydreaming about his results and those of the other scientists, he got lost in his thoughts, not realizing that he passed Mandess' office. Catching himself three doors too late, he turned and headed back, at which time he heard Mandess' voice one door away.

"They will be in a field alright, it will not be in a quantum field, rather a field of souls, keeping their minds in prison to dark matter. The Illuminati are planning this *now* and we cannot delay further action."

Another voice inside, was arguing with Mandess, "I will not be in on this one; the Mandela Effect was somewhat tolerable, seeing if we could tap into time. However, this Mandess, of stealing the souls of mankind, is madness!"

Mandess emphasized his point, "If you are not in on this, then you and your family will be affected by *it*. I cannot make any promises to you, otherwise."

Mandess put pressure on the man to carryout the plan, whatever *that* might be. Turnipseed was completely caught of guard and thought, "What in the world could have another man in utter fear, in which he would make a plea like that?" He waited briefly, as the door abruptly opened.

Mandess stood there in his fragile looking frame, with hatred in his eyes, like a laser beam glaring into Turnipseed's soul. Merrill felt naked to his stare, as Mandess uttered in disgust, "What are you doing here boy?"

Turnipseed opened his notebook, holding the project that needed to be signed off. "I just need your John Hancock, Dr. Mandess."

Mandess probed Turnipseed while giving his signature to the document. "How long have you waited for me to come out?"

"I just walked up Dr. Mandess, why?"

Still suspicious of what and how much he knew, Mandess eyed Merrill with a sneering smirk on his face. "You need to watch where you are, so that you are not jumping in on people's private conversations for your own benefit. Just because you are here in PRINA does not give you the license to put your nose into other people's business."

Having given him the document back, Mandess pointed for Turnipseed to leave, "Take off, will you."

Turnipseed turned around, headed back to his office, looking back awkwardly at Mandess, who would not take his eye off of him until he had rounded the curvature in the building where he could see him no more. Mandess then opened the office door once more to speak to the man, whom he had been conversing with, "Tomorrow night, meet me here and we will go over the matter."

Turnipseed walked back to his office, with chills going up and down his spine, wishing that he had not heard what he did this day. It made him unsettled as to the work of Mandess, and PRINA. He had always thought and believed the best about PRINA, but from the sounds of it, *this* was not what he had signed up for.

Uncertain of whom he should go to, Merrill was anxious, not paying attention as Dr. Martha Webber bumped into him while in route to have her project approved for the week.

"Hey Dr. Webber," Turnipseed said, "Do you have a moment?"

"Why yes Dr. Turnipseed, I do. We are close to my office, why don't we go in there."

Entering into Dr. Webber's office was comforting, seeing her mementos of home, and drawings from her grandchildren, gave the sense it was not an office but a treasure trove of memories. They entered and sat down, with her sitting behind the desk and Turnipseed sitting in one of the chairs on the other side. She sensed his uneasiness, and went to shut her door. She could not help but wonder if he had figured out what was truly going on at PRINA; she had suspicions of her own.

Dr. Webber was a good person, a grandmother of five, and a devoted wife and mother. She and her husband moved from England to be in Switzerland so that she could carry out her field of studies at PRINA. She had received private funding for her project, hoping to find cures to terminal diseases.

Dr. Webber wanted to check on Turnipseed's status since he appeared anxious, "Are you alright Dr. Turnipseed?"

"Please Dr. Webber, call me Merrill." He felt as though she was old enough to be his mother.

"Very well Merrill, are you alright?"

"As a matter of fact Dr. Webber, I don't know the answer to that question, and to me, this feels as much like a mystery as our study of physics."

"What's on your mind? Did you discover something while here?"

"I just overheard Mandess speaking inside of his office. Whomever he was speaking to was intimidated. I am not sure, but it sounded as though he said that he was not worried about the quantum field, but rather concerned with the field of the souls of mankind."

She was visibly disturbed upon hearing this information, and her looks could not keep it hidden. She had known much of the findings that have been under the table regarding antimatter and dark matter. This confirmed her suspicions.

Merrill saw her concern, and knew she too was frightened He asked, "Dr. Webber, are *you* alright?"

"As a matter of fact Merrill, no I'm not; this has bothered me for some time now, and even more so after hearing of your encounter. I have known of certain findings that seemed to be under the table regarding the relationship of antimatter and dark matter, as it related to the interaction with mankind. These findings that I am about to tell you will confirm your discernment."

She paused and continued, "I believe Merrill, that it is our second brain, our gut, warning us that something is happening here, larger than we know, that goes against the ethics of our field.

"I have to share something with you. While at PRINA late one night, I walked past a conference room where a scheduled meeting was taking place. A man, whom I believe to be Mandess, was speaking. I could not see him, but I am familiar with his strong dialect. He said that the Hadron Collider could open doors to other dimensions, and had in the past, taken souls across to the other side. It alarmed me and disturbed me to the core. Moreover, he continued, saying that we could bring dark matter from the other dimension which would be demonic in nature, as well as continuing to send souls through to the other side, removing them from this universe into the parallel universe."

Dr. Webber then shared with Merrill her concerns of the relation of antimatter and dark matter, as well as the so-called *lab experiments* that were discussed in this same conference that she was eavesdropping on. "Their discussions made mankind the rat in their lab experiment, as the weapon of antimatter was to be released in certain locations to prove their findings. These evil physicists desire nothing good with this particle accelerator, but instead have a sinister intent. I truly feel the other *thing* coming through the portal from the other side, is demonic in nature; their discussions regarding antimatter and the paranormal made sense to me." She went on to share the finite details of how they shared about antimatter working with dark matter, luring demonic entities.

Merrill was completely blown away and appalled by what Dr. Webber shared. Her discussions in relating demonic interactions with antimatter made him sick. Had she not overheard the meeting, she would not have knowledge of this. It was no coincidence at all. The possibility of dark matter coming in from another dimension, to interfere with the minds of mankind, causing chaos in nations was highly likely at this time. What was more disconcerting is that the HC was going to be turned on again next week. There was such little time.

Dr. Webber was glad to tell someone else; she felt that even her husband might have thought she was crazy. Now that she was able to tell someone else, especially a colleague in the field, gave her peace. "To be honest Merrill, I have felt for some time that more than just *our experiments* are being conducted during these times when they fire up the particle accelerator. Somewhere inside of my gut, I feel that there are sinister plots going on at the same time, which has nothing to do with our experiments at all, but rather opening doors to other universes."

"You know, since you mention it Dr. Webber, I remember having a crazy dream the other night, where this huge crystal tower was rising, and in the midst of it was a blue flame, with this Ancient Language streaming within it, like particles in the particle collider. They were bursting forth and going across the atmosphere, as these human warriors were fighting demons. They were dressed in an incredible armor that seemed to have special powers. I know this sounds crazy."

"No, by all means Dr. Turnipseed, it is not crazy at all, continue please."

"Well, these warriors had this same blue flame within them, and used a whip that had these keys in it, along with a sword and shield, fighting off the hordes of hell. Then I heard a name mentioned, Milly Teschlon, to which the demons shrieked in torment, and I instantly knew that whatever part she played, it had to do with what was going on here with PRINA and our release next week for the Hadron Collider.

"Further on in the dream, a black hole opened up to a parallel universe, where there were what appeared to be rice fields of mankind's souls, hooked up to perilous looking, sludge machines, keeping these souls brainwashed. I thought of what we were doing here at PRINA and the possible connection with the Mandela Effect, as well as the evil that was happening in my dream; nothing else can explain it."

Dr. Webber looked at Merrill, knowing that what he spoke witnessed to her soul, and determined that the two of them had to do something with the information that they had. She reflected on their conversation for a minute before speaking, "Merrill, I tell you what, see if you can find this Milly Teschlon and contact her about your dream."

Merrill was relieved to hear her response and looked forward to finding out who Milly was. "William, in the tech department, knows how to do a search for individuals. I'll give him the name and ask him to do the search."

"Sounds good," replied Dr. Webber, "keep me updated; we will call this, Project Blue Flame."

Merrill nodded as he left her office, feeling some solace about their conversation, and his ability to do something, no matter how small, in order to protect people from the evil plots that Mandess was behind. Merrill gave William the task of searching for Milly, which returned three women by the name of Milly Teschlon. Looking through the three women, he was able to take one off the list, since she recently died. Now his search was narrowed down to two.

"Good, that leaves me only two," he said to himself, while sitting in his office. His desk was covered by the documents of his hypothesis for the project that was to commence next week. He had a brief time to finalize all of his documents for the researchers on his team, but making contact with Milly was more important to Merrill.

He called the first Milly Teschlon, and left a voice mail stating his name and where he worked, hoping that she could return his call before the day was over. This Milly was in Europe so calling her at this time was not a problem.

However, Merrill saw that the other Milly Teschlon was in the United States, and knew that it was just past midnight there, and that he needed to wait until later. "I will just have to wait on this one, and will set my watch to call her," he thought. Making a note, and setting the alarm on his watch gave him a backup plan to ensure that he made contact.

Shortly after setting his alarm, he received a call from the Milly Teschlon in Europe. He answered the phone introducing himself again, and mentioned that the call might sound crazy, especially with him being a complete stranger. He went on to tell her that he had a dream of a Milly Teschlon, and was curious if she went by the name Milly, to which the caller responded, "No, I go by the name Mill for short, a nickname that stuck when I was three years-old."

Merrill knew that she was not the right one; in his dream the voice specifically mentioned, Milly Teschlon, so they said their goodbyes. He went back to work on his documents, waiting towards the end of the day before calling the Milly in the USA.

Waking up

The smell of southern butter pecan coffee woke Anjali, and she climbed out of bed to spend time with Alan, who had earned brownie points, getting the coffee ready. They enjoyed getting up extra early during the week, as well as on weekends. The Doctors Mercer had a relationship that could make anyone envious; they still acted like newlyweds.

"Thanks Hon, so glad you got the coffee started. How long has it been on the stovetop," Anjali asked. They preferred everything done the old fashioned way, trying to resist as much technology as possible. Their vintage red Dansk Coffee pot, designed by a Dutch Architect, was their pride and joy, as they made percolated coffee each morning, being immersed in the ambiance of the smell of fresh coffee floating throughout the house. Coffee was something not to be simply gulped down and done in passing, but to the Mercers, was an experience to be savored, which they did fully.

"It's about ready; I started it nearly an hour ago," Alan responded, "So, it will be the perfect darkness that I know you like. I tell you what, while we are waiting, why don't we share the dreams we were given last night by El Elyon. I had a dream and am certain, you did, too."

"Absolutely," Anjali said, as they pulled up a bar stool to the kitchen bar. Alan poured coffee for Anjali, having added the butter and coconut oil with Stevia, making her a Keto-latte.

Alan then picked up his gadget, *The Rock*, and demonstrated to Anjali once more, how it operated. He had done it a few times over the months prior, but enjoyed the demonstration, feeling the device gained more credibility as he gained more experience in presenting it.

Anjali loved his mannerisms and delivery during his demo, and let him carry on. However, this demonstration was different than the ones before, in that, during this demonstration, he gave her the details about his dream. Alan reminded Anjali of the tests that he had conducted with *The Rock* in July, summarizing the results of measuring the small earthquakes. The two of them were blown away at the effectiveness of it then, and more so now at the fact that it would protect Springfield from the assignments of Beelzebub.

They nibbled on their bacon, another Keto favorite, sipping their drink, when Anjali shared about her dream with the ancient relic, and how El Elyon wanted her to read from it, while Alan operated his device. He was overcome with honor, thinking that not only was his device so awesome to be used in this battle, but his wife would be standing beside him, doing what she loved, as he did what he so enjoyed.

Bacon grease now covering their fingers, they finished up at the kitchen bar washing their hands. Anjali then went into the family room where the relic had been sitting inside of a glass box on a stand, and opened it to pull out the ancient paper, looking at the ancient text.

"This is hard to comprehend Alan, who would have ever thought we would be doing any of this in Springfield." Anjali continued to admire the document, as Alan put his hand on her right shoulder, while he stood behind her agreeing. The two had to get ready and head out the door, where they would then meet up later and prepare for the meeting this evening.

Alan, pumped up about the night's gathering, walked out the door, kissing his wife while commenting, "I love my life, and I love my wife!"

They laughed and headed to their respective jobs.

Just Getting Going

Milly's alarm went off. It was 7 am and time to get rolling for classes. She was glad that it was Friday and excited about tonight's meeting, looking forward to all that it would bring, as she prepared for the day. Her Mother had made her Keto-coffee and brought it in, giving her the large cup that had the smell of butter piping out in the hot steam.

"Yum," said Milly, "what a way to start the day." She looked at her Mother smiling and, reaching for her hand before she walked out of the room, "Thanks so much Mom, I love you."

Lavern looked back at her budding daughter and blew her a kiss, "You are welcome my little philosopher."

As she was finishing the final touches for her appearance, Milly's phone rang. She saw that it was an international call, and was wondering who in the world would be calling her from outside of the country. At first she didn't want to pick it up but heard El Elyon speak, "Answer it Mildred."

She quickly picked up the phone and heard a distinctive voice on the other line, talking with a thick, heavy European accent, not knowing exactly where they were from. "Hello, is this Milly Teschlon," the voice asked.

Milly was perplexed as to who would be calling her and responded, "Yes it is."

"Milly, this is Dr. Merrill Turnipseed from PRINA in Geneva Switzerland. I'm sure you have no idea of why I would be calling or what we do here, but I was given a dream with you in it."

She was amazed that someone from PRINA was contacting her, and she wanted to put the phone down to jump and shout doing a happy dance, but heard Parker in her head saying, "What!"

"Yes Dr. Turnipseed, I know about PRINA, and am amazed that you are calling me," she said.

"Call me Merrill please, Milly."

"Thank you Merrill, so what was your dream about."

"I dreamed that there was warfare occurring with demons attacking mankind on this earth, and that there were human warriors dressed in great armor that shone brilliantly and had supernatural powers. Also, there was a huge crystal tower with a blue flame, having ancient looking language within it, shooting up, like particles in hot lava. As the warriors in my dream fought the demons, your name came up, where a voice said *Milly Teschlon*, to which demons shrieked with terror. It occurred to me that something that you and the group of warriors were doing was coming against the gates of hell."

There was silence, and then Merrill asked, "Does any of this make sense?"

Surprised and gathering her thoughts she said, "As a matter of fact, it makes complete sense; and if I may share with you, we have visited a Prophet of El Elyon who has shared with us about what PRINA is doing presently, in opening up a dimension to a parallel universe, that is detrimental to mankind and interacting with the demonic realm."

"Milly, I believe that I am to inform you of what it is that I sense going on here, as well as educate you a bit, so that you know what you are dealing with. Do you have time for me to share on the matter, and literally that is what I want to share on?" He knew he had to share on the information that Dr. Webber gave him after their meeting, detailing matter, antimatter and dark matter.

"Absolutely!"

Merrill cleared his throat and began. "As they have been discovering in some of their tests regarding the Higgs Field theory, with the particle accelerator, it is close to being confirmed that it exists, meaning, that wherever matter is not present, anti-matter is. It is with this area in particular, the Higgs Field, that reality as we know it can be altered, touching the minds of mankind, pulling on the dark energy within them that they cannot see; we are made of both matter and antimatter.

Any part of the soul that is given over to the dark side is tied to the antimatter. Whereas the good parts of our soul are tied to matter."

Merrill took another breath and continued. "Antimatter is a hostile dimension outside of this universe, that can be tapped into from this present dimension through the particle accelerator, which can harness that energy and use it as a weapon. Moreover, the demonic realm can absorb antimatter, because it operates within another dimension, where it has access to it. The phenomenon that occurs regarding this is, that antimatter can be neutralized in the spiritual realm and used. Therefore, when antimatter is produced here at PRINA, it attracts demons from another dimension to this one, where they seek to harness this power and use it against the souls of mankind."

"PRINA has been working with the particle accelerator to open a door to the other dimension, in order to pull out antimatter, and bringing it into this world, where many demons are attached to it. Antimatter has a specific energy signature that draws darkness, and this same energy signature is seen in everything that there is. In other words, there is light and darkness in all things. We as humans have opportunity to decide that which we are going to yield to."

Milly was so blown away, listening to all of this logical information, explaining the light and darkness, wishing that Tony was around to hear the brilliance of Dr. Turnipseed. She came back to the conversation immediately, realizing Turnipseed was still teaching her.

"A person has a connection to both realms at the same time, that which is of this earth, and that which is not of this earth but of another dimension, and is evil. This is why it is so important to watch what you think; because whatever your mind is set on, if it is negative thoughts or if it is good thoughts, will determine which dimension you draw energy from. Guard your emotional state; that determines where you are putting your thoughts, thereby where you draw your energy from."

"Dark matter, on the other hand, is *unidentified matter* that comes into our universe through the *antimatter,* brought in by the particle accelerator, which then pulls on demonic entities, destabilizing the mindsets of mankind. Therefore, during the experiments that are conducted, such antimatter forces are at work, pulling at the antimatter, or can I say, the darkness in others across the earth, giving them horrific thoughts and nightmares. Thus, if our mind is not focused, we can be susceptible to this antimatter that is released next week, which will then give opportunity to the demonic realm to bring chaos against mankind.

"This was seen in the past, where there was dark matter in the basement of a university, and the paranormal activity of demonic activity increased, and the students had chaotic and vile behaviors, so much so that the dark matter had to be removed. The school covered up and kept quiet about the activity, because it sounded like something from *The Exorcist*.

"This antimatter from the Hadron Collider will pull on the antimatter that is within a person. However, antimatter, in time, opens the door for dark matter to enter, which pulls on the other dimension that demons are from.

"For someone to be demonically possessed, they have to have a build up of the dark matter operating within them that, in time, will draw demons and make that person a house for hell. The dark matter within these people that are possessed, as well as those who are oppressed, opens the demonic dimension, where it can then attack others. They become a drink of hell, and that is what we have to watch out for."

Milly was silent as she waited to see if more would come from Merrill. She was rewarded for her patience as she waited on the last bit of information.

"I have overheard some things that have me greatly concerned, which is that this next week they plan to open a parallel universe, to send the souls of mankind over to, operating through the antimatter which will increase, to pull on the dark matter from the other dimension, so that the connection is made, making the minds of mankind inept to think for themselves, and a zombie to reality."

This confirmed all of Milly's fears, of what she had heard from the Prophet. He was right, she thought, in all that he shared with the group the evening before. Now, Milly had the logic and confirmation to share at the meeting tonight to give this wealth of truth to others, so that they would be able to fight in the battle.

Grateful beyond words, Milly extended her thanks, "This is such confirmation to us Merrill, and I cannot thank you enough for this phone call, that will have a great impact in our city, and from the sounds of it, in the earth for the souls of mankind. Your bravery and dedication to your field is stellar from what I can tell through your voice, and it is my hope that you know that your part in this battle, although it may seem small to you in your eyes, is actually rather large."

The two were silent for a minute, when suddenly Merrill exclaimed, "El Elyon be with you!"

And Milly found herself declaring back to him, "El Elyon be with you!"

After hanging up, Milly stood still, making hand gestures, where her arms went up and down by her side, like mini jumping jacks, as her mouth opened with silence, trying to put into words what she felt. Then she looked for her keys, grabbed them and headed out to Strytan. All that occurred from the meeting the last night at the Prophet's house, to the dream simulation that she had, and now Merrill from PRINA, blew her away!

Chapter 15

TV stations were encompassing a corner of The Quad, where camera crews had set up. All had hot coffee from *The Grind*, sipping on the addictions that Tony had made, as they waited for *something* to begin. Milly was baffled to what was going on, and eagerly found her way through the ocean of news reporters and their crews, as she searched for Parker.

Seeing Parker across The Quad waving at her, she went his direction, listening to the students, all the while around her talking about "the happenings" in the middle of the night. Their conversations were giving tidbits of information, like crumbs falling off of a table, as she passed through the crowd.

Arriving face to face with Parker, Milly asked, "What in the world is going on here? I have not seen so much action on campus, since when I was in middle school, and there was a possible bomb threat here at Strytan."

Parker answered, "Tony is waiting for us at *The Grind* and wants to give us the information that he has. I have heard a little, as well from people in passing, but believe that he has more since the news crews have been keeping him busy all morning. Let's go."

Milly agreed as they headed to meet Tony. Noise all around, the coffee shop was busier than normal. Excitement filled the atmosphere, like runners gathering at the starting line for the New York Marathon; there was a buzz of anticipation.

Tony looked at them, giving them the thumbs up, and said, "Give me a second, I just made you guys some new addictions; I've been experimenting. Here they are, just grab them, while I get my own and meet you outside on the patio."

Parker and Milly picked up their drinks ready to pay, but Tony informed them that the cost was covered, "This one is on me guys; we have something to celebrate."

They walked to their normal conference table waiting for Tony, at which time Milly asked Parker, "What have you heard?"

"Well Mill, you might have to take a sip before I tell you; it's really big."

He looked at her as if he was not going to speak, until she took a sip, "Ok already, I'm sipping, now go ahead and spill it out!"

"Some of the students here at midnight, began freaking out while in the dormitory asleep; they heard alarming noises outside on The Quad. Not all of the students heard it, only about 20 or so." He positioned his arms upward, while his elbows rested on the table. "So get this, the students that could hear it, came outside, and guess what they saw?"

Tony jumped into the conversation as he plopped himself down on the seat, "They saw a huge crystal tower rising with blue flames shooting out of it," he said as he leaned inward. "They also claim that they saw a lot of paranormal activity occurring in the dorms."

"Paranormal activity?" Milly asked.

"You know Milly, demons," Parker replied.

Tony lifted up his lab experiment cup, "I've got connections people," he said in jest. "Also, the news crews are saying that all of the students have the exact story, and since they are all from different dorms, they are saying it is not something made up, but rather that it sounds legit. Administration had a psychiatrist come to campus early this morning, and they are now meeting with the group of students, to verify if it was a group hallucination or if it is valid."

"Oh my goodness!" exclaimed Milly.

"That's not all either, you guys," Tony informed them as he continued. "Some of them claim to have seen angels flying in the night sky, and a few of them claim that they saw a mark on the foreheads of the other students who were outside with them."

"Do you know what this means," Milly asked.

"It means more people are seeing in the spirit, by El Elyon. They might not understand what is going on now, but they will; I will talk to Kaufman and Mercer, as well as Peyton, to see if the three of us," she said pointing to Parker and Tony, as well as herself, "can get a meeting together, so that we can share our own experiences here on campus, excluding our encounter with Dean Knight."

Tony and Parker said in concert, "I'm in."

"Great, I will go speak to them now and catch up with you guys later."

Milly jumped up from the table, headed towards Truman, and noticed that the building was now glowing with an amber color, as Greek words were written above it in a fiery blue opal: ***kai gnōsesthe tēn alēthian kia hē alēthia eleutherōsei hymas***. The words then changed into English, which read: ***You shall know the truth and the truth will set you free***.

Then she remembered TRUE MAN! Truman Hall, named by Augustine Castellanos, was established to bring truth to Springfield, through those who would be in this time, and seek the signs of that truth. For Milly, that truth came through being painted with the Wisdom of El Elyon. Simultaneously, she heard a huge door being opened, to which she heard El Elyon say, "My Wisdom is soon to be poured out, gather the troops Mildred, and speak truth. They will be set free in their soul, so that they can join the fight."

She knew that He was referring to the students who had witnessed all the happenings last night at Strytan. And then she heard El Elyon speak again, "Mildred, *his name* is not happenstance," to which she wondered who El Elyon was referring, then He continued. "*Augustine* means to increase, and *Castellanos* means castle." She gasped while obtaining revelation about Truman hall; that is where the students gathered last night she thought.

El Elyon spoke, "I Am bringing My warriors to My castle to increase Wisdom upon them." She knew instinctively that the meeting with the students should be held in Truman Hall.

She entered the building and bolted up the stairs to the second floor, where she happened to find the three professors in discussion, with Kaufman's door closed. Kaufman saw Milly through the window, to which he waved for her to enter. The excitement she was experiencing was more than she could contain, and the fact that her ketones on the blood ketone meter, read 2.7 let her know that she was high on ketones, as well. She was a ball of fire, feeling the flame of El Elyon burning brightly, waiting to release all that was within her.

Books were laid out on Kaufman's coffee table, as he and Professor Peyton were in the chairs, and Mercer on the couch. This let her know that they were up to something good for tonight's meeting, and she was curious as to what. Mercer motioned for her to sit beside her on the couch, and Milly dropped her book bag, sitting down to gaze upon the open books.

She looked closely and could not believe it, as she saw a drawing of the crystal tower sketched both in her Great Grandmother's book AND in an illustrated book written by a man, Alex Groton, who was from Springfield. Under the tower in the book, Alex had written, *I saw it once, and will never forget its power.*

"Who is Alex Groton," Milly asked, "and what does this have to do with what is going on now?"

Mercer picked the book up slowly, showing Milly the cover, where Truman Hall was on the front, and Alex Groton was standing in front of the steps. The picture sent a charge through Milly's soul, like fire in her bones, as she then read the title: *True Man*. Inside, where the prologue was written, Alex had the Greek words *kai gnōsesthe tēn alēthian kia hē alēthia eleutherōsei hymas.*

"That is crazy, professors!" Milly exclaimed. "That is exactly what I saw on the building, as I was headed here to talk to you about the students, who witnessed the tower last night."

"So you're saying that you saw this Greek phrase over Truman," asked Kaufman.

"Yes, and as soon as I did, I saw the English words appear, *you shall know the truth and the truth shall set you free*. Immediately, I heard El Elyon mention about Augustine Castellanos who built TRUMAN Hall. I learned this information about him, from Father Sanderson. He said Father Augustine named Truman Hall for the symbolism of becoming a TRUE MAN, through knowing Wisdom, representing philosophy and history, in order to write about the truth."

"That is right, I remember that story," said Peyton. "Father Sanderson and I talked about that a couple of years ago, and it set my soul ablaze with hope, knowing that we had *that kind* of history here at Strytan."

Milly, still intrigued asked, "What is this book that Alex Groton wrote, and what is he saying about the tower?"

"It is interesting." Professor Mercer added, "He wrote that he saw the tower during the early to mid 1930's, which was the time of your Great Grandmother. It appears that he was a college student at the time, and he was also majoring in philosophy and history. He briefly mentions your Great Grandmother, stating here," Mercer opened the book to Milly, "that she was the saint of Springfield, and had much Wisdom in the hardest of times."

Milly was wowed for sure, and the overwhelming sense of her connection to his story, sent chills all over her arms and legs. She could not help rubbing her legs and arms, when she asked, "So, is he alive?"

Peyton looked at Milly with his face tilted down, "I'm afraid not Milly."

"Man, I wish someone was alive that knew what happened then, so they could tell us about it."

Kaufman responded, "It seems that Groton is referring to Truman Hall being given some extraordinary powers during this time, which led us to believe that this might be the place we need to meet next Wednesday when things happen at PRINA."

"Oh, about PRINA," Milly said. "I totally forgot to tell Parker and Tony, because of all the hubbub on campus with the students who saw the tower last night, which I wanted to ask you guys about first. Would it be alright with you, if Parker, Tony and I meet together with them, to share some of our experiences? I would not be surprised if they could help us next Wednesday."

Kaufman looked at Peyton to get his ok, and then Mercer, to which she agreed. "Ok Milly, go ahead and meet with them, I don't see anything wrong with it. In fact it might help a lot."

"Thanks; I know that it will set them at ease somewhat to know that they are not the only ones experiencing it, and that they are not going crazy," Milly said, empathizing with the students. She got lost in thought pondering on what happened to her over the last few weeks and then returned to the conversation. "We will wait 'til after the news crews have gone, and meet up with them most likely over the weekend."

"What about PRINA," Kaufman asked.

"Oh yes, I forgot again," she said. "This man, named Dr. Merrill Turnipseed, who says he is a physicist there, called me this morning from Geneva, Switzerland, because I was in a dream he had. He said that many warriors in armor were fighting demons and he talked about the tower with the blue flame and Ancient Language being in it. Next, he went on to give me details about what exactly is going on at PRINA. Telling me the scientific part of antimatter, dark matter and demons, as well as us guarding our minds. I wondered if I could share it tonight at the meeting."

All the professors were shocked, and looked at Milly for a moment before responding, "Of course you can Milly," said Mercer. "That is astounding news!"

Kaufman and Peyton shared their enthusiasm, as they continued to shake their heads in disbelief, at the incredible connections the group was making. Time was accelerating, as it got closer to the scheduled release of PRINA's particle accelerator.

"Well group," Kaufman said as he looked at Peyton, Mercer and Milly, "I guess I will be seeing you all in a little bit. Time is moving on, and we must get to our respective places," to which, everyone got up from the place where they sat, and exited.

Now is Time!

Milly was in her Bug with Parker and Tony, filling them in on the details about Dr. Merrill Turnipseed, to which they had arms flailing about outside the convertible top, jokingly rebuking her for waiting until the end of the day to tell them. "I know you guys, I'm so sorry, between all the dreams we all had last night, the phone call, and coming to school to hear the news about the other students, the day has just flown by, and I am trying to keep my brain attached. Which by the way, with my ketone levels this high at 2.7, I have that runner's high feeling continually and forget because of the blissful state that I am experiencing."

"Ok Mill," said Parker. "We will let it slide this one time, but do not let it happen again."

"Ok. Ok. I won't."

"Say," Tony asked, "are we meeting in Truman Hall tomorrow with those students?"

"Yes," Milly replied. "I talked with Kaufman, Mercer and Peyton, who all agreed that we could use Truman Hall. Let's use the conference room on the second floor, since it is more of a comfortable atmosphere. There are couches as well as chairs, making it feel more homey."

"Sounds good to me, and you know a little coffee goes a long way with people who are nervous and confused, so maybe I could talk to *The Grind*, to see if I can bring in a set up and make them all a Keto-Coffee, giving them some oils for the brain recovery," Tony said with a little chuckle, while nodding his head.

"Perfect," Parker and Milly said simultaneously.

They arrived at the Doctors Mercer and headed in for their regular seats. It had become a second home, since they were meeting here regularly preparing for the big happening next week.

While Milly, Parker and Tony walked into the Doctors Mercer, little did they know that across the street sat Serugar, Vladamore's underling, who was sneering at their appearance, because it vexed him greatly. Other underlings surrounded him, to which, he pointed at them, barking orders, "Let Vladamore know they are meeting again! The angels are here guarding them and a firewall of El Elyon is around them, so we cannot get the information that they are sharing."

Afraid, the underlings trembled in their brownish dark serpent creature shapes, quivering at the thought of having to speak to an irritated Vladamore. Sheepishly, they went to the area underneath The Ancient Gatehouse, and got word to Vladamore, of what was going on.

He loathed the news, and foamed at the mouth, gnashing his teeth, wishing he had some of the black rock from the underworld to gnaw on; it was different than the rock under The Ancient Gatehouse. He clawed on the rock before him that easily gave way to his claws, which looked like knives sharpened in the rock's form.

Spewing forth, Vladamore reproved them, "Why have you brought me this news you fools? Tell Serugar that I want something done right now! I do not mean later, you worthless creatures! Tell him that he is to work at all attempts to get the news from this meeting!"

Foam disgorged across the assembly of underlings standing in front of Vladamore, as they were covered in the nasty film, leaving his presence immediately, lest he claw them. Vladamore had to get more workers, so he called on the watchman, Constugard, as well as the one he called the Dark Knight, Bobby. He went to the black ball where he spoke to Beelzebub. Afterwards, he called upon Bobby Knight and Constugard, as he conjured them into his lair for the dark meeting.

"Constugard and Dark Knight, I see you have heard my summons. I have need of you both; we have issue with the warriors of El Elyon. They are meeting this night to discuss matters, and they have information that is detrimental to our plan for this coming week. I need you to do what you are able, to bring me this information."

Constugard made an ogre type sound, grunting, which was his way of agreeing with Vladamore. He only served Beelzebub, but when necessary, aided the generals, which were in the area, in order to make Beelzebub's visitation more amenable to all the powers of darkness. He did not want to see Beelzebub incensed.

Bobby Knight, under the spell of Vladamore answered, "I will do as you say."

Vladamore ended his dark meeting with, "Time is growing short, and if we are going to do something about these pestilences, *NOW IS THE TIME*!"

The Meeting of Great Minds

It was time, and all in attendance at the Doctors Mercer, were eager. This night had been anticipated to occur even before the people present were born, which made it all the more surreal. Kaufman and the Doctors Mercer stood up front, as everyone else sat in their seats. They knew that the meeting would go extra long, expecting that a reasonable finishing time would be close to midnight.

Kaufman called the meeting to order, letting the group know the urgency of this particular night, since PRINA would be firing up its hadron collider next week. "I don't have to remind you of the importance of this coming week. We each have sensed the expectation of it, and have received our instructions in last night's dreams. Moreover, we have made priceless connections with one another to abort the evil plots against the souls of mankind."

Kaufman felt like a captain in front of his troops. "I cannot thank each and everyone of you enough, for participating in what has seemed an arduous, unrelenting and difficult task, to learn in a very brief time. You have had to learn about the supernatural, and quickly master spiritual warfare. That is a great feat ladies and gentlemen.

"I would like each one of you, to share the dreams that El Elyon has given you; this will help us strategize, as we stay in one accord. I am recording tonight's meeting and will type out the notes to email you, so that we are on the same page. A heads up before we get started, we will meet again on Tuesday, the night before the scheduled battle, and for those who attend the Prophet's house," to which he nodded at Milly and Parker, "we will be meeting there on Monday."

Kaufman walked across the front, like he usually did in his classroom, took a deep breath and began, "As for my dream, the details of it proved that this battle is greater than the souls of Springfield. That point, cannot be emphasized enough. At first I wished that I had not been shown all that was in my dream, but was given strength to endure the truth of the matter."

Kaufman paced to the left, stopped and continued, "PRINA's device will be set off, with hell's intent to capture as many souls of mankind, in order to pull them through into a parallel universe, where they will be put to sleep under a deep mind control substance of dark matter. They will be living in an alternate reality. Many who are unaware of the Mandela Effect, and are under its clutches will be caught in this spider's web and with the intents of PRINA be brought into the parallel universe."

"I was shown the distinctiveness between the body, soul and spirit, which you and I have come to know two of these very well, body and spirit. Since we have come into these recent spiritual matters over the past month, we have seen things that our normal eyes could not have. Therefore, we have come to know the distinctions between the body and spirit. However, until my dream, I did not know the distinctiveness of the soul. In the parallel universe, people's souls from earth, were brought through a singularity, where they would appear somewhat normal to you and I, if we were to have a conversation with them. The only difference is, their soul would be bound up in another reality, that of the parallel universe. They would be living a different reality and believing that they existed in this one."

"We have but a brief moment in *this time*, in order to work diligently in the spirit, to circumvent what the demons have planned. I know that I will be working alongside Milly on Wednesday, which she will share more about, with her own dream, and the hope that is still available for those souls who are already under the enemy's mind control and are asleep in the parallel universe. As for those who are not in the parallel universe yet, we will fight to wage war against the powers of hell in order to prevent the capture of their souls."

Kaufman reached his hand out towards Anjali and Alan, leading them to share their dreams. Alan held up the device he created, *The Rock*, and explained how he created it, as well as the testing he did of *The Rock*, this past July. Parker, on the edge of his seat, soaking in every finite detail about the device, listened to the scrupulous care Dr. Alan gave in designing it. Amazingly, Dr. Mercer was clueless that it would work against a neurological attack until the dream; he simply built it in blind faith.

Anjali then shared her dream, holding the ancient relic in her hand, giving the vivid description of the electrical storm that she saw occurring, and how Alan's device, with El Elyon's lightning, would bring disruption to Beelzebub's grid. She explained the supernatural occurrences and that they would experience increased lightning, with meteorologists already predicting a storm coming to the area next week.

Hearing the dreams thus far, from Kaufman, Alan and Anjali, encouraged the group, who were visibly excited as it prepared them for the battle. Parker then gave his dream, relating his past scientific experiment on brain waves, and the importance of positive thinking. He shared the data from his project, which he happened to have on his laptop. Parker emphasized the need to focus on the good thoughts given them by El Elyon, so that the enemy could not deter them from doing their particular assignments. He finished, by stressing to them that the main plot of Beelzebub and his cohorts would be to disrupt their thoughts.

At the end of Parker's talk, Alan joined in, describing how Parker was in his dream, assisting him with *The Rock*, and that the two would be working together. Parker and Alan did a fist pump and then sat down.

Professor Peyton, Father Sanderson and Tony each shared their own dreams, which helped the group connect the dots of the individual role that each person played on the team. Much like a bicycle wheel, having spokes to keep it stable, each member of the team had their own part to play for Wednesday.

Kaufman looked towards Milly for her to come up front, waving her to take center stage. Boldness filled her, as she was overcome with strength beyond her understanding, unsure if it was the ketones in her body or if it was El Elyon. Whatever it was, she was grateful to be feeling confident about what she would share.

El Elyon showed her the blue flame entering her belly, and coming up to her chest, where she felt warmth spreading, knowing that the supernatural power of Wisdom was being poured out. While standing in front of the group, Milly again heard the sound of a loud door opening in the heavens, to which El Elyon spoke and said, "Mildred, after you speak, let My warriors know that the door will open and a great degree of My Wisdom will be poured out. Tell them to be at peace at what they experience."

She replied back to Him in her thoughts, "I will El Elyon."

"First, I want to share with you that we will have more joining us for battle on Wednesday; the 20 or so students that you might have heard about today from Strytan's campus, who experienced the tower and paranormal activity last night, have already been contacted via email, and are meeting with Parker, Tony and I tomorrow at 2 pm, in Truman Hall. We will be filling them in on all that they need to know so that when the battle is heightened, they will be equipped for what to do and not be taken off guard."

She stopped momentarily, deciding what to speak on when it came to her. "Next, I want to share my dream, and then afterwards, a couple of other things that occurred to me today that are pertinent."

"I was taken above Springfield, able to see the souls of all different age groups and races, as I believed it to be people that were already in town. As the dream continued, I was brought to the Strytan Clock where I was given anointing oil that came from what El Elyon called, *eternity-time*. I have come to realize that this battle is an eternal one, operating outside of this realm. Like Professor Kaufman said, where souls are caught in between two universes."

"In my dream, I was given a special oil of which I was actually able to witness its power, while with Father Sanderson at a deliverance session at Saint Timothy's Cathedral this week." She looked towards Father Sanderson's direction, and he smiled nodding for her to continue. "While in the session, he brought a special box of oil out, which illuminated a drawing of an olive tree with Greek writing over it from 1 John 2:20 about an anointing that causes you to *know all things*."

"When I shared about my vision with Father Sanderson after the session, he gave me the history of its use, which was first made by Father Castellanos, who was the man that had Truman Hall built, housing the Philosophy, History and English departments. I am to use this oil to bring souls, that are already in the parallel universe, back to this reality."

Reaching for her water, she took a swig, and then continued, "In the dream, I was shown that when the portal opens, I will be busy anointing those in the other dimension, whose souls are imprisoned, to be awakened to come back to this dimension. What caught me off guard is that the people in my dream in Springfield, are the souls that are presently caught, over in the other dimension."

She felt a lump in her throat and didn't want to cry, and knew that she was fighting back tears. Mercer saw the conflict within Milly's soul and went up to the front to put her hands on the back of Milly's shoulders, while standing beside her.

"Go on Milly," Mercer said, "We are listening and you have no need to hold back your feelings with us; we will be fighting the most malicious fight known to mankind and, being human, causes us to experience many emotions."

Tears began to pour down Milly's cheeks as she grasped for a tissue, putting it in her hand, wiping her face on each side, trembling. "It really got to me when I saw the people in Springfield in the beginning of my dream," she said choking on her words. "They were all different ages, and appeared to be having a good time. Some were children, others were adults, and there were even some families. To think that these souls are presently over in the parallel universe as prisoners, is more than I can fathom."

She paused. Her legs trembled, and then her arms began quivering. Tears flowed down like a fountain hitting the floor, to which Milly collapsed, weeping profusely. Mercer was over her gently speaking into her ear. "Milly, you can do this, we all have need of your gift."

Parker was torn up, knowing his friend so well, and never once seeing her cry. He wanted to run up front and grab her, to hold and comfort her, but knew that now was not the time; Mercer had this.

Mercer continued to aid in emotional support. Milly's moaning stopped, and she gradually stood back up in front of the group. She should be embarrassed she thought, but she wasn't. She knew that this was a safe place to be the authentic her, and let the others know what she was experiencing.

Patting the tears on her cheek, she took another swig of water saying, "I'm sorry, I had no clue that this would happen." Father Sanderson wiped his own tear, feeling Milly's pain, knowing that the weight of the world was on a young woman who was coming into her own, and was now fighting for humanity. He smiled and nodded for her to continue.

Knock, knock, knock.

Anjali looked at Alan surprised, shrugging her shoulders and then looking at the group, "Is anyone expecting someone?" Everyone shook their head.

Knock, knock, knock.

Alan walked to the door, perplexed as to whom it could be. Upon opening, he found to his surprise that it was Robert! He was glad to see the Prophet, and introduced him to the others who had not yet met him.

The two of them walked to the room, facing the group, where Robert stood in front beside Milly. Everyone was excited to see who this Prophet was, and appeared overjoyed with his presence.

"What are you doing here Robert?" asked Alan.

Robert looked at Alan, and then Milly, "Why Lad, El Elyon sent me Himself, and it is a good thing He did; He said Milly would be needing some help right about now."

Milly gave Robert a tight hug, squeezing him as if he were her long lost relative. He was glad to see the welcome, and wanted to aid her, by settling her nerves so that she could finish what she had to say.

"Mildred Teschlon," Robert said in his thick Welsh accent, "You have need, lassie, to let them know the pertinent information." She smiled as he gave her a wink, while he walked towards the wall, standing beside it.

"I will, thank you Robert!" Milly was grateful for the extra support and also looked at Mercer, mouthing thank you. "I have to share with you the other things that have occurred. Because someone from PRINA contacted me today." Those in the group were excited, who had not yet heard. She shared the discussion that Dr. Merrill Turnipseed had with her over the phone, with the difference between antimatter and dark matter, as well as how it relates to matter.

"When this attack is carried out by PRINA, whom Beelzebub is using, they will be creating antimatter out of nowhere. This antimatter will be coming from another dimension, which is the parallel universe. As the antimatter is brought here, it then draws dark matter, which is important; that is what demons feed on. Within each of us there is both matter and antimatter, representing light and darkness."

"Like Parker said, if our minds are not guarded and thinking on the Ancient Language, we will be vulnerable for the PRINA attack to pull on the antimatter within us, which is where all violence in this world manifests. El Elyon has assured me, that at the end of this meeting, something will take place to deal with the antimatter in us. This is important to help protect our minds during battle."

"For the other students, whom we will be bringing in, we are going to let them know as well; if the antimatter level gets too high, it is going to be calling out to demons, which will bring even more paranormal activities of the demonic realm. This is probably what went on at Strytan last night; we had so much of the Tower manifesting with the blue flame, that the antimatter and dark matter manifested, so that people saw demons."

Tony jumped up, as Milly motioned for him to come help. "Tony is studying physics, and I thought it would be helpful to us, if he gave more of a demonstration of what Dr. Turnipseed was talking about."

Milly paused and remembered to say one last thing before handing the floor over to Tony. "By the way, when Dr. Turnipseed told me the dream he had, where my name was mentioned, he said that we were warring against the demons, and that when they heard my name, they shrieked in fear. I believe it is because we have the blue flame, that the demons fear us. We are covered in El Elyon's armor and have His Sword, along with the keys in His whip."

Tony tagged in for the continued discussion. "Yes, let me draw it here on this white board, to make it comprehensible. Seeing it this way will open your understanding. First of all, antimatter is difficult to control once it is produced.

"Something to which we can compare antimatter to, is an atomic bomb, giving us the idea of what uncontrolled energy within an area looks like, bringing disorder. Antimatter is the same way; once it is produced in the Hadron Collider, it is highly uncontrollable. One gram of antimatter is like four atomic bombs, that is how powerful it is."[xx]

The group was amazed at hearing the depiction that Tony gave. He knew he had their attention and continued. "Here, we are talking about antimatter that PRINA *creates* from its experiments, because this antimatter is other worldly and is brought in. It has to be contained and isolated from the rest of the world, in order to keep it under control, which is very difficult."

"Scientists at PRINA have one good discovery they are trying to prove, which is, that they believe they have found the Higgs Field. The Higgs Field was first theorized in 1964, to be true. Wherever there is not matter, the Higgs Field is present. Physicists at PRINA believe that by 2013, they will actually discover this Field. This Field of energy exists and interacts with other particles. For instance, while we are standing here, looking at each other, there is energy all around us, which *is* the Higgs Field. Particles within this Field are interacting all around us, although we cannot see the particles."

Tony stopped and looked at everyone, "Are you still with me?" Each person nodded.

"You and I are made up of matter, the chair is made up of matter, the wall is made up of matter, and so forth. All that which we cannot see is a part of the Higgs Field. The Higgs Field is where reality can be altered. Thus, as we look at the Higgs Field, we know that it contains antimatter, which we cannot see, touch or feel, although we are daily interacting with it. This antimatter, outside of PRINA's work, has existed in this earth, so we are used to this particular Field. However, PRINA is adding to this Field.

"Therefore, when you look at matter, and then antimatter, we can relate it as two dimensions, where matter is of the earth, and antimatter from another place. However, the antimatter that you and I are used to, again, is that which has already existed around us and within us. You and I are composed of both matter and antimatter; it is in EVERY living organism and has a certain heat signature.[xxi]

"Whereas, the antimatter at PRINA has never existed until they created it, so what they are doing is bringing more of another dimension into this earth. Since the 1800's, paranormal activity has been greatly studied by a certain group of physicists, who found out that it was a *dimensional slip* in our time, allowing entities to interact with this world all the time. It was then determined that antimatter was absorbed by paranormal activity, meaning that if there was a lot of antimatter pulled in, there was a lot of demonic activity."

"Because antimatter is within every life form, when the increase of the antimatter created at PRINA is brought into existence, that antimatter actually changes the *energy* of the life form, where the life form is now highly expressive of that exact antimatter energy, leading to behaviors of violence. In other words, people do what they would not normally."[xxii]

The group was getting it, and light bulbs were going off in people's minds. Synapses firing on all cylinders had everyone high on brain cell activity.

"You and I have good and bad within us, what we will see here as matter and antimatter, which makes us connected to both realms on an energy level at the same time. As Parker made mention about our thoughts, if we are thinking good thoughts, we draw energy from the good realm of matter. However, if we are thinking negative thoughts, we then draw energy, or dark matter, from the demonic realm, where we are fueled and affected by hell, literally. There is always a connection of antimatter with dark matter, which we will get into now.

"Your emotional state determines which realm you are drawing your energy from. When the heat signature within a person changes because of the *antimatter* affecting them, then they are actually able to draw *dark matter* from another dimension, based on their emotions."[xxiii]

"Let us consider the demonic activity as dark matter; what antimatter does, once it is produced at PRINA, is to attract dark matter. Once dark matter is brought into this realm, it has a connection still to the other realm, bringing demons with it. Dark matter is chaotic in nature and uncontainable."

"What we are also going to see, is that scientists have discovered that *even people* can bring dark matter energy into this realm. This occurs mainly through the expression of their chaotic emotions and activities. We see this with The Ancient Gatehouse; they are able to bring dark matter in from the dimension of hell, based on their satanic ritualistic activities.

"But this is the thing; dark matter in Geneva, Switzerland can cause the dark matter here in North Dakota to react, because they are linked, and this is what brings global chaos. They are betting on the fact that if they bring new dark matter into the world, that it will cause a domino effect.

"Because humans contain both the signature of good energy (matter) and bad energy (antimatter), while PRINA is producing more antimatter, it will pull on the other dimension's dark matter bringing global chaos. That is where the drawings of Mildred Lee come in, with the cords releasing the slime across the region. The depictions in her book of hell's cords coming from an underground tank, I believe, are the amplification of antimatter, which will cause a reaction of the dark matter.

"The only way that we can overcome this chaos, is to make sure that we pull from the blue flame of El Elyon and focus on the Ancient Language, that has been given to us for us to overcome this attack.

"Now imagine, if we have a person here," he said as he drew a stick person, "which I have given this one a big belly, for the purpose of this discussion. Within their belly is a bunch of circles that represent the release of antimatter *within them,* which for us, represents darkness."

"Now, if that person has a lot of antimatter operating within them, it is going to attract demons, which is what we will quantify as *dark matter.* This dark matter comes from another dimension and is uncontrollable."

Tony pointed at the stickman that had holes within the belly. "These holes signify the area in which antimatter within the person is pulled on, by the new antimatter that is being brought into this dimension by PRINA. When the antimatter builds up to a certain point, it will then draw dark matter in, releasing chaotic manifestations of psychosis in the person's mind, where they are given over to a violent state of existence, and it is in that moment, that I believe, Beelzebub plans to take the soul of that person into the other dimension."

Mouths were opened, as he finished making this point. He paused, realizing how much he needed to bring the point home.

"Let me go a step further and say that the blue flame within you of El Elyon is at total opposition to this dark matter. With that being said, if there is a person operating in dark matter, and they are around you, you will feel vexed and tormented, because of that antimatter that is already in existence within you. But you have been given the blue flame, to overcome the antimatter's reaction, to bring your emotions under control."

Milly joined him back up front and thanked him for the detailed demonstration and finished her portion with one more thought. "Today when I was at Strytan, I saw Truman Hall glowing as an amber fire in the midst of campus. I've seen the crystal tower in The Quad, that has the blue flame within, and this building is directly east of The Quad, at the point where the sun rises. Upon the building today I saw Greek writing converted into English, which read, ***you shall know the truth and the truth will set you free.*** El Elyon's Wisdom is truth, and Truman represents the true man, the one that has the philosophy of the Wisdom of El Elyon. As we fight this battle, we have to remember that, although there is great darkness, that the sun will rise in the east; light will come!"

Milly heard the door opening again up in the heavens, and knew that El Elyon was about to pour out His Wisdom. "Get ready," she said, "because El Elyon said He would pour out His Wisdom upon us at the end of this meeting, and it is coming."

Robert stepped up beside her, "Yes everyone, prepare yourselves for He is about to visit us in power, and I suggest you get out of your chair and onto the floor."

Immediately, everyone pushed their chair aside, and upon their movement to the floor, it seemed that the roof of the house was lifted off, where the group was able to peer at the dark sky, seeing the stars of the universe. There stood a huge door, and behind it was light, when suddenly it opened and poured out a brilliant light, that came rushing like Niagara Falls into the house and upon them.

Each person was on the floor, under the weight of its visitation, which was releasing the atmosphere of eternity within them, causing the antimatter within each individual to be burned up, where they would not be susceptible to PRINA's release of antimatter and dark matter.

The group was prostrate on the floor, feeling the immense painting of Wisdom from El Elyon, when then they heard His voice; "I have painted you, as My philosophers of truth in this earth. You will write about it within the atmosphere, as I make your tongue like a pen of a ready writer, proclaiming in power with My Sword, that which I have done and will do, defeating the gates of hell. You are My warriors and have been prepared."

The entire group was caught up into another dimension, as it seemed like the universe was all around them. The door opened in the heavens, and then brought them in, which was the point to which they lost consciousness lying still for an hour. Afterwards, the members of the group began to come to, checking on one another, where each individual was now up and each, sitting in a chair, stunned at the supernatural occurrence that just took place.

Robert slowly got up, and asked Kaufman to join him at his side. The two men stood in front, when Robert patted Kaufman on the back, and exclaimed to the group, "Well Lads and Lassies, I believe we are ready!"

Chapter 16

Crouched on a lamppost hanging over the street, Constugard sat like a gargoyle peering at the Doctors Mercer, while the group had been meeting. In scathing disgust he grumbled as he saw the group being lifted up to the door in the heavens, where they were painted with Wisdom. He grunted and snarled, then gnashing his teeth, at the utter torment he felt, knowing that the Ancient Language would be heard all over the area.

Beelzebub would be in a tirade for sure, he thought, loathing the thought of Beelzebub releasing the sound from the voice trap of the Ancient Language, to torment the underworld, for not obeying. Beelzebub would arrive shortly, and Constugard hated the thought of giving him the news, that the brilliant light of Wisdom had incinerated the antimatter within the souls of individuals within the group.

Constugard stood up, as dark charcoal grey wings came from behind his back, lifting him in the night sky, carrying him back to The Ancient Gatehouse. The smell could be detected miles away in the spirit, as Bobby Knight and the other Gatehouse members carried out diabolical rituals in the basement, where shrills and shrieks oozed through the bricks, seeming like a wall around the property. The gates of hell were getting larger a bit more, as the cords continued to spill out of the building in the spirit realm, and be carried all through the street, where they hoped to spread as much diabolical slime over the next few days leading up to the date of PRINA's release of antimatter, pulling on the souls of mankind in the region.

Vladamore conspired with his leaders, having them pull out all stops, to push the town of Springfield, and its university, into the most chaotic place in Area 9, where they intended for riots to break out in the streets. Heradacio and Dadanel were releasing their artillery of grenades in the spirit, planning on the cannon balls to be set off shortly thereafter.

Rafael and Tubal watched the underworld's movement in the midst of Springfield, and had a host of angels alongside them, retrieving the demonic grenades, picking them up and casting them in a special angelic emerald sac, suffocating the satanic smoke and extinguishing the weapon 's potency, completely.

Angels of different color, wearing the finest battle armament, traversed the landscape. Many angelic hosts had copper colored tint to their spiritual body, while others had a white effervescent tint, and still others had a dark tint. Their armor was varied, as well, from silver, copper, and gold, having markings of the ancient Tav, with a lion roaring upon their breastplates. As they went to and fro grabbing the enemy's weapons, the roar from their breastplate could be heard, as the sound extinguished all the evil within the demonic artillery. Evil smoke would be released as the grenades were being thrown in the emerald sac to be done away with.

Knight and his men were in The Ancient Gatehouse, finding that their satanic rituals were not as effective as they hoped, since they could sense the angelic host in the area, fighting against them. Knight came pounding up the basement steps, blood dripping from his hands, as he shouted in the main room, "CONNNNNNSTUGARDDDD!"

Constugard loathed any crony of Beelzebub thinking that they had authority over him, and came growling in front of Knight's face, as his crouched figure was now elongated, to where he stood 9 feet tall, against Knight's 6'10" frame. Constugard was face to face with Knight, snarling and growling, "What do you want with me, do you know who I am to Beelzebub?"

Knight realizing that he was overstepping his boundary with the demon, back peddled, "I know you are a great military sergeant and aide to our liege, and I have need of your assistance so that we can ensure his success in this area before his arrival."

Constugard loathed humans and only tolerated Knight because he was of use to Beelzebub for the moment. As soon as he was no longer needed, Constugard wanted to be the one to slice him apart with his claws, getting rid of the vomiting flesh creature that would try and bark orders at him.

"I do what I am designed to do for my liege," Constugard snarled to Knight, letting him know his proper place. "I already have seen the group lifted up to the door in the heavens, where they were then painted with El Elyon's Wisdom, do you not think that I do not know how dreadful this is for my liege, and that steps are already being taken?"

Knight stepped back, realizing that he was not going to ease Constugard's present state, and knew that he needed to return to the basement with the other members, doing their evil deeds, where the dark matter from the other dimension would find its way to Springfield, to enlarge the gates of hell. That was the only way the gates of hell increased in a region, was from the dark matter of the parallel universe, luring demons to its location.

Constugard turned from their conversation, went back to the top of The Ancient Gatehouse, continuing his watch against the angelic host of El Elyon, being ready to wrestle them should they come near. He was going to maintain his watch throughout the night, knowing that Rafael and Tubal were close by. Rafael's name was known among the underworld, as one of El Elyon's greatest warriors, and Constugard was not going to let him anywhere near Beelzebub's lair in Springfield.

Off in the distance, brilliant bluish silver wings were spread nine feet out, as the moon, giving it all the more brilliance, lent its light to the figure tracing the angelic form. It was Rafael, combing the area, safeguarding the group, as well as the people of Springfield.

Rafael wore his silver colored armor that sparkled like stars within the metal, gilded in the heavens by El Elyon, who took from the stars in the nebulas to design the brilliant piece of armor. *Star armor* was the strongest metal that there was, and the serpent creatures despised it; they no longer had ability for armor at this level of performance. Rather, the demons had to settle for the metals in the earth, reaching within the depths of the ground, to take and melt, building demonic armor having spikes and chains interspersed.

Rafael saw Constugard sitting over The Ancient Gatehouse, and could hear the moaning coming from the building, where diabolical activities were being carried out, as the gates of hell enlarged. Rafael motioned to Tubal, who took the silver shofar out of its sac and blew it in the heavens, when angels began to form a circular pattern in the night sky, like a wheel within a wheel.

The inside circle turned clockwise, while the outside circle turned counter-clockwise. Gold speckled dust in the heavens came in the middle of the angelic host, releasing specks of light throughout Springfield where the gold dust landed on homes, businesses, Strytan, and throughout, acting like the cloak of a garment over those who were within the location.

Vladamore's teeth gnashed, as he saw the angels bringing the gold dust within the realm, knowing that El Elyon's Light was being used as a cloak in the darkness. The darkness could not extinguish or put out this light, and was very unreceptive to it, as Vladamore snarled at Tildash and Morder, "My commanders, you are infinite fools, not worthy of hell's taunts; as you have allowed El Elyon's angels to release the Light, protecting the area."

Morder knew that there were still other things that could be done, there was timing to the cloaking device brought by the angels; it worked for only 48 hours. Morder informed Vladamore, "We need to summon the princes so that they can send their army against the angels within two nights, so that they cannot form the wheel within the wheel, unlocking the clock of eternity into the earth, where they can release the Cloak of Light."

Hell could not do anything for the next 48 hours in Springfield. They were kept from harming others, and it bought time for both sides to do their war strategies for the upcoming Wednesday. This gave both groups five days to prepare. Friday night was coming to a close as the midnight hour approached. The angels heralded in the night skies, raising their swords to El Elyon, shouting upon the sleepy town of Springfield, "El Elyon be with you!"

Awake!

Wind blowing in Milly's room as the cool night's breath came upon her, carrying the gold dust released by the angels, brought much comfort, carrying her into a deep sleep once more, to know the time which she was in. El Elyon was making Milly firmly confident in who she was, realizing the power that had been given to her with the painting of Wisdom and the unction of El Elyon's Spirit.

The crispness came across her nose tickling it lightly, to which she rubbed it instinctively, and then caught a glimpse of the gold dust that came into her viewing. Little specks of gold dust on her hands now, gleamed with the brightness of the stars. Light so brilliant that it blinded her vision causing her to grab for her backpack on the floor, fumbling around with her hands to reach for her sunglasses.

"What is this?" she asked inquisitively, trying to comprehend all that was occurring. Tubal was standing in her room, as she jumped up from the bed standing with feet firmly planted on the floor, sunglasses on her face asking him, "Tubal, what is happening?"

He smiled at her touching her lightly on the shoulder, releasing El Elyon's peace, and then opened a vial of oil containing liquid gold essence, lighting up here and there with sparks of ember light as it organically moved within. Opening the vial, he told Milly that he was releasing an eye salve from El Elyon, which would cause scales to fall from her eyes where she would see in the spirit in greater capacity. She would not have to depend on the cones and rods within her own eyes to contain the capacity of what she saw, but rather see through purified eyes in the spirit. She had not seen to this depth yet. Now because of the oil, she was allowed to peer at the Light of the gold dust, which was being laid upon the area.

With eyes closed, she removed the sunglasses and Tubal anointed her eye lids, where the organic liquid essence seeped through her skin, showing the x-ray of the eye, the cornea, pupil, rods, cones, and the optic nerve, sending a charge through the optic nerve seven times, like a pulsating electric current. Suddenly, she felt a crusting over her eyeball, to which Tubal said, "Now open your eyes."

Slowly opening her eyes, a crusty film covered them causing Milly for the moment to be anxious. Tubal lightly touched her again on the shoulder releasing the unction of the bronze shoes of peace on her feet, to which she became calm. He then blew lightly upon her eyes, when the scales began to drop off of her eyeballs, falling to the ground giving her the ability to see 10 million colors all at once!

She was overcome with amazement; not realizing that, that amount of color existed in the universe, much less the earth. Tubal responded to her reaction, "There is much more color than this Milly, in the heavens."

She peered at the gold dust on her hand and cloaked all over the road, seeing the beauty of the Light that shown all around, as if the ground had become the heavens, with thousands upon thousands of stars shining throughout. "What is this Tubal, this gold dust of Light?"

"It is El Elyon's blanket of protection, that we use in times of war, buying us time for further strategies, where Beelzebub's army cannot harm the area for at least 48 hours. After that time, the blanket will have dissolved where he is then able to attack. However, the demonic princes were not aware of our gathering last night in the heavens. We not only released this over Springfield, but in every inhabited city within Area 9. This has bought enough time for our council to meet again, and plan."

Milly was taken back all the more with the most striking appearance of Tubal, as his sapphire garment sparkled like the universe itself, now showing nebulas within, and even a part of it reflecting the Pillars of Creation. His garment was the universe and was all the more beautiful she thought. His hair was braided near the front, as it too, was pulled back slightly having his dark hair flow down upon the armor. She was beside herself, realizing that his garment had looked that beautiful all the time, but it was not until her eyes were open that she could see the entirety of its beauty.

SHE WAS AWAKE!

Never had she felt this alive and awake, and all she wanted to do was run through the city to look at everything and everyone she could, in order to perceive the beauty of El Elyon's perspective of them. She needed extra poise in order to bear all that she was taking in, unsure of how much of the beauty she could stand; it was more than she realized.

"Milly, it will take time for you to get used to, but it will come," Tubal said. "Be patient, and wait for the strength of the blue flame and the Ancient Language to fill you, giving you the ability to contain all that you are seeing and bear it."

"Wow Tubal, you are not kidding with that!" Milly exclaimed. "All the beauty that I am seeing is so overwhelming that, at times, I want to shut my eyes, not understanding how I can handle seeing all of this; it is too much."

"El Elyon will help you, and just like an infant learns how to walk, you are learning how to see. With this vision you will be able to see the hearts and minds of the souls that are caught in captivity in the parallel universe, knowing which minds and hearts are ready to be set free."

She looked at Tubal confused, thinking that all she had to do with the oil, once there, was to pour it out on everyone.

"No Milly," replied Tubal. He heard her thoughts and knew what she was thinking. "You can only pour it out on the minds and hearts of the souls that are ready to wake up from the deep sleep. There are those whose soul is given over to the darkness, and to pour out the oil upon them will be a waste. We are very respectful of the oil and do not want to spare one drop that will not be used."

Tubal waved his hands palms facing each other, one over another in a circle, presenting an open vision much like a holograph, where Milly saw the door that opened up in the heavens. "Wisdom was poured out on you when El Elyon opened the door. And now, each of you have the ability to have your eyes opened on a greater scale than you have known, where you can bear the splendor of El Elyon's light enabling you to fight successfully against Beelzebub's army."

"When you meet with the students at Strytan, know that you will see that which has attacked their soul in the past, and what they are meant to be, in His army, so that they can be delivered from hell's mental assault. El Elyon's Spirit will be with you giving you instructions."

Milly thanked Tubal, as he leaned toward her crowning her with a brilliant silver crown that was a simple solid band. It had writing of the Ancient Language upon it, with five sapphires distributed around the band.

Rafael came into her room just as Tubal was crowning her, and encouraged Milly to continue the fight. "You Milly, are a mighty warrior of El Elyon uniquely skilled with many gifts for this time. This crown represents the five gifts in which you walk boldly in the unction of, Wisdom, Knowledge, Understanding, Might, and Counsel. Each of these sapphires, have those aspects caught within the stone, where El Elyon has spoken to each one, which He chiseled from His Mountain, placing them carefully in this crown."

She was mesmerized with the simple beauty of the crown and spun around in her room, delighting at her appearance in the mirror. She could see the angels behind her while staring at their image, when they slowly faded giving her wishes goodbye.

The Students

Saturday early afternoon, found Milly, Parker and Tony scurrying to prepare for their meeting in Truman Hall's conference room, while they put their finishing touches on the day's meeting with the students. Eager and nervous at the same time, they were unsure of whom the students were and what to expect, only that there was a sure connection from all their supernatural experiences.

Tony had the coffee piping hot, with a mini coffee bar housing a small coffee shop set up for when the students entered the room. The cool lab experiment coffee cups were lent from *The Grind* for the meeting. The conference room was the coolest of all, looking like a throw back to the 1960's with brown leather Scandinavian looking couches, and orange colored oversized chairs, large enough for 1 ½ persons. Coffee tables all around had coasters placed on them for the students to set their drinks. A group table at the side of the room was set up with handouts that Milly had compiled.

She looked at Parker and Tony, "I guess we are as close to ready as possible. All the students responded to my email and were eager to come today. During the meeting, if you feel led to share anything, please feel free. I have a small outline of things we can share with them, where we can tag team wherever we feel most comfortable. We will be as relaxed and laid back as possible, and I am sure we will get a flood of questions." She slapped the sides of each of their shoulders and cheered them on, "Let's get to it guys; here they come."

From outside the glass walls, she could see them coming to the wooden doors, housing a glass window to peer through. Slowly they matriculated into the room, gravitating towards the coffee bar where Tony was playing the barista boy, wearing his favorite t-shirt, proclaiming that his addiction was coffee. He set the group at ease, as some began laughing, realizing that the barista boy at *The Grind* had a small fan club that spoke of him on occasion, as they carried around the addictions that he made. Seeing his familiar face made them feel welcome.

Parker was standing in the middle of the seating area, holding up his addiction, waving the group to the arrangement of seats where they could make themselves at home. Milly had been welcoming the students upon entering, seeing them spill out across the room between the coffee bar and the seating arrangement. A buzz was in the room, as the anxious, almost paranoid students now were feeling as though they were in a special club, having been marked by an experience that forever changed their lives.

Parker pointed to the main coffee table that had permanent markers and nametags, where each of the students could write their name and put it on their shirt. A tall fair skinned young man with shaggy brown hair, who was on the basketball team, towered over the table writing on his nametag, "Anthony." Parker welcomed him and began to talk to him about the new season for the Eagle's Basketball.

A set of twins were in the room, two young ladies that were a light dark tone of brown, Majestic and her sister Caprice, wrote on their nametags and joined in the conversation with Parker and Anthony. Other students began gathering around the table, filling out their nametags and enjoying the fellowship of coming together outside of the special event, to learn of who each other was.

There was Tiffany, a beautiful young black female who was 5'11" hanging out with Tracie, a thin white young white female at 5'6", looking up to Tiffany, as she reached up and hugged her. She was thankful that Tiffany acted fast the other night; having been frightened, Tiffany brought a lot of ease to the group.

Jayden and his girlfriend Loriel were present, looking forward to the meeting and glad that they could look to others instead of only themselves. Christopher and Matthew were brothers, one a couple of years older than the other one, both with sandy blonde hair, standing at 6'2", laughing and joking with the group as they enjoyed making new friends.

Bella and her sorority sister, Angie, from Theta Mu Alpha were present, glad to see that some students from their other classes were in attendance. Mike, Niles, James, Christy, Sherri, Charis and Brie were a few of the others in with the group. They all began to finish their nametags, at which time Milly began calling the meeting together. She nodded at Parker, who then shut the doors, and then to Tony who came to join her with the others.

"Hey everyone, I know that this meeting does not find us in the greatest of circumstances since the thing that makes you all unique is what you experienced. I will let you know that Parker, Tony and myself," to whom she pointed, "have gone through these occurrences over the past month, and had many questions about all that we experienced, and found it to all of our benefit to have this meeting."

The group continued drinking on their addictions, as Milly spoke. "I am warning you ahead of time that we will be throwing a bunch of stuff at you, but I have brought a handout giving you some information about things that occur in the spirit. Some of it has scientific evidence given by a physicist, whom I talked with the other day from PRINA. If you have not heard of PRINA, it is actually in Geneva, Switzerland, where a certain activity will be carried out this coming Wednesday, which brings us all here today."

"Before we get to that, I want to let Parker come speak." Milly nodded to Parker, passing him the torch, as he came to the forefront with a calm about his person.

"Let me start off by saying I agree with Milly on all these points, that we have experienced the supernatural occurrences here at Strytan for over a month, and at first, it freaked me the heck out, to where I didn't know if I wanted any of it. However, I have to say that after a week or so, I began to think of how cool it was to see things that others couldn't."

"When Milly first started experiencing the supernatural in front of me, I could not see what she saw and did not comprehend the level of focus and maturity that was needed to be normal; once you see the supernatural you cannot *unsee* it."

Others nodded in agreement, making noises of "mmm hmm," letting each other know that they could not *unsee* the other night.

"I will tell you this though," Parker continued, "We were fortunate to have others, who were in the journey with us, and were introduced to experts, I guess you could say, in the field, giving us guidance on what we are going to share with you tonight about spiritual warfare."

Majestic and Caprice's eyes bugged out, as they then looked at each other mouthing, "spiritual warfare?"

Parker nodded at them both, saying "You got it ladies, tonight is going to be spiritual warfare 101, 201, and 301, all packed tight in this evening." He motioned to Milly, who then took the floor back.

Milly pointed to the handouts, which she had just passed out, as each student held one. "What you have in your hands is information about what you will come to know well, in regards to spiritual warfare." She could see some confusion on the faces, seeing Anthony, Chris and Matthew looking at one another with a puzzled look.

"How many of you have family or friends in the military?" Milly asked. A few hands slowly raised of people who knew of someone. "Well," Milly said, "they have been trained to fight for our country in the natural, but what I am referring to here is fighting in the spirit." She had their attention.

"All of you saw the tower the other night and were able to see its mark upon the foreheads of those who are in this room. Right?"

They nodded as Charis and Brie made mention they saw each other's mark, as well as Jayden and Loriel, Niles and James. Each was motioning to the other agreeing with Milly. The group was bonding over the event that seemed traumatic at first but now was beginning to make sense.

"Right, you saw things that others on campus could not see; you saw the crystal tower with the blue flame that had Ancient Language engulfed within. That blue flame is what was marked upon you, with the ancient Hebrew Letter, Tav, which looks like an X."

The students were repeating, "wow," like a wave going off at a football game. They had no clue what the mark was, and now that Milly was bringing the information to them, and it was laid out on the worksheet, things were making much more sense. They were looking at the mark that Milly had on the sheet. She went further into detail about the spiritual armor each of them had and then taught them the difference between the whip with the keys in it and the Sword that would speak to them.

She shared, without disclosing the student or the class, what happened as time stood still and she had interacted with a demon, listening to the Sword to bind it up with the keys within the whip. After each and every spiritual encounter that she had binding up the demons, she would return to the normal space-time continuum, with the natural time in this earth, which was another dimension from that which she speaking on of eternity time.

She gave the students the example of eternity-time, and how it seems as though all other things remain frozen, while you seem to be the only one moving within the framework of that space, to which the Sword would always let you know when it would happen, along with the glowing of the amber whip. Milly went into further details about the battle that they were facing with what PRINA planned on doing in Geneva, Switzerland on the coming Wednesday in Springfield, and then handed it over to Tony, who would take them further into the physics of it.

Tony spoke to the group, having his whiteboard, and doing his teaching on both the Wave-Particle Duality to show the power of the blue flame and its energy inside of the students, and then discussed the antimatter and dark matter that PRINA had planned on releasing this coming week, where they were able to comprehend their ability to see the paranormal activity.

The students were spellbound as Tony gave the intricacies of science and the interaction with the supernatural. Anthony was a science major himself and sat speechless as the discussion went on, shaking his head in amazement, then nodding it in agreement. Majestic and Caprice's eyes were still bugged out, as they sat on one of the sofa's with their legs crossed, overwhelmed at what they seemed to have gotten themselves into wondering what they could offer.

Sherri, Christy, Mike, Chris and Matthew were pumped up, sitting on the edge of their seat, laughing at some moments, while chiming in with, "Wow" and, "No Way," or "heck yeah," at other times. The energy level was building up, as the meeting continued.

Milly knew that the group needed a break and stepped up after Tony's presentation. "Hey guys, I know this is more than you expected for a small meeting, and its already been two hours, so let's take a 15 minute break and meet back up afterwards."

The group slowly got up out of their seats, looking at one another with wide eyes and stares, uncertain of what they would hear shortly, not knowing what point would be made next from the group leaders. They knew it was more than just getting mere information.

El Elyon spoke to Milly before reconvening the meeting. "Mildred, I have given you the ability to see and the anointing oil that will cause you to know all things. Show them the display of the power I have given you with My Ancient Language, as I then open their eyes to see. Do what the Sword instructs and let it all unfold."

Milly knew that she could trust what El Elyon spoke and did not question it. Rather, she stepped out in blind faith as the group came back into the room to begin the last part of the meeting. "I'm going to tell you what we need from you all, and why we are meeting today, and then afterwards I am going to show you a demonstration of what you have been given."

People were sitting straight up, knowing that Milly was cutting to the chase and not going to take them on a long journey around the same mountain. "We will be fighting the battle of all battles in the spirit realm on Wednesday of this week. We will be empowered by the Tower that is on The Quad, releasing the blue flame with the Ancient Language, which is our fuel and power source to fight the demons. Some of you saw the paranormal activity the other night, and that is but the beginning of what will happen come Wednesday, so we have a very short time to prepare you."

She looked into their eyes with determination and purpose, like a general preparing his troops. "You all have brilliant shiny armor that will protect you from the demons, and will each have a whip with the keys of El Elyon to take care of demons, binding them where they cannot harm others. Moreover, the Sword you carry on your side will reverberate with sound, speaking to your soul, as you understand the translation of all that it says."

Majestic and Caprice, could not hide their expressions, as Majestic stood up and said, "I am a woman who can kick demons to the curb!" Caprice joined her, where they both did a Z-snap bumping hips, giving "uh huhs" and then sitting back down. The group laughed and then returned their focus to Milly.

"You got that right ladies, you can kick some demons to the curb, and for sure with the power you have been given. As a matter of fact, I will demonstrate it now, as I ask Angie and Bella to come up here." They apprehensively looked at Milly, who assured them that she would not embarrass them in any way, setting them at ease to join her.

As they both stepped up, Milly said, "Angie you have a hearing problem, not because of something that is natural but because there is a hindering spirit plugging up your ear, which looks like a rope stuffed inside."

Angie, surprised at Milly's boldness, stated, "Wow Milly, no one knows, but I have been deaf in my left ear ever since I was 13 years-old. My parents thought it was a pool accident, but I felt it was something different."

Milly held up her sword, to which at that moment everyone's eyes were opened in the spirit, and they were pulled into eternity-time, where the members of the group began shouting, "Whoa!"

"I command you hindering spirit, to come out of Angie's ear by the authority of this Sword!" Immediately the group saw a huge rope coming out of Angie's ear, looking like a large rope to tie a ship to the port. They began shouting, "Whoa man!" as the rope came out of Angie's ear, and she began shouting, while jumping up and down, with Majestic and Caprice now at her side with the same excitement repeating, "Sister, you are set free!"

Milly then looked at Bella, "You have had a struggle the past several months with alcohol and it's because of the generational issue within your family lineage that has you bound. It is a demonic spirit attacking you."

Bella began busting out in tears, as Majestic and Caprice put their hands on her shoulders. Milly picked up her Sword cutting the cord off of Bella's belly that had her bound to the addiction. "In the authority of this Sword, I cut the cord to addiction of alcohol and command it to loose you and go into the wilderness!" Immediately a demon came oozing through her skin like a dark sheet being pulled out of her belly, and began shrieking in pain.

The group members were blown away as they saw and heard the demon. Bella looked up at Milly, grabbed her tightly, hugging her, thanking her for setting her free of the oppression. "Milly, I cannot thank you enough!"

Majestic and Caprice began hugging Bella, and speaking words of encouragement, as she began to shout, "Woo Hoo!" The group lined up, where Milly then one at a time, came against demonic attacks in each person, sending out demons that oppressed them, as well as lifting off the lying serpents that had hooks attached to their soul. The group cheered as each person was set free from the assaults against their soul.

As Milly saw the oppression lifted off each person, she was then given a vision, looking much like a moving holograph, where she prophesied to the gift within each one. People were blown away saying, "I always wanted to do that," or "I never knew that I could do that." Each was blown away and enthralled to hear the prophesies over the others, as well. Left in awe and amazement, the group members began saying,

"We can stay here as long as you like guys; we are not leaving! We believe!"

Milly, Parker and Tony all armored up in the brilliant shiny armor for El Elyon's warriors, gave each other high fives, as now the team of students stood up around them, in their armor, looking in amazement at the meticulous detail given to it. They were spellbound by the supernatural, and Milly continued through the night, showing them how to use the whip with the keys, and confronting the demons in the spirit realm.

As the group was winding down, Milly had them stand in a line to put the unction of the anointing oil upon their head and eyes, to know and see with Wisdom. Tony and Parker were as pumped up as the other members of the group, and could not wait for Milly to anoint them as well. Such electricity was charging through the room, as everyone had the hairs on their arms standing up, chills down their backs, and experiencing a ketone rush in their brain, where it seemed that their synapses were firing away.

Milly anointed each of them declaring, "El Elyon's wisdom be upon you, as you fight the battle in the gifts He has given you, having your eyes opened by His Wisdom to know the Ancient Language that unlocks the door to all Wisdom, where you have the unction to know everything!"

Once she anointed someone, the blue flame would come into the person from the tower outside on The Quad, and the mark upon the person's forehead shone brightly. The experience was mesmerizing, as now the students who had come in uncertain at the beginning of the afternoon, at 2 pm, were now close friends and allies in a battle to fight for the souls of man, hours later at 10 pm. The meeting was a total success!

As they adjourned, Parker stressed the need for the group to keep the information to themselves, so as not to draw unwanted attention that would make anyone in administration suspicious of activities that would be, what they would consider, to be a group hallucination. Rather, it was easier to keep the information to themselves.

Milly instructed the students that the time in which they were to meet in front of Truman Hall would be when they sent the call out, most likely in the dawn. The students agreed with her, walking out together, giving each other high-fives and carrying on conversations, where the noise from inside of the room slowly faded, until it was now Tony, Parker and Milly.

Letting out a deep breath, they looked at each other as Tony said, "Well, that was intense!"

Parker and Milly started laughing, slapping Tony on the shoulder, saying, "Make us an addiction will you!"

Chapter 17

Sunday morning, cool temperature and the holidays around the corner, set an atmosphere of joy in the midst of Springfield. People were out and about early this morning at the local bakery, *The Sundry*, which made every kind of dessert imaginable, the lemon herb and tarragon leaf pecan muffin was the most favorite. The smell of pumpkin and pecan in the air as you passed the bakery, set people's nose to holiday cheer.

A special merriment in the town was partly a result of the angelic work the night before that blanketed Springfield for 48 hours. Hello's and good morning's coming from people's mouths, with a friendly smile, made this small town idyllic.

Everyone on the team was taking advantage of the day off, spending time with family and friends. All the meetings they had attended the past few weeks, and with the upcoming battle, gave them need to take a small respite.

The new students, now with the group, hung out on campus using the conference room at Truman Hall. They were still getting to know one another, and discussed what went on at Saturday's meeting, as well as the upcoming battle on Wednesday where they would fight. Each person, bringing a snack to the meeting, was ready to enjoy some sports, as they pulled in someone's desktop computer to watch the local Strytan Eagles basketball team, where Anthony was playing.

The Doctors Mercer had their usual routine, with brewed coffee from the stovetop, and bacon to accompany the coffee. While Kaufman had met with Professor Peyton and Robert at Sundry's bakery, Father Sanderson, was preparing for Sunday Mass, and Reginald Fielding prepared his sermon for his Sunday morning service.

Parker and Tony were hanging out at *The Grind* on the patio, where the two would split up for the day's activities. Tony would join Dana for Mass at Saint Timothy's Cathedral. Later in the evening, the two guys planned on eating at Milly's house, where she had invited them over for a meal.

Milly climbed out of bed, as the butter pecan flavor coffee tickled her nose hairs, making its way into her nasal passage, setting a tantalizing taste on the back of her tongue. "Oh, I am so ready for a good cup of java," Milly said.

One foot in front of the other, she walked downstairs where her mom and dad were, looking forward to her morning Keto-Coffee and discussion with them. This was the day she knew that she had to spill the beans on all that she had been doing with the group, as well as about the upcoming battle. Only now, she needed to find the right moment.

"Mom, Dad," Milly called as she traipsed down the stairways. "I'm smelling the brew, and I'm ready for my Keto-Coffee."

Laughter filled the downstairs, where Lavern and Daniel were looking at childhood photos of Milly, while relaxing in the sitting room recalling fond memories. "Hey guys, what are you laughing about."

Lavern held out a photo of Milly when she was five years old, where she had a sword in her hand and a knight's helmet over her head. "Do you remember this one Mill? You were crazy about knights in armor when you were little, and we bought you this sword and helmet with a shield for your fifth Christmas. You would not stop playing with it and kept wearing it each time you came home from school, up until you were about ten or so."

Milly had totally forgotten about the knight's battle wear that her parents got her, and looked closely at the few photos of her at different ages with it on. She saw her fifth, sixth, seventh, eighth, ninth and then tenth year wearing the uniform, completely blown away. Why did she not recognize then that something more was going on, having been so drawn to wearing battle armament.

"What is it Mill," asked Lavern, as she looked to Daniel, puzzled at the expression on their daughter's face.

Daniel reached out to touch his daughter's shoulder, "Milly, are you alright honey?"

"Guys, you know what, I have never been better, but for me to truly *be alright*, I have to share something with you two."

They were a bit perplexed, uncertain of what their daughter would disclose this morning, and hoped that it was nothing disconcerting; their morning was going so well, and they wanted Milly to enjoy it, too. "Seriously guys, there is nothing wrong, but looking at these pictures explains a lot. I understand things more clearly than ever. But before we sit down to talk, I have to get my Keto-Coffee, so Dad, would you please do the honors?"

Daniel kissed her on the forehead, "You got it my little warrior!"

Lavern reached her hand out to Milly, grabbing her daughter's hand, squeezing it tightly, as if to release the satisfaction she and Daniel had about Milly's life. They could not be more proud or happy about what Milly was becoming, seeking two degrees at Strytan that would help her on the road to a successful career.

Daniel brought in the drink, passing it off to Milly, "Proceed Knight Milly," he said jokingly, "your court is ready." He sat next to his wife on the loveseat, while Milly sat across from them in one of the wingback chairs.

Getting in full comfort mode, Milly tucked her legs underneath her, while she sat snuggled in the big chair, drinking on her butter pecan Keto-Coffee. "Ok, now promise you two will hear me out before you freak out."

Daniel and Lavern were not sure how to make out the request. They knew their daughter said there was nothing bad to discuss. However, they sensed that it was from *her* perspective of the matter, and things were worse than she believed. Cautiously, they looked back at their daughter and replied, "Alright, we will listen."

Taking one more sip before beginning her conversation with her parents, Milly spoke to El Elyon in her mind, "I need Your help, please give me wisdom."

El Elyon immediately strengthened Milly with the blue flame, responding, "I'm here."

"Ok, you see all these pictures of me with the knight's armor on?" Milly asked.

Uncertain of where she was going with it, they felt greater peace, wondering what that had to do with anything. "Yes," they responded.

"Well, I don't know how much you know of Great Grandma Lee and what she did here in Springfield. But several weeks ago, I discovered that she had three diaries that were recovered by a small group, of which two of my professors, Kaufman and Mercer, are a part. Mercer is in antiquities and Kaufman is my philosophy professor."

Lavern was shocked to hear the news of her grandmother's dairies. She remembered her own mother mentioning that she kept journals, and had written a bunch of stuff that she could not make sense out of. She vaguely remembered her mother showing them to her when she was little, and recalling some caveman language, along with drawings, being confused as to what any of it meant.

"I briefly saw your Great Grandmother's diaries when I was young and forgot that she had them," Lavern said. "How is it that they came across the diaries?"

Milly took another sip and reached out to her mother, assuring her that all was well. "Apparently, she left them with the priest of Saint Timothy's Cathedral, before she died."

"That is where she used to go to Church," Lavern said.

"Well that makes sense," replied Milly.

"What makes sense?" Daniel asked.

"Ok, what I am about to share might be a little far fetched for you guys to understand, but here goes." She repositioned her legs letting them touch the floor, as she drank the rest of her coffee, almost gulping it, then set it on the table.

"About a month ago, I began having visions of an ancient room, with old stone steps, a floor and stone walls. I was led to a room where there was an ancient desk, chair and small bed, where a voice called for Mildred, and then I saw this little girl get up from the bed and begin writing an Ancient Language, on a sheet of very old paper."

Lavern and Daniel looked at their daughter, not knowing where this was going. However, hearing that she was having visions was something that was out of the ordinary for sure. Lavern was not to far removed from this; she remembered hearing her mother discuss her grandmother's visions, as well. Now sensing what Milly was unfolding to them, made more sense of her grandmother's odd behaviors, while growing up.

"Go on Milly," Lavern said to her daughter.

"Professor Kaufman asked Parker and me to begin cleaning the basement in Truman Hall, which we didn't think much of, until we went down there to do the work. It was then that I began experiencing an open vision of walking on the old stone, and down the ancient steps, leading towards the philosophy department's files in the basement. Then in the basement I saw the old desk and chair that was actually in my dream."

Lavern and Daniel stared into each other's eyes, and then back to Milly. Daniel, wanting to make sure they were on track asked, "So what does this have to do with these photos of you dressed as a knight?"

"We will get to that in a bit dad, let me finish this part first," she pleaded as she looked at her father.

He nodded in agreement and Milly continued. "Once there, with this experience happening a few times, I saw in the vision where a relic was hidden behind the wall in that particular room in the basement. Sure enough, Parker looked, at which time he pulled out the ancient relic that was in my dream, housing a very old document that had two different ancient languages on it, one was Hebrew and the other Aramaic.

"Both Parker and I began talking to Kaufman and Mercer about this information, at which time we were connected with someone who was an expert with this particular ancient relic, Robert, whom also had knowledge of Great Grandmother's diaries. He informed me of her work in Springfield in the 1930s and how she worked with advanced knowledge that stupefied many in the town, that it could only be supernaturally given, since she was still fairly young, and a woman at that, in a time where women were still making their way after having the right to vote given to them in the 1920s."

Lavern and Daniel looked inquisitively at each other, realizing that Milly knew more about her Great Grandmother Mildred, than they did. "Well, I discovered that the Mildred that was in the first vision I was given, was Great Grandmother, and she knew the Ancient Language from El Elyon, as well as was trained by Father Augustine Castellanos, who was the priest, at Saint Timothy Cathedral."

"Her diaries correlate with the ancient relic that was discovered, whom the group believe to be authored by Father Castellanos." She inhaled, then exhaled, checking on the status of her parents. "Are you guys with me?"

Daniel and Lavern were now holding hands as they listened to the story that their daughter was describing to them, wondering what more could be shared. "Yes," said Daniel, "go on Milly, we are listening."

"More things happened, where in dreams and visions, I was seeing the universe, and in the midst of being lifted up in it, I met two angels, Rafael and Tubal, as well as seeing a door being opened by El Elyon in the heavens, to release Wisdom. I know this sounds absolutely crazy, but seeing these pictures brings more understanding to me, for what I am about to share next.

"In the midst of these supernatural experiences, I saw armor like this knight's armor in these pictures here, only more detailed, upon me, where I was being instructed about a demonic battle to fight, involving an assault against the brains of those here in Springfield, almost *zombifying* the people.

"I know this sounds like a made up tale but I can assure you that Parker and the barista boy, Tony, can witness to all that I am sharing with you, as well as Father Sanderson from Saint Timothy's Cathedral."

Milly's parents knew Father Sanderson well; he attended Mildred Lee's celebration each year, being a main sponsor and worker for the event. The likeness of Milly's experiences in the supernatural, along with the child photos they had been laughing at earlier, began to bring a witness, no matter how extreme, to their hearts.

"Mom, Dad, I know this is hard to grasp but I am telling you that something evil is planned, and I am not a conspiracy theorist But with the startup of PRINA's hadron collider this week, it is not good; the results of what they are doing in dealing with antimatter, will open the door to utter chaos upon earth, which has been backed by Steven Hawking who has warned physicists of what would occur. Moreover, I received a phone call a couple of days ago from a physicist there, Dr. Merrill Turnipseed, who had a dream of me in it, and located me, to share what was actually occurring at PRINA. You have to believe me."

Daniel was very familiar with PRINA, as a colleague in his office, talked frequently about the technical and scientific issues of what they were doing, warning Daniel for months that something would happen if they set the particle accelerator off again. Moreover, Lavern had memories from her subconscious triggered, when remembering the odd behaviors of her Grandmother Mildred Lee, who spoke of similar occurrences in visions and experiences in the supernatural, with her own mother.

Lavern and Daniel looked at each other with their hands cupped, patted each other's hands in affirmation, nodded and then looked at Milly. "We believe you," they said.

Milly was more floored than she thought they would be. "What, you believe me, just like that?"

"Yes," Lavern said. "I know that it is very far fetched sounding, and if I had not known the oddities about my own grandmother's life, then I would have definitely thought that you had lost it. But I remember mom telling me about her behaviors, and how she would always predict in the 1930's, things that were coming to the nation, writing letters to the President, and to those whom she could get an audience with. I never told you that people thought that she was crazy, except that all of her predictions came true."

Lavern looked at Daniel, "Honey, what do you think?"

Daniel spoke with firm confidence, realizing that his co-worker's concern with PRINA was valid, especially if this scientist that Milly spoke of, called her to warn her of PRINA's intention. "If I didn't have a coworker with such a huge obsession with PRINA and had not heard him pretty much preach about it over the past nine months, I would have thought you were a bit off, and seriously would've asked you to seek medical help."

The three of them laughed, as Daniel continued, "But Freddy, my coworker, would give me article after article, and send me video after video, which I looked at on occasions. The articles and videos backed up his suspicions."

The three of them clasped hands, to which Daniel said, "Now that we are here Milly, what is next?"

"Thank you both, I was so nervous telling you. Well, the battle starts this Wednesday, as PRINA kicks off their hadron collider." The three of them dropped hands, as Milly filled them in on one last matter. "By the way, I meant to tell you that I, along with those in the group, and the students that you heard about at Strytan the other day, with the tower." Milly paused and waited for her parent's response.

"Oh yes!" Lavern exclaimed, "I remember hearing about that, what fantastical reports I heard from it all."

"Well," Milly said, "We all can actually see a crystal tower in The Quad of Strytan, which has a blue flame in it, and is the place that El Elyon gives us strength for the battle."

"Oh my word! So it is true," Lavern asked.

"Yes it is." She looked at her parents to offer them comfort, by assuring them that when Parker and Tony arrived later for dinner, the five of them could discuss it further. Her parents agreed to not discuss the issue till then, and they looked at each other, when Lavern said, "Well, I don't know about you, but I could use another Keto-Coffee!"

They stood up as Milly leaped forward to do a group hug, "I love you guys dearly!"

Dinner

Parker and Tony arrived, looking forward to a home cooked meal from Milly's mom, Lavern. Entering the Teschlon's home, with the smell of chili invading their nostrils, set their anticipation levels higher, as they were salivating for Lavern's famous chili. The Teschlon's were carbing up, which is the Ketogenic diet term, for getting off the diet and eating more carbs than normal, so as to enjoy the evening's meal. They carbed up at least one weekend out of the month, and for sure on holidays, birthdays and anniversaries.

Lavern's recipe was known all over town, as the best chili ever, using her special hot sausage to give it the extra kick. She spent hours cooking it on the stove top, as she first cooked the Tennessee Pride hot sausage, and then added 3-4 cans of tomato sauce, with the 2 packets of chili seasoning, and finally the chili beans. It was the perfect flavoring and needed nothing else.

Daniel welcomed Parker and Tony to their home and for the meal. "Hey guys, are you ready for a good home cooked meal?"

"You know it!" Parker exclaimed.

Tony was chomping at the bit as he emphatically stated, "Absolutely! I smelled it as soon as the door opened."

"Great," Daniel replied, motioning to the dining room, "We will get it going in a minute, as we have the trimmings on the dining room table, of sour cream, cheese, corn chips and tortilla chips."

The group sat down to eat, feasting on a meat lover's delight, with chunks of sausage and beans in every spoonful, topped with bits of chives, cheese and sour cream, along with the side serving of corn chips. Milly and her mother put their corn chips inside of the bowl, while Daniel preferred to keep his on the side since he liked his chips crunchy. Parker and Tony followed Daniel's trend, enjoying each bite of the hearty meal.

"Oh my gosh, Lavern, this is amazing chili! I missed this so much from having it last year in my freshman year." Parker continued eating while making sounds of pleasure, letting the group know that he was happy with Lavern's chili.

Milly looked at her mother giggling, giving her a wink to let her know the chili was a hit. Daniel wanted to catch the guys off guard, and while taking another bite said, "So what is this about the tower with the blue flame and the Ancient Language."

Holding their spoons still to their mouth, Tony and Parker looked at each other, wondering if they had gotten Milly into trouble. To which, Daniel responded, "Relax guys, eat, we already know and had our own suspicions. We are going to enjoy this meal and night, so that you warriors will be ready for Wednesday's battle."

Parker put his hand over his heart, saying, "Daniel, you got me, and I thought for a minute that the meal was going to turn into a lecture. Man, oh man, I'm so glad Mill told you guys."

Tony looked at them in all seriousness saying, "I only have one thing to say in my defense."

"What is that," Daniel asked.

"Keto-Coffee. I'm making some after this meal, at which time we will talk about the specifics, as I give you both a small physics lesson on how to get a greater foam of butter with the spin." With a straight face and then a smile, he replied, "Come on you guys, lets finish this awesome meal."

After dinner, Daniel fired up the fire pit on the back patio, while Lavern put blankets on every seat. There was nothing more enjoyable than a hot cup of your favorite drink in the cold brisk air of the night, near a fire pit, while sitting under a blanket. The group headed outside, where they conversed over all that Milly had told them.

Tony educated Daniel and Lavern on the operations of PRINA's hadron collider and how the antimatter that it produced, was other worldly, opening up a portal to a parallel universe, where both dark matter, and assignments from the enemy, would bring many under its mind control. Daniel mentioned the articles that his friend, Freddy, had shown him.

Tony was taken back as he asked, "Freddy who?"

"Freddy Milner."

"Yeah, he and I have coffee regularly after Mass on Sunday. We have been talking about the stuff at PRINA since Steven Hawking came out with his warnings to the physicists there." Tony was relieved to know that Daniel already had some understanding, and between what science was proving, along with Mrs. Mildred Lee's diaries, there were many confirmations to the fact that the three students were not crazy, especially since the recent encounter with the other 20 students on Thursday.

A wonderful night, with great food and fellowship could not be topped, feeling as though it was the last meal before the battle. The three students were content, and enjoying their discussion with Mr. and Mrs. Teschlon. They laughed, talked, shared and discussed important topics in their nation, as they finished the perfect night.

Facing Fear!

Monday had come too soon. Milly headed out of the house, blowing her parents a kiss as she grabbed her stainless steel coffee cup. Lavern and Daniel stood by the window, doing their wave of goodbyes, as Milly jumped in her blue Bug and headed to Strytan.

The gold dust was lifting off the area, and there was possibility for the enemy to attack. The merriment that was in Springfield over the weekend, was now gone, and the atmosphere shifted to a sense of urgency.

A switch flipping inside of the soul set everyone in the group to a heightened sense of determination to be at their peak performance mentally, emotionally and spiritually. They had to be on extra guard this week; the volume of the seriousness of the task was louder than their daily routine. Most wished Wednesday would already come.

Kaufman was in classroom preparing for the session. Milly and Parker walked in, and he nodded, acknowledging their presence. They took their seats, and noticed Lassiter was acting oddly, as he seemed more sheepish around them, almost as if he were in fear. Milly then saw in the spirit, seeing the seven heads of Leviathan yelping at the presence of the blue flame within Kaufman, Milly and Parker. Their united front brought a greater strength against hell.

Time froze, students remained still, and all the clocks stopped moving. Kaufman, Parker and Milly each saw their armor, and the shields fastened on their back. Each of their blue flames joined together, forming a huge great sword, cutting the cords of Leviathan off of

Lassiter's mind. Immediately, the ruling power Leviathan was cast into the wilderness, and Lassiter reached for his head, now alive to the spirit realm, as he was unfrozen to see what they saw. He saw the blue flame of El Elyon entering his head where the cord of Leviathan had left, and began weeping.

All the other students were still frozen, and each of their clocks were still. Lassiter looked at Kaufman, Milly and Parker, who were all in armor, and asked, "What just happened?" He was stunned, feeling relief and being filled with hope, which he had not felt in a long time.

Milly received the nod from Kaufman to speak. "You have been set free from the ruling power of Leviathan that has oppressed you for some time."

"Oh my gosh, I cannot thank you enough; I have been so depressed to the point of suicide because I have felt like I was leading a double life, giving into evil behaviors that I loathed but could not stop committing! And what about all these other students, can they not see us?"

Parker put his hand on Lassiter's shoulder, "No man, we are in the spirit right now, and the only ones who can see us are those who are in the spirit with us."

All four of them looked outside of the door and noticed Dean Knight walking by, seeing Jezebel still behind him sending messages of hate towards Parker, Milly and Kaufman. Jezebel was not fond of Leviathan but did not want to see El Elyon's warriors cutting off the ruling powers from those who had been bound; it meant that the tower was enlarging at Strytan.

Kaufman looked at the other three students and said, "We are about to resume, get ready," to which each person was back in normal time. Lassiter was so blown away by the supernatural occurrence that he waited for Milly to turn her face toward him, when he gave her the peace sign with his fingers. She grinned and turned back to the lesson.

Looking at the class, Kaufman in all seriousness posed the question, "Give me your thoughts as to the quote."

"We can easily forgive a child who is afraid of the dark; the real tragedy in life is when men are afraid of the light." Plato

Students chimed in with different thoughts, referring to the darkness that they were dealing with, in their own soul. Discussing their need to be unafraid of truth, because it would reveal the inadequacy of the fear, which they cling to. Kaufman leaning on his desk, taking in the group's explanations and philosophy, realized that the class was having its own group therapy. He knew that before the coming battle, that Parker and Milly, as well as himself, needed to face any fears that would be resident within.

Slowly, Lassiter lifted his hand, and everyone expected a smart aleck remark, as each person rolled his or her eyes. Kaufman noticed his hand raised and pointed towards him, "Yes Lassiter, what are your thoughts on Plato's quote?"

"Professor Kaufman, I have been sitting here listening to people's transparency, and must say it is enlightening."

The class hushed stunned that Lassiter could be genuine. Now they were willing to listen; he had earned their trust for the moment.

"Yes Lassiter, in what way?" Kaufman asked.

"When we consider that Plato says that we can forgive a child who is afraid of the dark, we see that this is the first part of recognizing that it is the immaturity within the soul, that causes fear. He does not say that a man is afraid of the dark, but rather a child. However, if we continue to be afraid of the dark and do not experience compassion from those whom we believe to receive it from, for our fear of the darkness, then if unresolved, we, in our immaturity, are given over to fear all the more."

Now, Kaufman was standing and walking slowly towards Lassiter's desk. Listening intently, as he lifted his hand up to his chin. "Yes Lassiter, go on."

"Well, Plato's last line then says that the real tragedy is when men are afraid of the light. When I see this, I see someone, who in their childhood, afraid of the darkness, makes that their room; their fear becomes their obsession. All fear is, is the obsession of what we cannot do." Lassiter looked around at the class, seeing the eyes of the students, realizing their amazement.

"Therefore, if fear is the obsession of what we cannot do, or what we believe we are not, then that obsession actually becomes our world, the room to which we cannot leave, making us thereby afraid of the light; we are a prisoner of darkness."

Kaufman and the students were blown away. Milly looked at Lassiter, giving him thumbs up and smiled. Parker sat there ruminating on Lassiter's statement, realizing how much *he* was that person that had been afraid of the light.

Kaufman purported one last thing. "Lassiter, you say this with great confidence and much wisdom, how is it that you have come to know this?"

"Professor Kaufman, I was that little boy who was continually afraid of the dark as a child, going to my father when I was afraid, only to find his door closed and having no one to speak to me in my darkness. Instead, I made that my room, my world, and then invited everyone into my darkness, not making friends with those who were unafraid of the Light, because it was a place of comfort and familiarity."

Milly had a tear coming out of the corner of her eye, realizing how oppressed Lassiter had to be, before the ruling power Leviathan was cut off. Warmth spread across her chest as she realized El Elyon had given her compassion for her enemy yet again, seeing others through His eyes.

Kaufman was speechless, looking out of the window, thinking on the importance of the upcoming battle, as the freedom to Lassiter's soul made him all the more aware of the freedom needed to the souls of those who were in the parallel universe. It was his hope that on Wednesday they could set many free.

"Well, I think that about says it everyone," said Kaufman. "What a great note to end today's class on, and I hope you all have a good day, see you on Wednesday."

The students got up and hung around a little bit more than normal, talking to one another, as well as Lassiter. Milly and Parker waited for him, once the other students finished.

"Hey Lassiter," said Parker. "That was incredible man, I was blown away by all the deep revelation you had."

Lassiter smiled, thanking him and shook his hand. Then Milly put her hand on his shoulder and said, "Lassiter, you never have to be afraid of the darkness anymore, because you have come into the Light and are friends with those who fellowship in that Light." She winked and turned around to leave the room.

Lassiter remained standing at his desk, weeping, hoping that other students did not turn back to see him. Kaufman walked over to him, brought him towards the window of the classroom, and patted him on the back. "It's alright Lassiter, you no longer are afraid of the Light."

The Grind Conference

Parker and Milly headed to *The Grind* being enticed with the pumpkin spice aroma coming from the vicinity. They hurried in, when the smell was amplified.

"What is that smell," asked Milly.

Tony stood behind the coffee bar with a huge grin. "That is the flavor for the holiday season Milly, I'm making you and Parker one right now, a Pumpkin Spice Keto Latte. Because of our service to the other students on Saturday, the manager said I could give you two a free addiction today."

"Oh Great!" Parker exclaimed.

Milly and Parker took their addiction and went to the patio where the sun was beating down, keeping the students warm in the cold temperature. Scarfs around necks, toboggans on, added to the atmosphere of the season, as students sat around with their favorite hot drink.

Tony joined them, making himself an addiction as well, sporting a sweatshirt for the day, with the blueprint for the required science so that the body produces ketones. People would ask him continually what the science information was on his shirt. He loved keeping people in suspense so he could give them a small workshop on whatever information he could disseminate to their brain.

"So guys, this is the week," said Tony, as he kept his gloves on, holding onto his lab experiment coffee cup, repositioning his scarf over the left ear, to keep the wind chill off of his earlobe.

"Yes it is," Milly said in soberness of mind, taking a sip of her pumpkin spice latte, which eased all worries for the moment. She wanted to take in each moment, not missing anything lest she not fully have lived life. Feeling confident that no harm would come to the group on Wednesday, she could not help but think that they were all still putting their lives on the line.

"Listen Milly, you be at peace," Parker said. Tapping her on the shoulder, "Earth to Milly, earth to Milly."

They both laughed, and she responded, "Ok Park, I get it! I won't worry."

Parker began to share with Tony the spiritual warfare that occurred in their philosophy class, and Milly joined in, with the Plato quote that Lassiter illuminated to the class. Tony was wowed by the testimony the two friends were giving him, and was grateful he had met the two, forming a friendship that would not only be a lifetime but eternal; they operated in eternity-time.

Staring at Parker and Milly, Tony could not help but say, "Guys, do you realize that our friendship is not a lifetime friendship but rather an eternal one?"

"What do you mean," asked Milly.

"Well, not to get too serious, but just thinking of things from a scientific standpoint. Our friendship, although based in the normal space-time continuum of earth, still reaches further than this time, into what we have learned of as eternity-time. As a result, the level of maturity and depth of discussion that we have is based on a deeper part of our soul, where eternity has been planted, making our friendships richer because of that connection."

"Wow, Tony you are getting all serious on us, dude," said Parker.

"No man, listen to this; it is important for Wednesday's battle." Tony had understanding of how protected they were going to be, as they were in sync as one military unit protecting one another.

"When guys are in the military and go off into battle, they become one unit, and it is based on their task, as well as their friendship, being formed within that group that was brought together for that task. There is an extra element of connection based on the fact that the war brought them together. Unlike people that are not in the military, we cannot understand that connection; it is deeper than we know; we have not been there."

Milly listened, and felt peace wash over her soul, knowing that Wisdom was being given to Tony to speak, so that their fears would be dissolved. "I'm with you Tony," said Milly.

"Well, we are not too far from that kind of friendship, but even more so; our dimension of time as we know it, has been enlarged, encasing a greater wealth of knowledge and wisdom of that dimension, because our souls have been stretched for a greater capacity of relationship, having our perspectives changed."

"Wow," Parker replied.

"Think about it guys, when we did Saturday's meeting, we had already had the antimatter the night before, burned out of us, and as we reached out to the other students, we were able to do so from a deeper level, or can I say a greater philosophy. We could speak to the history in those students' lives to see them changed." Tony sat, still pondering on what he just spoke, as Parker did his Kaufman tilt.

"Man you should have been in class with us this semester in philosophy dude!" Parker could not help but feel that there was an extension of Kaufman's class now taking place at *The Grind*.

Tony looked at Milly, "Say, you know when you saw those things in the spirit that were harming the students, you were able to speak to it; you knew their history. But you didn't stop there; you brought a new philosophy to their soul of the blue flame with the Ancient Language that it forever changed them."

"Tony that is deep," Milly said, "but yes I know what you are talking about, which brings the two fields I am majoring in together, philosophy and antiquities/history."

The three looked around, as they heard birds chirping, students laughing, and the smell of pumpkin spice in the air. No more words, only silence, as they rested in a dimension that only very few understood, knowing that their friendship was not limited to the bounds of earth.

Chapter 18

Orange, yellow, light green, and red, the leaves were a bouquet of colors, as Milly and Parker drove to Robert's house through the fall landscape. This was the last meeting they would have at the Prophet's house before Wednesday's battle. Milly looked at the scenery, missing it already.

Parker knew his friend's silence revealed her inner struggle, and asked, "What's going on Mill? Why the sad face?"

"I am *so* going to miss everything, once this battle is over. Having made friends with everyone at the Doctors Mercer, as well as knowing Robert. To think that it is coming to an end is bittersweet." She was fighting tears, knowing they would arrive at his house soon.

"Listen Mill, I don't believe it is the end of our friendships, but on the contrary, I believe it is the beginning much like Tony was sharing earlier. Think about it. We as a group have something not only to offer Springfield, but to every place in the world."

"What do you mean Park?"

"For example, there might be, let's say, *unique problems* going on somewhere else in the world, like Rome or Egypt, and *our group* might be the only people to help out." Parker knew somewhere deep within, that this was the start of a long-term friendship amongst the group members.

"Listen Milly, I don't know how I believe this but I am certain that we are all going to be working together from here on out." Parker paused, and then exclaimed, "Heck Milly! We are the Ancient Language Seekers!"

She laughed, "If you say so Parker, I believe you."

They arrived on time, seeing the Mercer's car parked in the drive. Getting out of the Bug, they headed into the house for the meeting. Giddiness welled up within their souls like two kids waking up to see their presents on Christmas morning. When they reached the door about to knock, Robert said, "Enter, you two."

"It was a pleasant thing to have others expect you at their place and make you feel welcomed," Milly thought. She smelled something that was like cinnamon rolls and wondered if Robert was carbing up since the battle was around the corner.

"You wonder if they are the real thing Milly," he said, knowing her thoughts, "those are Keto cinnamon rolls and have only 1 carb and no sugar. Get you a plate, and bring it in here to have with your coffee."

Both she and Parker went into the kitchen getting the nice white dessert dishes on which to plate their cinnamon roll. They grabbed a fork, came back into the sitting area, and sat in their normal seats picking up the coffee that Robert had made them.

"Kaufman was just telling us what transpired in philosophy class today, where a young man, named Lassiter, was set free from the ruling power of Leviathan," Robert said, as he kept his eyes focused on Parker and Milly who were devouring the cinnamon roll.

"Sorry Robert," Parker said covering his mouth, trying to chew some more so he would not be speaking with a full mouth. "By the way Robert, those cinnamon rolls are good, I never would have thought they were only 1 carb and no sugar." Robert nodded receiving his compliment and listened to Parker's story.

"It was amazing!" Parker shouted. "The power of the blue flame in all three of us united and created a huge sword, cutting the cord of that spirit!"

Milly was still eating on her cinnamon roll and made an "mmm hmmm" sound in agreement. Robert enjoyed seeing the two youngsters enjoy his dessert.

"It's good, aye?" Robert asked as he looked to Milly.

"Oh my, absolutely!" She put her plate on the table, and continued drinking her coffee relaxing as she watched Parker tell his story. He was demonstrative with his arms waving as he acted out the scene, giving a mini synopsis of what happened in the spirit.

"Lad," said Robert, "its interesting that you brought that point up about you three uniting; because that is exactly what we are going to discuss tonight in our last meeting before the battle. The fact that you joined forces together in the spirit, your power with the Ancient Language was magnified giving you a larger weapon to fight the powers of darkness."

The Jade Hammer

Robert stood up at his regular spot during the meeting leaning his arm on the mantle. Next to his face, he was staring and lingering on the brilliance of a jade hammer about 4 inches long and 2 inches wide that was propped by a small gold stand. "Do you see this small jade hammer?"

The others stared and replied yes, acknowledging the small treasure. Robert picked it up from the gold stand, turning it over slowly in his hand. "I was given this from my father, who was given it from his father, who then received it from his father, and so forth. This hammer has been in my family, now for six generations."

Professor Mercer was excited to hear the history of the jade hammer, being a lover of antiquities. She put her coffee cup on the table and sat with her legs like royalty as she listened to Robert's story.

He stood still in front of the coffee table looking at the Doctors Mercer, Kaufman, and then to his left at Milly and Parker. Before telling the story about the jade hammer, he winked at Milly. "You will have a story of your own soon, for *your* family."

Robert looked at the others, and began his story. "This jade hammer was given to my ancestor, William Edwards, who was a well-known prophet in his time in my homeland, Wales.

"The druid king, in William's day, released much darkness in my homeland where most were afraid to come out of their cottage. A thick black fog settled over the land. Many druids pillaged the villages, abducting young people, to offer them as a sacrifice to their pagan god."

Each member of the group was enthralled; as a captive audience, they enjoyed what seemed like folklore. He continued, "My Grandfather told me the story of William and the power of The Ancient Language in his day. One day the druid king had taunted the villages more than normal because of all the undercurrent of revolt that was rumored. He threatened the villages all the more to quash these undercurrents. At one particular gathering, he brought a huge jade rock, which he claims was given to him from an Asian monk. William did not believe him; he knew that the druid king stole it from the monk, who had been through the city months before.

"The jade rock set in the center of one of the villages, in the middle of a blustery winter night. The druid king charged the people that he would take their children if they did not send someone to fight him. He was determined to make someone battle him, so he could overcome their finest, intimidating the entire nation of Wales, to shut up the undercurrents of revolt.

"It was then that William faced him; he despised the taunts of this druid king, who also continually put down El Elyon and His warriors."

Robert held the jade hammer up in his right hand and continued in his thick Welsh accent. "At this gathering, El Elyon's warriors were stationed on one side and the druids on the other. The druid king, like a lion pacing the area, challenged William to battle. Like a band of marauders the druid army had knives and clubs in their hands ready to strike, while William had only a prized silver box in his. El Elyon's warriors carried nothing, because they knew that it was a spiritual battle and that the Ancient Language would win their victory in the spirit; they knew the blue flame well. They were altogether familiar with their spiritual armor and weapons.

"The druid king was taken back that he could see no weapons amongst them, and decided to first call upon a demonstration of the power of each God based on which One would be able to transform the rock into something magnificent. The druids in Wales are very much into witchcraft and sorcery and always try to show off their supernatural ego.

"William gladly accepted the challenge. He was unafraid when it came to demons and did not even flinch at the Druids. He was so powerful in his time with the Ancient Language, that he cast many demons out of people, where they would scream his name, William Edwards!

"We are not used to this type of overt demonic manifestation as it was in the time of William. Most of the oppressed came from dark backgrounds, having parents who were druids committing dark pagan rituals. Their children, as they got older, wanted to get out of the dark magic practice and would come to William for freedom, for they knew that he had knowledge of the Ancient Language that had lightning with it.

"He would have them renounce pagan practices, and fought in his spiritual armor with the sword and the whip, setting many free from dark ruling powers. He trained many of El Elyon's warriors during the spiritual battle of his time where the towers were rising, so much so, that the entire nation of Wales was set ablaze with the blue flame and taken over by the Ancient Language."

Professor Mercer repositioned her red-framed glasses, now sipping her coffee. Alan, taking in the story along with the ambiance of the fire and coffee, relished the moment, while Kaufman had stares of philosophical inspiration written all over his face. Milly and Parker were like two children hearing a fireside story.

Robert lifted the green jade hammer. "William Edwards was not afraid and took the druid king on. Before the supernatural battle had begun, there was a battle over the jade rock. William took an old silver box that had Ancient Language inscribed all around it. He opened it up, and there laid a metal hammer, which was his weapon.

"William picked up the weapon and said, 'our tribe for El Elyon is like a hammer and will destroy your pagan altars!' Would you know it, the druid king got hotter, running toward William to kill him, when at that moment, lightning struck the jade rock, exploding the jade material all around leaving this small jade hammer in the midst of it.

Robert finished, "The warriors of El Elyon unified in William's time to come against the druids, and in the midst of them was a large blue sword, with the Ancient Language, that cut the cords of hell's gates off of the nation of Wales!"

"Wow," said Parker.

Everyone was surprised and stared intently at the jade hammer. Kaufman, still needing evidence asked to see the small piece, to which Robert handed it to him explaining, "I think you will find something a bit extraordinary with this small treasure if you look closely, Lad."

Kaufman pulled the jade piece closer, looking at the intricate detail of the hammer, and then he *saw it*! Strikes of lightning were moving throughout the jade hammer, as if the lightning that had made it was captured within. Kaufman's eyes were huge, as he then with great pleasure passed it to the Doctors Mercer and the two students for their viewing, as well.

Robert laughed, "No tool of man can create that special treasure, Lad."

Milly and Parker were amazed, as well as Professor Mercer, who had never seen anything so astonishing in all of her study of antiquities.

Robert added, "The lightning can only be seen by the warriors of El Elyon; they can see in the spirit. I bet you know something about this Anjali?"

She replied, "Why yes Robert; in my dream there was a cobalt blue sapphire table that had lightning caught within it. El Elyon told me that it was His voice, and that those who were able to hear Him, could comprehend what He spoke each time that there was lightning."

"You got it Anjali. You will be able to hear El Elyon giving battle orders simultaneously to His warriors, as His lightning increases during the battle. Demons will not be able to hear it, only His warriors and angels. This lightning will have you unite your powers, one with another, at which time you will see the appearance of a blue sword overhead, coming against the ruling powers. Today in Professor Kaufman's class was a mighty demonstration, so that you would know how to unite together.

"There is a special oil that my ancestor, William, was given from El Elyon before this battle. He called it, the Oil of Unity. As William followed El Elyon's instructions, putting it upon the warriors, as well as himself, he found that all of them were in one mind and accord. They operated like one person, as though they were different parts of a body.

"Through each battle that they fought, the oil would pull on the blue flame, not only from the tower within the region of Wales, but also from the angelic hosts; they too have a blue flame that is resident within, as they themselves are united with El Elyon, being carriers of the blue flame. Each of them has a different measure of the flame.

"The presence of El Elyon within the angelic host will be communicating with you, giving you more strength imaginable, to where you work in concert with them where each of you understand what is to be done, so you battle as a fine tuned machine much like a symphony being played by instruments. You, Kaufman, are the trombone, while Anjali is the flute, and Alan is the French horn. Parker you are like a trumpet, while Milly is like the violin, and the angelic host are the drums, and so forth. When you work in concert with one another, you make a beautiful sound, a symphony!

"The precious thing with this specific Oil of Unity, is that it protects every warrior, where no life will be lost." Milly was excited to hear this and perked up all the more when she heard Robert mention it.

"You mean no demon can kill us by any means?" she asked.

"You're absolutely right, it is a shield like an invisible force around a spacecraft, deterring the weapons of its enemy. Any means by which demons try to harm you will be averted. You will be able to tread over the scorpions, which are demonic spies sent against you, as well as the serpents of hell, and they shall by no means harm you!"

El Elyon's peace was upon the group, as they then wanted this particular oil upon them so that they would be protected. Robert held the bottle that was shaped like a wine bottle for serving olive oil in. At first glance it looked like olive oil, but upon his turning it, amber flecks dispersed throughout making it glow at times.

"I will put this upon each of you present, and on Wednesday will put it upon all those who remain in the group." Robert knew that the news would set them at ease and was glad to see their expressions. He still needed to move onto the other issue, which was the matter of each person's task for the day of the battle.

"Alan and Anjali, the two of you will be at the front of the campus, right before The Quad, where Alan will turn on *The Rock* device, and Anjali will read from the Ancient Relic. Parker, you will be there beside the Mercers assisting in using your armor and weapons to battle the demons. It is important that once this process begins, that you and Alan unite your weapons, while Anjali reads the Ancient Language in its entirety, at which time I suspect the clock will begin to sound."

The three looked at each other, while Alan chimed in agreeing that it was what El Elyon showed each one of them in a dream. They would follow the instructions emphatically.

"Great," responded Robert. "Now for Norman and Milly. Your instruction is very important, and you will have to keep in constant contact with the angelic host as you are in concert with their strategic warfare. Since the both of you will be going over into the parallel universe, this will prove to be of great service. Before you enter the other side, you will actually be taken to the crystal war room where the angels have council over the sapphire table that Anjali has shared."

Kaufman, on the edge of his seat, did thumbs up to Milly, saying, "We got this." He was charged up thinking of the privilege to see the fantastical place, before entering the parallel universe.

Robert chuckled, "You both will be going to the parallel universe in an unexpected way, but I will not share that at the moment; El Elyon wants to surprise you. He gets delight out of giving us surprises. Trust me, you will be more than overjoyed when you find out."

Milly was elated and wanted to know right this second how they would be going across. Like a child waiting for Christmas, she knew that she would have to wait for the surprise. She never expected to go to the angelic war room, and delighted in the fact of knowing that she would go places many others had never gone.

In a serious tone, Robert urged them, "Act as quickly as possible while over there; the portal to the other side will close after about two hours. PRINA's plans are to have the accelerator on for two hours at a higher intensity, which is the planned time of attack to come after the souls of mankind here, to cross them over. However, we are going to take advantage of that by crossing the souls from the parallel universe back to our universe."

Both Kaufman and Milly nodded, acknowledging the seriousness of timing. Robert clasped his hands together, rubbing them quickly in excitement and said, "Alright Lads and Lassies, let's take a small break before I put the Oil of Unity upon you." The group stood up, and disseminated into the kitchen to stretch their legs and grab another cinnamon roll with coffee.

The Beginning

After the short break, each of the members went back to their seat, preparing for their final time at Robert's before the battle. He opened the special oil, passed down from William Edwards, and asked that each individual stand in front of the fireplace before him, one at a time.

Kaufman came up first, at which time Robert put the oil on his right index finger, turning the vial upside down being careful not to spill a drop. He pulled his finger away, which was now covered in the fresh oil, and then smeared the forehead of Kaufman in the manner of the Ancient Tav, saying, "The Oil of Unity be upon you, giving you strength for the battle."

Kaufman felt woozy for a minute with his knees buckling up under him, making him think he was going down to the floor. Robert placed his hand on Kaufman's upper back speaking, "Your gift is mighty to see that which needs to be seen, like an eagle watching its young. In order to protect them from the enemy, you will have this foresight to protect many in the clutches of hell."

Next, Anjali came up when she took her red-framed glasses off, feeling the touch of Robert's finger rubbing her forehead slightly. As his finger touched her, she felt lightning throughout her slender frame, and heard the sound of thunder. "The Oil of Unity be upon you to give you strength for the battle."

Robert smiled at her, as she then opened her eyes, and he spoke, "To each of you, the Oil of Unity is something unique marking you especially with your gift." He then looked at Anjali, and said, "Your gift is to hear the Ancient Language and El Elyon, so that you can speak with His power, destroying darkness."

Then, Alan walked up to the spot where each person was taking their turn standing, and Robert turned up the vial of oil again putting his finger upon Alan's forehead, marking him in the sign of the ancient Tav. Robert then said, "You have a mind to perceive with the mind of El Elyon, knowing a greater strength beyond your humanity as you reach to know His mind, and bring His thoughts to others. The Oil of Unity be upon you to give you strength for the battle."

Alan could feel the synapses within his brain firing in greater capacity, and felt his understanding opened up, to where mathematical equations ran through his mind, bringing to life the reality of *The Rock* that he created and the other inventions that would come in time.

Next, Parker came up to receive the smearing from Robert with the Oil of Unity. As soon as he stepped up to the area Parker's knees dipped a little, at which time he said, "Whoa man! I can feel the power of this oil."

Robert looked at him, touching his shoulders lightly and said, "The Oil of Unity be upon you to strengthen you for the battle, where El Elyon has brought forth His great Knowledge, giving you insights into neural pathways within the brain, as well as metabolic cell-life within the person, causing you to discover the reality of truth to cure disease, and know the abundant mental capacity a person that is given by El Elyon."

"Man oh man," Parker said, "This is some kind of crazy power here; my brain feels like it is on fire, where I know a bunch of stuff I didn't before, about cell metabolism in the brain; I almost feel like I can hear your thoughts!"

Robert smiled, as he then looked to Milly, while Parker was finding his way back to his seat. "Milly it is time," Robert said waving her up to the area.

She stood up slowly, a bit hesitant, and came to the spot where each person had stood. Milly was nervous, unsure of how she would be affected by the oil, having watched everyone else. Her eyes closed, she heard Robert turning over the vial, noticing the sound of it returning to its upright state as it swooshed in the bottle. *Swoosh*, she heard with her ears. He then lifted his finger off of it, smearing Milly's forehead with the ancient Tav.

"You, mighty warrior of El Elyon, will be known as a lifeguard for your generation, opening up depths of the knowledge of truth, and the power of understanding, along with His mighty Wisdom, so that others will be set free to know a time which they have not known, of eternity. You will walk in a great strength to bring peace beyond this time, dipping others in the place of this beauty, as they come to know who they are. The Oil of Unity be upon you and give you strength for the battle."

Milly was shaking, fire rushing inside of her bones, traveling throughout her body, made her feel like a fish filleted and gutted. She was caught off guard, not realizing what was happening, as she felt herself slowly falling, when Robert caught her and led her back to her chair.

She sat down, with her eyes still closed seeing visions of the battle that was to come, as she saw each of her team members fighting demons, working cooperatively with the angelic host, and standing for the truth of El Elyon to speak the Ancient Language and burn in the blue flame. She was caught in a fantastical place and desired to stay there, but knew that time would not permit it.

Opening her eyes slowly and looking at the others, she said, "Utttttterlyyyyyy mind blowing!!"

Beelzebub's Arrival

Beelzebub finally arrived in Springfield late Monday night, looking for Vladamore, contemptuous of the news that he would receive, after seeing the tower of El Elyon rising and the Ancient Language getting louder. It was complete torment to his ears, as he hissed and howled, while covering his ears, "Who can bear this?"

Constugard perched over The Ancient Gatehouse, filling Beelzebub in on the details. "Welcome my liege." He was hunched over, and drew back a distance fearing that Beelzebub would take out his vehement anger on him. "There is much that needs to be done. The general,

Vladamore, has slacked on his job failing to implement your strategy my liege, to overturn this town. He has allowed a little girl to undo him making you look like a fool!"

The serpent creatures were not for each other; they did not know unity like humans did. After the blue flame was stripped from them, they were fully given over to the vile nature of darkness. Only out for themselves, looking for opportunity to put down another serpent creature, it was a cutthroat world with them.

Beelzebub was fuming, "Vladamore!" he yelled, "Where is that wretched fool!"

Beneath The Ancient Gatehouse, Vladamore heard Beelzebub calling his name, knowing that he would get a reprisal for the present state Springfield was in. A coward to tell Beelzebub what had transpired, Vladamore looked to throw blame onto his team. Scurrying upstairs to meet Beelzebub, Vladamore joined his liege and Constugard on top of The Ancient Gatehouse.

"My liege," Vladamore said addressing Beelzebub, as he hunched down, frightened that he would be clawed. "My team of commanders and artillery builders are pathetic and cannot carry out a single order that I have given them."

Beelzebub was fuming at the mouth, spewing venom towards Vladamore, as he yelled, "You dirty maggot! You alone are the one to blame, and if you were the general that you used to be, none of these quandaries would be present here in Springfield. Face it! You have slacked on your job, Vladamore, and are out of your league, not realizing that you have been defeated because of your own puny mind, where you have failed to outwit and outsmart a little girl!"

Afraid, Vladamore was angry as well, about the whole dilemma. Seeing Serugar, his underling, across the street peering from behind the tree, let him know that Serugar was spying to see what would happen. Although serpent creatures did not truly know loyalty and only acted out of fear, Serugar had an odd connection with Vladamore, and was seeing if his general was getting a bad beating from Beelzebub.

"What must I do to help my general," Serugar whispered while in the bushes. Talking to himself was a normal behavior, as he carried on, "I have to help my general, I must make him look good."

Hunched over, recoiling from the long claws of Beelzebub that were near his serpent creature body, Vladamore expected to feel the jagged slice come upon his throat, like a knife, from Beelzebub's claws. Beelzebub held them an inch away from Vladamore's face, as his reddish brown hand remained still, while foam spewed from both Vladamore and Beelzebub alike. Vladamore would not defy his liege, but he would not be treated like a dog either!

Serugar came closer to the building of The Ancient Gatehouse, wondering what he could concoct to give his general some time to spare. He then realized that the meeting that was to take place on Tuesday would be *the thing*, which could upset El Elyon's plans. And he quickly climbed up the building like a lizard, arriving to sit on the edge of the rooftop to bring more news.

"Serugar," said Vladamore, "There you are my underling; have you any news to bring?" Beelzebub turned to look at the tiny creature, loathing the sight of the underling, as it had zero to offer him, nothing that would pacify his anger.

Beelzebub began foaming dark foam from his mouth, snarling at the creature, when Serugar then spoke. "Good evening my liege," he said to Beelzebub, while bowing with his head all the way to the ground.

"Get up you worm of a creature," said Beelzebub, "what news do you have to bring?"

"My general has the team scouring the area for the great meeting that is to take place tomorrow, in order to foil the plans of El Elyon's warriors, knowing that they will meet their devastation and ruin after we take them out."

"Shut up you maggot of a creature," shouted Beelzebub. "Stop gloating in your general's work; there is nothing to orate about with this creature," he said as he pointed at Vladamore. "Need I remind you underling, that your loyalty is to me!" Beelzebub was now towering over Serugar, as Constugard sat there, snarling at the small underling wanting his master to slice him.

“Correct, my liege,” Serugar said, while trembling. “I am to serve only you.” He looked up at Beelzebub as if to persuade him. “And in my service, I have come to inform you that the little girl and her friends are meeting again one last time tomorrow. If we work fast, we can try to foil their plans by taking her out. If we take her out, we have the victory. I do not know what El Elyon wants with her, but whatever purpose it is, she is vital.”

“What have you purposed underling,” Beelzebub asked while slightly easing up on his demonic venom that had been spewing from his mouth.

“What else my liege, we have to kill her,” Serugar said point blank. “That is what general Vladamore has planned all along, letting the humans think that there was hope, only to wait till the last minute to blow up their plans. If she is out of the picture, then the whole deal is off; they cannot carry out their plans without the girl, they call Milly.”

“Has she not been protected by Rafael, the angelic messenger,” Beelzebub taunted in his face, seeing how Serugar would respond.

“My liege, there is a window of time, where Rafael and Tubal will be joining the angelic council, giving us opportunity to take her out. Although there is a firewall around her, if we can get to her, if we but try my liege, we can take her out.”

Serugar took a breath, and inhaled through his nose that seemed stuffed with mucus. Some of the mucus oozed out, to which he wiped it, and then said, “I believe we can do it my liege. It has been Vladamore’s plan all along.”

“Fine then!” Beelzebub screamed in Serugar’s ear, “Make sure it happens!” Serugar went running off, leaving Vladamore and Constugard with Beelzebub. The mad liege walked to Vladamore and snarled over his head, “You better hope this works maggot or you are out of here!”

“Yes my liege,” replied Vladamore, as he then hurried down to underneath The Ancient Gatehouse.

Bobby Knight was inside, working with his members, planning diabolical plots across the city where they could cause chaos. They had dirty bombs planted in different locations, and were still looking to throw the town into chaos, distracting the Ancient Language Seekers from their task.

Surrounded by his members, knowing that Beelzebub had arrived, Bobby Knight lifted up a chalice filled with blood from one of their recent sacrifices declaring, "drink up my brethren, we will abolish all goodness in this town, and make our liege the crowned prince of the area, defeating El Elyon's warriors and angelic hosts!"

The group drank up, and upon their faces you could see demonic serpent creatures superimposed, revealing the nature of possession of the soul of each man. They sold their soul to hell, and were fully given over to its weighty measure of chaotic nature.

Watching

Tuesday morning had come, and Serugar was working with Dadanel and Morder, as well as Heradacio, to use all their weapons in deployment against Milly. Today would be the day for them to get the *little star* of Springfield.

Bobby Knight was used by the dark powers, as he waited for Milly to pull into Strytan. He was not taking any chances this day and would not disappoint Beelzebub. His rank in the dark society, The Ancient Gatehouse nationwide, was high and this would ensure his dominion over the dark society for North America.

He knew that Serugar and the other demons planned to instigate an attack against Milly, as they brought him enough compounds to make several remote bombs. He and the other members spent most of the night putting the bombs together.

Serugar, and the rest of Vladamore's team, was surrounding the vicinity of the university waiting to see if the little princess was killed, in order to begin the release of pandemonium. If Milly was not dead they would have to release the chaotic plan tomorrow at the time of battle.

Milly pulled up to Strytan in her blue Bug, jumping out to meet Parker at *The Grind*. Bobby Knight had been looking out of his window, with the curtain pulled back. He picked up his phone and sent out a text, "the blue Bug with the convertible top, in lot J. Take care of it now!"

Meanwhile, Milly saw Parker, to which she grabbed him, walking arm and arm for a minute on their way to *The Grind* for their conference, "Today is the last day Park, get ready for the epic battle tomorrow."

He tried to remain calm while they walked saying, "I cannot wait; I feel as though I was created for this moment. Had we not become friends Mill, we would not be here to witness the greatest time in our lives, where what we do matters most."

They walked into *The Grind* to order their drinks, when a man dressed in a jogging suit came running through parking lot J, and then bending down to tie his shoe by Milly's Bug, placed a dirty bomb underneath. The bomb was to be operated by a remote button, used from a phone. He got up and continued his jog, texting Bobby Knight, "its done!"

The remote was tied to a burner phone that Bobby had gotten the night before. He was waiting for the right moment, when he would see Milly get into her Bug, to push the button and take her out. Looking in the dark ball that he brought with him to the university, he conjured up Vladamore and instructed him that the bomb was in place, and to send the artillery of bitterness, as well as the slime from the cords of the gates of hell, to be ready to release as soon as the bomb exploded, should Milly be found dead. Otherwise, hell's fury would have to wait until tomorrow.

The day had gone by, when on her way out, Milly met up with Parker and Tony one last time at *The Grind*, before making it to her car. Now, getting ready to leave campus, she slowly walked to her Bug. Her stomach suddenly was queasy, and she had an impression that something was wrong. Milly kept putting one foot in front of the other, as she got closer to her vehicle.

Meanwhile, Bobby Knight was looking out of his office window, speaking under his breath, "get closer Milly Teschlon, closer." The burner flip phone was open and he had his finger waiting till she got close enough to press the button, as he kept saying, "closer, closer, closer."

Suddenly, his administrative assistant, Julie, walked in hollering, "You have to come see this, Dean Knight." Her arms were flailing around, and without realizing it his finger hit the button. A loud explosion was heard in the parking lot while smoke went up in the air. Parker and Tony were worried that the demonic horde was after Milly, and they went flying as fast as they could to parking lot J.

"Milly," cried Parker, at the top of his lungs.

Tony and Parker were both frantic and trying not to panic until they knew that their friend was safe. As they arrived near the area in which Milly was parked, they found her on the ground, lying near the debris of a large tree. Apparently, the bomb did not affect her car, but rather a tree, which had been planted by the druids in the early 1800's, before Strytan was ever built. It was blown to smithereens. How did the bomb end up there?

Druids had come to the States early on, and planted as many trees to take over cities and regions within the USA, to practice their dark magic and sorcery. This druid tree was now in fragments all over parking lot J.

Milly, lying on the sidewalk was unscathed by the explosion. Tony and Parker got to her, when Parker lifted his friend up to see her eyes opening.

"Are you alright Milly?" Parker asked frantically.

"I believe so, what happened?" She was out of it and did not know what had occurred.

"Milly, it looks like the powers of darkness were trying to kill you! Thank goodness we had the Oil of Unity put on us last night; who knows what could have happened had Robert not anointed us!"

Parker and Tony assisted Milly to her feet, at which time, the Springfield police were arriving. News cameras were on campus, and there was hubbub around the parking lot, with security officials blocking the area off, and keeping students at a safe distance, to comb the area with their canines for any other devices.

Bobby Knight had messed up for sure, missing his window to take Milly out. He was hideously upset, screaming in a tirade at Julie, who had come to warn him of a raccoon that had gotten loose in the office.

"Out of nowhere, a raccoon appeared," she informed him, when the creature came and stood by her desk, and had caught her off guard alarming her.

He chewed Julie out for coming into his office, and that he had an important phone call, which she had interrupted. Absolutely steaming mad, uncertain if his plan worked, he wanted to get down to the parking lot as fast as possible to find out for sure.

Pounding out of the building like a bull going through Mexico City in the Running of the Bulls Festival, Knight was determined to find out if Milly was still alive. Right behind him, were Professor Kaufman and Professor Mercer, who both had a gnawing feeling in their stomach that it could be against one of the students on their team.

They arrived at parking lot J, finding Parker and Tony, while paramedics in the back of an ambulance were examining Milly. Milly's parents were alerted, and on their way, to check on their daughter's safety.

El Elyon had given both Daniel and Lavern a dream the night before, about Milly being in an accident and covered by two huge hands, that would not let harm come to her. They did not tell their daughter, so as not to cause any alarm. El Elyon's Spirit gave a peace to them, so that they did not panic on the way to the scene.

Arriving at Strytan, they got close to parking lot J and leapt out of the car to find their daughter. The paramedic saw them running and put his hands up, as if to convey Milly's safety, so they could have the news before actually putting their eyes on her. Seeing them off in the distance, Milly now stood up and had a huge smile on her face, as she opened her arms wide, where they came alongside of her picking her feet up off the ground to squeeze her tightly.

"Are you alright Milly?" asked her mother and father.

"Yes, I'm fine. I don't know what all went on, but the crazy thing is, when I was walking out to the car, I got queasier and felt nauseous. So I came to the sidewalk to sit down, putting my head between my legs, when all of a sudden I heard this sound, like a pitcher throwing a baseball in the major leagues, like a *whoosh* sound. Then, I saw a huge type of black ball device thrown beside that huge ugly tree over there, and it exploded."

"I felt cupped in two huge hands, where none of the debris could come near me. I felt stunned," she said trying to regain her composure, "I only knew that for the brief moment that I was queasy as I sat down over here on the sidewalk. I felt *taken out* of the moment, and was nowhere really. Then suddenly, I opened my eyes while lying down, to see all of this."

"Thank goodness you are alright Hon," said Lavern, who would not stop squeezing her daughter.

Daniel looked over at Bobby Knight; he never felt good about him, and knew stories of The Ancient Gatehouse, and had an eerie feeling that somehow he was connected to the explosion. Dean Knight felt like a laser was on his forehead, as he looked over and saw Daniel Teschlon's stare. When they locked eyes, Daniel knew, and Bobby knew that he did. He turned quickly to run off before Daniel walked over there, to speak. Bobby Knight was a coward at heart, a small dog with a loud bark, and had no backbone when confronted.

Security and the police had investigations taking place over the area as they combed for any leads. Milly slowly made it to her car, feeling completely fine, mostly just stunned, when her mother told her that she would drive her home.

"I still have to go to the meeting tonight Mom, and if you and dad want to come, I think you should. I know that this attack was from Dean Knight's doing; he is so evil and works with hell itself!"

Lavern and Daniel looked at their daughter, concerned greatly but still at peace, knowing that she was protected, and that no matter what they did, they could not keep their daughter from her destiny. It was in the family blood.

Daniel put his hand on his daughter's shoulder, "Milly, we will be at the meeting; it means a lot to us for you sharing what you did this past weekend, and whatever we can do to support you, we are there. Where is the meeting, warrior?"

She laughed and hugged her parents, "Its at the Doctors Mercer at 7pm."

Tony and Parker walked over, as well as Professors Mercer and Kaufman. When they stepped up to Milly and her parents, Milly introduced them to one another; her parents had not met the professors yet.

Immediately after the introductions, the group and Milly's parents saw the huge crystal tower on campus, overflowing in the blue flame that was spewing all around, with the Ancient Language all within. They looked down Main Street, and then saw the eagle's wings lit up with the fiery blue opal, alive and moving like an organic compound.

"What in the world," Daniel and Lavern shouted.

"What, you mean guys can see that?" asked Milly.

"Can we see it, of course we can, doesn't everyone else," asked Lavern.

Professor Mercer put her hand on Lavern's shoulder and said, "No Lavern, the group is the only one." Lavern was blown away; as Mercer was talking with her, a blue mark appeared on Mercer's forehead, with the ancient Tav.

"Oh my word," said Lavern, "this is more than I can take, so this is what you have been experiencing this whole time Milly?"

Milly now touching her mother's other shoulder, said, "Yes, Mom, welcome to *eternity-time*!"

Chapter 19

Physicists were moving left and right at PRINA, where they were scheduled to start the hadron collider at any moment. It was 3pm in Geneva, Switzerland. Scientists and engineers had done their preemptive testing, completing their checklist, as the technical room gave the nod for the proceedings of the Hadron Collider's launch.

The entire complex was the shape of a huge elliptical circle, and within the core of it was the elliptical encasing of the hadron collider container, which could be viewed through a 20-inch thick glass window. Every 50 feet around the window, was a key operated switch to one of the chambers inside of the collider. This ensured the safety of the large piece of massive piping in which the particles would collide. The process to releasing the particles was much like the military launching orders for firing a missile; it required much attention to every detail so that the collider was successfully turned on. Every protection mechanism was put in place so that no preemptive measures for firing it without authorization could be executed.

Each person, who was to manage the key and switch, was in place. They waited with anticipation for the green light that was stationed above the switch, along with Swarski's voice over the speaker, before carrying out their duty. Once the light was on and they heard their instructions, each switch operator would turn the key, and flip the switch, opening their part of the particle accelerator chamber. Once each person had performed their assignment, then the overall switch would be thrown releasing the particles.

Swarski on the overhead could be heard doing the countdown, with his thick Swedish accent. All the staff knew him, as the "Key guy."

"Get ready ladies and gentlemen, as we commence," Swarski said. Everyone was on standby with keys in place. "3,2,1 TURN and FLIP!" All was quiet in the facility as you could hear keys turning and each switch being flipped.

Swarski acknowledged, "Now is time for lift off!" PRINA considered the start of the hadron collider like NASA sending astronauts into outer space. Swarski was the manager of central control when it came to turning the hadron collider on and off. He took a deep breath before ensuing with the final countdown, as all staff anxiously waited to hear the descension. "10, 9, 8, 7, 6, 5 4, 3, 2, 1, WE HAVE LIFT OFF PEOPLE!"

Swarski's excitement was contagious, as scientists and engineers began shouting and jumping up and down, opening champagne bottles to toast. Celebrations were off the charts with music blasting throughout the facility. Most of the scientists and engineers were wearing costumes of all sorts, from fairytale stories, to cartoon characters, as well as scary creatures, dancing in madness. Anyone watching would have thought it some type of masquerade ball.

Chants were going throughout the facility, "Collide, collide, collide!" Dr. Merrill Turnipseed made his way through the bizarre activity, as he passed other physicists recording video, with handwritten posters, "What you used to know has changed, welcome to a NEW TIME!"

Dr. Turnipseed's frustration increased, knowing that he could not turn things back. Attempting to appear somewhat celebratory so his behavior would not give away his intent, he finally made it to his office.

"I must contact Milly," he thought.

Picking up his phone he fumbled, as a knock came to his door. "Turnipseed, are you in there?" It was the voice of Mandess who was given knowledge by the demonic hordes that Turnipseed was working for El Elyon. Holding his breath, he did not answer nor move. The knock turned into a bang, where Mandess was now screaming over the loud music, "Turnipseed, are you in there?"

His voice alone was eerie, causing fear to shoot through Merrill's belly; it wasn't the voice of a human, but rather Mandess' voice changed to that of a Mad Man, that of Madness! It had to be a demon, Merrill thought.

Turnipseed closed his eyes, remaining under his desk, with his flip phone in his trembling hand. Sweat poured onto his brow, and continued down slowly, as it then dripped over his eyeglasses, leaving a stream of water. He monitored his breathing, making sure that he would not allow the amygdala within his brain to get him into panic mode, and repeated the mantra, "Everything is alright. Everything is alright."

Immediately, he noticed by his desk these amber colored shoes over a pair of large feet attached to someone or something that had to be at least 9 feet tall. The light from the figure flooded the room encasing him entirely. He thought, "Surely Mandess will see this light and know that I am in here."

Mandess walked away screaming at the top of his lungs. Turnipseed then heard the voice of the person or thing that was attached to the body by his desk saying, "Merrill Turnipseed you may come out, for I have been sent by El Elyon to guard you."

Merrill crawled out from under the desk and saw an angelic creature, having the most brilliant armor of gold bedecked with rubies, wearing a matching gold band crown with rubies, which accented his long blonde hair. The sleeves underneath the armor were a glamorous iridescent white, trimmed in gold.

"My name is Amori, I have been sent to you by El Elyon, to contact Milly Teschlon. I will guard you and your family, as we make our way out of this place so that we can move you to a safe area."

Merrill nodded in astonishment, still trembling but now for a different reason. The angel's brilliance and rich authority, none like he had ever seen, oozed all through each fiber of his spiritual being much like the wave particle-duality where the strength and authority of his nature was made known. It was hard to be in Amori's presence and not be overwhelmed.

"What must I do," Merrill asked with his voice trembling.

"Contact Milly Teschlon, and then we will make our escape."

Merrill dialed Milly's number, to which she answered.

"Hello," Milly said.

"Milly, this is Dr. Turnipseed, the launch of the hadron collider has commenced and the particles are colliding. Get ready! The storm of antimatter and the opening of the parallel universe is coming!"

She thanked him quickly, hanging up and feeling nervous herself. Amori immediately picked Merrill up, like a man picking up a 20-pound sack of potatoes under his arm. Unsheathing his sword, Amori pointed it upward, to which a portal of light opened and he shot through it with Merrill in his care, leaving the vicinity. Other angelic hosts already had Merrill's family at a special location, and Amori was now taking Merrill there to join them under the angelic protection.

The Storm

The Ancient Language Seekers had a call list. Milly called the two people she was supposed to contact, Kaufman and Mercer, to whom, they each called two people, and so forth. At their last meeting on Tuesday night, they set a call chart in place, for when the word would come that the battle was to begin. Although they had their alarm clocks set, it was not for certain the exact timing of PRINA's hadron collider launching. The fact that Turnipseed called made it easier for the group to be on time for the battle.

Kaufman called Robert, who was to meet the group and the students in front of Truman Hall, where he would anoint the remaining people with the Oil of Unity, for their protection. Members of the group were in a fastidious pace to get to the location, as the skies darkened overhead.

Thundering could be heard rippling through the atmosphere, *boom, boom, boom*, as lightning erupted sideways branching off into different rods of light, projecting a theatrical show, as if a huge battle was already taking place in the heavens.

Meteorologists had come on the local news, warning of closings for schools and businesses, until the storm passed. With the storm elements of intense lightning, and strong wind gusts up to 40-50 mph, people were warned not to go outside.

Milly alerted her parents to Dr. Turnipseed's call, letting them know that she had to make her way to meet the group and that they could stay home, to wait for her call. They were timid at first, not wanting their daughter out of their sight, when Rafael and Tubal made themselves visible to Lavern and Daniel.

“She is safe with us,” Rafael said, as his glorious presence overwhelmed Milly’s parents. Lavern, holding her hand over her mouth, nodded, while Daniel fell back looking upward at the tall figures, amazed. He was speechless, seeing the silver blue colored garment of Rafael, covered by his majestic armor, with a massive sword in its sheath. Next, seeing Tubal’s shofar on his side caught Daniel’s attention, as his eyes then scanned his sapphire garment that sparkled like the night sky, covered by the splendid gold armor.

“Trust me mom and dad, all will be well,” Milly said smiling. She waved at them, while stepping into Rafael’s arms.

Rafael held onto Milly, as his expansive nine-foot wings spread out overshadowing both of them. Tubal’s wings spread out simultaneously, and both angels unsheathed their swords pointing them upwards, at which time a portal of light opened above them where they then flew out.

Lavern and Daniel looked at each other, hugging one another, wondering how they ever found themselves in such a fantastical occurrence. The fact that their daughter was involved, gave them mixed emotions, from being nervous to giddy. They never experienced such extremes of emotional energy, and knew that El Elyon had to be with them. Immediately, they saw in the spirit, as a huge blue fire surrounded their house where, within was the Ancient Language that constantly spoke.

“Wow, Lavern do you…” Daniel said as his wife interrupted him.

“Yes I do Daniel! OH MY!”

Likewise, the angelic forces stationed with the other members, took them like a shooting torpedo to Truman Hall. The new students recently recruited, were present, as their own angels gathered them for the battle.

Robert stood in front of the group with a massive angel, Timani, who shone like the brilliance of a star. His copper colored body glistened, as he wore an orange garment, glimmering like the setting sun filled with gold dust. His armor, a deep gold, had insets of diamonds sparkling from it. When you stared at his presence, your eyes were captivated, feeling that you were watching the most beautiful sunset.

The group lined in rows of 5, were ready to go to war. The front row consisted of Kaufman, Alan, Anjali, Milly and Parker, who were clad in their spiritual armor. Robert went past the first row, to anoint the rest of El Elyon's warriors, declaring over each person, "The Oil of Unity be upon you and El Elyon give you strength for the battle."

All were anointed, when Robert and Timani returned to the front. Timani nodded to Rafael who took long slow strides through the troops of the Ancient Language Seekers, making his way up front where he stood as a general, unmoved in front of his troops. In a valiant voice he shouted like a trumpet, "Take a knee!"

The storm was still brewing and winds were blustering 'round them, when the crystal tower suddenly appeared, and the blue flame erupted within into a beautiful light show. The eagle's wings on Main Street were all the more luminescent with the fiery blue opal flame, appearing like a runway now for the warriors about to take off for battle with their angelic hosts.

Instantaneously, the entire group was now inside of the tower, immersed in its great expanse with the blue flame erupting all around them, speaking the Ancient Language. It was the Ancient Voice, the voice of El Elyon! Inside, the warriors were protected from the storm and saw the swirling crystal tower ascending upward, where the spherical pathway on the outside was like a ramp that led to the heavens. At the top of the tower was an opening, much like a volcano.

Rafael spoke to the astonished group, who was down on one knee. An angel stood before each one with their sword unsheathed, ready to carry out Rafael's instructions. He began, "You will be knighted warriors of El Elyon for this battle, knowing that you are a carrier of the blue flame, the Ancient Language. Each of you has an angel, who will take you into the battle, fighting with you for the souls of mankind. This knighting is a sacred anointing that you must receive before you fight."

As Rafael spoke, the angels standing before each individual, held their sword in front of their own face almost touching their own spiritual nose. They looked straight ahead, not at the human before them, but as if they were peering off in the distance, seeing that which was to come for these heroic warriors of mankind.

Rafael, in a majestic battle voice carried out the ceremony, "Angelic hosts, pull your swords forward to knight them!" Each angel held their sword straight out, about three feet over the head of the person who they were to knight. As all of this took place, each individual was under the power of the Ancient Language, unable to peer at what was going on. Rather they had their eyes closed and head bowed.

They felt the presence of the Sword that was in the hand of each angel, as it touched their left shoulder, and the sensation of lightning bolts went through each warrior's body. "You are knighted by El Elyon for battle, you are His warriors," said Rafael, as the angels then touched their right shoulder. Lightning bolts continued to shoot through them. They were poised by El Elyon to contain the energy of the power given to them in the *knighting*.

Rafael then said, "Arise warriors, the battle has begun!" He looked at Milly, and waved for her to come to the front, to lead the group off into battle. Suddenly, the angels filed out from in front of the warriors, and stood to the outside of the group, surrounding them as a wall. With the huge shields on their back, fastened to them like a door to a house, they stood facing the warriors, while their shields were a wall around the group, providing a more resplendent military send off into the fight.

Milly walked in boldness to the front, as her garment, a sapphire blue tunic that sparkled as a sea of precious jewels, glistened similar to Tubal's garment, where stars and nebulas were inside of it, covered by her gold and silver armor. The bronze boots covering her feet, along with her attire, shone under the brilliant light of the tower, refracting its colors on the crystal walls.

She stood, boldly speaking, "Warriors of El Elyon, you have arrived here today as different people from when you began. You are extraordinary, fighting the battle of Light and darkness, the epic battle that has warred and groaned through all of eternity. Each place where the Light shines the brightest is in the darkest of areas."

With her shoulders held up, she walked back and forth in the front of the group while speaking, "You have had to overcome your own darkness, as the power of the Light of the Ancient Language has entered your hearts, where you have now entered into the Wisdom of El Elyon. The power of His Sword speaks to you the Ancient Call, which was before you were born. This Ancient Call has christened you from eternity. Your destiny was written in the heavens ages ago, before your birth, declaring the victory that you would bring in this hour."

The members of the group stood with resolute faces, smiling as their soul was embraced by the words that Milly spoke. It pierced them with the richness of the Ancient Language that was speaking through her, to bring Light upon them in greater intensity. Lightning radiated within each individual, amplifying each word. They could perceive the Wave-Particle Duality theory, where the Ancient Language poured upon them like waves from the ocean, strengthening them supernaturally.

"The Light pierces the darkness, and the darkness cannot overcome it, nor put it out! This Light burns brightly within each one of you! You warriors of El Elyon are being sent forth as a lightning bolt of the Ancient Language, speaking that which will be, as we defeat all of hell!"

Cheers erupted, as each warrior stood holding their raised swords.

Milly shouted, "El Elyon be with you!"

Everyone responded back, "El Elyon be with you!"

The angels came to the individual assigned them. One by one, the angels spread out their wings, nine feet in length, where they then shot upward, out of the top of the tower, taking each person to their respective place in battle, as they had a dramatic exit down Main Street, where the luminescent wings were like an airport runway.

The Shrill of Darkness

The hordes of hell were on high alert. Beelzebub had received information of PRINA's movement, as they started the hadron collider. There, standing before all the demonic hordes in the underworld, now back at the area of the dark black rock, Beelzebub shouted, "It has begun, my army, as we seek to destroy the souls of mankind!" High-pitched sounds could be heard throughout the dark underworld in their jeering, as underlings in the back jumped up and down, and the serpent creatures all throughout held their heads high, opening their mouths, releasing a putrid odor smelling like sulfur.

Hell's fury was being unleashed, as the cords began to ooze out into the streets of Springfield and all of Area 9, from the locations of The Ancient Gatehouse. Clear, reddish and greenish colored ooze, spread like gangrene from the gates of hell. Demons, like rats living inside of the walls of a house crawled throughout the city, chunking demonic grenades throughout, which let out the bitter smoke attacking the souls who were not immune to its workings.

While the storm brewed overhead, darkness filled the sky, and the serpent creatures shrieked in laughter throughout Springfield. They watched as the ooze spread throughout the streets, and the putrid fumes of the smoke entered houses that were unprotected. Now came the cannon balls filled with lying serpents, released immediately after the grenades.

Serpents of all different colors now crawled through the streets, looking for the places, in which they could enter, to attach to the souls therein. Screams from inside of homes could be heard, as well as angry shouting, where these serpents would enter, creating havoc all within, as people were involved in demonic brawls. Hell began to control those who were easily given over to the darkness, and insanity broke out.

Some homes were protected by the blue flame, which created a firewall around about them. The people in those places of protection were uncertain as to the cause of the pandemonium in the city, but knew it was wise to stay shut up in their place of safety.

Vladamore came out, feeling at home amongst all the darkness and chaos, gloating in what he believed would be a huge overturning of El Elyon's plans. He could see the demonic grid in the sky that glowed a reddish color revealing the darts within. The antimatter being released at PRINA was now filtering all throughout the globe through the demonic grid, releasing an eerie sound, like that of hell, of moans and screams with a screeching noise.

Within the homes not protected from hell's fury, was a devilish sound, as the antimatter that PRINA brought into the world from the other dimension was dispersed throughout the globe to create worldwide chaos. Places not surrounded by the blue flame were being bombarded with the antimatter. Gunfire could be heard within them, as people screamed in horror at the behavior they were witnessing from those whom they loved. It was as though they were living a nightmare of *Invasion of the Body Snatchers.*

Leviathan, Jezebel and Divination were over Springfield, looking for the zombified souls that they could possess, using them as puppets to do their work of evil. Once the antimatter entered a person who was given over to darkness, black matter was pulled in from the other dimension, where Jezebel, Divination or Leviathan would attach at a faster rate, having full control of the human, to capture their soul.

These ruling powers were sucking the life of the person out of their body. It seemed their soul was being drawn out like a shadowy figure, much like that with Peter Pan's shadow, where the soul was separated from the person's body.

Vladamore laughed in his shrilling tone all the more, seeing the souls of different humans coming out from their bodies, where they now could be taken into the parallel universe. Demons grabbed onto the souls once the ruling powers pulled them out, tying them up by a spiritual noose, dragging them through the air. Vladamore's plan would work for sure, he thought, and his liege would be all the more pleased at his diabolical success in Springfield.

Let There Be Light!

El Elyon's warriors were being carried to their positions, as darkness filled the sky while the tumultuous weather continued to overshadow the area. Lightning flashed throughout, with thundering all around. Alan, Anjali, and Parker were taken to The Quad area of Strytan. Although not far from the tower, the wind gusts made it humanly impossible to be outside and the wings of their angels protected them from the fierce winds.

Angels stood guard, as Alan removed *The Rock* from its sac, setting it upon a large pillar that had been chipped from the crystal tower. The crystal quartz pillar from the tower, created a greater frequency response wave for the device that Alan had made, like a guitar being plugged into an amplifier. The special material that composed the tower was both a house for the blue flame and an amplifier of the Ancient Language.

How ironic it was, Alan thought, that he named the device *The Rock*, and he was now placing it on top of a crystal quartz pillar, which was basically a large rock. Who would have known?

Alan turned it on, as Anjali stood nearby. Parker, with his angel Jalina, who appeared feminine in nature, battled alongside of him to thwart demonic powers all around. Demonic underlings, like hornets coming into a hive, swarmed them. Parker and Jalina were cutting the demons off, as their speed increased, like that of light, around Alan and Anjali, becoming a shield of protection about them. Thumps could be heard as the blades of their Swords cut the serpent creatures.

These were no ordinary blades, but ones made from the metal core of the Ancient Rock by the sapphire pavement, this material was shiny and stellar, in the hands of its warrior. Once this blade cut into a serpent creature, they would fall and dissipate into ashes, leaving no trace of their existence.

Anjali stood in the middle of The Quad, as Alan's device was now turned on, emitting frequencies with the lightning in the sky, thereby taking control of the demonic grid over Springfield. It made it, so that souls could not be taken from the area into the parallel universe. The souls that had been cut asunder from their bodies were being lifted up into the sky by the demons that were assisting in pulling them toward the singularity, into the parallel universe that had been unlocked by the hadron collider.

The singularity was above the storm and was not visible to those underneath. Alan's device was on, and shut down the ability for Beelzebub to take the soul's of mankind out, and Anjali was prepared to read the ancient text of Psalm 48. She opened her mouth to speak, her voice was amplified across the airwaves, and the blue flame came out of her mouth like a sword.

The Ancient Language could be seen within the blue flame. The sound of the language began to torment the other demons in Springfield, where Robert, Tony and the students, had gone to battle, with their angelic hosts beside them. Warriors were able to go with immense speed, wielding their swords to fight the demons as they entered into the homes and places not protected by the blue flame.

Tony entered a home where the children were holding guns against the heads of their parents, as he saw in the spirit, the lying serpents and antimatter that were controlling them. He took his sword and cut the lying serpents off of each one, which immediately caused the children to drop their guns to the floor. The angel beside him, Lazafiel, had a sac in which the putrid smoke from the grenades of hell, were sucked into it, expelling the darkness from the house, when the snakes then immediately left.

Christy and Sherri, who were alongside Tony, took their hands with the blue flame lit up brightly on their palms, placing them on the heads of the parents and the children. Tears flowed from all the family, as they hugged and wept, pleading for forgiveness for their horrid behaviors. The blue mark of the fiery blue opal Tav appeared on the family's foreheads, and immediately they were filled with the blue flame. Afterwards, the blue flame encapsulated the entire house, being a wall of fire around about, bringing the power of the Ancient Language within.

The group went into other homes and buildings under demonic attack, fighting to save the souls of mankind. About 20 percent of the souls had been lifted out of the bodies in Springfield, however were unable to leave earth and crossover into the other dimension because of Alan's device. The bodies', whose souls were separated from them, were still being puppeted by the ruling powers.

Immediately, angelic host assisted Father Sanderson and Pastor Reginald Fielding, who were going after the souls in the heavenly sphere. They warred against the demons, wrestling them with their weapons to recapture the souls, while the angelic host assigned to them, were binding the ruling powers, to further keep them from stealing other souls of men, women and young people.

Father Sanderson and Pastor Fielding saw the souls hooked on a noose being dragged behind demons, like a shadowy flag flying in the wind. As they recaptured the souls, they put them into huge sapphire colored sacs with a gold drawstring, to later return them to their body.

Father Sanderson and Pastor Fielding were above the storm, seeing the lightning strikes of El Elyon on the clouds, thundering into the dark antimatter that was the epic storm over Springfield. Meteorologists were experiencing the effect of the antimatter on their soul, and began having nervous breakdowns while on live television. WKJR Channel 36 thought they could not take anymore; the camera crew had the meteorologist and anchors on live when, on air they all fell to the floor screaming in hysteria. The pandemonium had engulfed them, where the antimatter was pulling upon their soul; it was a weapon against all that was good.

Vladamore was reveling in the chaos, especially since it was televised, knowing that the insane response to the antimatter would be released over the airwave frequencies, amplifying the demonic sound all the more, where others would be affected. People that were in places surrounded by the blue flame, watched the broadcast not understanding what in the world was going on, when they immediately fell to their knees bent over, and the blue flame came upon them as they spoke against the frequencies being released over the airwaves. Now, it was distinguishable, the places of light that were fighting and pushing back the darkness.

The homes and places unprotected by the blue flame, upon hearing or watching the news broadcast, would erupt into pandemonium. People would become aggressive and violently assail one another. All of the team of El Elyon's warriors had their hands full, dismantling the lying serpents, removing the putrid smoke, and bringing their Sword to touch the ooze released from the cords of hell, so that the power of the blue flame would burn up the demonic particles.

As chaos erupted in the news studio and across into other homes, Christopher and Matthew came into the building, with their angelic host, and began battling the lying serpents on the necks of the television crew, meteorologist and anchors. Although Christopher, Matthew and their angels could not be seen by the naked eye, the people inside of the television studio knew that someone or something was present, giving them aide. They began coming to their right mind, standing up and grabbing their head, realizing what had been occurring with them, while on live television.

The meteorologist profusely apologized, asking viewers to overlook the insanity that the team experienced for the brief moment. While continuing to explain the situation to the viewers, Christopher went over to him, and laid his hands on the top of the meteorologist's head, when the blue flame filled him, and wisdom came upon him.

He began alerting the viewers, "Please viewers, resist the antimatter particles being released into the atmosphere." The television station began to experience interference, and was shutdown. Some of the viewers caught the warning and began huddling together in a small circle, hugging one another, and somehow the expression of compassion began drawing the power of the blue flame from the towers into those areas, where warriors and angels quickly assisted, in overcoming the demons, and bringing the blue flame and the Ancient Language with them.

Springfield was beginning to light up like a Christmas tree in the wintery nighttime. Blue fiery lights were a beacon of hope in the midst of PRINA's chaotic intention to overcome the globe, was a volume of wave particles traveling through the atmosphere, interrupting the demonic sounds released from the grid, destroying the poisonous darts within. Angels all over Area 9 were having the same success as the warriors and the angelic hosts in Springfield. The darkness that became a plague across the globe was now being pushed back!

Alan's device, *The Rock*, was sending frequencies all through the region, providing ample opportunity for the battle of the souls of mankind to reach a victory, where souls were protected in the earth. The singularity had become the place and point, where now Milly and Kaufman would crossover into the other dimension.

The Ride Over!

Picked up by their angelic host, Milly and Kaufman were in flight. Milly was carried by Tubal, while Kaufman was carried by a beautiful dark angel, Meriza, who seemed the color of the dark sand of the desert, shining a coppery gleam essence, in the appearance of a male, with long dark hair and eyes that were a deep golden amber. Rafael was ahead of them, as both Kaufman and Milly were carried up to the Angelic war room.

Arriving at the palatial war room on top of Granite Peak Mountain was a thrill. Milly was inspired and amazed, as they were above the storm clouds where they could see the battle across the area. Angelic hosts and warriors fighting the demonic hordes of hell sent energy through Milly's blood, as it coursed now in sync with the Ancient Language. Her veins within had a fiery opal blue flame flowing through, stirring her spirit up to fight all the more. As she drew closer to the war room and the war table, ***lâcham***, she could sense it was near and able to see its splendor as she peered through the mountain with x-ray vision. Her spirit leapt, knowing that the name meant, "to fight!"

Milly opened her mouth while in flight as they edged to the top of the mountain, shouting "***lâcham***," from the top of her lungs.

Tubal looked at her and began to laugh, declaring, "Yes El Elyon's Warrior, you will fight this night! We are entering the War room, where you will be able to see the sacred table."

Kaufman felt the same instinctive surge of emotion and power going through him, and followed suit, as he opened his mouth shouting, "***lâcham***!" The two of them were like children at a theme park, feeling a renewed strength of adventure, which would be much needed for what they were soon to incur.

Eyes opened to the palatial crystal war room, looking much like the tower at Strytan, they were amazed to see its massive expanse, as they entered through the top with the angels bringing them into the fantastical place. Wings stretched broadly, the angels entered the cavity with an opening of 20 feet wide in diameter, to lower Milly and Kaufman onto the floor, as they passed the many tiers within. Milly felt like a gumball coming through a gumball machine, descending through the immense space. Seeing the words of the angelic hosts etched into the crystal walls in the Ancient Language now, could be heard by them, as the Ancient Language began to reverberate the conversations that had taken place.

Quartz Crystal emits frequencies, and for this particular tower, emitted the discussions of all the different angelic voices that had been within the palatial crystal war room, as well as the voice of El Elyon. Milly and Kaufman could hear the lightning that normally occurred in the midst of the angelic council, where El Elyon would respond to their celebrations of expected victory.

Milly, lifted up under her arms by Tubal, landed upon the crystal floor standing in front of the sapphire blue table, ***lâcham***, where she saw the lightning of El Elyon shooting throughout. The thunders could be heard as the lightning occurred. Kaufman was amazed, as well, looking at the brilliance of the massive cobalt blue table, caught in the majesty of its appearance.

Rafael, Tubal and Meriza, stood before the two humans. Rafael looked at Milly and Kaufman instructing them, "Here is where you will receive final orders before you are carried over into the parallel universe." All was perfect within the palatial war room, while the storm outside in the natural and spiritual was the worst disturbance in history.

Milly and Kaufman walked to the table, where they saw a holograph suspended above. The holograph was like watching a movie of what they were to do. As they entered the parallel universe, going through the singularity they would ride on the backs of eagles. Watching the holograph astonished them, and excitement bubbled up in their bellies, as they felt their spirit man doing flips in their stomach.

The spirit of man, which is attached to the belly of a person, speaks frequently to El Elyon's Spirit, and communicates to the soul, through the neurons in the stomach, which sends messages to the brain and then to the heart. On many occasions, the spirit man can create new memories, and stir up past memories to assist the soul in need.

Milly and Kaufman stood in awe, knowing that what they saw revealed was prophecy, as they watched their entrance into the other dimension while viewing the holograph. They could see into the parallel universe, where the hordes of hell watched the souls of mankind in rice fields, keeping them bound up to the sludge of hell. Kaufman watched as he used his sword to cut asunder the demons monitoring the souls, while Milly would be using the oil to pour out upon the different minds in the many rice fields, waking them up to the contraption on their head. The oil would then destroy the metal contraption feeding them sludge. Immediately, the shadowy soul would climb up out of its prison, at which time Milly would open her sapphire bag, known as the *Sac of Souls*, to recapture the soul and return it to earth along with the others.

In the holograph, Kaufman was continually battling demons as Milly did what she needed to do, while Rafael, Tubal and Meriza would assist them. Suddenly, the holograph disappeared and lightning began to strike throughout the table. The thunder that came thereafter actually turned into the sound of a Voice, the Voice of El Elyon, and Milly and Kaufman could hear what was spoken.

"My great warriors, this is a perilous task, and time is of the essence. With the singularity being opened for only a couple of hours, it is necessary for you to execute your assignments, and make it quickly back from the parallel universe. If you do not, you will be caught forever on the other side, where My presence will not be with you, and the blue flame will be removed at the closing of the portal. It is with great caution that I warn you, of the importance of the time in which the gate will be shut. I have placed eternity within your hearts, so therefore, you will be faster than you are in normal time, carrying out your tasks where it will seem like lightning speed. Be brave and courageous for I Am with you!"

Milly looked at Professor Kaufman, as they both nodded at each other. Immediately, each one had a helmet upon them of luminescent golden amber, which looked like a fire burning. They knew that it was time, and walked to their respective angel, Kaufman to Meriza and Milly to Tubal. Rafael looked at them both, and declared, "LET THE BATTLE BEGIN!"

The angels spread their expansive wings, to which El Elyon's lightning responded throughout the crystal tower. El Elyon was giving His power and strength to the angelic host, informing them that the same would happen if they did not exit the parallel universe before the closing. The seriousness of the hour was upon them. Each angel and human was sober, knowing the peril that was at stake individually, as well as to all the souls they hoped to recapture.

The fiery blue flame lifted under their feet from the sapphire table, ***lâcham,*** giving them a dramatic exit from the palatial crystal war room, as they were boosted upon the mountaintop. The singularity could be seen in the sky, as the portal to the other side was eerily dark, where no light shone. Kaufman and Milly looked at the angels, who then spread out their wings, preparing for the ride over.

Coming from a distance were huge massive eagles, a beautiful white color that blended with the look of snow. Each had a 20-foot wingspan the size of a small plane, and was about 20 feet long. It was time, and they would begin their ride, as they set their watches to 1 hour and 50 minutes before the closing of the portal.

Chapter 20 The Final Outcome

High on Granite Peak Mountain, above the clouds, Milly and Kaufman steadied themselves on the edge, knowing instinctively that they would have to leap upon the eagles. The first eagle rounded to the edge of the mountain, to which Kaufman nodded for Milly to leap. Jumping, she landed upon the glorious bird, holding onto its gigantic feathers, thrilled at the supernatural elation she was feeling. Kaufman leapt on the next one, and both were off as they followed the angels into the singularity, to enter the parallel universe.

The closer they got to the black hole the darkness on the other side was tangible. It had a presence completely opposite of the blue flame. Wherever the darkness was, there was a presence like a cloak of heaviness, which brought fear, dread, discouragement and disappointment. Because the antimatter was burned up within Kaufman and Milly, they had an advantage over other humans, entering the other dimension. The darkness would not have as much of an effect on them, as long as the singularity was still open and the connection could be made with the blue flame on earth.

The blue flame poured out from the angelic war room, from the top of Granite Peak into the other realm, like a ribbon leaving a trail behind them, as Kaufman and Milly continued their entry in. The two traveled through a dark tunnel, with the blue flame behind them casting its brightness, lighting the way. They saw Rafael, Tubal and Meriza straight ahead, as the portal was opened to a dark greyish world where there was no sun.

The eagles followed behind the angels who were now spiraling down, from the top of the sky at the portal's opening. Milly squeezed the eagle's feathers, concerned that she would fall once they began to spiral down, at which point the eagle spoke. "My name is Constance, and you, Milly Teschlon, are *safe* with me. I was privileged to carry your Great Grandmother, as she had a similar feat to perform."

Milly was shocked to find out that eagles could speak, and that this particular eagle had also carried her Great Grand! She replied, "Thank you Constance, El Elyon be with you!" Constance looked straight ahead, with a strong face into the distance, where the rice fields of souls could be seen. These eagles had eyesight four times sharper than a regular eagle on earth. Eagles were considered watchmen everywhere throughout the universe in the spirit and in the natural. Their job was to see what was coming, as well as to protect those in their care.

Kaufman discovered the name of his eagle was "Justice." While Milly had been talking to Constance, Kaufman had briefly spoken with Justice. The two eagles assured their riders that their safety was of the utmost importance, and that each eagle would be watching out for them, coming to their aid. With the angelic host and the eagles, Kaufman and Milly would be safeguarded, while in the parallel universe.

Upon entering, the group saw that there were about 100 rice fields of souls who were being fed sludge from hell. Milly did not want to panic trying to figure out the math, realizing they had less than an hour and forty-five minutes to cover all the fields. Tubal could discern Milly's mental struggle and assured her, "Milly, we operate in a faster time than this one while here, because eternity is planted inside of us. Therefore, our movement is close to that of the speed of light."

She was relieved to discover that they had an advantage over time, not only on earth, but also in the parallel universe. Suddenly, Milly was brought to reality when she heard the sounds of men, women and young people calling out, "Please! Free us from this darkness!"

Unsure of where the voices were coming from, Milly soon realized that it was the souls of those in the rice fields, calling out to her, sensing that she had the special ointment. The power of the ointment in her sac had such potency, that the presence of it could be felt by the souls who wanted their freedom. Other souls were growling as Milly passed, disgusted at her presence, detesting the oil, wanting the illusion of their fake reality.

Kaufman motioned to Milly, as he and Justice dipped downward in a spiral, to cut asunder the first demon over the watchtower of the first rice field they had come to. Unsheathing his sword, he steadied himself while Justice swooped, as the blade touched the demon, the creature turned to dust. Kaufman took out the remaining demons over the first rice field, and quickly motioned to Milly to pour out the oil.

Demons here did not have the advantage that the group did, in going the rate of the speed of light. However, they were each given a special receptor that, when activated, helped them go almost close to the speed of light in order to fight intruders. Never had they needed to use it until now. After the first field was attacked, the news began to spread to the other fields for the demons to initiate the receptors in order to increase their speed so that they could have a fighting chance.

Milly looked at all the souls in the field and knew instinctively, the ones who wanted freedom from their bondage. She opened the golden sac, pulling out the wooden box that she had gotten from Father Sanderson, as it still was ablaze with the olive tree and the Greek words. Upon opening the vial, Constance took Milly quickly over the top of the heads of all the souls in the first field, and she poured it out on those who cried out. However, those who were disgruntled, Milly knew would be a waste, since they would not receive the oil. Only the souls longing in faith could receive the power of its strength to be set free.

Immediately, as the oil hit the tops of the heads of the souls, a shadowy figure climbed out of the forms within the water, to which she realized that the souls had been in a prison. These particular forms that were in the water, although human in shape, were instead a prison made of special metals that kept souls contained magnetically. The greenish grid that could barely be seen in the sky, created a polarity in the atmosphere, where the forms in the water were highly magnetized encasing the captured soul. These forms, made it possible for the soul of a human to operate as a battery, powering this dimension.

Like a person climbing out of the sewer, the shadows were climbing out of the forms. Milly had the sapphire sac, which was the *Sac of Souls*, on her side. Once the sac was opened, a spiritual vacuum would draw in the freed souls. One soul after another was sucked into the sapphire sac, upon their release. As they entered, you could hear the pleasure within the fantastical sac; the souls rejoiced in the freedom that they received.

Milly was concerned that the demons might hear the commotion, and she opened the sac to whisper, “Be quiet please, lest we be detected.”

The souls hushed, as Kaufman and Milly, along with the angels hurried to each field. When they got to field number 44, the demons had been alerted by this time, having turned on their receptors in order that they could increase their speed. Having heard of the strange activity at the prior fields, the demons were readied with special weapons, wanting to catch the group off guard.

The demon on the watchtower remained still, as the group entered the field, at which time three demons jumped upon Rafael, Tubal and Meriza, grabbing their heels, putting a hook in the end of each one’s spiritual foot. Rafael made a wincing sound, as he then saw the demon’s weapon of a harpoon type instrument made of special material, hooked all the way through his heel.

Each of the angels rid themselves of the demonic instrument, as they continued to battle. Although angels did not bleed, they had a liquid substance that came from within as they appeared to be cut in their spiritual form. Blue liquid, that of the fiery flame of El Elyon leaked out of Rafael’s foot, as well as Tubal and Meriza, weakening the angels. They pulled their strength from the blue flame, and the demons knew that if they leaked out the substance, it would then weaken them to fight the battle.

The demons hideously laughed and leapt up and down on the heads in the rice field, forgetting that souls were caught within the forms, when the demon on the watchtower yelled, “Get off those souls you fools!”

Milly would normally panic in this type of situation, but instead found herself calm, where she was able to make considerations of what to do to come to their aid. She listened to the blue flame that was within her, as El Elyon spoke, “Milly, the whip on your side! Use the keys of the Kingdom as a cord to pull the blue flame coming from the angelic war room, closer to the angels, so I can fill them with My strength.”

Milly saw her whip lighting up to the amber color, and the keys within began to jingle. She let it loose flicking it, as she looked behind her to grab hold of the blue flame that still looked like a ribbon, pulling it close to Rafael, Tubal and Meriza, who were then filled and strengthened. Once they were imbued with its strength, they unsheathed their swords, along with Kaufman and began cutting asunder demons left and right. A hive of demons came at them, jumping left and right all over the field. Milly could not understand why there was more activity over this field than any other.

Constance then sent a message to Milly's mind, "This is the field of the souls of the young, who are to be great leaders in their nations. Beelzebub seeks the places of ruling and reigning in nations and looks for those who are being groomed, to bring them into the deceptions of darkness, so he can puppet them on earth, while their soul remains imprisoned here. When you set *these souls* free Milly, many who are being groomed as world and national leaders will no longer be under the guise of this deceit."

Milly heard the young voices crying out, as she then knew instinctively what nation they lived in. Different languages flowed up to her ears, as each one was scribed in the air floating into her eardrum. Upon entering her ear, she knew the translation for each language. One Asian girl feverishly pleaded, "Help me! My father does not know I am here, and I am to rule on his passing. Free me!"

Another voice came into her ear, a young African boy shouting, "Free me! Free me!" In a haunting tone it continued, "I am a prince in my nation. I will rule one day. My parents do not know that I am not in my body. Take me home warrior of El Elyon!"

Milly had chills going up and down her spine, as the hairs on her arm stood up. She knew that the warfare over this field was great because Beelzebub's capturing of these souls would end up deceiving entire generations of nations. The younger generation was the seed planted, of what would occur decades later in a nation.

Kaufman, led by Justice, was instructed on which demons to destroy, diligently putting his sword to them. Then out of nowhere, a demon jumped on top of Justice and began clawing at Kaufman. Kaufman yelled out in anguish, feeling the claw marks enter him like the blade of a knife. Meriza rushed over, swinging his sword upon the demon to bring its destruction.

Milly knew that the oil she had, was infused with a healing agent, and went immediately to Kaufman's aid pouring one drop upon his left leg, healing it right away. He thanked her, and she returned to pouring the oil out upon the heads of the souls in the field. One by one, they were climbing out of their forms, being drawn into the sapphire bag, where the blue flame began burning brightly within.

The blue flame filled the souls, refreshing them while in the sac, giving them comfort for the soon return home to their bodies. The more peace the souls felt, the stronger the blue flame burned within in the sac.

Kaufman and Milly went from field to field, trying to beat time. Little by little the singularity became narrower, to which Rafael said, "We have one more field, and if we do not hurry warriors, we will not make it in time."

Milly and Kaufman rushed knowing that they were racing against the clock, as they anxiously looked at their watches. Their execution was stupendous and they would make it on time, Milly thought. Then, without realizing it, a demon jumped upon Constance stabbing both Milly and the eagle. The two screamed in unison, as their pain echoed throughout the dark dimension.

"AAAAAAAHHHHHHHH" Milly's voice echoed, bouncing off of the grid onto the forms, causing electrical surges in the atmosphere, where lightning began to fragment throughout the area.

Milly saw the blue flame oozing from her leg. While in anguish over her leg, grabbing it to keep the blue liquid from oozing, a demon cut the sapphire bag loose from Milly's side, leaping off of Constance, taking it with him into the rice field, where he jumped from head to head.

Milly was in trouble and, unable to react, she yelled for Rafael, who already knew of her plight. He motioned to Tubal and Meriza to go after the *Sac of Souls*. They could not afford to leave the parallel universe without the sapphire sac!

"Ugggggghhhh!" Milly said in utter torment. She did not know if they would make it back through the singularity before it's closing. What made matters worse, was the thought of what would happen to all the souls who were hoping to get home. Instead of joy, they would be imprisoned again or destroyed. She focused her thoughts on El Elyon while feeling the pain in her leg. Constance also, had a gaping wound and was weakened. The two seemed to barely be making it, when suddenly El Elyon spoke!

"Get the oil Mildred, and pour it upon you both, it will heal you quickly." El Elyon spoke with urgency, "You must hurry; time is short!"

Milly opened the oil, pouring a drop on both she and Constance, which sent lightning throughout their bodies, restoring all that the demon had done. Next, Milly released her whip, reaching for the blue flame, with the keys in her cord, and drew it closer to she and Constance, as they were filled with more strength.

The demon below who had the sac was leaping on top of the heads of those in the rice field, running toward the factory that had sludge coming out. He was hurrying to destroy all the souls in the sludge machine, so that they could never leave. Tubal, Meriza and Rafael, fighting off demons to get to the conniving thief, were being hindered to retrieve the bag. Kaufman was still busy fighting his own battle and would not be able to attend to the sac.

Milly knew that it was up to her and Constance to recapture the *Sac of Souls*. In the face of danger, she tried to be brave. Constance, who was now healed, spoke to Milly the instructions she needed. "My dear Mildred, the blue flame has made you brave and you must trust me with what I am about to tell you, because you will need courage. The strap that goes around my neck, girds my belly, and has a place where you can put your feet. You must go underneath my belly, and fasten yourself, so that when I fly over the demon's head, you can reach for the *Sac of Souls*."

For a moment deep within her soul, Milly felt a connection with her Great Grandmother. She wept, knowing that El Elyon was allowing her to think of her Great Grand, in order to fight in boldness and with courage. Still flying towards the demon, Milly began to gradually move underneath to Constance's belly.

Still nervous as they were in flight, El Elyon brought the blue cord into her heart, at which time she heard the voice of her Great Grandmother,

Mildred Virginia Lee, speaking. The blue flame released a prophecy from decades earlier, which was spoken for Milly to receive at this moment.

"Milly, my dear Great Granddaughter," said the voice of Mildred Virginia Lee. "I knew that you would be born in a time that was perilous. I was given many visions and dreams about what your generation would have to endure, and know how difficult your task must be. You have to be brave child. What you have been called to do is much larger than you could ever know. El Elyon's blue flame within you, will give you the necessary strength to fight well. Be brave my little warrior and trust the Ancient Language, as you fight your fight! My fight has ended and you Milly must carry on! El Elyon be with you!"

Milly was now underneath Constance, with her feet locked into the straps. Tears flowing out of her eyes into the wind, she whispered back to the voice of her Great Grandmother, "El Elyon *IS* with you Great Grand!"

She knew that her Great Grandmother was already with El Elyon in eternity, and the prophecy that was left for her to hear in the parallel universe by the blue flame, made her courageous in the face of danger. Instantaneously, she heard Constance shout, "NOOOOWWWW!"

Milly let her body fall, trusting that her feet would remain locked in the straps while the rest of her was freely flying upside down. As they glided over the demon's head, she took her whip out hearing the keys jingle, and flicked it towards the sac, hooking it by the drawstring. With her other hand she took her sword, slicing the demon to smithereens! She got it!

Straightaway, she poured out the last bit of oil onto the heads of the souls in the last field, opening the sac for them to join with the others. One by one the last bit of souls from the parallel universe climbed out of the forms and had their souls set free coming into the sac. With time shortened, Rafael shouted, "the portal is closing, we must return!"

Milly, still in the straps underneath Constance, saw Kaufman in front of her, behind the other angels, as the hole kept getting smaller and smaller. Nearing the portal, she saw that the hole was now closed up to about 15 feet wide, and with the size of Constance, having Milly attached, they would need the hole to remain at that width, until they reached it.

One after another, the angels made it through, first Tubal, then Meriza, and after them Kaufman and Justice. Rafael saw the narrow time in which Milly had to make it. Seeing Milly still strapped underneath Constance's belly with the sapphire sac in hand, Rafael knew that the two would not make it. In order for Constance to fly faster, he would have to retrieve Milly with the *Sac of Souls.*

Like a bullet coming from the barrel of a gun, he dove and grabbed Milly, then shouted to Constance to head for the portal. Holding Milly underneath his right arm, Rafael's wings moved swiftly to get them out, at which time a demonic prince leapt forward from the singularity, just missing Constance.

The prince was raging in his demonic tirade. His appearance was a serpent creature body covered with the appearance of the universe, where he could cloak himself easily while in the heavens. Horns coming out of his head and an evil face with snarling teeth and a massive nose, made the universe on him appear ugly. He was determined to fight to the bitter end!

It looked as though all hope was lost, when suddenly the great warrior angel Mishal showed up behind the prince, slicing him in two, where a side of the demonic prince fell to the left and the other side to the right. Rafael shifted his wings to that of a missile making it through what was now a five-foot wide opening. He and Milly shot through like a bullet, with the singularity closing fast behind them.

Milly drew her whip as she flicked it, reaching for the blue flame in front of them, pulling them through in greater speed. The keys clanked within the whip and Rafael began to shout, as the souls in the sapphire sac could be heard celebrating. It was electric all around them as the sapphire sac had lighting coming from it with the blue flame burning brighter within each soul, giving them the comfort to know that they were close to home.

Upon Milly and Rafael's exit through the tunnel, the singularity was closing swiftly underneath their feet. Clouds that once were dark were now dissipating and the sounds of angelic hosts shouting victory could be heard all over the heavens!

"El Elyon has defeated the darkness! We have won!" the voices shouted. Tubal took his shofar out while suspended in the heavens, releasing a victory sound through the trumpet blasts. All of the heavens were rejoicing, knowing that for another time in earth, man had been protected from the diabolical plans of Beelzebub.

The towers all over Area 9 could be seen from the heavens. Milly, still safely kept by Rafael, was rejoicing as she saw many crystal towers across the land, from which the blue flame flowed out with the Ancient Language.

Back at Strytan

Rafael and Tubal assisted in transporting Kaufman and Milly back to Strytan, where they met the others in front of Truman Hall. The crystal tower on The Quad shone brighter, as now many townspeople gathered around rejoicing. The students and the rest of the team members were in front of Truman Hall, which glowed an amber color, with the Greek writing being converted into English, '*You shall know the truth and the truth will set you free*!'

Those who had endured the dark storm in Springfield and had been set free of the antimatter and dark matter were celebrating, as they themselves were marked with the mark of the Tav on their forehead, realizing how they were kept from hell's gates. Speaking of hell's gates, there was one last thing to deal with. Milly had to find out about Dean Bobby Knight.

Seeing Tony in front of the other students she asked, "Have you seen Dean Knight?"

"As a matter of fact, Milly, we all did," he said, while pointing at the rest of the students. "He came out here in a maddened state and began screaming, when there appeared this greyish shadow leaving his body, at which time he had a stroke, falling down on the sidewalk."

"I saw a demon come after the shadowy figure, and in an eerie shrill sound, the demon said, 'it's time to go into another dimension; your prison will be a rice field of man's souls, where *you* will be kept.'"

"We all looked in awe and knew that we were not to mess with the demon nor try and recapture Dean Knight's soul. When the paramedics came to find him, they said he had a massive stroke."

Milly knew that Dean Knight was getting his reward for all the evil he did here in Springfield. Despite justice being served, she had a moment of pity for him. Parker could see his friend struggling and patted her on the shoulder.

"It's finished Milly! The Ancient Gatehouse got demolished; a lightning bolt hit it, and utterly took it to the ground!" Parker exclaimed.

Joy filled Milly after hearing the news of the destruction of hell's gates. She stood looking around at the cheering townspeople, who were free of the dark plight. Wanting to join in on the celebration, she was brought to the task she still had left, when she saw Rafael.

Milly remembered about the *Sac of Souls*, seeing the sapphire sac on her side. Slowly lifting it up, preparing to hand the sapphire bag over to Rafael, she knew it was time for her to say goodbye.

Rafael walked up to her, as the others were unable to see him. He stopped and bent down gently to her face, wiping away her tear. "Well done good and faithful warrior of El Elyon, you have saved souls not only in this earth, but also rescued these in this prized sac from the parallel universe," he said motioning to the sapphire sac.

Tears stopped flowing down Milly's cheeks, as she tried to be stoic. Rafael reached for the sac, "I will take these souls to the bodies to which they belong." She handed them to him, putting her ear to the bag one last time to hear their joy, as all the souls thanked her. Milly did not know how to say goodbye and this one was difficult.

"When will I see you again Rafael?" Milly asked.

"You will see me again *when it is time* Milly Teschlon; I am sure there will be much darkness to fight in days to come," Rafael said assuring her.

"Before I depart, I want to leave you with this small treasure from El Elyon. You will not be able to see the tower all the time as you do now, but know that it burns brightly and remains here when the need arises. The need for this hour to fight against the darkness was great, so the power of the tower was made known to destroy the gates of hell and its intent of destruction against the souls of mankind.

"We have won Milly, you have won, and the tower's strength will be made known to you now through this small treasure."

Milly opened the beautiful turquoise velvet colored sac that had a small silver drawstring, seeing a wooden box inside, much like the wooden box for the oil. It lit up in amber etchings with the crystal tower on the outside. Gently opening it she saw within a necklace, bracelet and ring, each with the Ancient letter of the Tav, that was made of a fiery blue opal.

Milly wept as she pulled it up to her face, kissing it, grateful to be given such a treasure. Looking at Rafael she mouthed, "Thank you!" Before she knew it, Rafael spread his huge wings and took to flight. She looked off in the distance, seeing him leave, at which time the skies turned blue again, and the sun came out, bathing everyone's face in the beauty of a day, which would never be forgotten.

The tower vanished before their eyes, although Milly knew it was never far away. Putting on her jewelry, she touched the Tav and brought it up to her lips again to kiss the eloquent treasure. "I will never forget what You have done, El Elyon, for the souls of mankind. Thank you for the privilege of being Your warrior."

She turned and walked toward Truman Hall to meet up with everyone else from the team, when she heard softly, as a wind blew against her back, "I Am always here Mildred, and never far away. I need you to do one last thing, which you already know. Write in the Ancient Language, that which I have told you to scribe."

She felt as though she was back to the beginning of her great adventure, thinking of her dream when she first began encountering all these spiritual, supernatural experiences. The dream of seeing a little girl on a bed, getting up to write at an ancient desk and sitting in an old chair. She remembered her dream fondly, of the little girl pulling out an ancient paper to write on, in the script of the Ancient Language.

Parker looked at Milly, who was lost in thought, "Earth to Milly, earth to Milly," he said as he grabbed her, pulling her close to hug her. "Man Milly, this has been some ride, huh?"

"Yes Park, it most certainly has."

Anjali walked over to Milly and put her hand on Milly's right shoulder saying, "Kaufman told me everything Milly, I am so proud of you." Milly began weeping as she hugged Professor Mercer, thinking of the task of saving all the souls in the parallel universe, while Alan, Anjali and Parker worked on saving the souls on earth.

"You all had a huge part, Professor Mercer," said Milly, "the souls on this earth would have been taken had you not done what was needed."

"One thing Milly," said Professor Mercer.

"Sure, what is it?"

"I am giving you extra credit for this project," Mercer said winking, as Milly smiled and winked back.

As they ended their conversation, Milly saw her parents running to meet her, hurrying across campus. They informed her that Tubal had updated them on Milly's status and assured them of her safety. Milly and her parents, were in a group hug, grateful to be holding one another, and shuddering at the thought of what would have happened had Milly and the others not helped.

Standing in the midst of campus, the Teschlons were still, others around them chattering, discussing about the tower, and the crazy pandemonium that erupted in the midst of what seemed to be a quiet Midwestern town. No one ever expected all the occurrences and insane supernatural experiences, that would be unexplainable to the natural mind, but the townspeople were their own support group, in the middle of a college campus where many witnessed the tower and the blue flame.

The Ancient Language had defeated the gates of hell in Springfield, as Vladamore and his minions rode out of town as quickly as possible, knowing that Beelzebub would wreak havoc on them, as soon as they returned. Vladamore would rather take his beating and demotion than to be turned away from hell itself. Serugar followed his general, still obligatory to whatever he ordered.

After the majestic crystal tower's vanishing, Father Sanderson and Pastor Reginald Fielding came together to collectively assure the townspeople of Springfield, that if they had any further questions regarding the supernatural occurrences, they would be of assistance in the coming days, weeks and months, if necessary.

Dana was hugging Tony, as he lifted her up and swirled her around, they kissed one another, glad that the other one was alright. All over campus there was a buzz, the sound of community, care and of course coffee, where people were now headed to *The Grind* to get their addiction.

Kaufman walked to Milly and her parents, thanking them for allowing their daughter to participate in the wild adventure. They laughed and agreed to the *wildness*, saying that it was more than an adventure for sure. He asked them if he could briefly have a word alone with Milly, to which they agreed and walked off.

"Milly, I must say, that in all my years as a professor, I have never seen such a promising student as yourself." Kaufman peered through his glasses as he noticed her eyes, and then looking off towards Truman Hall, he spoke once more. "I truly believe, Milly Teschlon, that you have been painted with a Wisdom beyond your years, which is why I have this to give to you."

Milly was surprised to hear Kaufman saying any of this, and even more so, to see what he would give her. Out from his back pocket, he had a small notebook, held together by a band. On the cover were brush strokes of paint, where strokes from the top of the book to the bottom, were flowing, yellow, red, orange, green, blue, purple and so forth, all around the book.

She took it replying, "Thank you Professor Kaufman, I am honored to hear you say that and blown away by this small notebook."

"I think you should open the cover and look on the front page," he insisted.

Milly opened it, to where she was able to read, "*To Milly, one painted in Wisdom, as she uses the brush of the strokes with the same paint, to smear it on others. Write YOUR words Milly Teschlon! Sincerely, Norman Kaufman.*"

Tears fell onto her cheeks, and down upon the paper. She touched the words, as though each one leapt into her soul. Trying to hold back the floodgates, she kept looking at the writing and said, "Thank you Professor Kaufman, I am truly grateful."

He touched her shoulder and replied, "No, Thank you Milly Teschlon, Thank you!"

Professor Kaufman walked off, as Milly stood in front of Truman Hall, then realizing what El Elyon wanted her to do. She went towards the steps into the building where the sounds of all that was going on outside had faded. Back at the basement door, she found herself at the place where everything had started. Slowly opening the door, she looked into the basement seeing ancient stone steps. Light shone upon each one, giving a warm atmosphere to the underground rooms.

She could hear El Elyon's breath coming up with the flooding light, as He inhaled and exhaled, where she knew that He was with her. Milly descended down into the basement, where she could hear the Ancient Language speaking to her soul, like the sound of a violin playing in her soul. The language had become a part of her, and it carried her off to a tranquil place.

Slowly hitting the landing of the basement, she saw the stone corridor and the ancient light sconces, as she walked to the Philosophy department's storage room. Opening the door, she saw the desk and chair, where sitting upon it was an inkwell and ancient paper. She walked over to the desk and sat down, while listening to the Ancient Language pouring out on her heart and mind, as the song of the violin grew louder.

Upon sitting, she opened the drawer and found a wood carved relic tube, where upon it was the etching of the crystal tower, and ancient letters. Picking up the quill at the inkwell, she began to scribe in the Ancient Language on the beautiful aged paper, seeing it convert into English and back into the Ancient text. Her heart skipped like a deer near the water brook, as she scribed each word.

She looked at the text and trembling read it aloud, as it felt like fire was consuming her soul.

The Deep Place!

From the deep place, you formed my soul, with living waters crying out Your Name, forever explaining the nature of Your flame that so richly dwells within my inner man, letting me know my value and worth!

My heart and mind are rearranged by the sound of Your Name, which is a symphony of instruments in concert, building up to the place in time where Your breath is released upon my soul, awakening me!

I am renewed and refreshed, seeing that I have stepped into a treasury of jewels beyond man's opinions and scrutiny, that I am forever undone by the singularity that has opened wide, and pulled me in, like a vacuum outside of time, causing me to be in the safe place of Your arms, as I feel You breathe upon me, giving me purpose and destiny!

I am undone by the Sword on my side, that is forever reverberating the sound of Your Name, and the sweet melodic tunes that have created an aroma around My heart, as You mark me with Your sacred mark, calling me to Yourself, where I have stepped into the blue flame, to know the Ancient Language that calls out to my soul and spirit!

Here, You cause my soul to soar upon the wings of eagles, and I am lifted to the open door that stands in front of me, of eternity, knowing that Wisdom has been given to those who are marked and called by You!

Your mark is my jewel, the treasure of Your Wisdom, bedecking me like a Princess ready to fight in battle, knowing that she has already defeated all of hell itself, as I feel Your breath and hear the sound of the Ancient Language that has touched my tongue, and loosed it in power to use the keys of the kingdom and cause all of hell to tremble, declaring the presence of Your majesty!

This is the symphony of my soul, that swirls like a whirlwind around me, giving me strength and purpose, as I am armored in Your glory, revealing the nature of Your Light, living and moving in the Blue Flame of Your presence, that has become my dwelling place!

Milly, stunned at the verses and text she wrote, wept profusely opening her mouth, as she proclaimed, "Thank you El Elyon! I can never repay you for all that you have done for mankind! You are my jewel, and Your blue flame has forever etched my heart, making me the warrior that I was always meant to be, as you removed all doubt and insecurity."

She felt the wind of El Elyon move across the room, breathing upon her, and she nodded her head, knowing what to do. Picking up the ancient looking container, rolling the paper up to stick it safely within, she closed the tube, removed the loose bricks where they originally found the ancient relic, and put this new one in its place.

As she went to the door, she turned back, to now see an ordinary basement storage room, where everything was clean and in place, from where she and Parker had worked. Closing the door, she peeked back in, whispering, "We will see you soon, El Elyon, for we are ***The Ancient Language Seekers***."

Contact the Author

Thank you so much for reading this first full fiction, which I have written. I would so appreciate it if you could please give me a review on Amazon.

Sincerely,

Robin Kirby Gatto

Author contact info: robingodsfirewall@gmail.com

Author's Other Works

All of my books are featured on Amazon and you are able to find a complete list of my books, under my name, Robin Kirby-Gatto. Here are some covers of my books.

The series that I have are five in all, first which is the *Glory to Glory Sisterhood*, with my better works being *At His Feet* and *Destiny*. All my works from 2016 forward are much better, with the maturity in revelation and writing, which I would highly recommend works from 2016 to date. The next series I have is *God's Fire Wall School of the Prophets*, where I begin to use anatomy with my teachings by book 3. Another series I have is *God's Fire Wall Healing of the Soul*, which is a series based on the blueprint of man's soul. Next, I have the full fiction trilogy, *The Ancient Language Seekers*. Finally, I will finish the first book of my last series, *The Watchman*, which will be Rev 22:2 and involve teachings with Nikola Tesla. Covers to some of my books are on the following pages.

SESSION 4 THE SPIRIT OF KNOWLEDGE

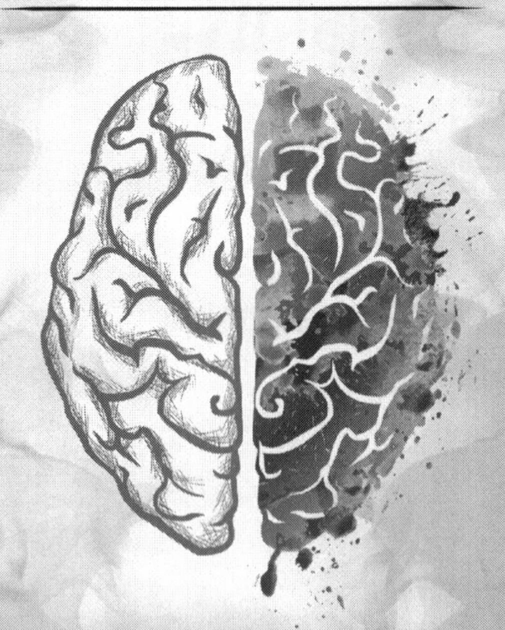

ROBIN
KIRBY-GATTO

GLORY TO GLORY SISTERHOOD

AT HIS FEET

HEALING AND DELIVERANCE

ROBIN KIRBY-GATTO

GOD'S FIRE WALL SCHOOL OF THE PROPHETS

SESSION 3 THE SPIRIT OF WISDOM

ROBIN KIRBY-GATTO

GOD'S FIRE WALL HEALING OF THE SOUL

SESSION 1 - THE LIGHT

ROBIN KIRBY-GATTO

---

[i] *Ecclesiastes 1:15-18 KJV*
[ii] *Ecclesiastes 1:15 KJV*
[iii] *Ecclesiastes 1:16 KJV*
[iv] *Ecclesiastes 1:17 KJV*
[v] *Ecclesiastes 1:18 KJV*
[vi] https://www.mechon-mamre.org/p/pt/pt3407.htm
[vii] Strong's Concordance Hebrew word # 5732
[viii] Strong's Concordance Hebrew word # 1080
[ix] Psalm 48:12 KJV
[x] Strong's Concordance Hebrew words # 4026 and # 1431 "Tower"
[xi] Psalm 48:4-6 KJV
[xii] Strong's Concordance Hebrew Word # 4428 & 4427 "king"
[xiii] Strong's Concordance Hebrew Word # 8539 "marveled"
[xiv] Strong's Concordance Hebrew Word # 926 "trouble"
[xv] Strong's Concordance Hebrew Word # 2648 "hasten away"
[xvi] Strong's Concordance Hebrew Word # 7461 "fear"
[xvii] Strong's Concordance Hebrew Word # 2427 "pain"
[xviii] Strong's Concordance Hebrew Word # 3205 "travail"
[xix] Genesis 11:3 KJV
[xx] https://www.youtube.com/watch?v=JnxFYS6PK9g
[xxi] https://www.youtube.com/watch?v=JnxFYS6PK9g
[xxii] https://www.youtube.com/watch?v=JnxFYS6PK9g
[xxiii] https://www.youtube.com/watch?v=JnxFYS6PK9g